The Reluctant Ascent of Nevil Warbrook
in his own words

The Reluctant Ascent of
NEVIL WARBROOK
in his own words

Volume One

Intimations
of Mortality

AVEBURY

Intimations of Mortality is the first of Nevil Warbrook's journals to be published by Avebury. The title was chosen in consultation with Edith Warbrook, Nevil's ex-wife, and with Deedee Bowbells, Nevil's colleague at Creative Havens and the acclaimed author of *Calypso and Wine*.

Nevil Warbrook is best known today for the restoration of Sir Tamburlaine Bryce MacGregor's *This Iron Race*. Originally published in the 1860s, MacGregor's work was subjected to extensive censorship by his publishers and Warbrook's revised and restored text was an attempt to recreate the text as MacGregor intended for publication by Hare & Drum of Edenborough. *Intimations of Mortality* serves as a companion to the author's restoration of Sir Tamburlaine Bryce MacGregor's text and ideally should be read in conjunction with book one of *This Iron Race*.

Avebury wish to express their profound gratitude to Eurydice Glendale, and Sister Ethelnyd of the Iona Fellowship of Grace for saving Nevil Warbrook's journals from destruction, and to Nevil's son, Gerald, for agreeing to their publication. We also extend our gratitude to Hendryk van Zelden for his advice and constant support; thank Nevil's agent, Desmond Catterick and Associates; his friends at Avebury and his colleagues and acquaintances at Creative Havens and Belshade College for excusing the sometimes unflattering opinions expressed herein. To all others mentioned in the text we request your tolerance and understanding.   .

Nevil Warbrook's journals will continue in *Blood & Water*.

6 February; White Bear, Devizes

It comes down to this: if I do not lose weight, I shall die; if I do not curb my drinking, I shall die; if I do not take more exercise, I shall die; and, according to that ghastly inflatable contraption that measures your blood pressure, if they don't get me a burst artery will.

Sobering news on the eve of a chap's sixty-second birthday; especially so when Daddy didn't live to see his sixty-third.

"Wasn't your father a poet?" Dr Saunders asked (this was two hours ago) from behind her black-rimmed glasses.

"He was. Thomas Warbrook was rather well known in his day."

"Died young," she said, and just as I thought Dr Saunders might have an interest in poetry, she said the date of death was in my patient notes.

I said my father's early death had robbed us of a significant voice among the late twentieth century poets, and we could only guess at what he would have written had he lived another decade or two, but my thoughts were already elsewhere.

Eleven is the age at which a child (boys, anyway) realises their happy state cannot last forever. Perhaps it's the acquisition of that second digit (the zero in ten not counting); or wearing long trousers with attendant restrictions on boisterous activities that might scuff one's knees; or that schooling suddenly seems to have a purpose, like a train with a destination and not a nice destination at that. Anyway, at age eleven I became aware of my waning childhood and symbolising that awareness was my father's French, eggshell blue Aller motorcar.

I don't suppose I ever thought of it as *eggshell* blue. Not then. If I apply an adjective I learned much later, to a childhood memory then what exactly am I remembering?

Stick to the facts. A blue Aller parked at Camber; a

tartan travel rug spread on the sand (Mummy was proud of her Scottish heritage); Mummy and Daddy sitting on said rug; Mummy with her sunglasses on, even when it was cloudy; Daddy taking off his jacket and hat, though never his tie; and me playing on the sand and wishing it was Cornwall where there were rock pools to play in.

The only queer note in the entire day (apart from being dragged round Rye's antique shops where Mummy's eye for a bargain was matched by Daddy's concern for expenditure) was Edwin, my imaginary friend, who refused to *aller* from the Aller and sat on the back seat waiting to go home. He was afraid that if he joined me on the beach we might hurry away and forget him.

The seats were a dark-blue, plasticky material. Absorbing the sun during the day they roasted the back of my legs all the way home.

I lost Edwin in Tonbridge when I was twelve. Probably that's when all children lose their imaginary friends. It's something to do with the growth of neural connections between the left and right hemispheres when the brain stops being two communicant halves and becomes one. I recall we had travelled by train to see Auntie Eileen—Daddy had had a bad year and the Aller was *allering* another family—and Edwin stayed behind when we all got off onto the platform. I think he was expecting us to return to the train later, as we always had to the Aller, and I last saw Edwin with his face pressed against the carriage window en route to Dover.

Dr Saunders was staring at me.

"Sorry. Mind wandered," I said.

"According to your Well Man appointment six months ago, you drink approximately twelve units of alcohol a week. Has that changed at all?"

I admitted to confusing units with pints.

"Still," I ventured, "twenty-four is hardly excessive."

"Almost everyone," Dr Saunders said, "underestimates how much they drink, but even twenty-four units is considerably above the recommended limit. Do you drink alone, Mr Warbrook?"

"Not in the pub," I said.

"And at home?"

"Only a night cap before bed. And sometimes a glass of wine with dinner. So, what's the verdict? You make it sound like I'm at death's door."

It was then she delivered the bad news which I paraphrased at the top of the page and having, somewhat tactlessly, said that if I didn't take better care of myself I would soon be following my father, she instructed me to keep a daily record of my alcohol consumption and weigh myself weekly; both accounts to be presented at my next appointment. In the meantime, if I experience tightness about the chest or dizzy spells, I should call the emergency services.

I have never met a woman less ruffled, or more in need of ruffling, than Dr Saunders, whose starched white blouse is so unyielding it wouldn't look out of place in the sculpture gallery at the Ashmolean, but her instruction had the desired effect and I walked straight into W B Jones, stationers, and bought this journal. The cover is faux leather in a shade of terracotta and each day occupies a generous two pages. That is far more than Dr Saunders requires, but it has reminded me of a conversation with Elfa Jonsdottír at last October's Exmoor Haven.

The weather that week was delightful, and it had prompted Elfa to be particularly adventurous with the Inspirational Walks. Icelanders are extraordinarily strong-willed people, and one does not say no to them. Hence a three-hour trek across the heather had left me footsore and stiff in the saloon of the Withered Arm in Porlock.

Elfa, who is half my age and frightfully athletic, took pity on me and began rubbing my aching calf muscles whereon I mentioned that I was soon to be sixty-two, the very same age my father was when he passed away.

"Anything more will be a bonus poor Daddy never enjoyed."

Elfa paused massaging my aching calves, my stockinged foot resting snugly in her lap, and said, "You should make a saga. You can call it Nevil's Saga and in it you must vrite all you do. Then you see vhat you do in the years denied your farzer. Yes?"

Elfa is probably the sanest and most down-to-earth of all my colleagues at Creative Havens—even if her crime fiction is far too macabre for my taste—and, as I said, one does not say no to an Icelander, but I had put her suggestion aside until Doctor Saunders' prophecy this morning.

And so, the page fills.

Postscriptum: two glasses of house Merlot with lunch'.

Post-Postscriptum: I miss the eleven-year-old me. I miss Edwin. I even miss the Aller.

FILIAL DUTIES

7 February; Tea Bush Café, Salisbury

As I have done every birthday, except one, since my father's death twenty-two years ago, I set off early for Salisbury.

The skies were leaden as I drove over the Downs. According to the chirpy young woman delivering last night's weather forecast there is a twenty-five percent chance of snow today. Quite how one prepares for a quarter chance of snow, I cannot tell, but I am taking no chances. I have a tartan blanket, a Thermos of tea, and a garden spade. Lunch' and a bunch of daffodils—my father's favourite flower—I bought in Devizes.

It was certainly cold enough beside Daddy's grave and by the time I'd finished reading his poem, 'The Reddleman,' my lips were frozen. Even the daffodils shivered. Happily, clusters of yellow and lilac crocuses beneath the elm trees were just coming into bud so something is trusting in spring's arrival. Jackdaws roosting in the trees kept up a fearful racket throughout. Couldn't see what was disturbing them but I had the curious impression I wasn't alone.

Observances concluded, I drove into Salisbury and parked on Cathedral Close. From there I passed on foot what had once been my father's home—happily, whoever has care of the place has not ruined the garden, though the roses need pruning—and stopped at the Tea Bush to warm up before I drive to Amesbury to see Mummy. Ordered muffins and a pot of tea and grabbed the chance to scribble a few words while I wait to be served. Place is busy with shoppers taking their lunch'.

Next door to the tearooms is a small department store. They have a display of stuffed toys in the window. Mummy always kept cats and while a live one would be against the rules at Crossstones House they cannot object to a stuffed toy. Obviously, I don't want to sit here with it, so I'll pick it up on the way back to the motorcar. It's bright yellow and cheering and God knows Mummy's condition is pretty grim. Apparently, there is, as one kind, if not altogether cheering carer remarked last year, as much comfort in the visit of a stranger as in the visit of a son, and if I fear Mummy does not entirely know who I am, I am not to think my attendance wasted.

Muffins and tea have appeared.

Later; Cathedral Close, Salisbury

How deuced annoying. My own fault, I suppose, though it seems unfair to blame myself for something so unforeseeable.

The muffins had scarcely made an impression on my tummy and the tea did not have the warming properties for which I had hoped. So, I glanced along the menu board and noticed they had spiced parsnip soup. Knowing that was bound to put some fire in my tummy, I ordered a bowl with rustic bread. I did not have to wait long but as the waitress passed the shimmering golden bowl before me, I spotted something else golden-yellow enter at the door. It was the stuffed cat, or one very like it, in the clutches of a small girl. The girl was followed by her mother, and both joined the queue at the counter.

It was a moment before I realised the child was staring at me. I glanced down at my soup but not before she had tugged on her mother's hand.

A maternal shadow had loomed.

"Is there a problem?" the woman asked.

"No. I don't believe so."

"Then why were you staring at my daughter?"

"I assure you; I was not."

The girl emerged from behind her mother's legs and glared at me.

"I was looking at the toy cat. It's a very big cat."

The girl reacted as though I had attempted to drag puss from her arms. Neighbouring tables had fallen quiet, and ears had turned my way.

"The cat?" her mother asked without trace of believing me.

"I saw the cat, or one like it, in the window of the shop next door. I was going to buy it after I'd eaten. I saw your daughter's cat and immediately thought it might be the same cat. I was certainly not staring at your daughter."

"Buy it?" the woman said.

"For my mother."

Before she could comment with another disyllabic reply, I said that my mother had dementia and lived in a home where they didn't allow real cats.

"My cat," the girl said, having inherited her mother's laconic habits.

"I hope it's not the only one they had," I said.

"They got it from the display," the mother said, having mustered several words at once. "Come along, Alice. We'll sit near the window."

I finished my soup in silence then crept out and into the department store. Of course, the cat had sold and in desperation—I really did have to get to Amesbury—I bought a rabbit instead. Only hope Mummy likes it.

The snow has arrived but I'm taking a few moments before I drive home. The car park is anonymous. Everything, the sky, the stone walls of the house, has a sepia look.

Seeing Mummy always leaves me wretched. At least she knew I was not a stranger, but I cannot be confident it was me she recognised. I distinctly heard her say my father would be proud of me, which didn't seem right at all, and rather has me wondering whose father she had in mind and who she thought I was. She is, I fear, away with the faeries. At least she was happy with the rabbit, though she insisted on calling it a hare, so I can console myself that I brightened her day.

And that would have been that and—sensibly—I would be heading home by now, but for two interventions whose meaning I am trying to grasp while memory is fresh. The first was from Judith Malmsey who invited me into her office for a cup of tea and chat. I, having reminded myself all bills were up to date, pointed at the flurries of snow beyond the French window and asked if matters could wait.

Judith, who is the day manager, pointed out that the snow wasn't yet lying.

"Perhaps not here," I said, "but the Downs at Avebury are rather higher."

Judith smiled, but I could tell she wasn't letting me go so easily so I followed into her office.

"You don't know anyone called 'Rookwood' do you?" she asked once I was seated. "A family friend, perhaps? Or someone your mother knew before she married?"

It took me a moment's recollection before I said there was a Rookwood up at Oxford with my father.

"Can't recall his exact role, but he was something of a guru to a few undergraduates. Why do you ask?"

"Your mother has mentioned him. Is the gentleman still with us?"

"Good Lord. I shouldn't have thought so," I replied. "He

must be a hundred by now. What has Mother said of him? I can't imagine they ever knew each other."

"She insists that she has seen him."

"Really? Where has she seen him?"

"At night in her room," Judith said.

"Ah, well," I said. "Unless you're leaving the front door open at night, I think we can rule that out. Besides, she has just seen me, and I'm not convinced she knew who I was so I wouldn't put too much store by it."

"Oh. That is surprising,' Judith said. 'Your mother knew you were coming today. She was quite insistent."

I was now trying to screw my mind to recall anything Mummy had said that might indicate she was confused, but apart from that curious comment about Daddy being proud of me I couldn't think of anything unusual. In any event, I assured Judith that Lester Rookwood was most unlikely to be visiting my mother.

Then, just as I had left Judith's office, one of the carers approached me. A pretty Spanish girl, I recalled her name was Conchita. She kept glancing up the stairway and back towards Judith's office. I asked if I could help her.

"Mr Warbrook. May I speak a moment?"

I saw no harm in it; though of course I was concerned given the snow and hoped it wouldn't take long.

Conchita drew me aside and from the front pocket of her apron produced a long black feather.

"I find this in your mama's room this morning," she said.

I suggested Mummy had found it in the garden and thought it looked pretty.

Conchita said they had not had the garden doors open all winter.

"Also, it not the first. Please."

Conchita took me aside and opened the door to a store cupboard. It had all the usual things one expects; vacuum cleaner, mop, and so on but she ignored them and indicated a marmalade jar full of black feathers.

"There is one every morning," she said. "I told not anyone."

"Why ever not?" I asked.

"It is ... Forgive. I do not know English: a *presagio*."

I didn't know what she meant.

"In España," she continued, "it means there will be a death in the family."

I understood *presagio* meant a presage or omen and tried to reassure her. In a house like Crossstones there would be old chimneys, queer draughts, and the like. But her brown eyes gazing up at me suggested I would not convince her.

"If I were you," I said. "I'd throw those horrid things away and tell Judith you have birds nesting in the roof. Now, I must be going."

"Please," she whispered. "You have care. In España death not come to one who feather given, but one close to them."

"And this is England," I said, "not *España*. I'm sure there's a sensible explanation."

And so, I departed into the dusk of the car park where I am sitting with the engine running and the heater on full blast. Given Dr Saunders has only requested medical information and Elfa Jonsdottír will have no interest in these musings I suppose I am really writing this to myself so I can admit that my visit to Crossstones has been thoroughly unsettling.

Nota bene: look up Lester Rookwood in the *Oxford Dictionary of Biography*. Can't imagine he's still alive: not with the debauchery he got up to. Also look up Spanish folklore regarding jackdaws and crows. Now, home.

Postscriptum: Am now home and abed. Thoroughly exhausted. Two fingers of Owl Service malt whisky for my nightcap. If Dr Saunders disapproves, I will claim extenuating circumstances.

Post-Postscriptum: Sixteen stone, eight, as recorded this morning.

Touch and go last evening. Fortunately, the Highway Authority had gritted the hill at Bishops Cannings and the Rover purred onto the Downs. Could have done with my driving gloves as the heater packed up near Marlborough and though the travel blanket kept my knees warm, I had to prise my fingers from the blasted wheel when I arrived home shortly before seven.

Last hundred yards were the worst of it when I left the main road and negotiated the lane. Luckily, no one was about so I crawled along and made it into the drive. Only alarums were after I left the car as my shoes weren't up to the task and I slithered into the hedge. Hawthorn is damned unfriendly.

It's at moments like last evening that I wish I had a dog. A dog would have greeted me like a long-lost pal, but Boris and Tusker didn't even look up as I entered the kitchen. I was too weary to write anything further on the day, so I showed the cats the back door—neither was interested— then read for an hour or so until bed with a nightcap.

Have woken to fields swept with snow and the distant trees frosted. Only the Longstones, two outliers of the Avebury circle, were untouched and seemed all the darker against the white expanse. Birds were squabbling over scraps put out by my neighbour, Mrs Pumphrey.

Dressed and proceeded downstairs. The roads must be open because I have a letter from King James University wishing me happy birthday and reminding me my annual Privileged Membership granting access to the Reserved Manuscript Depository needs renewing. The card is kind enough, even if I am paying for it, and it looks smart alongside a sentimental offering from Mrs Pumphrey and a rather nice card from Molly Poppins at the Linden Tree guesthouse, but it's galling that despite the occasional necessity of the R.M.D., I am paying for the privilege of being chilled to the bone while some ghostly harpsichordist runs their fingers up and down my spine. At least, that is what it feels like after a few minutes in The Cell. It would be nice if Privileged Membership paid for the services of the cleaning staff as whatever effect magick books have on me, or on Van Zelden, spiders seem perfectly immune. Rang the alarm bell in a complete blue funk a year or so ago convinced a ghostly presence had grasped my hand only to discover in the cold light of the library that I had plunged it through a cobweb intricately woven between the table legs. Required several whiskies at the Stuffed Cock on the Royal Mile before I was back to my normal self, and would the university consider my claim for shredded nerves? Would they hell. Apparently, they have never found a cleaner willing to enter The Cell and librarians think dusting is beneath them. Since that ghastly fright, I have always checked for arachnid activity before sitting down.

Some curious literature about spider bites and magick, but it would only unsettle me. Best not to research some things too closely. I shall visit my bank next time I'm in Devizes and arrange payment. If I remember, I'll get a receipt, as there's every chance I can claim expenses from Hare & Drum.

HARE & DRUM
Lunchtime; Avebury Trusloe

Desmond telephoned with a reminder that Hare & Drum are interviewing me on Monday. Hardly likely to forget; a personal visit from one's publisher or representative thereof is unusual enough to catch in the memory. Blasted nuisance Dessie not giving me the chap's name. Claims he couldn't decipher the handwriting. I hadn't the heart to suggest he might have mislaid his reading glasses. As literary agents go, Desmond Catterick is past his sell-by-date. Still, what would I do with some whizz-bang chap fresh out of a glasshouse university, eh? Worse thought, what would he do with me? Or with a young filly wanting to remake me for the younger reader. Perish the thought. Had enough of women telling me what to do with Edith... not that I don't miss her dreadfully.

Thankfully, the rest of Hare & Drum's letter was typed,

and Dessie relayed the necessary. The fellow, whatever his name is, claims to recognise me. An unsettling thought as I don't have any idea what he looks like. Dessie hasn't met the chap either so I shall be blind.

I suppose that raises the possibility I have met this mystery man before, but no idea where that could be.

Publishers have a certain smell about them. Differs widely, of course. My last publisher, Little Brown Johnson, was decidedly whiffy. Should have put me on my alert, but too late now. After the receiver has paid out what's owed to the printers and to the assistant tea boy, and so on, I doubt the authors will get a fraction what's due them. Shame really, as they did a respectable job of my little production and *The Deeper Well, a History of Gaelic Poetry*, was selling rather well, not least in the Canadian provinces where the Scotch heart pines most for the land it abandoned. Curious exports, Scotland: whisky, shortcake, and nostalgia for grinding poverty and famine. And literature, thank God, without which you, Nevil, would have nothing to keep body and soul together so don't gripe about the popularity of past miseries.

Dessie had the most peculiar instruction. I am to wait for the Hare & Drum chap on the footbridge where the path to Avebury crosses the Kennet, barely a rivulet so far upstream, at twelve noon. From there, he and I will walk to the pub, which I have no objection to, for the interview proper. All very curious. I can see myself, however, waiting at the appointed hour and gurning at every passing stranger in case they are this Edenborough man of mystery. Hopefully, they will just take me for a rustic eccentric, and not someone of dubious morals.

Something deuced uncanny about meeting on a bridge.

Later; Avebury Trusloe

Studious day editing, having at last turned to the business of *This Iron Race, book two*. Poured myself a glass of Merlot to reward my industry.

Compared to the first volume, there is a marked difference between MacGregor's original manuscript and the published text. Too early to say for certain, but one feels that MacGregor had given up any hope Beresford & Lucas would publish the book he wished to write and from the outset wrote two versions; one for immediate publication and one for... posterity, one assumes: hard to say exactly. So long as his original manuscript remains legible and clear that may make my work easier. If it doesn't it could well become a great deal more difficult as I can no longer rely on the published text to guide me.

Nota bene: best not mention any of that to Hare & Drum. If I let on the editing work could be done by a halfway-decent secretarial typist, they might suggest reducing my fee. Besides, if MacGregor's manuscript becomes as convoluted as the first volume, then I will justify every penny.

The cats have been decidedly 'off' with me today. No idea what I have done to offend them. It is their loss if I must throw out two perfectly good portions of Kitty Nibbles. I shall have a word with Mrs Pumphrey as I wouldn't put it past Boris and Tusker to be dining next door when my back is turned. Had thought of retiring to The Red Lion this evening but bitterly cold out and last night's snow is still lingering. This glass and a hot toddy at bedtime will ward off the chill. Later I'll settle down to an evening of light entertainment on the gogglebox. Doesn't do to be highbrow too much of the time.

Postscriptum: one glass Merlot. Two fingers Owl Service single malt for my nightcap.

9 February; Red Lion, Avebury

Called in at the village shop for some stamps and a pint of milk this morning. They had my favourite flapjacks in so bought a bag of four. As I left the shop Molly Poppins was emerging from St James's where she has been doing the flowers for Sunday Service. The pint of milk was like ice in my hand, and I would have hurried on, but Molly's not one to let a chap escape.

"Did you get home alright?" she asked.

"From Salisbury? Oh, yes. Touch and go, but I'd rather sleep in my own bed than put up in a hotel."

"Awfully brave of you. Surely your father wouldn't have minded if you waited a few days."

"You didn't know my father," I said. "He approved of habit and routine. No. I'm glad I went. Did the snow trouble you?"

"Three guests cancelled," she said. "I'll have to throw out their breakfast bacon. Taken it out of the freezer and I'll never eat it all. You wouldn't want some rashers to take home?"

"Be a shame to let it waste," I said.

So, to cut a long story short, I have bacon for the next three days. I'd have had the eggs as well, but Molly reckons they'll last a while longer. The guests were a survey team from the Antiquities Trust.

Pub is quiet this afternoon, but the fire's blazing and I have a copy of the Daily Recorder to amuse me. Keeping one eye on the window. I don't have my torch with me, and it will be dark soon.

Postscriptum: two pints of Cropwell's Bitter.

Later; Avebury Trusloe

Felt a bit squiffy after leaving the pub. Probably coming down with a lurgy. Wouldn't surprise me, given the weather. Must speak to Jonathan about the jackdaws. They are getting territorial about 'their' pub and one of them dropped a stick on my head. Nasty scratch and I needed the antiseptic.

Had three of Molly's rashers with beans and fried bread for supper. Comfort food is what this weather demands. Perked up once I'd eaten. Recalled that Spanish girl's worry about bird feathers and looked it up in Baxter's *Avian Folklore*. Not just Spanish but found across much of southern Europe, the gift of a black feather means a death in the family. Didn't give any more details. Won't worry Auntie Eileen with it and Gerald would only laugh at me. Besides, there's no signal for his portable telephone in Borneo so I must rely on him calling me.

Daily Recorder mentioned there's a live broadcast of Van Zelden's latest extravaganza tonight. He's in New Amsterdam so it isn't showing here until the early hours. I won't stay up for it, but I might record it for later viewing. No doubt it will annoy me immensely, but one knows a man by his deeds.

Must remember to put the cats out tonight whether they like it or not; don't want another accident like last night.

Postscriptum: hot toddy at bedtime; two fingers Budgitts cheapo whisky with water.

10 February; Avebury Trusloe

To church this morning. My mind drifted during the sermon and when I heard Peter mention Russia, I assumed he was going on about the latest beastliness in Moscow. Then it all got confusing, until I realised, he was talking about Bishop Ussher and the actual topic was the danger of relying too much on the word of the Bible, Ussher having infamously deduced the earth was barely 6,000 years old by totting up dates in the Bible. Don't trust the Bible is only the latest of the Reverend Peter Chadwick's peculiar missives.

Actually, 'Peter,' as he insists we call him, was unfair on Ussher as the bishop attempted to make the Bible agree with known dates in history and it's not his fault the sciences of geology, archaeology, and biology weren't around to point out his errors. Wanted to mention that to Peter over tea and biscuits after the service but Molly Poppins waylaid me, and I never got the chance. Meanwhile, having thought the sermon was about Russia I had Moroshkin's 'Dance of the Swans' lodged in my earbone. If you know the tune, you'll understand just how annoying that was.

Nota bene: re Parochial Church Council meeting on Wednesday; Molly unable to arrive early to turn on the heating so yours truly will oblige. Fortunately, the Parish Room is across the way from the pub so shan't have to stand around freezing.

Not as chilly as yesterday, but grey skies and persistent drizzle. Decided against an hour in The Red Lion and headed home for lunch'. Afternoon spent editing. Increasingly certain MacGregor knew his preferred version of the text would not see the light of day. Am to bed early tonight as I must be wide awake tomorrow for my meeting with the representative from Hare & Drum. Despite the bitter weather I have decided on my tweed jacket as my coat is looking shabby. Next week I'm in Glastonbury for the first Creative Haven of the year. Five days of classes, tutorials, and jolliness—I don't think—but the income is useful. Wouldn't be above a visit to the charity shops in Devizes. Some bargains in the windows and at my age a coat doesn't need to be stylish. Presentable will do.

Can't get over the peculiarity that this chap from H&D knows me yet I haven't the foggiest about him. Assuming I recognise him, I shall immediately be on the spot trying to recall when we met and whether I said anything regrettable or promised something I never delivered on. It would be like an old pebble turning up with something very disagreeable underneath it.

All will be answered tomorrow at noon.

ROOKWOOD

12 February; Devizes Library

In my concise edition of the *Oxford Dictionary of Biography* the entry for Rookwood is miniscule and the date of death indicated by a question mark. I've had better luck in Devizes Library and learned that Rookwood disappeared in 1967 while on a walking holiday in Ayrshire. His body was never found, and it's presumed he drowned in the River Doon. In the unlikely event he faked his death he would now be ninety-eight so I can safely say he has not been visiting Mummy at Crossstones.

The entry on Lester Rookwood may also explain Mummy's insistence on calling the stuffed rabbit a hare. Rookwood, as I should have remembered, established a private dining club at Oxford which he called The Helios Society, and its emblem was a hare. The Helios had a reputation for licentiousness and Rookwood encouraged sexual exploration on a heroic scale. Regrettably, it does my father's reputation no favours to recall he was a leading light in it during his time at Oxford. Mummy was innocent of any association with Rookwood, but one assumes a conversation was had at some point and Daddy confessed all. Curious that almost sixty years later Rookwood and the Helios Society should float to the surface of Mummy's mind.

Nota bene: paid annual subscription to KJU and kept receipt.

O'BRIEN

Later; Crown Inn, Bishops Cannings

I talked so long with Mr O'Brien at The Red Lion yesterday I arrived home weary beyond belief and fell asleep on the sofa. Woke just in time for supper and made myself scrambled eggs—tummy was a bit unsettled so didn't want to risk anything excessive—and by the time I'd done the washing up—a task Edith and I always used to share, and which is thoroughly miserable undertaken alone—it was time to put out the cats and bed. Didn't feel any need for my usual nightcap so it was head down and away to Nod. Slept soundly but woke this morning with a faint ringing in my ears like distant laughter. I glanced along the road outside but couldn't see any children playing. Imagine the joy on Dr Saunders's face were she to add tinnitus to my ailments.

Happily, the ringing noise didn't last beyond lunchtime when I had to do my weekly shopping in Devizes. Thence to the library, which I have just related, and on to the thatched pleasantness of the Crown Inn at Bishops Cannings just below the escarpment of the Downs. It's a pretty village and not at all touristy, unlike Avebury. I should only have one or two as the Rover is outside. It would be unlucky to see a police car on the few miles home, but better safe than sorry.

Now: my observations of Mr O'Brien.

First thought. I have no idea where he knows me from, but I would surely have remembered a face like his, even though at this precise moment I am having a devil of a job picturing it. Uncommonly tall, though, I do remember that. Suspect he's a hit with ladies who like a man of mystery.

He had a curious way of holding my attention, rather as an insect pinned to a collector's tray, but with the legs still waggling away. Macabre thought. Best not dwell on it. Obliged him with an account of my first meeting with Van Zelden; I shall never forgive him for the trick. Brutal it was.

O'Brien was pleasantly knowledgeable of MacGregor's work, though off hand I'm struggling to recall anything he said. But he was attentive and curious. Certainly, got me talking, which is the mark of a halfway-decent journalist, though it was odd he didn't take notes. If he relies on his memory I'm bound to be misrepresented to some degree. Will have to ask Hare & Drum to send me the proofs before they print anything.

Postscriptum: one pint of Brakespeare's drunk and another about to be ordered.

13 February; Avebury Trusloe

Came down for breakfast this morning to find a mouse loose in the kitchen. If Boris cannot break his unpleasant habits, he could at least ensure his gifts are no longer mobile. Damn thing retreated under the fridge, and I had to move it from the wall. Eventually released the beastie outdoors and hopefully no worse for wear.

Interesting haul from behind the fridge: one beer mat from The Red Lion, the programme from a forgettable evening at Swindon Theatre, and a packet of condoms not purchased by me. Three of the original five were missing but

I couldn't see any evidence for how long they'd been behind the fridge. I suppose, it's possible they date to before Edith and I moved in; the alternative is too beastly to imagine. Threw them in the bin, along with the programme. The beer mat I can find a use for.

Finished off Molly's bacon then tried to settle down with my morning coffee and continue editing but was too easily distracted. Business with the condoms put me in a doleful mood as it reminded me how much I miss Edith.

Dominoes match at The Red Lion tonight. Hoping for revenge against The Green Man as we lost badly against them just before Christmas. Bert Tanner tried to buck up my spirits by saying it was all down to luck but that doesn't explain why he's so much luckier than I am.

Postscriptum: three pints Cropwell's Bitter, two doubles Owl Service malt whisky. Won two of my three games and drew the other. The Green Man trounced.

DEFENDER OF THE FAITH
14 February; Avebury Trusloe

Managed three hours of editing before 'lunch' intervened. Progress remains good.

Made myself cheese on toast with a splash of sauce to liven things up. Probably ought to investigate eating more greens as I expect Dr Saunders wants me to lose some weight. It was that spirit which took me out for a walk this afternoon. Still that bitter easterly wind, but at least the sky was a pretty shade of blue. Walked over towards Windmill Hill, but the last bit was too muddy, and I turned around. Not a soul about but a buzzard shadowed me most of the way.

Got back about three and managed another few hours of editing. All progressing smoothly.

Broke for tea early as I had to put the heating on in the Parish Room for seven. Takes an age to warm up. Found some frozen peas and had them with cod fillets in parsley sauce. Felt positively holier-than-thou. Of course, I then spoiled it with a slice of coffee cake.

Must have tweaked my left knee earlier and so drove the mile into the village. Left the Parish Room warming up and retired to the pub. Jonathan was at the bar and I took him to task over the jackdaws.

"And it's still sore," I said of my injury. "It could have had my eye out."

"Well, only if you'd been looking up and then you could have dodged it," Bert Tanner said. At that early hour he was the only other customer.

"I am not in the habit of dodging missiles," I said. "Even so, I consider my nasty scratch quite bad enough."

"Well, I can barely see it," Bert said.

"It's had three days to heal," I replied.

"Then why are you complaining of it?"

"Because I'd rather it didn't happen again. And why are you defending the blasted jackdaws when they're Jonathan's responsibility?"

Jonathan said he didn't see the jackdaws were anything to do with him.

"They sit on your roof," I said.

"They sit on everyone's roof, and in the trees," he said. "They're wild birds. They don't belong to anyone. If you want something done about them, and I'm not saying I object as they're a menace to the customers outside in the summer, you go ask the parish council."

"'Ere," Bert piped up, "Aren't you on the council?"

"Me? No. I'm on the Parochial Church Council but that's just to do with the church. Parish council is different."

Bert nodded sagely. "So, no point asking you about bin collections?"

"None whatsoever."

Bert returned to his beer. I had ordered a pint of Cobwebs Cask as my usual tipple was off that night and I wanted something to wet my whistle ready for the talking later.

"Jonathan, could I pick your brains a moment?"

"My brains? You're the Oxford-educated chap."

"Theology and Babylonian Studies wasn't the broadest of education. No, I was wondering what you thought of that tall chap I was with on Monday."

"Here?"

"Of course, here. In that chair by the fire. You gave me a pack of pork scratchings."

"Did I? Doesn't sound like me. Tall did you say?"

"Yes, unusually tall. Wondered what you thought of him. He seemed to give you a bit of a turn at one point."

"You sure it was Monday?"

"Positively. He was from my publisher."

"Don't recall. Mind you, it all got a bit distracting Monday so I might have forgotten. Bunch of Hell's Angels turned up. Not our usual Sunday crowd. Chapter from up north. Bit rowdy. Seems they were looking for some fellah, but I didn't catch a name. I'd feel sorry for him if they got lucky. Nasty looking bunch."

Obviously, O'Brien did not make the impression on Jonathan he made on me. I left Bert at the bar and found a more comfortable seat and a copy of the Daily Recorder. By this time, I had only some twenty minutes before I needed to open the doors of the Parish Room, so I drank up and did the crossword before leaving.

"I hope you remembered to turn the heating on," Molly's voice rang behind me as I was crossing the road to the parish room.

"I did. It should all be pleasant," I said and let us both in.

A wave of oppressive heat struck us.

"Heavens, I think I may have overdone it," I said.

"Should we open the windows?" Molly asked.

"No, I think not. Just need a little adjustment."

Staring at the controls I saw I had misread a seven for a three and had thus made the room somewhat tropical. I dialled it back to two.

"Bloody-Nora," said a voice from the doorway. "Like a Chinese kitchen in 'ere."

It was Terry Woodson, our head of Fabric and Works, a man whose common speech masks an unusual skill with wood and stone.

"My fault," I said, less the blame fell on Molly.

"You'd think the church has money to burn," Terry said. "You know it will be billed to us."

"I do know, thank you," I said.

"Well, so long as you know."

"It was an easy mistake to make," Molly said in my defence.

"Easy for some. Some is too much for abstraction and not enough for doing, that's my thoughts on it."

"I am the first to admit I am not a practical man, Terence. Perhaps next time you could have charge of ensuring the room is warm for us."

"Can't make the commitment. A man with practical skills is in demand, y'see. Could get a call at any time."

Next to arrive was Paul Durdle, one of our Church Wardens; followed by Fred Thirsk, our Captain of the Tower. Then Lucy Chadwick, Peter's wife; Sid Morris, who looks after the churchyard; Pauline Lamb, the other Church Warden who doubles as our treasurer; and lastly Prudence Turnstone who organises the Spiritual Outreach Committee and runs the catering. Fortunately, the repeated opening of the door had reduced the heat to something more reasonable by the time we were ready to begin.

Pauline Lamb took the chair, and I settled down to taking minutes. Matters ran smoothly until we came to preparations for Easter.

"I feel we ought to make an effort this year," Prudence said.

"Haven't we made an effort before?" Fred said. "We've always had the church looking nice for Easter."

That wasn't what Prudence meant.

"It only benefits those who attend the church, and they are only a small part of the village and its visitors," she explained.

"Visitors?" Sid asked.

"We don't need to go over this again," Paul Durdle said. "I agree with Prudence, and more to the point this is at Peter's request. We need to appeal to other faith traditions and even to those whose faith is too young to have traditions."

"Y'mean pagans and wicket folk," Sid muttered.

I corrected wicket to Wiccan in the minutes, though I sympathised with Sid.

Prudence looked smug; if Peter and Paul were on your side then you had won. Sid looked like a commander who'd lost his cavalry.

But I don't want to repeat an old argument here: while Peter is our vicar Sid and I have lost the battle and all we can do is bide our time. The church likes to move its incumbents on every few years, stops them going native, and provided Peter doesn't get his way with anything major, such as removing the pews and replacing them with café style tables and chairs like he tried last year, we'll eventually get *our* church back.

Meanwhile, Prudence and her Spiritual Outreach Committee have a free rein to come up with ideas before the next meeting and will discuss them directly with Paul or Peter. One solid decision made this evening affects yours truly: Prudence wants me to write a series of talks connecting Avebury with The Passion for the weeks leading up to Easter. Not sure if I'm to read them at church or if one of our lay readers will have the dubious honour. Initial ideas are the stones for the blocking of the tomb, blackthorn for the crown of thorns, the Kennet for the water spilt when the spear pierced Christ's side—not keen on that one—and Silbury Hill for Calvary, which admittedly seems a bit of a stretch. Sid's suggestion that I connect the ass to the Cherhill donkey sanctuary will be ignored.

Nota bene: wonder if the manor house gardens have any palm trees. Unlikely but worth a look.

Nasty moment on the way back from the meeting. There I was, barely doing forty on the Devizes Road, when a pair of motorcyclists roared past going like the clappers. Hadn't seen them coming and I nearly put the Rover in the hedge.

Enough. Cats are loitering by the back door so it's a glass of whisky followed by bed.

15 February; Avebury Trusloe

Received another letter from King James University this morning. I was all set to fly into a temper as I assumed it must be a reminder for my subscription, but no; this was much more welcome. They've asked me to give a talk on MacGregor's library at Arbinger. The audience will be the university trustees, invited faculty and students. The fee they're offering is modest, but they'll cover expenses. Checked my calendar and I am free the second week of May so have typed my reply ready to send off to them. I can combine the talk with a look round Arbinger and a visit to the Scottish Records Office. I've been delving into Mummy's family tree to see how far back I can trace my MacStrangie ancestry. Not found anything before the seventeen-eighties so far.

Fairly sure the university will pay for two nights' accommodation, but I'll see if I can stretch it to four and spend the week in Edenborough.

Rest of the day spent editing and making notes on the Easter talks at the church. Had the bright idea of writing something about pilgrimage and pilgrim trails. Jerusalem is of course a pilgrim destination, as Avebury is for many, and the ancient Harrow Way passes through Avebury on its way from Dorset to Winchester and Canterbury.

So that's stones, blackthorn, and pilgrim ways. Need one more idea. I'll have a think while I'm making tea.

Postscriptum: it's raining but put the cats out regardless.

Boris—or Tusker, hard to see in the dark—unimpressed and scratched me. Second time this week I've needed antiseptic.

Usual nightcap.

17 February; Avebury Trusloe

Church this morning then a leisurely lunch' at The Red Lion. Arrived home about three. Prudence had a few ideas for the lent talks. Safe to say I shall be ignoring them. Meanwhile my thoughts are turning to tomorrow morning and Glastonbury.

Creative Havens have provided a great deal of information—even more than last year—but as far as I can tell it's all much the same. I have five days of lectures shared with Deedee Bowbells, whose company is pleasant enough, a dozen one-to-one tutorials with the Castaways, plus an Inspirational Walk, which, as it's Glastonbury, means climbing the Tor. Józef Mazur is the guest reader.

It's not that I dislike Józef, but he is a gloomy presence. I suppose anyone who endured three years solitary confinement in Siberia would find human company difficult, but it's been several years since he left the gulag and his autobiography, *Dead Sun*, won lots of prizes so one would think he is over it. Only hope he doesn't start painting while he's there. He was with Clarissa and me during last year's Whitby Haven and by the end of the week the place stank of turpentine. I have a passing interest in art—Angela Spendlove is always trying to rope me into the Avebury Society of Painters—but I can't make anything of Józef's oeuvre. "Thunderstorm at Midnight" is my best guess, though why anyone would paint the same thunderstorm again and again I can't imagine. Then again, I can barely imagine Siberia, let alone three years of it without human company.

Mind you, even in translation the man can write, and, if the critics are to be believed, *Dead Sun* is extraordinary, if far too bleak for yours truly. My copy sits on the shelf above the downstairs lavatory.

Deedee is perfectly charming and hasn't let the success of *Calypso and Wine*—both the book and the film—go to her head. Of course, she hardly needs to work for Creative Havens anymore, but claims she enjoys teaching. Lucky her: I need the income and teaching is a test of my patience.

One little snippet among the paperwork sent by Creative Havens: the company might be acquired by Poseidon Travel. Didn't say what that will mean in the long term, vis-à-vis my employment, but hopefully it won't change anything. Why anyone would name a travel company after an angry sea god is beyond me. It's like naming an airline after Icarus.

Better stop now. I have a dozen tins of Speedo-Kat for Mrs Pumphrey who is caring for Boris and Tusker while I'm away and then I'll pack my things. Hour and a half to Glastonbury and want to arrive before lunch' so I can get myself sorted. The Avalon Centre is a decent venue but need to pick my room carefully. Bed was a bit damp last year.

Postscriptum: usual nightcap. Weight, sixteen stone, ten.

ET IN AVALON EGO
18 February; Avalon Centre, Glastonbury

Arrived shortly after noon. Later than I would have liked. Mrs Pumphrey caught me as I was leaving, and we had a lengthy conversation which revolved around Mr Pumphrey's antique chairs and Boris and Tusker's claw-sharpening habits. I recall saying that so long as they didn't starve I didn't much care how they spent their day. Mrs Pumphrey was unimpressed. Result is that Boris and Tusker will be locked in at my place during the day and she will pop round to feed them and let them out at night. One only hopes they do not take against me. Or against my furniture. Though nothing of mine is antique: merely old.

The manager at Avalon has assigned me a different room than last year. This one faces south so hopefully it will catch a little sun. Deedee Bowbells is her usual jolly self and Józef

Mazur is as haggard as ever. He asked me if I had enjoyed *Dead Sun*. Caught me unexpected and I could only say that I didn't think it was the sort of book one was supposed to enjoy. Probably a faux pas as he looked even glummer. Only caught a few glimpses of the Castaways. As usual, half are gadding around like butterflies with immense smiles and an air of expectation while the other half wander like lost sheep. One forty-something woman with red hair and skin like leather was wheeling a hand truck across the car park laden with wine: box each of Beaujolais Villages, Côtes du Rhône, and Italian Primitivo. I jokingly asked if she was setting up a bar. Obviously, she assumed I was a fellow Castaway because she replied with a manic grin and said, "It's the only way I think we'll cope." A young chap, about half her age, had brought a unicycle and was busy weaving between the bollards in the car park. Fortunately, they did not collide.

Won't meet them properly until this evening when we have the social. I suggested to Deedee and Józef that we all abscond to The Shotgun on Chilkwell Street, but Deedee overruled me, so we are stuck in the grim Gathering Room at the arts centre. Deedee is the Captain at this Haven, and she has the first tutorial session this afternoon. I get them tomorrow morning.

Nota bene: check what I'm supposed to be teaching them.

Deedee remarked that the weather is looking fine for Thursday, apart from high winds, so I suspect she's taking us up the Tor again for the Inspirational Walk. I suggested we might try the caves at Wookey for a change but apparently Józef suffers flashbacks when he's in confined spaces.

"Besides," Deedee said, "the walk will invigorate you. You do look a little weary and it's only the first Haven of the year."

Deedee's remark reminded me of Dr Saunders' instruction re chest pains and the ilk. How did I get to this state?

Lunch' was dreary. Chilled sandwiches and small portions of rice mixed with something indeterminate.

Nota bene 2: weigh myself during morning ablutions and not in the evening. I 'lost' two pounds overnight and could do with all the good news I can muster.

Later; George & Dragon, Glastonbury

I have taken my notebooks down to the oldest pub in town. Have a few spare hours between lunch' and dinner at the centre this evening and where finer to spend it than at the George & Dragon on the High Street. Ordered a glass of red and found myself a table up by the stained-glass windows looking on to the street. Pub's quiet but that's fine by me.

My tutorial tomorrow morning is on 'voice.' What it is, how to acquire it, how to use it. Made notes referring to a couple of my father's poems and to an early novel of MacGregor before he found his own voice and was still borrowing heavily from Emilé Breton. I'll also sneak in an extract from Józef's *Dead Sun* which will give them a taster of his reading tomorrow evening. Only need half an hour of teaching material. Then I'll set a twenty-minute assignment. Ten minutes discussion of process will take us to the break and in the second hour I'll invite them to read and critique each other's assignment work. Usually only about half want to read while the rest retreat into their shells. With any luck one of the readers will be so god-awful it will encourage the rest to join in. Ought to grab ten minutes with Deedee during lunch' tomorrow to compare notes on the Castaways.

I've brought the manuscript of *This Iron Race* to the pub but I'm feeling jaded so might wander round the abbey instead and then pop into St John's for a bit of reflection and prayer. The church is a haven of sanity on Glastonbury's High Street where it's easier to buy a witch's broom and cauldron than a loaf of bread. Place trades heavily on its alleged connection to Camelot and attracts more than its share of oddballs.

That said, I was pleasantly surprised to see a display of the new edition of *This Iron Race* in the Man, Myth, & Magick bookshop. Tempted to pop in and offer to sign a few copies.

Not sure what to make of this year's Castaways. More women than men, though that isn't unusual, and more colourful than usual with an assortment of tie-dyed skirts, yashmaks, and ponchos. Average age is up by a decade compared to most Havens, though that's probably the Glastonbury factor. Place favours the aging malcontent more than the youthfully adventurous. Trying to recall last year's Glastonbury Castaways but it's all a bit of a blur. The reader was the delightful Estefanía Roncesvalles, who set the male Castaways' hearts aflutter. Unfortunately, the piece she read was a poem from her latest collection set during a Wild-Women's retreat on the island of Lesbos, which more than lived up to its promise. One woman burst into tears and fled towards the car park and was never seen again and one chap complained to Roman Bold (I was his second in command) and he had to take Estefanía aside and pass on the complaint.

Roman isn't the most sensitive of chaps—odd, given he's half Italian, though ex-French Foreign Legion and devout Catholic, suggests one or two conflicts in Roman's soul—and it wasn't managed terribly well. Poor Estefanía ended up in tears and thought she was losing the gig. I had to reassure her—in fact over a shared bottle of Tempranillo in this very pub, if not this very table—that all would be okay but that reading such an arousing piece immediately before the coffee break had been unfair on the male members of the group. Poor chaps daren't stand up for several minutes.

Of course, this year's Castaways are here for Deedee Bowbells. Writers can smell money and Deedee has the Midas touch. She got half a million for the film rights alone. Don't think any of them said so much as a word to Józef over lunch'. Though I admit he never is one for small talk. One must lose the habit in solitary confinement.

Nice remark from one old chap—Nigel Bosworth or Boswell or something—said he heard my father deliver a reading in Oxford Cathedral. That must have been thirty years ago now.

"Impressive man, Tom Warbrook," Nigel said with uncalled for familiarity. "No one writes poetry like that nowadays. Have you followed him?"

"Not in poetry," I said, "though I dabble now and then. Literary criticism and scholarship are my thing."

"Oh," said Nigel glumly. "A critic."

"More academic commentary," I said. "I'm not a journalist."

I think Nigel had lost interest by that point as he didn't reply. Lunch' was pleasant fare. Deedee was eating hers with relish but Józef spent the hour toying with his. Man's thin as a rake.

Better put this away and drink up if I want to visit the abbey. Suspect they close at sunset and it's not far off that now.

Postscriptum: large glass Cabernet Sauvignon.

DREADFUL NEWS
Midnight; Avalon Centre, Glastonbury

A late end to the day. The evening's social was winding down around ten. Józef had gone off to his room and I was about to do the same when Deedee caught me by the elbow and asked me to wait until all the Castaways had left.

I assumed she just meant for appearance's sake, but as the last of them disappeared Deedee ushered me towards a doorway onto the terrace.

"Absolutely gasping for a ciggie. Need to talk."

I asked if it would wait, mindful it was freezing outside, and my jacket was scant protection.

"It's Józef," she hissed and pushed down on the release bar for the door. It swung open onto the darkness.

"I hope you can get us back in again," I said as it shut behind us. "Perishing out here. Siberian, you might say."

"That's not funny," she said.

"Even so. What are we talking about?"

"Has Józef spoken to you?"

"Only briefly. Asked if I'd enjoyed *Dead Sun*. Gave me a signed copy when we were at Whitby."

"Did you?"

"Hardly got into it. I admit the man writes like a dream, but there's only so much misery a chap can take."

"You must read it."

"Well, there are other books..."

Deedee had lit a cigarette and after drawing on it she interrupted me with a cloud of tobacco smoke.

"What did he say?"

"Don't think he was happy. Actually, I said it wasn't the sort of book one was supposed to enjoy."

"Oh, Nevil. It's so uplifting."

"Really?" I was bemused Deedee had dragged me into the cold to deliver her opinion of *Dead Sun*, but then she changed tack.

"He didn't say anything else? Have you noticed anything?"

I recalled he'd scarcely eaten anything at lunch'. Not much more at the evening meal.

"Does that tell you anything?"

I admit that I can be dull-witted at times. Edith always said I drove her to despair. I suppose I drove her to Rupert as well. Anyway, the penny dropped, and Deedee confirmed it.

"It's cancer. They can't operate. Reckons doctors have given him four months. Six months tops."

"Good lord."

"It's so unfair. After everything he's been through. Makes me realise how shit my own success is. I'd give it all away just to give him a few years."

I was stunned by her reaction and said, "I didn't know you felt like that about him."

Deedee choked on her cigarette.

"I don't feel any *way* about him. It's just... he's such a brilliant writer. So much better than me, than you, than anyone else on this stupid bloody 'Havens' crap. Don't you think?"

I admitted I hadn't given it much thought. Don Ribble,

our Lakeland poet, might run Józef close for wordplay, but a wet day in Ambleside doesn't trump three years in a Gulag.

"Has he told management?" I asked. "Only they'll need to reschedule…"

"He doesn't want anyone to know."

I was puzzled how Deedee should know if Józef wanted to keep it quiet.

"I picked him up on the way and drove him down. He just came out with it in the car. He was so dignified. I was in tears, and he apologised for making me cry. Can you imagine?"

Deedee was smoking furiously, and the tip of her cigarette glowed like sulphur in the darkness.

"It is horribly bad luck," I said.

"It's shit, that's what it is. How can anyone believe in a God when shit like this happens?"

"He tests us. Those who believe, anyway."

"Sorry. I forgot you're one of them."

"I do believe in God, as an underlying meaning to everything. Even though it makes no more sense to me than it does to you. What should we do?"

"Do?" she asked.

"I mean for this week. Should we do anything?"

"No. He'd hate I told you, but I had to tell someone. I want you to walk with him on Thursday. I'll have to lead them up the Tor, but please walk with Józef. He gets tired easily so watch him."

"Of course. And I won't let it slip. I've brought my copy of *Dead Sun* down with me. Want to quote from it in tomorrow's tutorial on voice."

"Good. Do read it. It's brilliant. And so humane. Let's get inside. I'm freezing out here."

And that was that. Deedee and I parted without another word. Don't blame her complaint against God. None of us are immune from doubt.

Good lord: a *presagio*. A death in the family. Could it be? No. Nonsense. Even allowing Creative Havens is a kind of family for me, what possible connection does it have with Mummy? Glastonbury must be getting to me. Still, poor bastard. *Dead Sun* is on the bedside table, but my mind is in a whirr tonight.

Postscriptum: three glasses of whatever plonk Avalon Arts were serving up.

19 February; Chrétien Tearooms, Glastonbury

Slept badly and woke with a headache. Still have a headache at one in the afternoon. Blame the wine they were serving last night. The cheap stuff is full of additives. Hence, I've called at this tearoom rather than the George & Dragon.

Bloody pretentious name but the tea is in a proper pot and my slice of walnut cake is moist and generous. Just had lunch' at the Arts Centre so cake is sufficient. Chrétien de Troyes did more than any other poet to preserve and popularise the Arthur story, even if he was French.

This morning's lecture on voice went passably well. Didn't feel quite up for doing the readings myself, but Nigel has a decent voice and was happy to help. Bit worrying when I suddenly found myself welling up during the extract from *Dead Sun*. Caught me unawares, but I fobbed it off by saying I was probably coming down with influenza. That might have the benefit of shortening some of tomorrow's tutorials.

Haven't seen Józef today. He was missing at breakfast and lunch'. He is reading this evening and I only pray he can get through it.

Bit of a contretemps during the excerpt from *The Barra Bride*. Obviously, some of the students have done their homework because one woman challenged me on my views of MacGregor and magick. Her hair was dyed with henna and her wrists jangled with La Tène bracelets, so I expected the worst.

Suggested to Alexandria—at least I think that's her name—she should take it up with me over lunch' as it wasn't apropos our discussion, but at least three more Castaways sided with her. One of them had spotted *This Iron Race* in Man, Myth, & Magick and argued they were only displaying it because of MacGregor's association with magick.

Rather went into a huff at that point; said, "If you would care to buy a copy, you'll see that my position is completely vindicated. MacGregor *wrote* about magick, but he no more practised it than *Windy Heath* proves Emilé Breton was a half-witted savage from Todmorden!"

Fortunately, most of the Castaways were indifferent to MacGregor's reputation and with their help I got the session back on track.

Alexandria is not on my list for tutorials. Nigel Bosworth (that is his name) is on my list so part of tomorrow morning should be in tolerable company.

Lunch' was dreary. Jacket potatoes with a choice of cheesy, spicy, or fishy filling but no identifiable ingredients in any of them. Potatoes were done in one of those ghastly radio ovens and the skins were moist and leathery. Tried to collar Deedee for a chat so we could compare notes on the Castaways, but she was distracted. She'd had a bad night worrying about Józef and then an even worse morning. Crispin Dearwood, the actor who portrayed Blake Tender in 'Calypso & Wine,' has been accused of something obscene with a python and won't be available for the sequel.

I suppose no matter how successful we become the difficulties never go away. They just become more peculiar. What *can* one get up to with a python that doesn't end in disappointment and a well-fed snake?

Nota bene: am now in two minds whether to sign the books in Man, Myth & Magick.

ITALIANS
Later; Avalon Centre, Glastonbury

The tearoom became crowded when a party of Italian schoolchildren descended en masse. Or should that be, *in modo massiccio*? I heard one of them mention *Venezia*, which invites one to wonder why the Italian education system would drag children from one of the finest cities in Europe to the backwaters of Somerset.

Fortunately, having finished my cake and tea, I was only bound to my chair by inertia, and it was easy to head out rather than endure the *fracasso*.

I wandered down the High Street with a vague desire to try my luck again at the abbey. There was a wedding in full sway yesterday afternoon and as I'm not in the mood for such things so soon after my divorce I did not go in.

Past the 'Celtic' boutiques with their incense sticks, Peruvian llama wool shawls, and faerie cards, and left onto Market Street by the witch's accessory shop with its grimoires, besoms, and matching chalice and cauldron sets in copper and bronze. Startled by a mannequin in the window cackling at me but it was only one of those 'living statue' performers.

And past Man, Myth, & Magick with its neat little display of "Edited by Nevil Warbrook."

The abbey is splendid, and one can't begrudge them the entrance fee. It's an extraordinary survival when so many of the grand monastic houses vanished into building stone centuries ago. Has a tremendous air of grace and age about it, only slightly marred by a white dove that had contrived to wander in and was flapping aimlessly across the tracery ceiling. The west window with its depiction of Joseph of Arimathea catching the blood of Christ in a cup is much later than the stone tracery surrounding it and a bit overdone for my taste. I asked one of the volunteer guides if it was always this quiet and she said they had only just got rid of a party of Italian schoolchildren.

"*Che sfortuna*," I murmured but I don't think she understood.

The abbey must have put me in a good mood because on the way back I turned into Man, Myth, & Magick and introduced myself. They were delighted to see me and overjoyed when I offered to sign some of the books. Ended up doing all thirty-seven and jokingly said, "Perhaps I oughtn't to sign them all, do you think? Not everyone puts value on a signature."

The woman smiled and said it wasn't a problem and her chap, or *a* chap anyway, rather worried me by adding, "It will be easy to get more in. The wholesalers will be discounting them soon."

"Oh dear," I replied. "That doesn't sound good at all."

"Way it goes," he said. "It's popular, though. We've sold nine in the last few days."

I did not enquire further as the bookselling trade is not my expertise. But I do wonder why a book that is selling well would ever be discounted. Will call Dessie to complain.

And thence back to Avalon Arts where I have retired with *Dead Sun* to the study room. If I am escorting Józef up Glastonbury Tor on Thursday, I shall need to be prepared.

Bleak grey sky, colour of nacre; flights of crows; the Quantock Hills a smudge of charcoal, black with distance.

DEAD SUN

1am; Avalon Centre, Glastonbury

Józef's reading was immaculate. If one closed one's eyes, it was impossible to imagine you were listening to a dying man. He also made me want to finish his damn book, with urgency. To keep one's sanity and decency after all he went through is inspiring and uplifting, just as Deedee said. It was... yes, I will say it: it was Christlike.

Deedee was in tears by the end and so were one or two of the Castaways. Yours truly also had a lump in his throat and didn't care who knew it.

Tutorials tomorrow morning. Hopefully won't be too strenuous. Think I can squeeze in another half hour of reading before I absolutely must turn in.

Postscriptum: Avalon's taste in wine has not improved. One glass only.

Slight buzzing in my ears all morning. Probably down to lack of sleep. It was two when I finally put *Dead Sun* down. Ashamed I ever thought it was bleak.

In consequence, tutorials this morning were a bit of a blur, but I don't think I short-changed anyone. For all his approval of my father, Nigel Bosworth writes the most god-awful sentimental rubbish, but he was the only one of the Castaways where I had to bite my tongue. The rest wrote presentable stuff, if predictable in their errors.

Grabbed lunch' at the Centre, 'soup of the day,' which was probably from frozen, and a rustic cob which was hard as flint. Rain has settled in for the rest of the day. Sweeping over the Levels, it rattles the windows and starlings line the telegraph wires like notes on a stave.

It is as though the waters are rising to cut us off from the world.

Couldn't bear the Study Room on a day like this, so I left the Castaways working on their assignments and hurried down to the bookshop which has a snug little reading room out the back. Comfy leather chairs and an almost collegiate atmosphere. Settled down with my journal, which I think is coming along nicely, and *Dead Sun*.

This evening I'm presenting a lecture on narrative structure. Plan to rattle though the epistolary, episodic, and picaresque novel, then framing narratives, nested narratives, unreliable narration, metanarrative, and metafiction. Idea is to broaden their approach to storytelling, though I much prefer a simple tale simply told without any buggering about.

Resisted the temptation to use the scene in the new edition of *This Iron Race* when MacGregor visits Beresford and Lucas as (a) Creative Havens frowns on tutors promoting their own work and (b) I don't want to provoke Alexandria again.

Now, back to Siberia.

Spent a pleasant two hours reading at Man, Myth, & Magick this afternoon before some clot decided the place needed 'cleansing.'

That did not entail a vacuum cleaner—which I could have tolerated—but incense and vapid strumming on a guitar accompanied by a young woman wailing as though in childbirth.

Whatever they were trying to banish, it certainly did for me, and I was back here well before dinner. No sign of Józef but found Deedee alone in the Gathering Room and managed ten minutes with her. She confirmed that Nigel is a decent sort but tone-deaf as far as words are concerned and Alexandria only wants to write about faeries and dragons, albeit she is tolerably good at it and will probably be published. Abigail, that's the woman I saw with three boxes of wine, asks questions with the urgency of a woodpecker but sits there with a vacant expression while the answer is delivered.

Alexandria has, so Deedee reckons, identified Abigail as a woman with unresolved maternal issues and offered to realign her spiritual centres.

"I suspect Abigail doesn't want to be realigned," Deedee said with a grin, "at least, not by Alexandria."

"What do you mean?" I asked.

"You don't know?"

"Know what?"

"Honestly, Nevil. Alexandria's a raving lesbian. She tried it on with me the first night."

"I don't see how on earth I am supposed to tell who she wants to sleep with?" I protested. "I'm hardly clearsighted."

"It's obvious if you know what to look for."

"Knowledge I have never sought," I said. Then to change the subject asked if there'd been further news on Crispin Dearwood.

"They've recovered the snake," Deedee said.

"From where?"

"You don't want to know."

"Good lord!" I said.

Deedee giggled.

"Actually, it's not that bad. Crispin is claiming he was looking after the snake for a friend—think it's his boyfriend, which explains my doubts over him as Blake—and the heater in the vivarium packed up. Poor snakey was just looking for somewhere warm to curl up for the night. The maid found them both in bed and misconstrued everything."

"And you believe him?"

"Not in the slightest, but if it means he plays Blake again I don't care. What have you been up to?"

"Reading *Dead Sun*. That bookshop, Man, Myth, & Magick, have a reading room out the back. Spent the afternoon, most of it, in there. I admit it is astoundingly good. Deserved all those prizes. Speaking of which, have you seen Józef today?"

"I think he's resting. Last evening exhausted him."

"Not surprised."

"Did you sign your books in that shop?"

"Yes. Yesterday, in fact."

"Thought so. I bought one. It's... unusual. Haven't read much classical fiction, but MacGregor seems modern somehow. I assume that's not your doing. I know how fastidious you are."

I could have spoken for longer, but I had my notes to finish for this evening's lecture, so I said I hoped she enjoyed the new edition and returned to my room. Dinner is some thirty minutes off. Feel unusually hungry.

Nota bene: top marks for not retiring to the George & Dragon this afternoon. Without making a great fuss about it or demanding praise, I am attempting to break my bad habits. Dr Saunders, take note.

Midnight; Avalon Centre, Glastonbury

I have finished *Dead Sun*. I understand why the man paints and it's nothing to do with thunderstorms.

Dinner this evening was the first time I can say the food was enjoyable: proper steak with all the trimmings. Even brought Józef out of his reverie and he was tucking in with relish. Entered my lecture with a feeling of wellbeing that lasted all of five minutes.

Alexandria—I still can't see how one is supposed to know—kept banging on about the fable being the archetypal story form and everything else is a pretentious self-indulgence by writers who think they are the story. Then another Castaway, Dave something or other, talks in a Lunden whine, said that all these complicated and archaic forms are irrelevant to modern fiction because agents only want stories with maximum appeal to the widest demographic which demands immersive third person and linear narrative.

Alexandria replied by telling him every writer should follow their unicorn, at which point I decided we had discussed the matter enough and pressed on with all speed. Fortunately, I could crib from my notes and managed not to leave any gaps for awkward questions. Went well until I lost my way at one point—turned over two pages of notes at the same time—but luckily Abigail was paying attention and put me right again.

Nigel approached me at the end and shyly asked if I would consider looking at his 'manuscript.' He said it was inspired by his divorce.

Oh God.

21 February; Avalon Centre, Glastonbury

Second tranche of tutorials this morning. Abigail is a surprisingly moving poet, though I suspect one or two of her works were written under the influence. Dave Ripper—he who argued that modern agents only want linear single viewpoint narrative—is perfectly competent at doing exactly that and may well add to the vast pile of soulless modern commercial fiction.

It seems harsh to tell a writer fixated on money that they would be better off as a lawyer or mugger and doing so would probably bring a complaint from Creative Havens, so one offers vague encouragement.

But really this morning has been much more about the weather as the sky is piled with cloud and it's blowing a hoolie. There were a few queries over lunch'—we're back to the jacket potatoes—but Deedee is determined to press ahead with the walk up Glastonbury Tor.

A QUEER TURN OF EVENTS
Early Evening; Taunton General Hospital

My memory is surprisingly clear until the very last words Józef spoke to me.

Fifteen of us, together with the driver—a surly local man who would be happier in a hay field—piled into the minibus for the short drive to the foot of the path up to the Tor.

Deedee requested it, I suppose, for Józef's benefit, and the driver clearly believed he had better things to do. I, as requested by Deedee, had attached myself to Józef like a shadow. Deedee was out in front, leading the group up the Tor. The footpath is narrow necessitating almost single file. I was shadowing Józef, and we joined at the rear so none of the Castaways would get left behind.

We approached the summit from the east, which is a longer walk but an easier climb and the Tor protected us from the worst of the wind.

"I enjoyed you reading last night," I said. "In fact, it persuaded me to stay up till two and I finished it. Extraordinary. Did you know you would write it during your confinement, or did you only know later?"

Józef's face was drawn in, the cheeks hollow. His lips have almost no flesh on them, but I believe they curled slightly.

"In the situation I was in, one does not know if one will live."

"No, I suppose not."

"And in the end, I did not live."

I did not understand him.

"Deedee has told you. No?"

"How did you know?"

"I assumed it from your awkward silence."

"Ah. I see. You put me in an awkward position. Promised her I would not let on."

"It is I whose position is *awkward*. I am dying."

"It is beastly bad luck."

"Not luck: only a final consequence. They believed I had psychic abilities and were determined to investigate, even eradicate. I do not know what they learned but the treatment ended before it could destroy me. So I thought."

This was more than I had heard Józef say to me in two years of Creative Havens. He was not angry with the swine, nor sorry for himself. I could never accept fate with his equanimity.

"I thought they stopped that sort of thing back in the nineteen-thirties," I said.

"Russia is a land of old habits," he replied.

"This will be your last Haven," I said.

"Most likely so. And we are here, walking towards a tower on a barren hill."

"There are sheep," I said, "It's not entirely barren."

He ignored me and asked if I had enjoyed *Dead Sun*.

"It's not the word I would use," I said. "I only wish I had read it earlier, before I knew... it changes how one reads it."

"The reader always brings his knowledge to the text. No writer can escape that. But I am glad you read it. May I ask what draws you to *This Iron Race*? It is hardly MacGregor's best work."

"Perhaps not as we know it, but he was ill-served by his publishers. It might have been his greatest work, along with its sequels. The published text does his ambition little credit."

"Do you give him credit?"

"I hope so. I trust so. Why do you ask?"

"I did not include everything in *Dead Sun*. It was my story, and I did not wish to obscure that; but the guards brought me books. They were liberated years ago from a rich man's dacha. They had been ill-treated, damp and stained. Yet had survived and so would I. Among them were works by MacGregor."

"He was popular, for a time, among the early revolutionaries," I said. "They approved of him mocking the Tsar. But a rich man's dacha sounds as though it must be pre-Revolution."

"Does it? There were many rich revolutionaries, both before and for a time after," Józef said.

We had begun to lag behind the group which had stretched out over many metres. I could barely see Deedee. We were climbing on a steady gradient, and I asked Józef if I was walking too fast.

"No. They will not start down until we have joined them and then they will be keen to do so because they will have grown cold and as there is nothing to detain us up there, we shall descend with them."

The path had also moved to the flank of the Tor, outside of its protection, and the wind caught us now. I had to struggle to hear Józef.

"When a man spends so much time alone," he said, "he comes to understand that the world is not as it appears. I was alone, yet I had many visitors. Not even a tyrant can keep a man from the true nature of things. I glimpsed my soul and stood at the edge of the Well of Shadows and saw all the lives my soul had led, both behind and before. MacGregor described what I could see with my own eyes."

"You did not suspect autosuggestion," I offered.

"I suspected everything and everyone. Do you know what I did to hold onto my sanity? Here."

Józef showed me the palm of his hand. The hollow of it was crossed with scars reminding me he had kept a shard of glass. His description of repeatedly cutting himself was still fresh in my mind.

"I saw clearly," he continued. "I have read your new edition of *This Iron Race* and though you respect MacGregor's intentions, you do not see clearly. However much he surprises you, you must be brave. I am convinced death is not the end, as you are, I hope, convinced. Even so, there is much I would have done. I think I must stop talking. The path requires my breath."

It had narrowed also and Józef walked ahead of me. There were steps, twisting back on themselves. Some of what Józef said I lost in the wind. Nor, I suspect, had he heard all my replies. Then the path met a narrow triangle of summit with the blunt end centred on the tower. Its stones were black against the churned-milk sky and the wind howled round and through it. Deedee and the others huddled beside the tower or crouched against the walls. Józef bent and turned away from the blast. The central arch was directly in front of me. A clear Gothic eye filled with wind and howling voices.

I stumbled. Józef tried to take my arm. His lips mouthed me to follow but the voices raged in my head. Then a curtain descended.

When it rose again, I was here, in Gerbil Ward.

I am sitting up in bed with my notebook and pen. I wear a blue and white hospital gown which affords no dignity. Certain of my clothes are in a plastic bag on the chair next to the bed but my trousers and undergarments are absent. It was fortunate my journal was in the jacket pocket. Doctor Ganymedes—he is a Greek-Cypriot—has poked and probed and taken various measurements. None caused undue alarm, but I remain under observation.

There are seventeen occupants of Gerbil Ward, besides me. It would be an unnecessary cruelty to describe them, but I am anxious not to spend the night.

Later; Taunton General Hospital

The ward is named after Dr Rodney Gerbil, a leading physician in these parts some years ago. Shame as I was amusing myself by naming the other wards after small rodents.

I am to be released within the hour. Deedee is coming to collect me. I am a little light-headed, as though I might be blown about like thistledown, but my heart rate is as it should be and my blood pressure normal. I have also had a psychological test which any modestly educated seven-year-old could have passed. The results of my blood test will not be known until next week.

Therefore, Dr Ganymedes has deduced that I am as well as I, or Dr Saunders, could hope and I am to occupy no more of the Wessex Hospital Trust's resources. He has diagnosed psychosomatic stress brought on by over-stimulation of the auditory nerve. I will probably feel a little faint now and then and am to undertake nothing strenuous. He has also barred me from driving.

His diagnosis is wrong, of course, but it seemed wiser to accept his opinion than risk further detention. Dr Saunders can figure out what it really was when I am home. Not driving is awkward as tomorrow is the last day of the Haven.

Ah! I can hear Deedee approaching. Hope she has remembered to bring my spare trousers. Annoyingly, Taunton GH has disposed of a perfectly good pair of corduroys. They claim I had a little accident.

ON TELEVISION

22 February; Avalon Centre, Glastonbury

It is an uncommon experience seeing oneself on the television: especially so when surrounded by a dozen people who are poring over every detail of one's performance. On the television men in bright red suits have strapped me to a gurney and manhandled me into a helicopter.

I have never flown in a helicopter and never much cared

to, but now that I have, I regret that my unconscious state rendered me unable to dislike the experience.

"Up, up, and away," someone said.

Deedee touched my arm. "I wanted to go with you but there wasn't room."

"It's a very small helicopter," I said.

"Why is it bright yellow?" someone asked.

"So you can see it," Nigel Bosworth suggested.

Abigail laughed and said, "It's not like it can sneak up on people."

Indeed not. But whatever afflicted me certainly did sneak up. Józef was closest when it happened, and I can tell he's itching to talk with me. I suspect he will have some notions I won't like.

Nota bene: require new trousers.

Later; Avalon Centre, Glastonbury

There has been a flurry of messages between Deedee and Creative Havens, and I am temporarily relieved of further duties. Józef has taken over my last commitments to the Castaways, and I am resting in the Study Room. It will be 'lunch' in an hour and after a few speeches and thank yous from all concerned, the Haven will end.

I had considered wandering down to the bookshop or the George & Dragon this morning, but perhaps that is unwise. I am not yet entirely myself. Any sudden movement of my head excites a peculiar roaring in my ears and a lapse in balance. I have not had earache since I was a child and hope it is not a recurrence. Deedee has offered to drive me home, though it is considerably out of her way. Dave Ripper has offered to drive Józef to Bath and from there he can get a train. Everyone shall depart homeward.

Józef has not yet managed to catch me alone so whatever he wishes to impart is still waiting. I suspect he will say that my sudden affliction had a paranormal origin. He may be right, but I am not inclined to leap to that conclusion until all other possibilities have been exhausted. Having said that, he was alongside me when whatever it was happened so he may have seen something.

Meanwhile, Devizes surgery has telephoned. Dr Ganymedes has been in touch, and I am to have a follow up appointment next week. Results from my blood test will be forwarded to Dr Saunders. Hopefully, she will then pass me fit to drive, and I can look to retrieve my motor car from Glastonbury.

Today the wind has dropped clean away but the floodwaters on the Levels have not abated and reflect a cool, grey sky.

HOME AGAIN
Late afternoon; Avebury Trusloe

Deedee was a little reluctant to leave me, but I assured her Mrs Pumphrey was nearby and all I had to do was call. Pleasant as Deedee's company is, I feel awkward about having unaccompanied women in the house. Even Mrs Pumphrey doesn't get past the kitchen door.

The cats are ignoring me, but I have not found any significant damage to my furnishings. House is perishing and I am sitting in the living room in front of the fire. Shall get up later and make myself scrambled eggs on toast. Ought to pop my head out the backdoor and say hello to Mrs Pumphrey. Haven't quite got the energy yet as it always turns into a conversation and never a terribly interesting one. If I don't call on her soon, there is every chance she will call on me to let the cats out as she tends to forget which day I am back.

I think yesterday's misadventure has caught up with me as I am astonishingly weary. My bags are still unpacked and apart from exchanging my brogues for a pair of slippers I have not changed since Deedee dropped me off. Can't face doing any work tonight and fancy I will gawp at the television and then go to bed with a hot toddy.

Managed to call next door just before twilight. Still unsteady on my pins so didn't want to risk it after dark and it seemed frankly rude not to thank Mrs Pumphrey for looking after Boris and Tusker. Both of whom, incidentally, slipped past me the moment the back door was opened.

As I hoped, she was in the middle of cooking Mr Pumphrey's tea—which smelled considerably more entertaining than scrambled eggs on toast—so the conversation was shorter than usual.

"They were no trouble at all, Nevil. But I do wonder if you are letting them have too much of their own way."

Frankly, she astonished me, and I asked for clarification.

"They completely turned their noses up at Speedo-Kat and I had to buy Kitty Nibbles instead. I hope you don't mind. It was seventeen Crowns, ten. I know the village shop is expensive, but I didn't want to go all the way into Devizes."

Seventeen Crowns, ten would have gone some way to buying the new coat I promised myself, not to mention new trousers to replace those destroyed by the hospital, but I felt too feeble to do more than grin and bear it. The Speedo-Kat was on special offer in Budgitts, and I ought to know better than forcing economies on the cats.

"No trouble," I replied. "Bit short right now, but I'll pop into town in the next day or two. Anything else untoward happened while I was away?" I had already decided not to mention my adventures. It was only broadcast on Somerset News so none here would have seen it.

Mrs Pumphrey cocked her head to one side as she pushed crocks around on the kitchen counter.

"Now you mention it, there was. This morning when I went in, I heard a noise upstairs. Well, I didn't fancy it in case it was an intruder, so I got my Bill and sent him up. It was a jackdaw in Gerald's old bedroom. No idea how it got there. Anyway, Bill left the window open."

"A jackdaw?" I said.

"You know. Big black—"

"Yes, I know what a jackdaw is," I said. "How on earth could it have got in? Was the door closed?"

"I wouldn't know. You'd have to ask him."

"How odd. Room hasn't been used in ages. Gerald is in Borneo, or he was last time he wrote. Only hope it's gone. Haven't heard anything."

"I expect it must have flown. That was the only thing I recall."

"Well, thank you for the cats, and the jackdaw. Goodnight."

I left Mrs Pumphrey wreathed in steam as she emptied a saucepan into the sink. Back indoors I went up to Gerald's room and closed the window: no wonder the house is freezing. No sign of the jackdaw, or indeed any sign it had been there. Queer thing the door being open though. Assuming it <u>was</u> open. But then, how else could the bird have got in? The window was closed and I'm certain the chimney is blocked up.

Find out in the morning. Now, drink up while there's still some heat in my hot toddy and off to sleep.

Postscriptum: two fingers of Owl Service whisky taken with hot water.

23 February; Avebury Trusloe

Retrieved one black feather and a stick from Gerald's room first thing this morning. Must have overlooked them last night. Feather reminds me of that Spanish girl at Crossstones. I have thrown it out. Don't want it in the house. Wonder if the bird was trying to build a nest: that would explain the stick.

Breakfasted on porridge. Can't stand that cereal stuff. Never seems to fill me up. Wholemeal. Came from Budgitts. That shop is a marvel. Much cheaper than the supermarket. Have now sat at my writing desk with cup of coffee to hand and am ready to commence work.

Postscriptum: weight, sixteen stone, four. No doubt thanks to the miserable food at Glastonbury.

Later; Avebury Trusloe

Solid day's editing *This Iron Race, book two*. Feel almost back to my usual self. Only dizzy spell was when I got up to let the cats out. Think the wind's picked up, but not forecast to rain or snow. Cats showed no hesitation and streaked into the darkness. Church at ten tomorrow morning so early to bed.

On reaching the landing I found the door to Gerald's old room had swung open during the day. Must get the lock seen to. No doubt that explains how the jackdaw got in.

Brought a bit of light reading to bed with me. *Nigger Goes West*, by Richard Hannay is a childhood favourite. Very undemanding stuff and frightfully old-fashioned. Not my original as Mummy sent all my old books off to a church jumble sale. Found this copy during a Haven in Norwich last year.

As a boy I always wanted a dog, and a black Labrador like Nigger seemed the perfect companion. Never quite got around to it and a bit late now. Besides, I'm away too often and it wouldn't be fair.

Postscriptum: usual night cap.

24 February; Red Lion, Avebury

To church this morning. Peter delivered an energetic sermon on the growth, or should that be regrowth, of faith in Eastern Europe. At least he and I were on the same page of the same book this week.

Had decided against mentioning my excursion to hospital last Thursday. Didn't want to worry anyone and it all seems to have cleared up now. Felt perfectly fine this morning. Weather's improved and it's been a nice calm day. Walk across the meadow between Avebury Trusloe and the High Street was a delight; all sparkly dew and cobwebs like silk, white horse grazing in the distance beneath the elms, sunlight slanting through the mist. Horse didn't seem to mind me crossing its field, which is as well as I've never been at ease with the creatures.

Post-sermon during the tea and biscuits Prudence asked if I'd made progress on her Easter talks.

"Only I am very aware that time marches on."

Said I had my four subjects but had yet to make firm notes. She was disapproving.

"I had hoped to see something this week, only Tim and I [that's her husband] have ten days booked in Florence."

"How fortunate for you," I said as sweetly as I could. "Unfortunately, I've had a week working in Glastonbury so haven't had much chance what with tutorials, lectures, marking homework and visits to hospital."

"Hospital?" she said.

So much for keeping it quiet. After that it all came out and, within seconds, I had a crowd of cooing women around me all concerned for my health. Molly was there of course.

"It sounds frightful," Prudence said.

"But as you can see, recovery is complete," I replied with as much self-belief as I could muster.

"A helicopter?" Molly said. "How daring of you. I'm envious."

"Regrettably, my mind's a compete blank on the whole thing. But that's why I haven't had a chance to do much work on Prue's Easter readings."

"Here," Prudence thrust a business card in my hand. It had Tim's name on it. "It's got our joint electronic mailing address. Do write as soon as you have anything for me to read. I so want it to go well, for Peter's sake."

As do we all, Prudence. As do we all.

Made my excuses a few minutes later but before news of my misadventures circled the entire room. I'm as happy to accept sympathy as the next man, but there were some details of my misadventure I really did not want to let slip.

Sun had evaporated the dew and the meadow merely looked green and damp. Happily, there was no sign of the horse. Spent the afternoon editing. If previously I suspected MacGregor had little hope of his preferred text getting past Beresford and Lucas, then today confirmed it. He was writing material that wouldn't be acceptable in print until the nineteen twenties. It's hard to say what people will make of it. I'm not entirely sure what I make of it.

Postscriptum: usual nightcap.

25 February; Avebury Trusloe

Shopping in Budgitts this morning. Weather grey and damp as I waited for the bus. Couldn't find a trolley at Budgitts and had to carry my bags across the car park and then to the bus station. Felt quite shaken and the ride home was thoroughly miserable. Nasty easterly wind.

Afternoon spent editing. Progress still fair. Haven't heard anything from Hare & Drum regarding their interview.

Postscriptum: glass of Budgitts vintage port instead of my usual nightcap. The Britannic Isles are safe once again after the evil French plot was foiled by Nigger the trusty Labrador. Happy memories. My eight-year-old self seems only a handshake away.

WORRYING DEVELOPMENTS

26 February; Avebury Trusloe

Foul start to the day. Quite apart from the gale outside which has left me feeling very unlike my usual self I received a letter from Hare & Drum.

Signature is illegible so I can't say if it comes direct from O'Brien, but he clearly passed on everything I said to someone and they are worried I may have crossed a legal threshold, whatever that is. Actually, I know what that is; it's an imaginary line seen only by lawyers and their spivs who are paid to worry about improbabilities. Upshot is, they are worried Van Zelden may take out a character defamation suit (whatever that is) regarding my 'allegations,' as H&D put it, of events at the Koningin Hotel. The devil is that although every blasted word I said was true I have no witnesses and have made no previous complaint. H&D are prepared to print my account but have approached Van Zelden for his side of the story.

Given I took on the editorship of *This Iron Race* to refute Van Zelden's claims it irks me immensely that it should offer him a platform for his horrid opinions.

Fitful morning's editing as a consequence. Thoughts refused to settle. Tried to get the fire going but it sulked in the hearth. Suspect the wind's in the wrong direction.

After lunch' I took the bins out and then cleared the front lawn of a branch blown down from the oak tree at the end of the drive. Had nowhere to put the damned thing so dragged it to the back garden and tossed it over the hedge, but as I did so I had the queer impression the Longstones were almost on top of me, rather than at the far end of the field. Very unsettling and needed a stiff drink to calm myself. Attempted to settle back into editing but failed miserably. MacGregor's words just swam on the page in front of me. Instead started reading the next of Hannay's 'Nigger' books, *Nigger of Nanking*, and spent afternoon wallowing in nostalgia.

Damn Van Zelden. Damn Hare & Drum.

Later; Avebury Trusloe

On reflection, I suspect the prophylactics behind the fridge must have been Gerald's. He stayed for a month or two after he left university and before his globetrotting began. I recall I was away for at least two Creative Havens while he was here, and no doubt while parental authority was absent, he made off with one of the girls from the village.

What a relief. The thought of Edith and Rupert abusing the kitchen was too much.

Postscriptum: glass of whisky and off to bed. Still blowing a gale but I insisted Boris and Tusker went out. Required the antiseptic again.

27 February; Avebury Trusloe

On the one hand, it's nice to know that Creative Havens cares for my welfare but I'm not entirely sure what to make of their generosity. I received this morning a letter, from the president of CH, but almost certainly from an underling, expressing their deepest concern for my wellbeing, along with a voucher for a week at a health spa near Malvern promising an invigorating course of light exercise, aromatherapy, massage, Yoga, meditation, and hydrotherapy. My immediate thought was to gracefully decline but right at the end of the letter it said the week included a health check and interview with a registered practitioner of alternative therapy (whatever that might be) and my future employment with Creative Havens was conditional on passing it.

I suppose the first thing before accepting is check with Dr Saunders whether I'm quite up to a week in a health spa. Wouldn't mind a doctor's note excusing me from Yoga as well, but I suspect that won't wash. Am hopeful that 'hydrotherapy' is the medical term for a nice warm bath.

Noted the dates in my diary: 25th to 29th March. The Wednesday clashes with dominoes evening at the pub but they can manage without me. Otherwise, the week is clear. Information from Midsummer Hill is vague on accommodation but assuming I have a room to myself I ought to be able to take work along with me. It may even prove more productive than a week at home as staring at the same patch of faded wallpaper sometimes dulls the enthusiasm.

Nota bene: not that I have any desire to see Dr Saunders again, but I had thought the surgery would have been in touch by now. No further dizzy spells but I am getting a peculiar sensation in my ears whenever there's a breeze.

Afternoon spent editing *This Iron Race*.

Later; Avebury Trusloe

To The Red Lion this evening for dominoes. Need to get new batteries for the torch. Light was stuttering as I crossed the meadow. Cold and damp with a bit of mist rising. Owl startled me. Must have been overhead when it hooted into the darkness. I was wary in case the horse had returned but it was absent.

Regrettably, I was not on my best form and even Sid Morris had an off-night. Despite Bert Tanner winning two of his three matches The Red Lion lost by six games to three

Queer sense I was followed on way back from pub. Couldn't see anything with my torch but I could hear something snuffling off in the darkness. Surely someone comes and puts the horse to bed each night rather than letting it wander.

Arrived home to find the house deathly quiet. Let the cats out and sat down with my slippers and a glass of whisky.

Postscriptum: three pints Cropwell's Bitter and usual nightcap.

BANK OF PARENT

28 February; Avebury Trusloe

Two letters this morning. One expected: Dr Saunders' secretary has booked me an appointment on Monday. Handily, I will be able to discuss this Malvern thing with Dr Saunders and hopefully get a clean bill of health so I can collect my car from Glastonbury. The other letter was rare as hen's teeth; I knew it must be Gerald even before I opened it as no one else requires such exotic stamps. I also half-guessed why he was writing and as a result am now contemplating getting the 'bus to Devizes and arranging a money transfer to somewhere unpronounceable in the Far-East. I suppose my plan to buy a decent coat must be put on hold for a while.

Telephoned Devizes Surgery to confirm my appointment for Monday: they confirmed receipt of my patient notes from Taunton. All is well.

Have brought my coffee into the study. I call it my study because it's the only room in the house from which the cats are forbidden. Speaking of which, I spoke with Mrs Pumphrey re the uneaten Kitty Nibbles, and she denied they were dining at hers. Perhaps they are supplementing their diet with the local wildlife.

Have re-read Gerald's letter to assess urgency of situation. I suppose if matters were truly grim, he would have telephoned, reversing the charges, naturally. On the other hand, I ought to do the shopping and Devizes is my only sensible option. Without the car I will have to carry everything and it's ruddy miles from the shops to the 'bus station in Swindon. The weather is dry, which is an advantage. No telling what it will be like on Monday.

So, that affects the present. I shall sit here and drink my coffee. Then, after a reasonable delay to allow for bladder comfort, depart for the 'bus stop.

Postscriptum: returned by early afternoon, all business done. Arms feel leaden and my back aches and all for two bags of provisions. Trying not to begrudge Gerald enjoying life in the Tropics at my expense. Not being very successful at it. Almost wavered towards the whisky bottle but at the last moment remembered I must account for my intake to Dr Saunders on Monday and made a pot of tea instead. Have now sat at my desk to work.

Post-Postscriptum: usual nightcap.

March 1; Avebury Trusloe

April may be, as the poet said, the cruellest month but February is surely the dreariest. In my childhood it was briefly enlivened by my birthday but as I grew older that seemed less and less significant until now, I would be pushed to say that it does not increase my dislike of the month.

Apologies. There ought to be governance against writing while harbouring the glums, but I have much on my mind. Still thinking of Gerald. I sent him two hundred

Crowns. It is less than he requested but that is the limit of my parental restraint. Edith will have had much the same letter from him, and he trusts, correctly, that she will not communicate with me, and I will not communicate with her.

If a son's love must be kept with ready cash, then I will at least be competitive. Between us, he should survive.

Dessie Catterick telephoned this morning. He informs me that Hare & Drum have authorised part-payment for the editing of *Book Two*, which is timely given the two hundred winging out to Gerald, but passed on their concern that my stance on MacGregor and magick may affect the book's promotion and sales.

"There is," Dessie said, "money in magick, as well you know it. Do you think you can be a little less hard on Van Zelden? What harm is there if MacGregor wasn't quite as strait-laced as you believe?"

"Actually, Dessie, having started on the second volume I can promise you MacGregor wasn't as strait-laced as anyone believes."

I didn't elaborate but suffice it to say some of the material is positively racy.

"Sly old dog, was he? Well, he wasn't the only one. Emilé Breton was one for the ladies as well."

I told Dessie that wasn't what I had meant. As far as is known, MacGregor was faithfully devoted to both his wives. I added that as far as I could tell, MacGregor had accepted volume two would never be published in his preferred text and this had liberated him.

"In fact," I said to Dessie, "the comparison is more with L. H. Durrants, Baudelaire, and Victoria Wolfe. He was writing material sixty years ahead of its time. Bit of a surprise, I must admit. Still unsure what affect it will have on his reputation."

"Kind of thing sells, Nevil," he said. "No one ever bought a book because it wouldn't offend their grandmother."

"Unless it's for their grandmother," I said.

"What? Oh yes. Jolly true. But have a think about this Van Zelden business. I caught one of his shows on the gogglebox other day. Frightfully clever and sell-out crowds. Worth thinking about."

I said I was thinking. Then he asked me about Norfolk.

"Norfolk? I know bugger all about Norfolk. Had a girl-friend who lived somewhere that way but that was forty years ago."

"Was she flat?" he asked. I said he was unfunny. He said he had a job he could send my way. I asked if it was paying. He said two hundred Crowns. I said I knew enough about Norfolk.

Later; Red Lion, Avebury

Toward late afternoon the weather improved, and I took myself off for a walk, passing out of Avebury eastwards, along the Harrow Way towards the chalk downs and Marlborough. I had not gone far before I spied a pleasant sign of spring: the snowdrops were in flower.

It is hard, even after a week such as I have had, not to feel uplifted by this brave, yet delicate flower. There were other signs of life too, but the snowdrops had the stage to themselves and were a delight to see.

Passing by Manor Farm a wooden signpost caught my eye. There is something majestic about such a signpost; it is as though the name boards were making decrees. Seeing 'Rockley' upon it suggested the subject of a future article for the church newsletter, albeit Rockley is outside the parish. It is not enough that Avebury is home to what Stukely erroneously called a Druidic Temple, but at Rockley is a quite genuine temple of that most romantic priesthood of brigands, crusaders and assassins, the Knights Templar! Little enough remains of their temple; indeed, the provenance of what does remain is disputed, but their presence in Rockley is historical record. Today, Rockley is little more than a dry valley high above Marlborough with a

62

single road serving a scatter of houses before petering out in a field, but it was once a place of learning and mystery.

But another day for that. I fear, I did not get remotely close to the Downs today. There would have been scarce time to ascend and descend before dark and I had no flashlight with me. Also, the wind was from the east and bitterly cold and when my numb fingers could no longer adjust my camera, I turned homeward. Reaching the henge itself, Avebury's resident jackdaws put up a fine display and I spied a young falcon receiving a thorough mobbing before I turned into The Red Lion for a glass of whisky and a sit by the fire.

What of Hendryk van Zelden? Dessie seems convinced that Hare & Drum wish for an outbreak of peace between us. Though I had thought our frisson was more of an attraction: public loves the whiff of disagreement. Damn it, it was more than disagreement. Bastard nearly had me pissing myself in public.

Now, now. Not good for the blood pressure. Calm down and sip your whisky. In any event, given the nature of the material I am finding in volume two I wonder quite what sort of man I am defending. MacGregor has shape-shifted from an upstanding man of nineteenth century letters into a forerunner of the 'Farmyard Fuckers' like Asher Hughes and his ilk. Oh, it's nothing I find obscene, or even remarkable today; but nor has it the old-fashioned quaintness of *Nigger of Nanking*. It would be easier if I understood what Hare & Drum want from the project. Surely, they can't have known what was in the second volume and at face value they shared my enthusiasm to defend MacGregor from Van Zelden's allegations. Perhaps they didn't anticipate volume one selling so well: if Man, Myth, and Magick is anything to go by it must be running off the shelves. Perhaps that has changed their complexion. They can smell money.

Postscriptum: edited for an hour or so after returning home. Thoughts: if H&D want a rapprochement between Van

Zelden and myself then I think it possible they may approach him to write a foreword for either this volume or for volume three, much as Sister Ethelnyd provided for volume one. Considering what I have read of volume two, I could tolerate that. Recall that I had recorded VZ's show in New Amsterdam, which I assume is what Dessie was referring to. Of course, it may put me in a worse mood if he's up to his old antics.

I suppose if it wasn't for him and his damn-fool attitude to MacGregor then I wouldn't be part way through editing volume two and volume one wouldn't be selling at all. If more people are reading MacGregor, then isn't that the whole point of the work? Probably. But he's no longer quite the MacGregor I thought he was. On the other hand, this is undoubtedly the MacGregor HE wanted to be.

Trust Gerald has now received the two hundred Crowns I sent. Had Gerald half Van Zelden's success I would worry a great deal less of him, and had Van Zelden half my son's fecklessness, I should worry a good deal less about him!

As it is, I worry about them both.

Post-Postscriptum: usual nightcap.

EASTER TALKS FOR PRUDENCE
2 March; Red Lion, Avebury

Church tomorrow and it reminds me I ought to get on with the Easter Talks for Prudence. Tell the truth, haven't done a thing on them since I saw her last Sunday and even if she is swanning around Florence, time is passing. So, after getting milk and a paper at the village shop, I've called in at The Red Lion to pick Jonathan's thoughts. He's been a local here far longer than I have.

Unfortunately, he's had to nip off to Devizes and won't be back for an hour and the young lad serving doesn't look like he's seen sunlight for several weeks so no point asking him. Out with the notebook and pen.

First: the stones of Avebury. Buried. Unearthed by Keiller. Stone blocking Christ's tomb. That should go last.

Blackthorn: plenty of that about. Nice white blossom around Eastertime. Bitter fruit. Ties in nicely with the Crown of Thorns. Harrow Way passing through Avebury on its way from Dorset to Winchester and Canterbury connects to pilgrimage. Avenue of stones towards West Kennet marking approach to Avebury. Could link that to Christ's journey to Calvary. Better to connect Avebury with Jerusalem as pilgrimage sites. Not particularly Easter-ish but might do. The church must be in there somewhere. Church founded on Peter. Peter denying Christ three times. Last Supper. Ah, bread and wine. Got it. So, plenty to go on. Now all I have to do is write them.

Shame the gardens at Avebury manor have no palm trees. Gunnera doesn't fit the bill. Devilishly prickly stuff and not something you'd want to walk on in sandalled feet.

Postscriptum: one pint Cropwell's Bitter.

3 March; Avebury Trusloe

I suspect Peter had been primed by Prudence before she departed for Florence. He asked me about the Easter Readings during coffee and biscuits this morning. Mentioned my ideas and hit a snag. He's not happy with including the bread and wine of the Last Supper: said it's a bit too High Church and can I think of something with broader appeal. Broader appeal than Holy Communion, eh? That's a tough one.

Damned good mind to include the donkey sanctuary, after all. Something about Christ encouraging kindness to even the humblest of creatures. You know, that might just work.

Anyway, I made notes for the piece on blackthorn last evening, so I have some progress to show. Meanwhile I've an afternoon editing MacGregor ahead of me. At least that pays the bills.

Postscriptum: usual nightcap last night.

4 March; Market Street Tearooms, Devizes

Naturally, I did not present Dr Saunders with this journal when I called for my appointment this morning. Instead, I took from it the information she needed and gave it on one page. After an unusually long perusal of the information, she looked over her black-rimmed glasses with the expression of someone bidding farewell to a decrepit pet just before the veterinarian enters the needle.

Not only had I disappointed her, but I felt a pang of conscience as I realised this woman cared that I had disappointed her. It was a look my mother might have given to me at age eight when after a particularly foolish attempt to dam a stream or catch frogs I returned home with arms, knees and shins covered in mud.

"I'm afraid my weight hasn't altered much," I said feebly. "It dropped a few pounds during my time at Glastonbury— I blame the dismal food rather than my illness—but since then it's gone back on. A month hasn't really been long enough to break my habits."

"So I see," Dr Saunders said. "One hopes you can do better. I understand the temptation to drink when you feel the cold, but it really doesn't help. The alcohol opens the capillaries, and you lose heat even faster."

I admitted that I was aware of this and, more to deflect attention from my dismal performance, I asked about my patient notes from Taunton.

"His name really was Dr Ganymedes, and it really was Gerbil Ward. Ha. Named after a Dr Rodney Gerbil, not the hamster-like creature."

"Why ever would you imagine they named a hospital ward after a gerbil?"

"I don't know. At the time it seemed perfectly plausible. I had just been whisked from the top of Glastonbury Tor in a howling gale."

"The report does mention the wind. The helicopter

could only just land. Have you experienced any unusual symptoms since?"

I mentioned the occasional dizziness. Only seemed to happen if I step out of the house but I haven't noticed anything in the last few days.

"Do you mind if I assess your reaction?"

"To what?"

"If I tell you, it won't be a true reaction."

Dr Saunders was fidgeting with her pen and had removed the ink refill from the plastic tube. She asked me to close my eyes and the next thing I knew a jet of air blew against my left ear. Of course, I jerked bolt upright and opened my eyes. For a moment all seemed well and then I collapsed in the chair as though my spine had been cut.

"Can you tell me what you felt when I blew in your ear?" Dr Saunders asked.

"Well," I said. "The last person to do that was my wife, my ex-wife, when we were courting."

Secretly I wanted to see if the starched Dr Saunders might blush, but nothing doing, so I admitted to a momentary dizziness.

"Presumably it's something to do with the inner ear and my sense of balance," I said.

"Not quite. Dr Ganymedes diagnosed over-stimulation of the auditory nerve leading to psychosomatic stress."

"I know that. He told me that. But what does it mean?"

"He means that you were unusually sensitive to the effect of the wind, hence your reaction to a puff of air just now."

I recalled then that I only felt dizzy when I went outdoors, and that it was indeed at its worst during high winds. I mentioned this to Dr Saunders and asked what might have caused it.

"It may be connected to an inner ear problem. I would assess your other ear but now you know what to expect I think the result will differ. I'd like to book you an appointment for a scan at Swindon Hospital. Would any date be suitable?

I consulted my diary, and we agreed the 18th of March. I then mentioned that the following week I would be in Malvern.

Dr Saunders asked the name of the spa.

"Midsummer Hill," I said. "I had wondered if, given your concern, I was quite up to some of the treatments they offer. The yoga seems particularly worrying."

"Yoga is excellent for upper body strength and posture," Dr Saunders said. "And it places little strain on the heart. Less, in fact, than walking a flight of stairs and you don't wish to be excused from your bedroom."

"No, Err. No, not at all. Personally, I'd rather not be going but my employer has made it conditional on my future employment. There'll be some tests you see. My employer, Creative Havens, runs residential writing retreats, but they are part of a larger organisation, and they also do health spas. Fortunately, I don't have to give them anything other than a week of my time."

Dr Saunders had been busy at her keyboard while I was talking, and now she announced that the cost of a week at Midsummer Hill was six hundred Crowns.

"If I were you, I should make the most of it," she said. "I assume they do not permit alcohol and all the meals are calorie controlled?"

I said I really hadn't thought about it.

"If you would like me to write to them on your behalf, I can do so. It might be useful for them to know your medical history. I don't think it will excuse you from Yoga, but you will get the most benefit from the week."

I agreed this was sensible.

"And perhaps a week without alcohol will break the hold your habit seems to have on you."

"It's possible," I said noncommittally.

"Let us hope so. I think you should take your illness in Glastonbury as a warning. It's true that medical abilities have risen dramatically since your father's death, but you shouldn't tempt fate."

Dr Saunders then looked almost sheepish. I do think if she smiled more often, she could be attractive.

"I have something I'd like you to see. It's my son's."

She showed me a schoolbook: *An Anthology of Twentieth Century English Verse*.

"I mentioned to David that you were Thomas Warbrook's son, and he asked me if you would sign it for him. Here, he chose this poem."

"A Bend in the Road," I said. "Written about 1963. Only too happy."

"Thank you. Now: I'll send your notes to Swindon for your test and then we'll book an appointment here when we have the results."

And after Dr Saunders agreed that I was fit to drive, provided I did not wind the car window down, I left. All in all, apart from disappointing Dr Saunders, and another hospital visit, and not avoiding yoga at Malvern, it went better than I feared.

I think I have time for another pot of tea, and they do a nice cream scone.

Postscriptum: weight this morning, sixteen stone, eight.

PROHIBITION

5 *March; Avebury Trusloe*

Having given some consideration to what I shall give up for Lent it seems I only have one choice. Perhaps the combined weight of medical opinion and faith will lead me to better habits. Therefore, let me announce it here: for the next forty days I shall give up alcohol.

Of course, one of those weeks is at Malvern so that won't be difficult—it's not as though I have any choice—but I shall miss the conviviality of the White Horse at Woolstone during my next Creative Haven. Assuming I pass whatever dastardly tests they have in store for me at Malvern.

Glumly, it occurs to me I ought to take those tests very seriously. Losing my contract with them would be a significant loss of income. Is giving up alcohol for lent the act of a reasonable man? Or is it the act of someone with a drink problem who's desperate for a remedy? Oh dear. One can dwell too much on these things. I suppose one can laugh it off and say it's not such a big sacrifice, but one likes to make these little observances.

I have itemized the alcohol I have in the house. One bottle French Merlot. One bottle Owl Service malt whisky bought yesterday afternoon at Budgitts—a waste of twenty-five Crowns in the circumstance—plus the dregs in this bottle which I shall see off tonight: easier to resist temptation if I have to open a new bottle. Anyway, draining the house of alcohol just so I'm not tempted during lent isn't quite in the spirit of things and I might put the wine aside to celebrate afterwards.

I don't suppose it risks doing more harm than good? One hears of people suddenly giving up a bad habit and having all sorts of complications. But then, if I do have complications, it proves I have a problem. Which I haven't. Therefore, I will be fine, if a little tetchy. It's not as though I have any other bad habits to compensate for not drinking. There will be the mockery of Sid at dominoes to contend with, but it's not as though it's a lifetime. Forty days is brief enough. I think I'll say it again and underline it this time:

I am giving up alcohol for Lent.

Ash Wednesday; Avebury Trusloe

Rained all day. No dominoes this evening as the back room is hired out to a wedding reception. No one I know, thank heavens, so I shall not be obliged to offer them my congratulations. Also, grateful that I do not yet have to announce my Lenten sobriety to Sid Morris. I'm sure he will find it immensely amusing.

Early to bed as travelling tomorrow.

Caught the eight o'clock Swindon 'bus and am now on the train to Bristol. There I will catch another train to Wells, and then on to Glastonbury by 'bus to collect the Rover. That's over three hours travelling but it should only take half that to drive home.

As there's nothing much to hurry back for it will give me a little time free in Glastonbury and there's a book I'm hoping to find: *The Christian Landscape* by Otteline Perrelle. It's fairly old, 1950s I think, but it's the sort of thing Man, Myth & Magick might have and there are a few other esoteric bookshops in Glastonbury I can try. In fact, I don't think the town has a normal bookshop as they all specialise in the odd and exotic. I have a fancy Perrelle's book might be useful for these blasted Easter pieces Prudence has me writing and as I'm going to Glastonbury anyway it would be foolish to pass up the chance.

Of course, it would have been much simpler if I'd got back to Prudence after a day or two's thought and said I didn't think her idea workable, but I do dislike letting people down and so I fudged it and hoped for the best. Alas, two weeks on it's too late to put my hand up and say "Sorry," I'll have to make the best of it.

Pleasant day for a journey at least. Bit of blue sky and calm air. Now that I know my dizzy spells are brought on by the wind, I've become acutely conscious of the weather.

Nota bene: ask in the bookshops if they have anything on psychosomatic stress relating to the auditory system. Must be worth a try as I can't be worrying whether I'll keel over in the slightest breeze.

Anyway, that's all assuming the car starts after sitting outside for two weeks. Hoping to visit Mummy tomorrow so if the car doesn't start it will throw a spanner in the works. But no sense getting glum about things that may not happen and there's sure to be a garage in Glastonbury, even if they might do a sideline in broomstick repair.

Postscriptum: should have mentioned that I polished off the last of a bottle of Owl Service on Tuesday evening. A generous three fingers. My last drop until the eighteenth of next month. Oh Joy.

MARSH SPRITES
Later; Chrétien Tearooms, Glastonbury

Green Knight Garages assure me the Rover will be ready by five o'clock. Ominously, that is also the time they close so if they are out on their estimate I will be stuck here till morning.

With that in mind, I've had a word with the manager at the Avalon Centre and they'll put me up for the night if needs be. I only managed to get the car going thanks to a ladies' hockey team who are down here for a spell of team-bonding. Luckily, they were all strapping girls and after they gave me a shove, I got the engine ticking over. Of course, given the battery was completely flat and didn't seem to be charging it was straight round to the garage.

According to the caretaker at Avalon, it's not unusual for cars to mysteriously develop a flat battery if left there for any length of time. He pointed out that the car park backs onto a rhyne and thence onto the Somerset Levels and said they have trouble with marsh sprites. Apparently, they like nothing more than a juicy battery. I did my best to humour him, but my battery is undeniably flat, and I suppose he knows the place better than I do. Hopefully, Green Knight Garages will have a sensible explanation.

On the bright side, a nice woman at Labyrinth Books managed to find a second-hand copy of Otteline Perrelle's book. I also asked if they had anything on psychosomatic stress which led to me giving an edited account of my helicopter ride off the Tor. After that she couldn't have been more helpful, and I soon had six books to choose from. Fortunately, most were inclined to the occult—I am certain no one has hexed me—but one stood out for its sensible medical terminology and though it was more expensive than its fellows it seemed the wisest choice. I have yet to look at it in detail—one ought to be seated comfortably at home before reading anything alarming—but I'm sure it will be helpful.

While I wait, I've called at the tearooms for a pot of tea and slice of cake. One way and another I have been on the move since eight this morning and this is my first opportunity to sit down without the scenery rushing by.

Perrelle's book is fascinating. My assumption that hawthorn or blackthorn would be appropriate local references for Christ's Crown of Thorns is wide of the mark and perhaps the common bramble or briar is rather closer. I suppose as the Bible is unclear on what plant the Crown was made of it wouldn't be inappropriate to use gorse. There's plenty of it growing on the Downs.

Something to consider for this evening, assuming I get home today.

Evening; home again

Green Knight Garages deny marsh sprites had anything to do with the condition of my battery and have replaced the alternator. Repair bill of three hundred and fifteen Crowns puts a significant dent in this month's finances. Had I not promised to give up alcohol for Lent I would have headed straight for the bottle. Tea is a poor substitute.

Blinding headache and shortly to bed after putting the cats out. Not glanced at Perrelle's book, or the book on psychosomatic stress. Best leave them till tomorrow after I get back from Amesbury.

8 March; Avebury Trusloe

I try to drive over to see Mummy at least once a month. It isn't always practical, what with work taking me away from home so often, but one does one's best. Not heard anything from Judith Malmsey regarding Lester Rookwood so hopefully that delusion has gone away, but one fears it is only

73

a matter of time before another takes its place. Mummy always had quite the imagination and it is coming home to roost. Speaking of roosting I hope whoever was putting jackdaw feathers in her room has gone away as well. I'll keep an eye open for Conchita just to be safe. Weather is dismal with low grey cloud and forecast of drizzle, so I won't have any reason to open the Rover's window.

Awfully tempted to call in at The Gingerbread House in Manningford Bohune on the way back but I shall not let myself down. At least, not after only two days of prohibition. Be strong, Nevil. It will be worth it in the end.

Had better see if the Rover starts. You never know, the marsh sprites might have followed me home.

BLACK FEATHERS

Afternoon; Gingerbread House, Manningford Bohune

It occurs to me that I am only giving up alcohol, not pubs. It is true that once inside a pub my resolve will be tested by familiar smells and the kindness of friends, but not tested nearly as much as refusing the pub altogether. Besides, I have my regular commitment to the Avebury dominoes team to consider and I can hardly insist they decamp to the village hall!

That said, walking into a pub and ordering a coffee and bottle of sparkling *eau de pays* feels deuced odd. Like swearing in church or littering in a graveyard.

What I hadn't expected when I walked in from the drizzle was the pleasant smells wafting from the kitchens. The Gingerbread House has something of a reputation for food and I hadn't realised how hungry I am. Prices are a bit eye-watering but there's nothing much tempting in my refrigerator at home.

What with Gerald's plea offsetting that nice little earner from Norfolk (The cash from which I have yet to see) and now the bill for the new alternator I should check my finances. Always embarrassing to be caught short at the end of the month. Still: payment for Glastonbury should hit my account any day now—Creative Havens are prompt payers; I'll give them that—so I probably don't have anything to worry about.

I suppose a peek at the menu couldn't hurt. They might have a tasty little entrée to soothe the hunger passions.

Anyway, I had my journal open to record my impression of Mummy this morning, rather than idle speculation on 'lunch'. She seemed a little glum and when I asked her how she was she dabbed her eye and said my father had been ignoring her lately.

Even after twenty-two years without Daddy and two years of Mummy's illness the shock whenever she says something like that never goes away. It is as though someone had shaken some unseen rug beneath my feet, and everything wobbles and threatens to fall over. Vertigo is the closest word for it. I recall involuntarily clutching at my chest as though experiencing one of the more theatrical kinds of heart attacks and my voice was an octave higher than usual.

I said something to the effect that I'm sure Daddy wasn't really ignoring her and perhaps he couldn't help being away. It's best to go along with her thoughts as saying Daddy is twenty-two years dead really wouldn't help matters.

"You must be right, dear," she said. "Even though you're not a bit like him."

Actually, I do resemble my father a little, but whereas he was thin as a rake all his life, I have inherited the MacStrangie tendency to put on weight after so much as a wafer biscuit. I suppose we are unalike in terms of achievement also, but I like to think that is down to modern times which do not value scholarship as highly as in my father's day.

Again, I did not question Mummy's opinion, but then she said something that truly shocked me.

She leant in closer and with a giggle said that my father had been visiting her at night after everyone had gone to bed and they would dance through the hallways into this very

75

room and thence out the French windows into the garden. "And after we had danced and made love, he would leave me a black feather. Only I've lost them," she said, suddenly distraught. "I've lost them all and that's why he won't come back."

Then she burst into tears, and I was quite unable to console her. One of the carers had to take her back to her room.

I don't know what to do. I simply don't know what to do. Obviously, I recalled the jar of feathers in the broom cupboard but could hardly say anything and Conchita was nowhere to be seen. Not sure they should be returned to Mummy anyway as they might only increase her delusions. Hoping she calms down again and all will be as normal. I'll telephone the home in the morning and ask to speak to Judith. If possible, I'll speak to Conchita as well. She seems to know more about Mummy than the rest do. Nothing I can do now except have a bite to eat I suppose. Devilled lamb's kidney with bitter chocolate mousse and tempura seaweed sounds exotic.

My father would have disapproved of such luxury and Dr Saunders will disapprove of the calories. I probably oughtn't to make a habit of dining here but as a rare treat I think it acceptable.

Postscriptum: managed to pull myself together this evening and complete the first of the Lent Talks dealing with the Crown of Thorns. Despite Perrelle's speculation I decided to stick with my first thoughts and write about blackthorn, not least because it's in bloom right now.

Reasonably pleased with it and will drop a copy round to Prudence tomorrow morning on the way to Swindon.

Nota bene: food at The Gingerbread House is excellent but next time pay closer attention to the prices.

9 March; Clegg's Café, Swindon

I decided on the way home from Manningford Bohune yesterday afternoon that my potentially parlous finances are no reason not to replace my lost pair of trousers. This I have done from Budgitts' *Prêt à Porte* range, and I am now recovering over a cup of tea and sandwich in Clegg's. Rather a comedown after The Gingerbread House.

Purchasing new trousers is possibly my most loathed activity in the world, though dancing may be worse. Luckily, it's easy to avoid dancing but one does occasionally need new trousers.

It's an occasion made worse by two factors: one of which I have no control over and the other which is an inevitable consequence of being a literary scholar: vis, I am short in the leg and permanently on a budget. Hence, I am reduced to scavenging the racks at the bottom end of both the metric and pecuniary scales.

I first picked out a pair of 96cm waist *chinos* (what, pray, is wrong with calling them trousers?) in a nondescript shade of grey they labelled 'surf' and retired to the fitting room. This proved a misnomer as the difficulties began near my knees and worsened with altitude.

I returned the chinos to the rail and selected a pair with a ninety-eight waist in 'Castile,' which is a shade between sand and beige. There was measurable improvement above the knees, but it was now I began paying attention to the 'straight' or 'comfort' comment on the labels. I can't help thinking that legs are usually straight, but it was apparent my legs are not.

The pair of 98cm chinos was also returned and having read the label, I returned to the fitting room with a pair of 98cm 'comfort' chinos.

One peculiar fact. The trousers I had worn to the shop are a 94cm waist and a little baggy around the middle. I suspect a centimetre is not always a centimetre. Colours, meanwhile, had ranged from grey, through sand, to a sort of bottle green the label described as 'cypress.' There were none in blue (the colour of the trousers I needed to replace) and the only other colour they had was 'snowdrift' which I fancy would spend longer in the laundry basket than on my backside.

The 98cm regular *chinos* fitted but gave the impression that I was one movement from disaster and the pockets gaped at the side, revealing a slice of brilliant white pocket lining. Why they cannot take vanity into account and make pockets gape with an expanse of material the same colour as the rest of the trouser leg I do not know.

They, also, were returned to the rack and, with reluctance, I picked up a pair of 100cm *chinos*, though I gambled and risked a straight cut of leg. Then to the fitting room once more, where, to my relief, they fitted in a manner that was dignified and allowed modest movement without imperilling my anatomy. I suppose I only have myself to blame as the dreaded one metre waist has been creeping up on me for years, but perhaps it will not increase further. There is certainly nothing in Clegg's to tempt me.

10 March; Avebury Trusloe

My little homily on the Crown of Thorns and our local blackthorn trees went down well this morning. Prudence got most of the praise over the tea and biscuits after the service, for she read the piece, but she was happy to share the acclaim and I had several come up and say how pleased they were and how they had never thought to look on blackthorn trees that way and where had I got the idea from. Too polite to point out that the connection is fairly obvious unless I had Christ wrap his head with a rambling rose. Anyway, I have four days to write and deliver the next talk which will now combine the Twelve Stations of the Cross with the long-lost avenue of stones from Beckhampton, of which the two Longstones, known as Adam and Eve, are the only surviving members. 'Adam and Eve to Calvary' has a ring to it.

But first, the continued editing of *This Iron Race, book two*. Unlike church homilies that will put bread on my table.

11 March; Avebury Trusloe

Decent weather this morning so went for a walk down to the Longstones and then back along the supposed route of the avenue. If one is to write about something it always helps to familiarise oneself with it.

Things were a little muddy after the recent wet weather, but enjoyable, nonetheless. No dizziness at all and I can almost say I feel healthier than I have in many months. Can my new regime be working? Time will tell. Certainly, my lunch' of low-fat cheese and wafer biscuits with apple and celery is frugal enough.

This afternoon I shall put my inspiration to the test and write the piece for next Sunday before I start work on MacGregor. Then I know I am free to devote the next few days to work. My week in Malvern is fast approaching and I cannot guarantee I'll have time or energy for actual work.

Nota bene: remember to remove my boots from the top of the boiler or risk the leather cracking.

12 March; Avebury Trusloe

Nothing much to report today. Homily for Sunday written, and I'm reasonably pleased with it. I'll drop a copy off to Prudence before dominoes tomorrow evening. Editing continues. I'm still troubled by the new text. Quite different from anything MacGregor wrote before. One might almost call it pornographic, except it is far better written than most filth.

Wonder if I should mention my worries to Hare & Drum. Can't imagine they looked at MacGregor's first drafts before sending them to me. It will certainly change a few critics' impressions of him and explains Beresford and Lucas's reaction. For the moment I shall press on regardless and discuss the matter with H&D once the second volume is completed. That way we shall have a better oversight of the whole work and, more importantly, I shall be paid. Worry them now and the whole enterprise might be cancelled.

Postscriptum: weight this morning, sixteen stone, nine.

Dominoes this evening was overshadowed by news that Avebury has lost one of its oldest shops. It is sad when any village loses one of its attractions but as Robert and Jeremy Black have run Avebury Antiques for over thirty-five years the loss is both part of our fabric and part of our history.

It was, I suppose inevitable. Both men are in that time of life where the years grow thin as wheat in a dry spring and since Jeremy slipped and broke his hip during January's snows, opening times at Black's Antiques have been erratic; Robert, more often than not, keeping to the backroom of the shop next to the stove and the kettle.

Those in the know understood he might be brought out into the front parlour with a firm knock at the door, but the casual visitor was never so bold. At least, so Robert mentioned to me, the quiet gave him a chance to catch up on his reading and he politely enquired how my own work was going. I assured him he had plenty more years left to read whatever I produced, and this seemed to give him some comfort.

Meantime, Jeremy, the senior of the brothers by some two years, continues to convalesce at their sister's in Bourne-mouth, but it is hoped he will return soon, and they will remain in the village.

The windows of the former antiques shop are a sorry sight and worse for being so central in the village. Given the peculiar bend in the road from Swindon, it is the first sight the motorist has of Avebury and its ghostly windows lend the place a dilapidated, uncared for appearance that is far from the truth. We all hope someone takes it over before the main tourist season. There is talk of a café, even, heaven fore-fend, one of those ghastly coffee houses, but I scarcely think it will find the trade nine months of the year. More promisingly, The Henge Shop may take over the premises, though of course that will only leave a vacancy at their present establishment in the High Street.

I suppose I look at it and think a bookshop specialising in history and local matters might do well, though I am quite aware that no one with any business acumen ever chose to be a literary scholar, so perhaps I am optimistic! If it doesn't find a buyer, it won't bode well for the future of the village.

NORFOLK

14 March; Avebury Trusloe

Doorbell rang early this morning and I had to get downstairs promptly. Postman had a large package and a billet for me to sign. Confused at first, but then I saw it was from Norwich and all was clear. Once opened on the kitchen table I found a list of criteria from Norfolk's Emerging Writers, along with a batch of short stories. The criteria also assume the judges are familiar with Norfolk and will mark stories down for inaccuracy and use of Norfolk stereotype.

That might be tricky. Quite what strings Desmond pulled to get me this little number, heaven knows. One ex-girlfriend from Saxmundham, a couple of book signings in Norwich and a Creative Havens gig at Cromer (in a particularly desolate January, if I recall) hardly makes me familiar with the history and culture of Norfolk. Perhaps someone cried off at the last moment, a not unreasonable response to the imminent arrival of two hundred amateur short stories, and Buggins was next out of the hat. Ah well. I remind myself it is Lent, and suffering takes many forms. Let us hope there are not too many stories about cats. My life is quite filled with cats as it is.

I only have to skim through them and select the best five. Or the five that are least bad. Fortunately, most bad writers give themselves away in the first few words. The winner will be chosen by Florence Ffyffe, whose fame far eclipses mine and who will probably be paid more to read those five than I am to skim through this lot. There are another four pre-judges out there and they are all Norfolkians.

Managed to get through fifteen of them this morning

before I lost the will to live. Afterwards I continued with MacGregor.

Postscriptum: on second thoughts, Saxmundham may be in Suffolk.

15 March; *White Bear, Devizes*

Just when a chap thinks he's over it and everything is ticketty-boo, the arse falls out of his trousers, and everything is suddenly naked and jangling like a galvanised frog's leg.

There was I, alone in the world, quietly about my business in Devizes, midway between the bank and the Asbo market (not its real name, but honestly, given the people who frequent the place it should be) when who do I spy coming the other way, hand-in-bloody-hand, but Rupert and my ex-wife.

It doesn't matter how many miles on the clock, how many grey hairs on bonce and balls, it sets a chap back to when he was five years old and snivelling his heart out because someone got a slice of cake, and he didn't.

Thank God I hadn't got around to buying the frozen peas. Though had I done so, Edith's path and mine might never have crossed today. As it was, I had dived sideways into the nearest porch, which happily belonged to the White Bear. Pretending a call of nature—there are enough occasions I don't pretend so it was hardly what one might call acting—I managed to make the gentlemen's cubicle before I blubbed. Quite what anyone at the urinals would have thought, heaven knows. Luckily, Devizeans are known for their cast-iron bladders, and no one heard me.

It's not the first time I have bumped into them, but it has never hit me quite so hard. Edith looked lovely and I even remember when she had worn the same lilac dress with me beside her. Rupert was wearing denim—the man's built like a beanpole—and those ridiculous maroon riding boots he always wears. Couldn't tell for certain but I think he may even be braiding his hair in that ridiculous horsetail fashion young footballers affect.

Anyway, I couldn't hide in the lavatory forever, so I got myself together and pretended all was normal as I ordered a pint of Moonraker non-alcoholic bitter. Might not stiffen the spine like a proper pint, but when you feel like walking wounded it's important not to look it to stop the buzzards circling. What desperately awful timing that he and she should appear together during the season of penance. As if things weren't testing enough.

Hopefully, Edith and boyfriend have buggered off back to chez Glendale's—a 'ranch style' palace with all mod-cons just visible if you crane your neck from the Swindon Road—and I can finish my shopping in peace.

If I am not careful the rest of my day will feel tarnished. Two years. Two years since Edith left me and there's not a day, I don't miss her and reproach myself for not being more attentive. It can't just have been the maroon riding boots that cost me my wife. She found something that was missing from home. Something I too have lost. "*Whither youth unto the green grass, for in autumn wither you as hay,*" as my father wrote in 'The Harvestman.'

I must look pathetic hunched in the corner scribbling away over my half-drunk pint of non-alcoholic beer with my bag of groceries. Divorced, they'll think. Or a widower—how tragic. Or lifelong bachelor. Alone. Alone, that's what they'll think. And they'll be right.

I should visit the gents again before I go. This sort of stuff goes straight through a chap.

Later; Avebury Trusloe

Arrived home to find a message on the telephone answering machine. I recognised Edith's number and nearly deleted it on the spot. I could only suppose she had noticed me scurrying into the White Bear and was delivering something to the effect that I should get over it all and start living my life again.

Which I should. I know I should, but when you've been hurt by a betrayal it takes a great deal of getting over. I didn't delete it—after all, this is the voice of the woman I loved, or still love, and listened to the message while drinking tea. She had spotted me in Devizes but hadn't noticed that I had seen her and Rupert. She was just asking if I was well as she thought I looked a little peaky. Well, I might say, anyone would look peaky if they'd just spotted the love of their life arm in arm with some bounder in riding boots. Then she asked 'who my friend was' which I don't understand at all. Perhaps she thought someone was with me but obviously she's mistaken.

Anyway, that was only some sort of preamble because she was really calling on behalf of Rupert's daughter, Eurydice. The girl's doing some sort of thesis or article, Edith was a bit vague as she always is about academic work, but the subject is MacGregor and Eurydice would like to interview me.

I've nothing against the girl—never even met her—and it's not her fault she's Rupert's daughter, but in the circumstances, I can't see myself doing it. I shall cry off, claim I'm too busy. But I shall be polite and suggest one or two books she might look at. Of course, now I'll have to telephone Edith but at least this is her private number so no chance of Rupert picking it up.

A HORRIBLY AWKWARD SITUATION

16 March; Avebury Trusloe

Telephone call this morning from Eurydice. She had intuited, correctly, that I was unlikely to return Edith's call and had taken matters into her own hands. I asked if her father knew she was telephoning me. He did not, but then she asked why should he know? She was nineteen and even if she was still living at home, he had no control over who she spoke to.

I admitted that was reasonable.

"Look," she continued. "I get this is difficult for you because of what happened, and I'd understand if you wanted nothing to do with me because of my dad, but we both know he's a dickhead, so we have two things in common."

I was taken aback by her honesty but then asked what the second thing was. She said we both adored MacGregor.

"I think adore is a little excessive," I said. "I admire his work immensely but I'm not in love with him."

"I know," she said, "you're in love with Edith. But that's okay. Edith is cool."

Honesty is refreshing but also a little bracing first thing in the morning. Before matters got too delicate, I asked her about MacGregor.

"I get this thing with you and that Zelden guy," she said. "But maybe there's something you're both missing. Anyway, I've got this essay to write, and I want to look at 'Lays of Brigadoon,' his poem. That was the first thing he wrote after Madeleine died, yes?"

I agreed that it was and mentioned that Richard Wagner wrote the music for the operatic version.

"But that was later," she said. "After the first book of *This Iron Race*?"

"First and second books," I said. "MacGregor was completing the third while overseeing the opera's production at Winchester."

"It's the poem that I want to focus on," she said. "I want to compare his poetry before Madeleine's death and afterwards. I was hoping I could interview you."

I admit to a sudden touch of cold feet. The girl's enthusiasm was palpable, but she was the daughter of the man who stole my wife. That may be unfair—no, it is unfair—but there it is. I made my apologies and said something about being too busy.

She said it was okay. She was disappointed but understood.

Can she really understand? What does a girl of nineteen know of love? I suggested she read Evelyn Bishop's *A Writer's Life*, but of course she already had. And she had read Crabtree's *The Wizard of the North*, though little good that had done her.

"I am sorry, truly I am," I said, "but the circumstances are just too horrid. Perhaps if you were to write to me, then I think I can answer anything you ask. But to meet... sorry, I don't think that would be right. I can't escape the knowledge that you share a house with my wife, my ex-wife. I hope you understand."

She said she understood. "No," she said, "I really do understand. I have to deal with this with my mum all the time. My dad's a dick. You're not the only one he's hurt. I'll write and thanks for offering to help. Bye."

I said goodbye and put the telephone down.

An hour later and I am still uncertain what to think. Am I being too priggish in not meeting the girl, or is it really too painful? I hope I am not punishing her for the sins of her father. That would be too awful. If she writes and I reply, then perhaps at some point we might meet to talk about Mac-Gregor. I like nothing more than talking about MacGregor and she is enthusiastic. I hope that I do meet her. Just not yet.

Later; Avebury Trusloe

Been in a peculiar mood ever since speaking to Eurydice. Didn't prevent me from continuing with *Book Two*, but perhaps I am seeing it in a new light. It was the girl's comment that 'Lays of Brigadoon' was the first thing MacGregor wrote after he recovered from Lady Madeleine's death that got me thinking. That is generally accepted to be the case, apart from the 'Black Books,' as MacGregor called them, none of which have survived.

Although I have seen nothing in my restoration to question that case, in terms of emotional permissiveness the content of the material in *Book One* went beyond that in 'Lays of Brigadoon' and in *Book Two* far exceeds it.

Seen in those terms, the text I am bringing back to life must lead to a reappraisal of MacGregor's state of mind after his recovery from deep depression. I cannot tell if these writings are the work of a fully recovered man seeking emotional honesty in his work, or if it reveals a man determined to martyr himself, or at least his text, in challenging public decency.

It is not that the material itself is extraordinary in its language or content when compared with that of writers working sixty years after MacGregor's death, but that is really the point. The only contemporaries of MacGregor producing work as explicit as this were pornographers and, while a few flourished in the shadows, a writer of MacGregor's stature and reputation surely had too much to lose by copying them.

That is not to say the text in *volume two* is anything like that produced by pornographers—there is none of the florid prose or obsession with sex one finds in nineteenth century erotica: no Portals of Venus or Gates of Sodom, thank heaven—but only that its content would have met the same fate under the law.

What, then, did MacGregor intend by writing a text that could never be published in his lifetime? And what effect will publishing it now have on MacGregor's reputation?

But, taking Eurydice's thoughts further, could one see this work as testament to his love for Lady Madeleine and Lady Helena? Was it love which forced him to a new level of honesty in prose?

That is the happiest of thoughts.

SACRIFICES

17 March; Avebury Trusloe

Peter talked about Lent this morning and all the things we might give up. I sat there feeling pleased with myself until he started going on about the starving in Africa and what they might give up for Lent and how they couldn't really give up anything. Peter seems to forget at times who his parishioners are. Instead of being happy with the sacrifices we are making he chastises us for having potable water and mains electricity. It left a bad taste in my mouth, especially when I noticed him tucking into a slice of Mrs Hartmann's walnut and Madeira cake after the service with a complete lack of self-reproach.

Quite a few are making sizeable sacrifices for Lent: Molly is giving up meat, though whether she will oblige her guests at the Linden Tree to follow suit she didn't say. Sid Morris is giving up cigarettes, though few expect him to last the course. Regrettably, a few have taken that view over my own Lenten promise, but I am determined to prove them wrong.

In other news, my talk on the Beckhampton Avenue and The Stations of The Cross went down well, though Prudence thought I was stretching the comparison a little and that it wasn't as convincing as last weeks talk on blackthorn. Ah well. One cannot please everyone all the time. One or two had never heard of the Beckhampton Avenue though I think they are new to the village so perhaps that is not so surprising.

Sid mentioned that the avenue, or its course, passed directly under my house.

"I had no idea," I said. "I'm surprised they allowed it."

"Those houses are what, fifty years old?" he said. "They weren't so worried back then, plus no one really knew if that avenue of stones ever existed until a bit later. Only found the holes of 'em, ain't they. Holes where they stood."

I said I believed that was so, "There are the Longstones, but no one believed an avenue connected them to Avebury. Under my house you say?"

"They surveyed it a few years back," Sid said. "Not long before you and your missus came to the village. But there's always been tales about that field."

"What field?" I asked.

"The one atween you and they stones. Y' must've seen how it holds the frost in winter."

"And what sort of tales?"

"Faerie rides, that sort o' thing," Sid said and then winked heavily to let me know I was victim of one of his tall tales.

"You almost had me there," I said.

"You spend too much time reading of such things," he said.

Perhaps I do, but that field really does hold the frost long after it's gone everywhere else.

"I'll be off," he said. "Might be Sunday to this lot, but I've had a call that wants some slates fixing. Reckon I'll see you on Wednesday then?"

"Someone has to take the minutes, prove we were all there," I said.

"There are them that does, and them that writes about them what does," he said and left before I could think of a reply.

If he knew how many times I have corrected his ignorant use of English in those minutes, he might have a higher opinion of writers.

It was time for me to say goodbye as well, but I singled out Molly and thanked her for the fine reading of my piece on the avenue and mentioned that Sid had spent the last ten minutes convincing me the stones once ran through where my house stood.

"Oh, but they did," she said to my surprise. "I thought you knew that. Everyone knows that. There's a cold spot right outside your house, have you noticed. In the middle of the road opposite your door."

I admit that after walking home from church I stood outside my door and walked back and forth a few times. Apart from feeling a bit of a fool I didn't notice anything.

Scrambled eggs on toast for lunch'. Said a prayer for the poor bloody Africans. Not sure what else I'm supposed to do. Completely unfair of Peter bringing it up. One doesn't attend church to feel guilty about living in a civilised part of the world.

Later; Avebury Trusloe

Afternoon editing MacGregor. Turned misty late on. Chilly night forecast with a frost. Went out about nine to get a bucket of coal. Pitch black. Cats slunk past me like ghosts and disappeared into the gloom. Where do they go at night? What do they find to do?

I headed back to the fire and a cup of tea. Why is Lent in bloody winter? It's just the time you need a bit of good cheer. Nothing on the telly and going to bed early. Noticed the calendar as I was retiring for the night and my appointment at Swindon Hospital is tomorrow afternoon. Oh joy.

PUBLICITY

18 March; Avebury Trusloe

Breakfast only just eaten and already a telephone call. Desmond has received an enquiry from a radio station in Oxford asking if I will do an interview with them and talk about MacGregor. Dessie thinks I ought to do it.

"Publicity, old boy," he said. "Never knock any opportunity."

All very well for him to say that but I've endured some dull and ghastly evenings in the name of publicity.

"Not doing anything that day are you?"

I checked my diary for the twenty-first—which is only in a few days time—and mentioned it was short notice but that I had nothing planned. Assuming the interview only takes an hour or so there are plenty of enjoyable distractions in Oxford. I could give Professor Hans Frum a call and arrange to meet at The Trout. Wouldn't mind having a chat about the material in MacGregor's first draft. Get a second opinion on it, as it were. Haven't seen him in ages anyway.

I asked Dessie what exactly Radio Nuage broadcast.

"Jazz," he said. "Apparently it's French for *cloud*."

"I know perfectly well what nuage means," I replied. "But why are they interested in MacGregor?"

"Dear boy," Dessie said, "That's like asking why the fish is interested in the hook. They mentioned something about a Felicity Asterisk, French chap. Publisher."

"Ah," I interrupted. "Would that be Félicien Alberix?"

"That's him. Thought it wasn't right. Chap named Felicity. What ever next? Who is he?"

"Published some of MacGregor's last works," I said. "Nearly published *This Iron Race* in MacGregor's intended text in the early 1900s. That was before MacGregor's fair copy vanished into the aether. Unfortunately, Lady Helena died before anything got off the ground. And Radio Nuage is interested, eh?"

"Seems so. No idea what they want of it. So, if this Asterisk"— "Alberix," I interrupted— "Yes, him," Dessie continued, "If he had published it then you'd be out of a job."

"Happily, so," I said.

"Speaking as your agent I don't think that's quite the attitude, old thing. Anyway, they want you in the studio at ten sharpish on Thursday. Think you can do that?"

"I have recovered my motorcar, so it presents no problem," I said. "Who is the interviewer? Who do I ask for at reception?"

Dessie obfuscated a moment. Obviously, he had lost the letter.

"Here it is. Name is Dave Bratt. Programme is called 'The Exchange'. Goes out seven in the evening."

"Oh, so it's not a live interview," I said.

"No, but just as well, eh. Don't want you saying anything impetuous on air, do we."

"I am never impetuous, Desmond. I shall be there at ten."

Said my goodbye in a slightly bad mood. Do wish Dessie wouldn't keep calling me old boy and old thing. He's only two years my senior. He gave me the address of the studio and Cowley isn't far from the delights of Oxford's centre.

Hopefully, it will all be over by lunchtime. I'll give Hans a call later and see if we can meet.

SHAKE, RATTLE, AND ROLL
Later; Swindon General Hospital cafeteria
My word! I feel like I have been struck like a gong and some half hour later I am still vibrating. The ordeal has left me

with a queer sense of drifting in and out of focus, so rather than drive home immediately, I have a cup of tea and a sandwich in the cafeteria.

Someone has decided the place should be decorated with children's drawings. Presumably, it's to cheer the place up, but one can't help feeling that this is where people go to absorb very bad news, whether news of their own health, or that of their nearest and dearest. I'm not sure the naivety of children is quite what one wants at such moments. But at least there's none of that dreadful background music one finds in so many cafes. That really would be too much, listening to the inanities of popular music while mulling over one's frailties. My table is next to a painting of a goldfish by 'Charlie,' aged seven. No telling if it's happily circling its bowl, or dead on a plate.

On arrival, I was passed moderately speedily from reception to a waiting room and then called to a numbered door. Inside was a nurse who asked my name and that of my doctor and then informed that I must remove anything metal upon my person.

I took out my purse, followed by my house and car keys, and then my watch.

"I think that is all," I said and placed them in the box provided by the nurse. She was smiling indulgently as one does when observing a child being foolish.

"Metal buttons, zips, anything in your wallet, such as bank cards, banknotes? Aglets or steel toecaps in your shoes?" She asked.

"Ah."

It turned out I was wearing rather more metal than I suspected and in a short while was reduced to my shirt and underpants.

"Any piercings?" she asked.

"Certainly not."

"Tattoos?"

"Tattoos? They're hardly metal."

The indulgent smile returned. "The inks can contain metallic elements."

"No tattoos," I said.

She was filling out paperwork and ticking off each item as I spoke. There were a lot of questions.

"Any surgical implants? Stents, pacemaker? Metal screws or fixings following surgery?"

"No, nothing like that."

"Any dental crowns?"

She said this with a sort of flourish, as though certain to catch me into an admittance.

"Is all this really necessary?" I asked.

"Absolutely. The magnetic field generated by the equipment can tear out a dental crown. You wouldn't want that, would you."

I admitted that, yes, I had a dental crown, but after some thought, and a quick inspection, it was determined to be ceramic, and therefore unaffected.

"Good," she said. "Almost done. Are you taking iron supplements?"

"No. Gosh! It doesn't have any effect on blood, does it? Only I recall there's iron in blood."

"We will not be removing your blood," she said with the same indulgent smile.

"Last section," she said and turned the page revealing more questions.

"Do you have clearsight, or the Gift of Grace as it is sometimes known?"

"Good Lord no. What has that to do with metal?"

"Please, this would be so much easier if I asked the questions. Is there any history of clearsight in your family?"

I hesitated a moment, thinking of Mummy and her claims of a midnight visitor. But of course, that was merely a delusion rather than anything else.

"No, not to my knowledge," I said. "Next you'll be asking me if I've ever seen a ghost."

The nurse glanced up with a curious expression of half boredom and half curiosity.

"Actually, that is the next question. Have you or anyone in your family ever seen a ghost?"

"Certainly, I have not, and so far as I am aware, no one in my family has either."

Of course, even as I replied I couldn't help wondering exactly what Mummy was seeing at Crossstones. The most likely answer is nothing at all, but I can't rule out Lester Rookwood's ghost calling on her.

"Excellent. If you will sign here."

She handed me the form with a finger indicating a dotted line below her blue ticks.

"What actually am I signing?"

"That you have heard and observed our precautions."

"Ah. So, should anything untoward happen it's not your responsibility."

"That's right. We have done everything to ensure you will be safe."

I did not like that word.

"And you're quite certain about no piercings?" she asked with a glance at my underpants.

"Quite certain."

Actually, I knew a chap at Oxford who had a piercing in his how's-your-father. A Prince George, I think it's called. I suppose if the device can remove a dental crown... Some things are best not dwelt on.

Anyway, with much of my effects now consigned to a box, I was given a surgical gown and a pair of disposable slippers and shown through into a second room which was completely empty, apart from a device resembling a chaise longue and the grotto of a diminutive Santa. Everything was spotlessly, almost terrifyingly clean.

The nurse handed me a pair of ear buds.

"Wear these," she said. "It can be quite noisy."

Noisy doesn't begin to describe it. I lay on the chaise

longue and after a moment of relaxing, it propelled me silently into the grotto, which, from the inside, resembled nothing more than an immense pipe. Everything was very white, and I was reminded of the isolation tank at Malvern, as it had the same disorientating effect. I looked about, trying to find something to anchor my eyes on, and eventually spotted my feet.

"Now relax," she said just loudly enough to penetrate the ear buds.

I did as requested and my feet slid below the soft hill of my tummy.

"I'll be next door, but we will instruct you when we're ready."

I dimly heard the door close and fathomed that I was now alone inside the machine.

"We'll be scanning in ten seconds," a voice said. "Lie perfectly still and don't be alarmed. We will be as quick as we can."

"...three, two, one."

The Earth moved. Or at least, it seemed very much as though it had. I had a sense of vast entities circling my head and every so often they would collide in ways that echoed through me. I tried to breathe normally and hold perfectly still, but ineluctably, my toes were slowly curling. I allowed my toes as they seemed sufficiently far from my head, which was the focus of events, that I didn't think they mattered too much.

As I lay there, thoughts swam into my head. I remembered Edwin. Mummy and Daddy at the seaside. Daddy shouting at Mummy over some ridiculous misunderstanding. Edith the day she walked out on me. The first poem I wrote. All sorts of silly, half-forgotten memories slid around in my head, half in-focus and half-not, moving like dappled shade on a woodland floor.

Then it was over, and the chaise longue slid out of the machine, and I could breathe properly.

After a moment the nurse entered and led me out of the room. I was in a sort of blur as she offered me my things and I began to get dressed behind a screen.

"Thank you, Mr Warbrook. We'll have the scans processed in about ten days and your doctor will be in touch. Have you got everything?"

I had reassembled myself and the box was empty.

"Yes, thank you. Was I brave?"

"Yes, you were. Ten days."

So, there we are. An experience, I admit, but one I fervently never wish to repeat.

Charlie has drawn a bubble coming out of the goldfish's mouth. I think we can say it is alive.

Evening; Avebury Trusloe

The mist lingered till midmorning before the sun burned it off. Pleasant sunshine after that. Couldn't resist glancing across the field towards the Longstones before I left for Swindon and just as Sid had said, the frost was lingering while it had gone from the surrounding fields.

Managed to fit in a couple of hours on my next Lent talk between returning from Swindon and teatime. I have something presentable but the more I worked at it the fewer connections I found between the stone blocking Christ's Tomb and the stones of Avebury. After all, when the stones of Avebury were re-erected, they really did find a body: that of an unfortunate barber—identified by a pair of scissors—either crushed when the stone fell or deliberately buried beneath it. Too late now, but I think I should have written about one of the long barrows at Kennet which were sealed with stones and did have human remains in them. We can all be wise after the event.

Had considered going for a walk once I'd finished—my quest for more exercise and a healthier life continues—but the fine weather hadn't lasted, and I wasn't tempted out. Grave danger of turning into a hermit, but at least the PCC meeting tomorrow evening will force me out of the house and on Thursday I have this interview in Oxford.

Hans has returned my call but is unable to meet as he and his wife are going to the theatre that evening. Shame as I had hoped to ask him what he recalled of Lester Rookwood. Another time.

Only hope I don't dream abut that ghastly machine. Once was quite enough.

BAD BEGINNINGS (AND ONE GOOD ONE)
19 March; Avebury Trusloe

Another package of short stories arrived from Norfolk this morning. Reminded me I have not yet finished reading the first batch. Given the two hundred I am getting for reading them will come in useful, I sat down with a promise to read twenty before lunchtime.

I say read, but reading is not usually necessary. The first paragraph is enough to show whether someone can write, and one only needs to properly read those that pass the test. Enough fail in the first paragraph to save a great deal of time. Excessive amounts of weather are a typically bad way of beginning any story but in a short story where every word counts it is deadly. The weather is a popular subject in Norfolk, especially when employed with the pathetic fallacy. Several stories started with angry storms, raging tempests, and furious blizzards.

There was one rather affecting story which I have set aside as one of those I hope Miss Ffyffe will consider worthy of winning. It starts predictably enough with a chap walking a beach after a storm—I may be ignorant of Norfolk, but I am aware it has fine beaches—who finds a bottle containing a message. So far so ordinary, but rather than leading the chap to treasure or romance or the rescue of some mariner, the message asks whoever finds it to write a reply and return the bottle to the sea. This the man does, and as a joke invites the sender to tea. The next day the bottle is there again on the beach and inside is a reply accepting his offer. I must admit the ending put the hairs up on the back of my neck.

Apart from that one story, there were at least two that concerned cats, three where the story turned out to be a dream, and several where the entire story took place in the character's head without a single line of dialogue or action on their part. And those were the ones with competent first paragraphs. It is fortunate I only have to find five worthy of passing on to Miss Ffyffe.

After lunch'—smoked mackerel on toast with a glass of apple juice—I continued editing *Book Two* but found I couldn't concentrate. Whether it was the morning of looking through those dreadful short stories that frustrated me, or that one story of the bottle on the beach, I can't tell, but I hope the feeling passes.

Unable to work on editing, I decided to do what I had not managed yesterday and walked down the green lane to Silbury Hill. I had hoped to include the hill, which I can just see by craning my neck out of an upstairs window, in my Lent talks, but nothing came of it. Whatever Silbury may have been, it is no Calvary.

The hill itself is too steep for easy climbing, even if one were prepared to risk the wrath of the Antiquities Trust, but it has a brooding magnificence quite different from anything one finds among the Avebury Stones and one usually finds oneself alone there.

Watched a pair of buzzards circling the summit before noticing grey cloud brooding over the Downs and headed home. Rain caught up with me just before I reached the door, and I was soaked. Clear again now and it looks as though it will be a dry night. PCC meeting this evening and I may walk into the village rather than bother with the car.

Postscriptum: weight this morning, sixteen stone, seven.

Late evening; Avebury Trusloe

Most of the Old Guard were absent at tonight's meeting and it fell to Molly and me to mount a defence against the latest idiotic idea. Fred Thirsk, our Captain of the Tower, had mentioned a few days ago when I bumped into him at the post office—he was collecting his pension and I was buying a pint of milk—that he had seen Peter Chadwick pacing out the nave and side chapel at St James's with pencil, paper, and tape measure.

"You know what he's up to?" Fred said.

"Another try at getting rid of the pews?"

"Doubt it. Not after Antiquities Trust backed us up. But it'll be something like it, mark my words. You'll have to watch for it as I can't make next meeting. Wife and I are over at our daughter's in Aldershot. Best of luck."

So, I attended tonight's meeting forewarned, but even so I was taken aback by the audacity of the proposal and the degree of support Peter had already mustered. Poor Molly had no idea what was coming, but bless her, she soon rallied round.

Peter's scheme is devilish. Unlike last time when he attempted to replace the pews with café-style seating, nothing of historic value will be lost from the church, but in some ways this proposal is even worse. After Paul Durdle had outlined the plan with the help of a sheet of graph paper, I spoke up:

"Just so everyone here understands. Peter proposes to overturn one thousand years of worship at St James's by moving the altar to the west end of the nave and turning the chancel into a crèche. I've no doubt a crèche is a jolly good thing for the village, but is exposing our historic rood screen to the fingers of young children a good idea? Meanwhile our Saxon font is moved to the north wall out of the way of the new altar and the pews turned to face west."

"We have to move the pews," Prudence said brightly. "Otherwise, Peter will be talking to the back of everyone's heads."

"Speaking of Peter," I said. "I assume you intend moving the pulpit as well?"

"The pulpit stays where it is," Paul said.

"We'd like to move it," Prudence added.

"But we can't," said Paul. "The Antiquities Trust would have to be consulted and would probably refuse permission."

"Some people don't seem to understand the church is a living thing and must adapt," Prudence said. "They'd sooner it was a museum."

"Perhaps," I said, "It is only living because it respects the past. So, along with a new altar we have a new pulpit."

"Peter doesn't want a pulpit," Paul said.

"He thinks it separates him from the people," Prudence said. "He wants to be free to move among us."

"Oh, like the Holy Spirit, I assume. So, the existing pulpit does what?"

"Presumably gathers dust," Molly joined in. "Except it won't. I'll see to that."

"The pulpit will not be disturbed," Paul said.

"Certainly not by anyone using it for its intended purpose," I argued. "Can I ask, is there anyone here who hasn't been consulted by Peter before tonight? I mean apart from Molly and myself. Only you all sound perfectly *au fait* with his idea. Does Sid know? What about Fred and Terry? Were they consulted? Does Pauline Lamb know anything about this?"

"We hoped Pauline would be here tonight," Prudence said.

Pauline's apologies had been read earlier. Her mother was unwell, and she had been called home. I knew perfectly well Fred knew nothing of the details and assumed Sid and Terry knew nothing either. All three are, along with Molly and me, long-term custodians of St James's while Prudence and Paul are Johnny-come-latelies. Lucy, of course, supports her husband in everything he does, at least in public. I immediately suspected Pauline was part of Peter's plot.

"Speaking woman to woman," Lucy said to Molly. "You understand the need to attract young families into the church, and especially to make the church part of children's lives from an early age."

I muttered something about grabbing them before they're weaned. Paul tutted.

"I do," Molly said. "But are you sure the chancel is the best place for a crèche? I mean, how often would it be open?"

"Every weekday," Lucy said.

"Oh, I don't think I'd like that," Molly said. "It's so useful to be able to come in and clean and dust during the day. And it would be off-putting to all our visitors."

"Visitors?" Prudence asked.

"Those who come to admire the church," Molly said.

"The church is for the faithful, not tourists," Paul said. "Haven't you always said as much, Nevil?"

"I think that's more Sid's take on things," I demurred. "But I do think running a crèche five days a week will destroy the atmosphere of a place of worship. And it's not as if the village lacks a crèche. The New Barn School takes children from the age of one."

"They hardly offer a Christian environment," Prudence said sharply. "The Henge Shop sponsors them, and you know what they're like."

"And have you, as our Spiritual Outreach Officer, spoken to the New Barn School?" I asked Prudence.

"I have not approached them, no," Prudence said.

"I agree with reaching out to families with young children," Molly said, "But I know one of the teachers at the New Barn School and I'm sure they would welcome support from the church."

"Exactly, take the church to an existing school rather than trying to put a crèche in the church," I agreed.

"Thank you, Nevil," Molly said.

"I don't wish to put a damper on your enthusiasm," I said to Paul, Lucy, and Prudence, "But tonight's meeting is not quorate. Presumably, Pauline's absence was a bit of a blow."

Prudence looked glum.

"Never mind," I continued. "I have noted that we are too few to pass a resolution and will be sending copies of the minutes to Sid, Terry, and Fred, along with Pauline, of course. I think I can safely say everyone will be attending next time."

What I meant was that with five of us voting against the proposal and only Paul, Prudence, and Pauline in favour (the vicar's wife traditionally not having a vote) Peter's plans would proceed no further.

"Now, is there any further business?" I asked.

"Yes," Molly said. "I would like to propose that the PCC approach the New Barn School on behalf of the church before the next meeting."

"Do we have anyone to second that?" I asked.

Prudence was glaring at Molly, but to her credit she wasn't swayed. I delayed a moment, hoping someone else would second the proposal and spare me from doing so, and to my relief Lucy put up her hand.

It was her turn to be glared at by our Spiritual Outreach Officer.

"I'm sorry, Prue. But if we can't get young families and children into the church, then we must take the church to them."

"Motion carried," I said. "I think that is your responsibility, Prue. I'll add it to the agenda for next month."

Prue looked as though she had swallowed a toad but agreed.

There wasn't a great deal of note after that and I signed off the minutes at a quarter past nine and after the usual round of switching off lights and heating we departed into the night. Lucy headed across the road to the rectory while Paul and Prue had parked up at The Red Lion. That left Molly and me briefly alone.

"A close-run thing, Nevil," Molly said. "You deserve a pint tonight."

Her voice had a bright gaiety to it quite at odds with the oppressive meeting.

"At other times I would agree with you," I said. "But I've given it up for Lent."

"Oh yes. Silly me. You mentioned you'd stopped. How is it going? I mean, do you miss it?"

"It wouldn't be a sacrifice if I didn't," I said.

"Never mind. Another time then. We showed them tonight, you and me. We stuck up for the old church."

"We did indeed," I said.

I was halfway home before I realised Molly would have joined me at The Red Lion had I been going there. She may even have bought me that pint. A close-run thing indeed. I am not sure I am ready for a woman's attentions; however innocent they may be.

20 March; Avebury Trusloe

Day spent at my writing desk. No distracting letters or telephone calls resulted in a good day's work with only the briefest of halts for lunch'—sardines on wholemeal toast was surprisingly tasty for something so virtuous—and cups of tea.

Struck me this afternoon how revolutionary Mac-Gregor's depiction of females is. Of course, Eolhwynne and Màiri Mulcahy in *book one* were spaewives, or ex-spaewives, so outside the norm of womankind, but Sarah Pinsker is an entirely ordinary young woman whose viewpoint is drawn with realism and sensitivity. The character is present in the published text, of course, but I think her depiction in the first draft is noticeably more honest and candid, even if one ignores the obvious erotic element. Will it change critical opinion of MacGregor? Indeed, I think it will, and for the better. I am encouraged.

Have now broken off for tea and do not expect to resume work later. Dominoes tonight against the Waggon and Horses in Beckhampton.

Later; Avebury Trusloe

An evening of mixed fortunes. I managed two draws and a loss and despite Bert's best efforts we lost 5-4. However, the battle of 'the bones' paled beside the psychological warfare once we had put the dominoes away. My attempt to enjoin Sid against Peter's plan to turn St James's upside down backfired when he took it upon himself to give his opinion of my Lent talks.

Suffice to say, he is unimpressed and while the words farfetched, simplistic, platitudinous (in all honesty I didn't think Sid knew the word) and plain nonsense did not all appear at once he scattered them through a rather caustic review that left me hurt and blaming Prue for the difficulty of the assignment.

"A good craftsman, such as you have claimed to be with words, doesn't blame his cack-handedness on the difficulty of the job. If it was that hard a job, he should never have taken it on," Sid insisted.

"I was hardly in a position to refuse!"

"And why not?" Sid asked. "If Peter asked me to mow the graveyard in five minutes or cut it to a millimetre, I'd tell him it can't be done."

"I didn't want to let her down."

"If you're that bothered about letting her down then why'd you oppose this daft business with the altar?"

"That's different," I said. "I opposed it because it damages the church."

"And writing stuff about the stones and blackthorn trees doesn't? You're messing up the True Faith with wicket magick."

"It's Wiccan, not wicket."

"All I am saying is there's more ways of damaging the church than shifting the furniture."

"You really believe my Lenten pieces are damaging the church?"

"I do. It took a deal of sacrifice by folk a lot smarter than thee and me to break the Old Faith in this land and we're fools to let it slide back. I know they call themselves Wiccans. It is I call them wicket folk. Blackthorn indeed. You know folk reckon blackthorn is a haunting tree."

"I know there is a deal of folklore attached to it, as there is to most native trees. But any Bible scholar will tell you a great deal of folklore is written into the Bible itself."

"That's as may be," Sid muttered. "But there's no blackthorn in the Bible is there. So, what's the next pagan nonsense you'll suffer us with on Sunday?"

"I'd sooner not say, given you will obviously denounce it. Anyway, regardless of how you feel about my Lenten Addresses, I hope we will see you at the next PCC meeting so we can kick this latest proposal into touch."

"You shall. I've other news from the post office. But it can wait a moment."

Sid went off to the lavatories leaving me with Bert.

"I'd ignore him, if I was you," he said.

"Thank you for the vote of confidence. I suspect he isn't the only one with misgivings. I'm not entirely comfortable with it myself, but it's what Prue wants."

"Though he is right that you didn't have to go on with it."

"Too late now. I am obligated."

"And she's not a woman to let down."

"No woman is."

Sid returned and took his seat again.

"What's this news then?" Bert asked.

"There's a party interested in the antique shop."

"That was quick. Robert has only just announced he's selling up."

"Reckoned a prime location like that would get attention," Sid said. "Seems the prospective buyers have been nosing round the village."

"Looking for what?"

"Competition, Sally at the Post Office reckons."

"And who are they? Do we know that much?"

"She gave me a name, but it meant nothing to me. Crocus... no that weren't it. Sounded like it though."

"Crocus," I repeated. "What about Kronus?"

"Yeah, that's what she said. Heard of 'em?"

"No. But I can guess. Kronus was a Greek god. Forerunner of Zeus. In fact, he was Zeus's father. He was famous for castrating his father and then eating his children, so they didn't usurp him."

"Thought there'd be a law against that," Sid said. "Reckon they and that lot at The Henge Shop will get on well."

"Shouldn't think so," I said. "Sounds like they are chasing the same market. I hoped the Blacks' place would make a cosy bookshop and café."

"There's books in that Henge Shop," Sid said darkly.

"I meant books normal folk might actually read," I said. "This will have to be it for me. Up early tomorrow."

"Unusual for you."

"Driving to Oxford. I'm on the radio."

"Local radio?"

"Yes. And mini-wave, I think."

"Shan't hear it down here."

"Then you are spared," I said.

21 March; Nuage Radio, Oxford

Mr Bratt is in a meeting, so I am waiting in reception. They are playing music but so quietly it hovers at the edge of hearing like a persistent insect. Reminds me of something I heard in Labyrinth Books in Glastonbury. Seats are comfortable and the young chap at reception couldn't have been more apologetic.

Journey up was uneventful. Fine day with a little sun. First day of spring, allegedly: night and day of equal length. Traffic in Oxford was dreadful, but it always is.

Sid's news last evening was disappointing. I had hoped for a shop that might serve the village rather than the tourists, but I suppose we just don't have the numbers and it would put our existing store out of business. Oh well. At least it's better than someone converting it into a home.

Better put this away and wait for Mr Bratt.

A BLOODY AWFUL COCK-UP!
Later; Eagle and Child, Oxford

I had no idea that could have gone quite so badly. Indeed, I don't believe it could have gone worse. I shall telephone Desmond first thing tomorrow and make my feelings plain. Have now retired to nurse my wounds at the Eagle and Child on St Giles. It's a writer's haunt I have fond memories of from my student days at Israel College, but it has yet to work its old charm on me this afternoon.

Where am I to begin?

Dave Bratt was a thin man, older than he seemed at first sight, and with his long hair affectedly worn in a ponytail. I recall thinking as I followed him to the interview room that he didn't look like my idea of a jazz enthusiast. I also noticed the smell of incense and platitudinous slogans on the walls: 'to err is human, to forgive is divine,' was one of them; and 'all are climbers on the sacred mountain,' was another.

For some reason I had supposed the interview room would have studio lighting, but of course as this was radio Bratt showed me into a gloomy cubbyhole of a room with a half-glazed partition in the middle of it. Through the glazing I could see a technician seated at a console.

"Chase will be here in a moment," Bratt said.

"What chase?" I asked.

"Chase Carnadine, your interviewer."

"Oh, yes of course. For some reason I thought it might be you."

"I'm the producer," Bratt said.

"Yes, but surely, it's not difficult to combine the two. I mean, how hard is it to interview someone?"

Bratt ignored my question and asked me to say

something for a sound test. I, for want of anything better to say, recited a line from 'The Corn Flail':

"At the sign of the Black Ram we drank his health and mine in honey, blood, and wine."

Bratt looked at me like I was mad.

"From one of my father's poems," I said.

The soundman put up a hand to indicate all was well and at that moment Carnadine walked in.

If I seem unusually calm describing all this it's because I want to convey the feeling of gloom as it came over me, along with a sense of utter betrayal.

Carnadine was younger than Bratt, but looked older as his head was completely shaved. His face was lugubrious with the cheeks hanging low at the side of the mouth, as one sees in the aged. The eyes were deep-set and dark, with the right eyebrow pierced with a gold ring. The only thing his appearance had in common with Bratt was neither looked like a jazz enthusiast. In fact, they both reminded me of Glastonbury.

"Sorry to be a trouble," I said to Bratt. "I have got this right? *Nuage Radio* is a jazz station, isn't it?"

"*Nuage?*" Bratt said.

"Yes, *nuage.* The name of the station. It's French for cloud. I, or I suppose my agent, assumed it was named after the Reinhardt tune."

Carnadine stared at me and for a moment the deep-set eyes under the bald scalp looked like a grinning skull. Then he calmly indicated the station name on a notice board.

"Exactly, *nuage,*" I said. But then as Carnadine moved his hand closer to the board a hyphen appeared between the 'u' and the 'a.' It did not spell nuage, but nu-age.

"Oh heavens," I said. "There's been a misunderstanding."

"Too late now," Bratt said. "We've booked you."

"Booked?"

"If you back out, we miss our recording deadline. There'll be costs."

I had got the idea that new-age types were fun and easy going, but it was clear from Bratt's tone that he was anything but. I had to grit my teeth and get on with it.

Carnadine began by introducing me and asked when I became passionate about MacGregor. It was an easy enough question.

"And you see him as a literary figure, a great author, nothing more," he said.

"And poet," I said. "His poetry became old-fashioned rather quickly, but he was certainly a great poet in the minstrel tradition."

"I don't think anyone would deny he was a famous writer, and poet," Carnadine said. "But how do you respond to suggestions he was something more than just a great writer?"

"You assume one can be something *more* than a great writer," I said. "But I assume you are referring to the wild accusations made about magick, are you not?"

Bratt asked the technician to stop the recording. Carnadine leant back in his chair. His gaze was unsettling, but Bratt was talking.

"No one is making any accusations, Mr Warbrook. Our listeners are interested in the work you're doing to bring MacGregor's book back to life."

"Life?" I protested. "It's not alive. I'm simply restoring the text."

"It was a figure of speech," Carnadine said. "Mr Warbrook. May I call you Nevil? Nevil, the general idea in an interview is I ask a question and you answer it."

I agreed that it seemed a reasonable idea. Recording resumed.

"I'd like to know what you make of this," Carnadine said. "I know you must be familiar with it, since it's from the book you edited." He then quoted something Sister Ethelnyd wrote in her introduction to *Book One*. I noticed he read from a photocopy rather than the actual book: "*In denying MacGregor any association with magick, other than as an informed author, Mr Warbrook does him a disservice.* Sister Ethelnyd is a friend of yours, isn't that right?"

"A dear friend, yes. But as with all friendships we have our differences. That happens to be one of them."

"So even your friends don't agree with you," Carnadine said.

"Not all the time, no," I agreed. "Do yours?"

"No," Carnadine admitted.

"I have made no attempt to keep my reasons for taking on the restoration of the text hidden," I said, hoping to speed up proceedings. "Mr Van Zelden made certain accusations against Sir Tamburlaine MacGregor, and I object to them. Many of his accusations rely on his misunderstanding of the original text, which is the exact text I am working from to restore the new edition."

Carnadine glanced up and I caught a glimpse of those dark eyes.

"With respect, that's not entirely true," he said. "You admit you only have the first draft material. MacGregor would have written a fair copy, wouldn't he? A definitive version you don't have?"

"That is true. His fair copies are lost. Perhaps even destroyed."

"And you don't know what changes he may have made to his first drafts."

"Not in detail, no. But in many instances his first draft material and the published text, his revised text, are terribly similar."

"But neither are the text he wished to write," Carnadine said.

I agreed that was so.

"You might consider my work an educated deduction based on the best evidence available," I said. "I make no claims that it is perfect."

Then, as I had been expecting all along, Carnadine repeated that cheap jibe from Van Zelden about sending a blind man to count the stars and it all got rather heated. Bratt stopped the interview several times and clearly was getting angry. Carnadine just continued as smooth as ever, as smooth as his shining head. And then it was over.

On reflection I may have become a little too heated and they will have to bleep out a few choice words.

Obviously, Bratt and Carnadine intended to frame the whole interview as a battle between myself and van Zelden. I suppose I am partly to blame for that with my colourful account of what happened at the Koningin in New Amsterdam, but I could never have anticipated quite so much interest in my bladder! Indeed, rather than ask me to justify my case that MacGregor's was never a practitioner of magick, Carnadine presented the difference of opinion as a spat between two grown men obsessively pursuing a chimaera.

"Does it matter if MacGregor dabbled in magick when everyone is doing it today?" he asked.

"I assure you most people have nothing to do with it," I said.

The only saving grace is I have not forsaken my Lenten promise, but it was a damn close-run thing. I arrived here in something of a fury and just stared at the bar until the barkeeper broke my gaze. I apologised and after some deliberation ordered a pint of Merit Bitter. It's ghastly stuff but the only thing non-alcoholic with the comforting appearance of a pint, and I retreated with it to a backroom once frequented by Oxford's literary greats. It was some moments before I glanced up and recognised my own father among them. I raised my glass to him.

One of the photographs had me puzzled until I realised it was a group portrait of my father and some of his chums beneath a chestnut tree, possibly in the little graveyard by Martyr's Cross. I recognised Hugo Grayson and Chorley Williams, but one figure had me puzzled as his face was blurred, as though he had turned it during the exposure. Then I noticed the regalia across his chest and realised it was a rare photograph of Lester Rookwood.

I suppose it is comforting to recall my own father wasn't without his troubles, but I am still determined to have words with Desmond in the morning.

22 March; Avebury Trusloe

I telephoned Desmond straight after breakfast. To my chagrin, he had not yet arrived at his office at King Charles's Circus, and I had to leave a message with Pea. Pea promised she would speak to him as soon as he arrived and ask him to telephone me.

Rather took the wind out of my sails as Pea is such a put upon soul it really is too much to lose one's temper with her.

The morning was bright and warm and normally I would have strolled to the village shop for a newspaper and something for lunch', but I was now chained to the house awaiting Desmond's return telephone call. This took an age, but he eventually replied just after eleven.

"I can't believe you've only just arrived at the office," I said after his usual brisk hello.

"Can't you? Breakfast meeting with the editor of Scorpio."

"Scorpio?"

"Magazine. Hoping to get work for some of my clients. Astrology. You wouldn't be interested I suppose?"

"Certainly not. Now listen. I had the most hideous day yesterday."

I launched into an account of everything at Nuage, rather, Nu-age Radio.

"Ah," he said at length. "I think I can see what happened."

"Do you? Well, it's a bit bloody late."

"It's the hyphen, isn't it. Not clear on their letter."

"Never mind the blasted hyphen. You completely dropped me in it."

"I suppose they were thinking of their audience and sounds like a good number of their audience are also going to be your readers."

"Well, those readers are going to be jolly unhappy because I assure you, I have not found a trace of anything like that in MacGregor's first drafts. Frankly, they might as well have invited bloody Van Zelden to interview me. They even mentioned that damned remark about a blind man counting the stars."

"Did they? Well, it is a jolly good line. Besides, had they brought him in to interview you it would really have got things going."

"It would have been a disaster. As it is, God knows what Hare & Drum will make of it all. Afraid it all got a bit heated. The whole pitch of the interview was completely at odds with what I'm trying to do."

"But Nevil, to get your message across you need a bit of publicity and to get that we need to stir things up a bit. Don't you worry; if that O'Brien chap isn't happy, I'll hear soon enough. Nothing we can do now. They broadcast it yesterday afternoon."

"I know it's too late this time," I said. "But don't drop me in it again."

PUBLICITY

Later; Avebury Trusloe

Felt better after speaking to Desmond. Considered settling down to editing but yesterday's business was still befuddling my mind, so I did what I had earlier wished to do and walked into the village. Managed to get the last copy of the Devizes Messenger and a pint of milk. Sorely tempted by a new delivery of flapjacks but reminded myself that they are high in sugar and kept my resolve. Nor was I tempted to continue up the High Street to The Red Lion, though perhaps noon always was a bit early even for me.

I was on my way back down the High Street towards home when the door of the Henge Shop burst open and Apple Tree, one of three sisters similarly named, ran out calling after me.

"I thought it was you. Just wanted to say you were brilliant."

"Was I?" I said. "You don't mean that business with the church?"

"Yesterday on the radio," Apple said, her face as round as her name.

"Ah. I didn't think anyone here would receive it from Oxford."

"We subscribe on mini-wave," Apple said. "For the shop."

"Really? Oh dear. It wasn't what I had hoped it would be. Brilliant, you say?"

"Yeah. You really made me want to read the book. You were so enthusiastic about it. And it was so funny when you got mad with him."

"Well, had you met him you might have understood why I got cross."

"I've met Chase. He came and did a piece for the shop. Went really well. Anyway. Just wanted to say it was great. If I get a copy, will you sign it?"

"Of course. In fact, I was in Glastonbury recently and a few bookshops there were selling it. I signed their copies. Apparently, it's selling rather well."

Apple laughed.

"I'll speak to the manager. Anything Glastonbury can do, we can do. Got to get back. Bye."

Alas, I suspect Apple is right. But then, what is the point of publishing the new edition if people don't read it? And they are the very people who should read it.

Ate lunch' in a thoughtful mood—not that one can exactly enjoy hummus and toast—then settled down for an afternoon of editing MacGregor.

ESSENTIAL THINGS

23 March; Avebury Trusloe

Breakfasted on grilled kidneys and toast this morning and intend a couple of hours work before driving to Devizes. Need a few things to supplement my diet at Malvern.

The third chapter of volume two is closer to the published text than was chapter two, but it is noticeable that whenever the supernatural is involved its depiction is clearer and more grounded. In the published text—that approved by Beresford and Lucas—it is easy to believe it is all imaged by Bheathain Somhairle, but MacGregor intended it to be as much a part of reality as the clothes on Bheathain's back.

At a loose end last night after finishing editing and with nothing on the telly to detain me, I recalled I had recorded Van Zelden's show in New Amsterdam and settled down to watch it. Of course, it was as infuriating as it was fascinating, but even if I have painful memories of our encounter at the Koningin I cannot deny the man's skill.

There was nothing on the scale of his trick with Stonehenge, but while that could be regarded as merely an illusion— despite the reports in the *Kilkenny Advertiser* of crushed cows, Stonehenge did not transport to a field in Eireland—the way he persuaded a young man to assassinate the American President spoke of a more subtle kind of magick. That the President appears to have played along with the scheme also spoke of Van Zelden's increasing fame.

Despite my loathing of the man and his attitude towards MacGregor, he has my grudging respect.

Later; Market Street Tearooms, Devizes

Rose's Delicatessen have furnished a pound of Gresham's mature cheddar—pungent taste but almost odourless so the guards at Midsummer Hill won't detect it—an Italian salami, large Meldon pork pie, a half dozen bottles of Bast's non-alcoholic bitter, and two packets of ginger snaps. Also took a gamble on a non-alcoholic Riesling. Not on Abigail's epic scale at Glastonbury, but it should supplement whatever gruel they serve at Malvern.

Usual necessities all came from Budgitts, including a dozen tins of Kitty Nibbles, a box of Dark Crusader chocolates for Mrs Pumphrey, and a packet of Dalesman Tea.

Nota bene: pack kettle in case one not supplied. Ditto set of cutlery and plates, as necessary.

Confident I can survive next week and grateful not to have bumped into Edith and Rupert, I have retired for lunch' to the Market Street Tearooms. One can be certain of not meeting any Ruperts here as it caters for the elderly visitor, but it has a pleasing domesticity—the chatter of the women behind the counter is entertaining and homely—and the sandwiches are excellent.

The weather next week is supposed to be cool with sunny spells. I have no idea if the residents at Midsummer Hill enjoy excursions, but I am hoping to visit one or two places nearby—the view from the Malvern Hills is spectacular—and it would be tedious if we are kept in all the time.

I have been rereading the brochure, but while everything is couched in unthreatening terms it assumes a great deal of knowledge by the client. Perhaps there are those who attend health spas the way some of us enjoy a week by the seaside, or a writers' retreat, but I suppose all will become clear soon enough. I have also looked at my contract with Creative Havens and even if they decide not to renew, I am guaranteed work between now and November, so if it does come to parting I have plenty of notice. That also means I have only one week at home after Malvern before I am tutoring at the Woolstone Haven. Regardless of how much I suffer next week, I simply must find time to work on *Book Two.*

Ah. The waitress has my pot of tea and sandwich. Best put this away for now.

Postscriptum: everything packed ready for departure. Check-in time at Malvern is between three and five-thirty so I need to be off by three o'clock.

24 *March; Avebury Trusloe*

Busy day ahead of me so an earlier start than usual. Tried to rush breakfast and burned my scrambled eggs. Terrible stink and had to put the saucepan to soak. Off to church in fifteen minutes and I have already spoken to Mrs Pumphrey and made arrangements for Boris and Tusker. As last time they will be in the house during the day and let out last thing at night. Mr Pumphrey is still protective of his furniture. Mrs Pumphrey approves I have supplied Kitty Nibbles rather than a cheaper brand. She will also take in any post as I anticipate a further delivery of short stories from Norfolk.

I think the cats know I am going away as they are studiously ignoring me.

Nota bene: leave message on front door advising postman.

Nota bene 2: ignore above as don't want to advertise I am away. Trust postman will leave package in the porch.

Third of my Lenten talks at church this morning: the stone blocking Christ's tomb compared to the Avebury Stones. No idea who Prue has reading it. Must admit Sid's denunciation rather got to me and I wish I had turned Prue down. Too late now. I'll have to write the next one in whatever odd moment I get at Malvern.

Better put this down. Morning looks damp and my motorcar can be temperamental.

STALE BISCUITS

Lunchtime; Red Lion, Avebury

The Reverend Peter Chadwick is a scoundrel. His sermon on the need to accept change if we are to bring Jesus into our lives could not have been more squarely aimed at me and the other stalwarts of the PCC if he'd put our faces on a wanted poster and pinned it to the church door. It absolutely takes the biscuit. Speaking of which, I spoke to Prudence Turnstone as the Jammie Dodgers and ginger nuts handed out after the sermon were decidedly stale. She had the nerve to reply: "I rather thought you approved of old and stale; we wouldn't want new biscuits, would we?"

Stupid woman.

Sid and Fred were there too, but as they had missed the last committee meeting Chadwick's message passed over them. Molly, however, was most upset and arrowed in on me after Prudence had smirked off.

"I can't believe he intended to be so hurtful," she said.

"Oh, I can believe it all too well. In his own way he's quite as bad as the iconoclasts who had the parish hiding the roodscreen. Wouldn't be surprised if he'd get rid of that as well if he thought the Antiquities Trust wouldn't notice."

"But it's Saint James's most prized possession," Molly said.

"Don't worry, he can't touch it. But I suspect his plan to relocate the altar and font will get past them. That's why we must be especially vigilant. I spoke to Sid last Wednesday over dominoes and he's against it. You butter up Fred. I can guarantee Terry won't like it as this is all 'Fabric and Works.' So long as we ensure each PCC meeting has enough of us, we can stop this at the voting stage. Meanwhile your idea of getting Prue to approach the New Barn School should deal with the crèche idea. That was awfully clever of you, by the way: really knocked the wind out of Prue's sails. Of course, might be a bit tricky as Sid dislikes the wicket folk, as he calls them."

Molly laughed a little and put her hand on my collar bone.

"Do you really think it was clever?" she said.

"Why yes. Inspired even. I don't know if you had thought it all through, but it was quite brilliant the way it worked."

"Yes. I suppose," Molly said.

I had an acute sense I had disappointed her. A sensation I am all too familiar with from years of marriage to Edith, but I can't for the life of me think what it was I said. Anyway, her hand returned swiftly to her side and presently she moved off to chat to Fred Thirsk.

I was briefly alone with my tea and a stale Jammie Dodger when Peter Chadwick sidled up.

"I am enjoying your Lenten talks," he said. "Excellent to see how you are combining the natural world, even the world of folklore, with The Passion."

"It was Prudence's idea," I said a little stiffly. "I am only the wordsmith."

"Jesus, too, understood the need for craft."

But not guile, I thought, that being Peter Chadwick's speciality.

"Have you looked around you, Nevil?"

"Around?" I said.

"At this room."

I took a glance but saw nothing unusual.

"It rather looks as it always does," I said.

Chadwick's hand went to the biscuit tin and from politeness I advised him against the Jammie Dodgers. His hand dipped in anyway and produced a biscuit which he then held as though it was the sacrament.

"That is the trouble," Chadwick said. "The crowd is the same as it always is, save for the few who pass each year. Where are the children, Nevil? 'Let the children come unto me and detain them not,' said Jesus, but where are they? Where is anyone under the age of thirty in this room? Would you have a vibrant church, or a church of old men and old women guarding their holy relics?"

He licked the jam and then swallowed the biscuit whole with a grimace.

"Revolting," he said and moved on.

Molly returned from having spoken to Fred and said he was completely on board.

"Good," I said. "At least... I think we may have to compromise."

"Compromise! I saw Peter talking to you. You haven't been nobbled? Surely, not you?"

Her eyes held such a look of disappointment and pity I could hardly look at her.

"Peter has a point doesn't he," I said.

"Does he? You said yourself he'll only be here a few years and then it will all be right."

"I suppose I did. But we will all only be here a few more

years, or maybe ten or twenty years. What then Molly? Who will arrange the flowers when you're gone?"

In retrospect, that wasn't the best of arguments, and with a look of horror poor Molly ran out of the hall. I shall have to think of some way of making it up to her. Perhaps my own cavalier attitude to the Grim Reaper isn't shared by everyone.

I left soon after but instead of driving straight home popped into the pub for a pint of Merit.

"Still on the wagon, Nevil?" Jonathan asked.

"Until Easter," I said. "Some of us like to keep up the faith."

Jonathan looked offended. I've no idea what he believes in but the only time I recall seeing him in church was for the funeral of one of his customers. I retired to a seat by the fire and nursed my pint.

Faith in what, though? Holy relics or the sort of church Peter wants it to be? Can they possibly live together or must one stifle and the other destroy?

Wretched business upsetting Molly like that. Must try and get her something in Malvern to make up for it. Assuming they allow me out on my own.

Ah, here's my lunch': mixed grill with all the trimmings. No idea when I'll eat proper food again so I'm treating myself.

THIEVES!

Late evening; Midsummer Hill, Malvern

First impressions when I arrived at Midsummer Hill after an uneventful hour and a half in the Rover were... well: impressive. A few traces of the Benedictine priory survive, but most of what you see is seventeenth and eighteenth-century brick. Cedars on the lawn give it a stately home appearance.

Inside, alas, most of the original features are gone and it was inside my troubles began.

Check-in was smooth. Log-burning stove made the entrance hall homely and there was even a spaniel warming its belly beside it. Dog leapt up as I came in and greeted me with lots of tail wagging. Some paperwork to complete which also went smoothly. My full itinerary depends on the results of a medical tomorrow morning, which is standard and prevents clients collapsing, I suppose. For the moment I am on something called the Paleo Diet which mimics what our ancient ancestors once ate, though I suspect woolly mammoth is not on the menu. Whether I remain on that diet for the rest of the week also depends on tomorrow's medical. Porter took my bags up to my room which is pleasant enough and spotlessly clean. Surprised to find it had a small refrigerator but where a hotel might have a minibar, I found only six bottles of Malvern Water.

It was then half past five and I took the suggestion from the lady at the desk to have a shower and dress for dinner, which was at six. I must say the shower is a work of art and my skin was left tingling. The lady said something about sloughing off our usual cares ready for the week ahead and I suspect I sloughed quite a bit in the shower.

I interpreted dress for dinner to mean smart but casual and arrived in my tweed jacket with white shirt and Israel College tie. Most had taken a less formal approach and there was everything from saris, through yashmaks, and even one chap dressed as a Peruvian shepherd. The majority are women beyond their childbearing years, though most of us are sprightly and determinedly youthful.

Woolly mammoth was not on the menu; I was served a rustic wholegrain risotto with local mushrooms. I assume they must have been frozen, though it was tasty enough. Dessert was a lemon and iced water sorbet with a stalk of mint sticking out of it. The Paleo Diet didn't seem at all bad, so long as I augmented it with my private cache, and I rather hope to stay on it as I didn't fancy some of the other offerings.

From seven we had an hour of induction which was dreadfully dull and I'm afraid I may have nodded off and missed some of it. Apparently, some of the practices at Midsummer Hill are loosely modelled on the Benedictine monks, while the outdoorsy activities are inspired by a one-time owner of the estate whose brother founded The Boys' Adventure Corps. Two things did stick in my mind and are pressing: lights out is at ten o'clock and morning activities begin shortly before dawn with something called Sun Arising. We are to assemble under the cedar tree at five-thirty wearing whatever we have slept in.

I hope to God it involves a bit of jigging about, or we will all be frozen.

After induction we had two hours of what they called familiarisation, which was a glorified term for wandering about. I was mindful of getting a decent cup of tea with a few ginger snaps, but for politeness's sake I dawdled around a bit. Found one large room which was obviously a gymnasium and another with half a dozen baths lined up in a row. Haven't bathed communally since boarding school and don't much fancy it now. Then I followed a curious ringing noise into a room lit by a single candle. Took a moment to discover eight or so women on the floor holding hands in a circle. They were humming while a woman in the centre of them rang a tiny bell. I simply stood in the doorway and listened until the woman stopped ringing, and everyone fell quiet.

"Can we help you?" the bell-woman asked.

I was suddenly the object of attention.

"Err, probably not; I suspect this is one for the ladies," I said.

Whatever it was I said, it seemed to be misinterpreted because their gaze became more intense and I backed away, saying, "never mind me, carry on do," before escaping.

Having familiarised enough, I headed up to my room and let myself in.

I immediately sensed danger. The room had the same austere cleanliness as before, but my bags were not on the bed and my driving shoes were not in the middle of the floor.

Concerned, I flung open the wardrobe and found my shirts, trousers, coat, and spare jacket all neatly hung. A set of drawers revealed my socks and underwear all segregated. My slippers sat by the head of the bed and my pyjamas were folded on the pillow. The same deference was shown to my journal—this journal—MacGregor's first draft and my typewriter, which were laid out on a table.

Of my kettle and cache there was no sign.

A plain white envelope also sat on the table. Inside was a typewritten letter stating that the following items (there was a list) had been removed for safekeeping and would be returned on my departure from Midsummer Hill. Such items were considered detrimental to my stay as all nutritional needs are catered for in the set meals. Alongside the letter was a pamphlet warning that excessive levels of fats and salt in processed foods cause heart disease, carbon dioxide in beer releases free radicals (whatever they are) which cause cancer and premature ageing, and tea acidifies the stomach.

The letter also advised that while I had been permitted to retain other inessential items—they must mean everything relating to work and my journal—the, and I quote: "holistic environment at Midsummer Hill is all-consuming and will leave little time or energy for extracurricular activities."

The utter, utter bast—

25 March; Midsummer Hill, Malvern

I had assumed that lights out might come with a gentle coo of warning, much like Mummy did when I was seven, but no; a church bell chimed in the distance and the whole room plunged into darkness. It was fortunate I was already in bed as it might have taken me a while to find it.

It is now eight-twenty and I have been up three hours.

Of course, as soon as I had a free moment I presented to reception. No one was attending the desk, but I rang a bell until a young chap came and explained my loss. The man—thin, about thirty and with the blank gaze of a fanatic—read the letter with, I swear, a flicker of amusement, and reminded me this was a health clinic, and the confiscated items represented the life I wished to leave behind.

"If I had any intention of leaving them behind, I wouldn't have brought them with me," I said with what I hoped was devastating logic.

"We often find an initial fear and reluctance among first-time visitors," he said. "These items will be returned to you at the end of the week. You may then choose whether to take them with you or dispose of them."

"Dispose! Have you any idea how much Gresham's Cheddar costs?"

He glanced at my tummy and suggested two months.

"Utter—" I bit my tongue and turned away from the desk.

Someone had let the stove go out and the dog was absent.

I would write concerning this morning's surprising events but my medical is at nine and I must not be late.

Dancing at dawn

Lunchtime; Midsummer Hill, Malvern

I have not been so violated since Dickie Toast and a bar of soap in the shower during my second year at Ripon. But that must all come later.

The morning began with assembly under the cedar tree on the front lawn. It was a chilly, pre-dawn twilight when I arrived, as instructed, in the clothes I had slept in, but with the addition of my slippers. These were spotted by a chap wielding a torch and he asked me to remove them. There had been dew overnight and the sensation of damp against my feet wasn't unpleasant but once under the cedar the ground was dry and bare. Even in the gloom it was clear everyone had followed the instructions regarding clothing, but there was more variation than I expected. My striped ginghams were a conservative choice, and a few chaps only wore shorts and at least one, whose profile I saw against the reflected sky on a lake, was naked. Several of the ladies wore modest pyjamas, like mine, but there were a few in nightdresses of various lengths and translucence. Not wishing to appear stuffy, I undid the top button of my pyjamas.

We were joined from the house by a tall slender woman who I recognised as the bell-ringer of the previous evening. She wore some sort of green top which barely covered her bottom and held one of those small, square-sided bells you see on Swiss cows, but with a much higher tone.

Hoping the nearest person might have a sympathetic ear, I asked when dawn actually was.

"It's six o'clock. I'm awake well before it every day," they replied. It was a woman. With her short hair, boyish figure, and pyjamas I had taken her for a man, but her voice was soft and friendly.

"Do you rise early?" she asked.

"I have seen the sun up," I said. "But only in the summer after a night of drinking!"

It was a weak attempt at levity, and it misfired.

"I can't anymore," she said. "I mean, I lived like that once, but it was killing me."

"Sorry to hear that. As a matter of fact, I am teetotal myself just now: for Lent you see. Do you miss it?"

"Lent? I'm sorry I don't—"

"No, no, I meant alcohol. Do you miss it?"

"Sometimes when I'm lonely. It made bad things bearable. I'm Madeleine. Everyone calls me Mads."

"I'm Nevil," I replied and to try to match her informality, added that friends call me Nev. But I felt dreadfully awkward, like you do when you ask someone how they are, and they actually tell you. I was also feeling the chill, as were several others from their vigorous rubbing. Could we really be doing this every morning, I wondered—I have now confirmed that we are—as it seemed even more pointless than the annual Midsummer Eve invasion of Avebury. Along with growing colder, it was also getting lighter, revealing more of my fellows. Madeleine was attractive, but many of the rest had, like me, suffered middle-aged spread and other impediments.

And then the bell-ringer called everyone and asked for quiet.

"Sol, we welcome you back," she cried. "Breaker of darkness, night-slayer, day-bringer, wearer of bright colours, sky warrior, grail of life, Sol Arise!"

Everyone was silent. Then, holding the bell above her head, she marched into the middle of the lawn. We fell in behind, but whatever solemnity the moment might have, was deflated by the fall of light revealing middle-aged people in their nightclothes.

At least the damp grass was a relief to my feet, though I could hardly feel them owing to the chill. The bell-ringer halted—unlike most of the rest of us she had a truly exceptional figure, and the green top was revealed as a chemise—and rang her bell frantically.

"Dance!" she cried. "Dance to the sun. Follow!"

And with that she flung herself in the air and the chemise rose to her waist. I averted my eyes. Then, to my horror, everyone was dancing: most with that awkward stagger the middle-aged employ at social occasions, but more than a few—all women apart from the chap entirely naked—with orgiastic fervour. Among them was Madeleine and whatever connection I felt I might have made with her rather shrivelled and died.

At least all the flailing warmed me up and the view of the sun rising in a glow of white and crocus yellow was spectacular. However, it occurs to me that on at least one morning this week it will be raining. Oh well.

Immediately after Sun Arise, we all filed into a large room with brown matting on the floor and rust-red walls illuminated by flickering lights. The door closed and we were asked to sit cross-legged on the floor. This was done with varying degrees of ease or indignity.

Madame la Cloche had swapped her cowbell for one with a deeper tone, which she now rang and invited us to meditate. I thought of breakfast and whether my income from Creative Havens was worth all the indignity. There was also an earthy smell, which I suppose is to be expected of half-naked people who have vigorously exercised sitting cross-legged.

Someone sniffed loudly and I glanced sideways to see Madeleine gently crying. I admit it wrenched my heart, but any thoughts of chivalry were crushed when Madame la Cloche said something about attaining the stillness of the rock amidst the rushing waters of life.

Feeling was now returning to my feet, and I took to clenching and unclenching them to relieve the pins and needles.

Presently the bell rang again, and we were all dismissed. I was aware of Madeleine leaving the room swiftly but didn't see which way she went. As I showered and dressed for breakfast, I felt some sense of normality descending, but to my surprise found it rather depressing.

Breakfast was surprisingly pleasant. The bread was a sad unleavened thing, but the scrambled eggs were excellent. I had no idea cavemen ate so well. Admittedly the herbal tea tasted nothing like my usual cuppa, but nor was it revolting, and I was quite by my bowl of flaked grains, dried fruit, and nuts, albeit I've no idea what kind of cow provided the milk.

My medical was a half hour after breakfast and before that we had something called sacred space. For this, we were encouraged to find a place where we felt safe and secure, and which would be our refuge during the week ahead. Several people headed out to the gardens, but I took my opportunity to call at reception, as I have described, before rushing to my room to write up my journal. Books, I suppose, have always been my refuge.

Blast. Must stop now. My second massage of the day approaches. Hopefully, the masseur will soothe my ruffled feelings.

Quiet time; Midsummer Hill, Malvern

Quiet Time is what they call the hours between seven and ten in the evening. No activities are scheduled, and we are at liberty to socialise or be on our own. Later, I wish to be social. Not something I expected to want to do, but I am haunted by Madeleine's comment on drinking and loneliness. No, not haunted: touched.

As there is nothing lonelier than writing up a journal, I will be brief.

The medical was half perfectly ordinary—in fact, Dr Saunders could have performed it—and half nonsense. I do not think dangling a pendulum over someone's chest counts for much and as for the suggestion that my chakras are out of alignment, well it reminded me of the mad lesbian at Glastonbury.

But at least that was harmless; unlike my coffee enema of which I will say nothing except that Dickie Toast's bar of soap has nothing on five feet of hose. Honestly, coffee is probably the only thing here worth drinking, and they stuck it up my arse.

The doctor—it was the same for my medical and enema—was an owlish woman with bobbed hair and glasses assisted by an earnest young technician in a green tunic. Afterwards, he took me, still wearing my surgical gown to a room with four large baths. Each had a kind of hinged canopy, like an oystershell and I was reminded of Botticelli's Venus. I was led to one and asked to sit inside while it filled with warm water.

"Bit complicated for a bath," I said. "And where are the taps?"

"Has no one explained this?" the filler-upper asked.

"No one has explained anything, dear boy. I am a lamb to the slaughter."

"This is an immersion chamber," he said. "It creates a sense of weightlessness and mild disorientation that frees us from the physical world."

I suspect we feel something like that at the moment of

death, so it wasn't a happy prospect. Nevertheless, once the water had reached a level where I could float free of the bottom, the canopy closed, and the interior flooded with pale blue light. I can't tell how long that lasted but then the light began to fade until it was deep blue, and I couldn't see a thing. Presently I began to waggle my legs and arms about just to feel the water against them, as otherwise I was losing track of where I was. I then had the strange sense I was not alone and for some reason a schoolboy memory of dissecting an eel popped into my head and next moment there were eels everywhere. Must have been the enema put the thought in my head, and only a sense of how absurd it all was had stopped me from screaming.

Of course, I did completely lose track of time and may even have dozed off before the technician returned and let me out.

I was still not to get back into my clothes, however, as next up was a massage, my first of the day, which was remarkably pleasant and it's a shame I wasn't in any sort of mood to enjoy it.

Then came lunch' and news that, following my medical, I had been taken off the Paleo Diet and put on something called Synergesis, which appears to consist of vegetables and rice.

After lunch', and now I must be brief, I spent two hours pretending to be a knight on a chessboard, most of it while wearing a blindfold so I was oblivious of the actual game other than the instructions I was given. Happily, I survived to the end and my side won.

That was followed by Yoga, which, given the stresses of this morning, nearly killed me, and then a half hour of 'primal screaming' which I would have enjoyed immensely—God knows I had enough to scream about—if I had any energy left.

Then shower, followed by more green things with pasta for dinner, which brings my journal up to date. And with that I shall close and go in search of a shoulder to lean on. I can't be the only one who's suffering. In fact, I know I am not.

Postscriptum: sixteen stone, six, as recorded by the doctor this morning.

NICA
Late; Midsummer Hill, Malvern

Rather subdued downstairs this evening. At first, I assumed everyone had had a bit of a rough day, one way or another. In an attempt to go with the flow, I left my jacket and tie in the wardrobe and unbuttoned the collar of my shirt. The Peruvian shepherd had swapped his outfit for a kind of French peasant look with scarlet jerkin and wide-brimmed hat. Man's thin as a rake so God knows why he needs to spend a fortune coming to this place. Apart from him there were only about seven of us socialising and I didn't see Madeleine among them. Madame la Cloche lazed in the corner of a sofa. It was the first time I had seen her without a bell and thankfully she was now fully-clothed. She was in conversation with the French peasant, but she glanced up as I came in. I poured myself a glass of spring water, which, to my surprise was pleasantly fizzy. There was also a bowl of pistachio nuts and I grabbed several of them as it was my first protein all day.

"I thought it might all have been a bit too much for you," someone said behind my back. I turned to see Madame la Cloche.

"The first day is often the hardest," she continued. "I'm Veronique, but everyone calls me Nica. You're Nevil Warbrook."

She was much more disarming and personable up close, and I resisted saying that I was happily aware who I was.

"I can't pretend today has been a pleasure from start to finish," I said. "But there are several others missing this evening, so I suppose I am made of tougher stuff than some."

"Really? I believe everyone has come down from their rooms," she said. "Some have gone jogging. There's a path around the lake. It's perfectly safe, even in the dark. I know this is your first time at Midsummer Hill and I was nearly going to send someone to see you were all right."

"Thank you," I said a little stiffly. "But I am perfectly all right. I am a writer. I'm hoping to work while I'm here. This week is not exactly my own choice."

"I saw your file. Creative Havens are paying," she said. "Head Office are keeping you in-house."

"They seem to think I am unwell," I said. "Had a bit of a turn while climbing Glastonbury Tor a few weeks back. I'm one of their writing tutors. Writing retreats, ah, rather like this, I suppose. Though less strenuous."

"We'll try not to be too hard on you," she said. "But you must also try not to be too hard on us."

"Whatever can you mean?"

"You spoke to Kedden this morning about some items missing from your room. He reported that you had been aggressive and made him uncomfortable."

"I'm sorry, but I thought the whole thing rather shabby. Had someone explained, rather than just taking everything, it might have been different."

"But you were aware that all dietary needs would be met."

"I was aware.' I said begrudgingly. 'It just didn't sound much fun. This new diet is certainly no fun."

Nica cocked her head to one side.

"Syzygy, or something like it," I said.

"Synergesis," she said. "For maximum cleansing and weight loss. You will feel the benefits."

I crunched a pistachio.

"I hope you'll be comfortable here," she said. "You'll get more from the programme if you don't fight it. We do have a small wardrobe of clothing more suitable for the week. You might want to find something that will help you relax."

"Thank you, but I am happy as I am," I said with a trace of defiance. Actually, I secretly yearn to be the person who can get away with flamboyant dress, but alas it just isn't me. We all know our limitations.

"May I ask...?" for the first time Nica sounded uncertain. "The work you mentioned. Is it *This Iron Race*?"

"Gosh. Yes, it is. You know it?"

"I read and reread it years ago. I have bought the new edition but not had a chance to read it yet. Is it very different?"

"It depends," I said. "In places very much so."

"It's the magick," she said. "I knew it."

"Only in part," I said. "The most striking difference is MacGregor was writing half a century ahead of his time, which is why his publishers refused it."

"Would you sign my copy? I know it must sound unprofessional of me."

"Not at all. I'd be happy to. Tomorrow evening perhaps?"

"Thank you."

"And can I ask. The fizzy water. Don't bubbles free the radicals or something? Like in beer?"

"The water is naturally carbonated," she said.

"Ah," I said. "That makes all the difference."

I waited around another half hour or so. Nica had other people to talk to and there was no sign of Madeleine. The French peasant tried to engage me in conversation, but I couldn't shake off that dawn image of him silhouetted against the lake. I was also weary and determined that I would finish writing this before lights out. So, I retired for the night. Lights out isn't for another forty minutes but I may well be asleep before then.

No work on MacGregor two days running. That must change, but where to find the time?

SILENT HUMMING

26 March; Midsummer Hill, Malvern

Bit of frost last night. Feet were like blocks of ice during Sun Arising. Madeleine smiled at me but there wasn't much chance to say anything more than a brief hello. Dawn was spectacular but by the time it arrived we were all desperate to get inside.

Once inside and gathered in a circle on our haunches, Nica rang her bell, and we were all asked to hum silently. The odd thing was that even though none of us were making any noise I could hear humming. Must be some form of auto-suggestion.

After breakfast I dashed upstairs for my thirty minutes of sacred space, determined to get at least a few passages of MacGregor edited. Almost managed it but got distracted thinking about my next Lent talk for Prue Turnstone. Life at St James's seems a world away, but I can't let it slip my mind. The half hour went too quickly and was followed by ninety minutes of tedium listening to everyone say who they were and what they hoped to get out of their stay. Madeleine mentioned that her mother died recently. She had looked after her during a long illness and this week was her way of reconnecting with herself. I admit I didn't understand much of that, but then I often don't understand people. She didn't mention her drinking problem, so I assume that's long behind her. When it was my turn, I said my doctor had referred me here and I hoped to get out of it in one piece.

Nica looked offended and not one person laughed.

Best part of the morning was a sauna followed by a massage. Unlike the previous massage, this involved placing hot stones along my spine, and the back of my arms and legs. A little alarming at first, as it reminded me of an intimate scene in *Book Two* I edited only last month, but after a moment's tension I relaxed and with the warmth suffusing into my bones it proved rather pleasant. It's all to do with aligning my chakras.

Then, just as I thought I was ready to eat something, we were told it was a fast day. One woman asked why we weren't warned earlier, and someone said no one warned the tiger when it was time to go hungry. Everyone accepted that as though it was the Wisdom of Solomon, but I'm fairly sure tigers have a limited concept of lunchtime.

First thing this afternoon we have something called Eirish Dancing. Never been too fond of the Eirish and I loathe dancing so don't hold out much hope.

Time calls.

Dancing is the sort of thing stars like Frederick Banistaire or Margarethe von Brunnen do, or rather did, as they are both long-dead. Anyway, it is not what we were doing. We had to maintain an undertaker's decorum above the waist while everything below thrashed about as if fighting off a squirrel.

It was murder on the knees, and I only hope I haven't done any permanent damage. Whatever the, frankly, dubious, physical benefits, it's supposed to increase serenity in our core being even when dealing with trying and testing experiences. Or as Maeve, our dance-mistress, said: everything at the centre is still, even as we combat all the world throws at us.

Where I was standing there wasn't much that wasn't flapping and flopping about and unless the world is within kicking distance, I don't fancy my chances.

Thankfully, the ninety minutes included a video of a professional dancer. It still looked ridiculous and there's only so much fiddle music I can take, but at least I got my breath back.

Madeleine looked very fetching in her leotard. Nice figure for a woman her age. The dawn nudist had to excuse himself partway as his elasticated leggings were chafing. Given his red face and a few giggles from the nearest ladies I can guess where it was chafing.

Then khaki garments and boots in assorted sizes were handed out to wear over our leggings and leotards before we were led outside by a short, muscular chap with no hair.

The morning frost had disappeared, and it was now drizzling. I was glad of the extra layer of clothing as 'Clive' led us round the lake and then up into woodland. I found Madeleine and asked if she knew where we were going.

"It's the obstacle course," she said. "I saw it while jogging on the first night."

"I thought jogging was last night."

"I've jogged every night," she said. "It helps me sleep. You?"

"I might manage a decent rush for a train," I said.

"Besides, walking gives me more time to think."

"That's what jogging helps me avoid," she said. "You're not enjoying the week, are you?"

"Is it that obvious?"

"Just a bit. It will be better if you don't fight it the whole time."

"That's what Nica said."

"Nica?"

"Veronique: the woman who leads us at Sun Arising. Keeps showing everyone her backside when she jumps in the air."

"Oh. I didn't know she shortened her name."

"She's nice enough," I said. "Chatted to her last night, while you were jogging, I expect. Not as mad as I had thought. Quite personable, actually."

"I think she's bossy and full of herself," Madeleine said. "But I suppose a woman like her only has to flash her bum and everyone thinks she's wonderful."

I really don't understand some people. Madeleine avoided me the next hour while we crawled under nets and along ropes and over logs. Someone—not I, I promise—remarked that if she'd wanted to join the army she would have. Must have given the dawn nudist an idea because he suddenly stopped and said it was too militaristic and asked to be excused because he was a pacifist.

For a moment I thought Clive was going to tear him in half—which he probably could have done—but suddenly he backed down, despite the red stripe on the back of his neck and excused him. Clive then started shouting at the rest of us with even more enthusiasm, urging us on and under and over.

"Come on," he yelled, "you'll be thanking me this time tomorrow."

I wonder what he has in mind. I still suspect that some people are quite aware of the week's itinerary while I am completely in the dark.

By now we were all horribly warm and filthy from

crawling in the dirt and I was rather glad to hear my name announced on the PA with instruction to attend hydrotherapy, along with three others, including the dawn nudist, who I must start calling Dave now I've figured out his name, but not, alas, Madeleine.

This would be a chance to relax in a hot bath while scrubbing Worcestershire off my hands and knees, or so I thought. The attendant was Kedden, the chap I argued with the first morning. I hadn't seen him since then and there was a slight froideur when he saw my face. I took it upon myself to find a moment to apologise, thinking that Nica would approve of me doing so.

We were instructed to undress and leave our clothes to one side. This was something of a moment for me as, unlike Dave, I dislike public nudity immensely. Fortunately, the four of us were all men, so that was one difficulty solved.

The baths were large, quite big enough for several to bathe together, if that was their thing, but above each was suspended a wooden platform, like a stretcher. I assumed these were for lowering invalids into the water and was surprised when Kedden asked Dave to lie on the platform on his back. The bath beneath him was already full but didn't look inviting. Hot baths have a certain smell to them, and this had no smell at all, except a vague disinfectant aroma. I was the third in line and, as Kedden lowered the platform for me, I saw my moment.

"Nica, I mean Veronique mentioned I was a bit harsh the other morning. Apologies. Bit of a difficult day. Perfectly understand. My things are...?"

"Safe in the kitchens," he said. "Everyone externalises fear in their own way."

Kedden moved on before I had a chance to say that my indignation had nothing whatsoever to do with fear and I lay down and tried to get comfortable on my back. Meanwhile, I had sensed a distinct lack of warmth from the water beneath me and looked on doubtfully as my neighbour lay down on his platform. The platforms were suspended from the ceiling by pulleys and cables ran down the room to the far wall. Kedden advanced on what appeared to be the controls and I began to suspect this would be every bit as horrid as morning ablutions at Ripon. I was wrong. It was far worse. There was a sudden whirr of wheels and before I could blink, the platform plunged into the bath with me upon it. It was freezing and sent me into a spasm of coughing. I must have gulped a pint of bath water before the cables heaved me free.

Dave arched his back and screamed in what sounded like orgiastic pleasure. My neighbour groaned. I attempted to sit up but was unable to get purchase on the platform before the cables whirred again and I descended.

I shall not prolong describing this torture. Presently, the heaving in and out ceased and we were suspended with just our highlands above water as cold-water jets concealed in the rim of the bath puckered our flesh. I could not doubt I was now thoroughly clean, and nor did it hurt much after the initial shock, though I was aware of mild delirium and Dave's continual yelps and squeals. Kedden seemed only interested in the neighbour I heard groan and I think the poor chap may have passed out. I now regretted apologising to Kedden as I am certain he took pleasure in my suffering.

Anyway, after some minutes of the water jets, Kedden moved to another panel and turned a wheel. Like a long-lost friend, warm water replaced the cold jets and I writhed, at first with pleasure and then with pain as blood returned to distant parts.

When it all ended and we were winched from the water, our flesh glowed like poached salmon, and it was as though electricity was coursing through my arms and legs. Much as I dislike the thought that the procedure had any benefits whatsoever, I admit that I have rarely felt as alive as I did in the moment after release from the baths.

That ended the afternoon's activities, and we were released to get dressed for dinner. I slipped away from Dave and company, intent on visiting the wardrobe Nica had mentioned last evening. Not too much in my size, but I found a snazzy waistcoat that I'd have been happy to wear at the Eagle and Child during my student days. Wouldn't suit me at all back at Avebury, but there is a certain freedom here to try out new things. Anyway, it should make me look less stuffy and out of place.

Now, six approaches and dinner is served promptly.

I WILL BE REWARDED?
Late; Midsummer Hill, Malvern

Dinner was unusually appetising this evening. Nothing more than veg with rice, but they had done something interesting with herbs and spices. That or I am reacquiring long-lost taste buds. Of course, not having eaten a thing since breakfast was an obvious factor in my appreciation. I wore that snazzy waistcoat to dinner, but I suppose everyone was too hungry to notice.

I was determined to get some work done that evening, ideally on MacGregor, though that blasted talk for Prudence is looming. However, inside the door to my room I found an envelope. Tomorrow we are travelling to Wales for a day of orienteering, followed by rock scrambling and something called 'wild swimming.' Then we will camp overnight in the forest and return Thursday morning. The note warned that, "Everything you elect to bring with you for Wednesday evening must be portable as you will be carrying it to the campsite."

Not slept in a tent since family holidays in Cornwall and I had no idea what constitutes 'wild swimming.' I did know that my back and legs were rather broken and an evening of sitting at my desk would not be ideal preparation for another day of strenuous activity. I could spare an hour and still leave time to get some work done and decided that a few lengths of the swimming pool would ease my joints and pains. It might also afford some preparation for whatever wild swimming entails.

I collected my towel and bathing costume and headed downstairs. Passing through the dining area on the way I was surprised to see Madeleine. She had leggings on and had a torch.

"Hi," she said. "Hoped I'd bump into you. I'm going for a jog around the lake. There are a few others, but they've gone ahead. You said you sometimes ran for the train, so I thought it might be good for you."

The woman had hardly glanced at me all day and now, when I was bone weary, she invited me along, alone with her. She had done something with her hair as well, pulling it back away from her face and neck. It took several years off her. Alas I was in no fit state to go jogging as even walking was painful and I simply had to decline.

"Everything is a bit too sore after this afternoon," I said. "I'm going for a swim; ease the joints a little. You could join me, I suppose."

"Sorry, no, really I can't," she said. "I must run. And I'm afraid of water. Have to be excused tomorrow. My baby brother drowned; you see. In a garden pond."

"Ah, well of course. Quite understand. No harm intended. Enjoy your run. Hope the owls don't get you!"

I'm not sure that was quite the right thing to say as Madeleine flinched slightly before heading out the door, torch firmly in her hand. Her companions must have been so far ahead she was running on her own. No fun at all in the twilight but what could I do? I could hardly have gone with her as I can barely hobble. No, it was managed as best it could be. I shall try to put things right another time.

The pool was unattended, but that suited a relaxing swim and I slipped into a cubicle to change. Unfortunately, getting into my swimming trunks was a repeat of my experience buying trousers and no matter how I wriggled it proved impossible.

I could have abandoned the evening, got dressed and returned to my room, but the lighting was subdued and if Dave could prance around naked at dawn and Nica was happy for everyone to see her bum, then they should have no problem with me discreetly swimming *sans* costume.

So, leaving my clothes in the cubicle, I stepped out onto the ledge around the pool and climbed in.

The water was bliss: exactly the right temperature and just deep enough to allow proper swimming without being out of my depth. I must have swum up and down, breaststroke and then crawl for some ten minutes before I sensed I was no longer alone. It was as though a shadow had shifted somewhere.

"I admired the waistcoat you wore at dinner. It suits you," Nica said.

I turned and saw her standing in the doorway. She held something large and rectangular, but silhouetted against the light I couldn't see it clearly.

"Ah, you have me at a disadvantage," I said.

"And I am happy to see some of your inhibitions are easing."

"My costume proved a little tight. Few years since I last wore it. Nor quite sure what I'm to do about tomorrow."

"Tomorrow?"

Nica had crouched at the edge of the pool to test the water.

"Wild swimming," I said. "I'm not in Dave's league when it comes to public... well, you know."

"I'm sure we can find something for you," she said. "Do you mind if I join you?"

"Oh, well, no. I suppose. It is yours, after all."

Not sure what else I could have said. Of course, it was awkward as all I had wanted was a bit of light exercise to ease my aches and pains. It became a good deal more awkward when Nica placed the thing she was carrying on a chair, and pulled her dress over her head, revealing nothing underneath. I suppose given her performance at Sun Arising I shouldn't have expected any different, but that was among a crowd of people and somehow it didn't seem to matter half so much in the chilly dawn as it did in a warm swimming pool.

Anyway, she dived in gracefully and surfaced a few yards from me.

"Don't mind me," she said. "I swim to de-stress. Helps me to see things clearly."

"And what do you wish to see?"

I broke into a gentle breaststroke while Nica rolled into a back crawl and swam to the far end of the pool.

"I don't know until I see it," she said. "You can't look for something until you know what it is you're trying to find."

"That sounds wise enough," I said.

I had reached the poolside and turned before propelling myself off. Nica likewise had turned at her end of the pool and we now gradually swam towards each other. Having my eyes ahead of me, avoiding a collision was my imperative, but perforce I also could hardly avoid watching her. Nica is far out of my league, obviously, but not shy about men at all. I suspect if she wanted someone, or something, she would have no hesitation in reaching for it. And I, of course, am not yet free of Edith.

Nevertheless, as our courses converged and then passed, I was aware of womanliness in a way I had almost forgotten.

"Do you write poetry, like your father?" she asked.

"Less often than I would like," I admitted. "My father's talent far outshone mine in that endeavour."

Before I had chance to wonder at her change of conversation, she continued.

"I write," she said. "I can express my feelings in poetry. It's the discipline of expression that makes me reflect on how I feel. I'd understand not wanting to compete with a parent though. Especially one so well known."

"One doesn't want to invite comparison by ploughing the same furrow," I said. "No, I am happy dedicating most of my writing work to others."

"You will be rewarded," she said.

"I hope so."

There was a dropped beat in the conversation as Nica

stopped swimming and came upright. The water reached to her shoulders. "Hope so what?" she asked.

"You said I would be rewarded," I repeated.

"I don't..." She was genuinely puzzled. "Rewarded for what?"

"Dedicating my writing work to others; MacGregor I assumed you were thinking of."

"No. I don't think I meant..."

She shook her head and fell backwards. At first, I thought she was going to swim but then she wasn't moving, and her face was under the water.

I called her name and lifted her head up. Her eyes were closed, and I tried to remember everything I knew about first aid, hoping she would recover without needing to announce our presence to anyone. But though she was breathing—I had checked she had not swallowed her tongue—really, I had no choice.

Kedden was the first to respond and to his credit he picked up immediately what was going on and jumped in fully-clothed.

"She fainted; I think. Perfectly okay one—"

"It's okay, Mr Warbrook. We can manage it from now."

"She's breathing," I said. "I made sure she was breathing."

Others had followed Kedden into the water, among them Dave, and Clive from the obstacle course. And Madeleine had come in, though she stayed at the side of the pool.

Kedden and Dave got Nica to the poolside.

"Did she swallow any water?" Kedden asked.

I didn't think she had. But Kedden rolled her onto her side and presently she coughed and opened her eyes. Everyone was relieved when she sat up, and someone found her a bathrobe.

I was still in the pool. I wanted to get out, as I felt terribly self-conscious, but was aware of Madeleine standing there. Lord knows what she might have been thinking after I had turned down her offer of a run. Then Nica turned to stare at me and, for a second, I was worried she thought something had happened between us to cause her fainting, or perhaps that I had taken advantage of her. But instead, she said something I couldn't hear and then she was crying.

I felt awful, and worse, a complete fool, so regardless of Madeleine's presence I got out and dried myself in the cubicle. When I came out everyone had gone, so I returned to my room and packed a few things for tomorrow's excursion.

That left an hour free during which I have typed most of next Sunday's Lenten talk. It's now half-past nine but I can't go to bed without finding out if Nica is all right.

Postscriptum: I found Kedden at the front desk. He looked pleased to see me, which is a first, and began to hand me a book.

"This must be yours," he said. "It was by the pool."

It was a copy of *This Iron Race, Book One.*

"Not mine," I said. "Nica was carrying something. I didn't see what it was. She put it on a chair. She had asked if I would sign it. My name's on the cover. I'm the editor."

"Mystery solved," he said.

"She's recovered?"

"Thanks to you," he said. "She'll be fine in the morning. Maybe someone will have to stand in for her at Sun Arising, but she'll be okay for the trip to Wales."

"Good. Good. Glad of that. Gave me a turn, I can tell you."

"It's not the first time," he said. "She senses things now and again. Hears voices. Nothing to worry about."

"I'm sure it isn't. Well, I hope to see her tomorrow, fit and well. Do return the book to her."

"Sure. And thank you for raising the alarm."

Strange turn of events. Kedden and I appear to be best friends and Nica hears voices.

Lights out approaches so time for bed.

27 March; Hereford Road, Herefordshire

No time until now to note anything down so am doing my best on the 'bus. Madeleine has avoided my eye ever since Sun Arising—led by Clive of the shaved head who, happily, remained fully clothed—so I've not had a chance to explain how Nica ended up in my arms with both of us naked in the pool. Nica, I'm happy to report, has joined us but is a little subdued this morning. Hardly surprising as whatever happened—assuming something did happen—must have been a bit of a shock. There was something she said I didn't catch just after she had recovered. She was giving me such a look at that moment. Not accusatory, more... surprise might be the word.

Brecon is well over an hour's drive away, which would have been an ideal opportunity to work on MacGregor, but given the fragile condition of his first draft, I cannot risk bringing it on a camping trip. So, I must sit here and admire the spring scenery.

Dawn was the most spectacular I've seen so far, but the clouds have been building ever since and now the sky is threatening. It does not bode well for the day's activities.

Lunchtime; forest, near Brecon

The day has become thoroughly miserable. Can't believe this is good for my health. Haven't time to write much and I don't want my journal getting wet. Also, this tree stump is none too dry and my bottom is feeling the damp.

From what we saw of it, Brecon is charming, but we drove straight through and then came off the main road and after a bit of swerving on narrow lanes, the 'bus parked at the edge of a forest. To my surprise, Kedden, Maeve (our dance mistress), and Clive were there to greet us with a trio of off-road vehicles. The rain had not yet started, and we were asked to line up with our belongings in the car park where Kedden divided us into teams of three. I am with Dave and a woman named Sophie to whom I've barely said three words. Each team was then given a small rucksack with enough food for the day and navigation equipment.

Dave, taking charge, opened the map we were given and examined the compass. His comments were encouragingly critical. Sophie and I looked bleakly at each other. I have the sense of direction of a bluebottle blundering about in a greenhouse and Sophie didn't seem any better.

"Compass is rubbish, but it's usable," Dave said.

"Have you done this sort of thing before?" Sophie asked.

"In the Boys' Adventure Corps," he said.

"Wouldn't that have been a while ago?" I said. "I mean, do you remember all of it?"

"More recently, done treasure hunts. Maps, coordinates, compasses; in a car, not on foot. Otherwise, the same."

"Then I think you are in command," I said.

"We should be a cooperative," Sophie said. "Make collective decisions."

"Surely not if one of us knows what he's doing. Frankly, I haven't a clue."

This did not seem to appease Sophie, and to be fair, we have not had the easiest relationship with Dave. It's one thing to know where we are and where we should be going, but quite another to decide how quickly we should get from one to the other.

I'm getting ahead of myself. We were then asked to elect a leader and I unhesitatingly chose Dave. Dave also chose Dave, and so Dave it was. Dave was given an envelope which contained a list of place names and map coordinates. He had already identified where we were on the map and announced that it did not match any of the places on the instructions.

"Do you suppose that's what the cars are for?" I ventured.

"Reckon so," he said.

It was. Each leader called out the person first on the list and the teams were assigned a name and a vehicle. We were Team F and assigned to Kedden, along with Team E, which included Madeleine.

It had begun to rain gently and as we all climbed into Kedden's off-roader Madeleine smiled at me and said that I would probably regret not going for more jogging.

"Not to worry," I said blithely, "I've been training for the Wild Swimming."

I had of course entirely forgotten in my haste to make light of last evening that Madeleine's brother had drowned in a garden pond. She didn't say anything more as we drove into the forest.

After a few miles of narrow bumpy track, Team E was dropped at a fork, and a few miles further on the track ended at a gate, beyond which was bare hillside.

"This is your spot. See you at the campsite," Kedden said. "Try not to get lost."

That was an hour ago. Dave assures Sophie and me that we are not lost. To his credit, he has led us so far to three waymarks listed on the instructions. At each we found a Midsummer Hill poster with a rubber stamp for marking our instructions to prove we had found it.

The food is worse than usual for being cold and Dave is impatient to leave. I must look lively.

UNDER CANVAS

Night; another part of the forest

I'm writing this in my tent by torchlight. Rain is pattering against the canvas and every so often something larger falls with a moist thud from the canopy of trees. I do not anticipate a great deal of sleep, but at least it is not made worse by having to share a tent with Dave, who has had to leave us.

More of that after I have spoken of this evening's activities.

When Sophie and I arrived at the campsite we found most of the other groups already established for the night. Fortunately for Sophie, she was sharing with Madeleine who already had their tent erected. Mine lay sprawled like a dead cow in the bracken and, after a few hopeless attempts, Clive took pity on me—or I had sufficiently infuriated him with my incompetence—and within minutes I had my home for the night. There was a certain amount of 'questioning' regarding the absence of Dave before Nica read out a short statement explaining what had happened.

The rain had at that point eased off, and we sat round a jolly campfire on which we toasted vegetarian kebabs and various other things. If it hadn't been for the pervading damp, it would have been our best evening meal so far.

"Is it always this wet here?" I asked Nica. "I mean, I assume this is a regular event."

"Last time we were here there was snow," she said. "Four people had to dig their way out after snowfall overnight."

Kedden spoke up to say that last October there was flooding, and they had to abandon camp in the middle of the night.

"No chance of that this time, I hope."

"I think we'll be okay," Nica said.

Thank God I had the sense not to bring MacGregor's manuscript with me. That would have been tricky to explain to Hare & Drum.

Then Kedden produced a guitar and he and Nica entertained us. Even Clive joined in and proved an inventive percussionist with just a few logs and a tambourine. It all reminded me of holidays in Cornwall with Mummy and Daddy, which made me ever so slightly maudlin. Madeleine looked radiant in the firelight as she swayed to the drumming and moths fluttered about the fire.

Then Nica declared that she had sung herself out and said we should have some spoken word. No one volunteered and Nica suggested I should read something. I protested as I'd brought nothing with me.

"But I have," she said, and produced a Wordsmith volume of my father's poetry. "It was in the library at Midsummer Hill. I took the liberty of thinking you might read from it."

How could I refuse?

"Actually, there is a poem that rather fits with today," I

said. "Dare say we've all found a few *bends in the road* and here is my father's 'A bend in the road.'

All roads incline to straight.
Ask then of the bended way
What diverted the surveyor's eye?
Or ask of thyself if it is thee,
Eyes close upon the present,
Who walks the road less travelled,
And sees the turn awry?"

"That was wonderful," Nica said.

"I didn't know he was your father," Madeleine said. "Do you write poetry?"

"A little; I'm more of an editor," I said.

"He's editing *This Iron Race* by Tamburlaine MacGregor," Nica said.

"Endeavouring to. I've brought the original manuscript with me. I mean it's at Midsummer Hill. Not in my tent. Too precious to risk it here."

"Is it true what they say?" Madeleine asked.

"Is what true?"

"That it's full of magick," Sophie said.

Madeleine nodded.

"I've always had an empathy with it, because of my name," she said. "His first wife."

Kedden was paying attention.

"Isn't magick dangerous?" he asked. "I mean, even talking about it. Here especially."

"Here?"

"In the woods."

"Oh, I see. That depends how much one believes," I said.

"I believe," Madeleine said. "I've always believed."

"Perhaps Kedden has a point," Nica said. "We don't want any bad dreams. Not out here."

"Well, if I may have the last word," I said. "No Madeleine and Sophie, it is not, as you say, 'full of magick.' Though I admit there is more in the revised edition than in the text you may have read. MacGregor had to tone things down for his publisher."

"I knew it," Madeleine said, her eyes shining.

It put me in a bit of a bad mood and left me wondering all over again whether I will succeed, or even if I *can* succeed at meeting the reader's expectations. I can only follow MacGregor's text.

Rain has picked up. Steady drumming against the tent now. Torch is attracting the six-legged wildlife.

Better explain about Dave before I turn in.

After lunch' we went relentlessly uphill, following a path through a valley. Only damn thing to see were the sheep and the clouds. I was concerned as the latter seemed rather low and I had visions of us climbing into them and getting hopelessly lost. Even Sophie's trouble-free spirit was a little subdued.

Then we came to a fork and for the first time Dave looked to be troubled by the compass. Sophie suggested left. Dave thought right. I hadn't a clue, but suspected Dave was right as he had been so far, though I wasn't prepared to back him up on it.

The map wasn't much use as the waterproofing had given out and everything was a bit of a blur.

"I suppose if we climb that we can see where we are," I said pointing at a hill.

Dave tried to find the hill on the map. I said we didn't need to find it on the map—I may have said bloody map—as it was perfectly obvious it was a hill.

"There is a path," Sophie said, pointing at a gap barely wider than a rabbit through the heather and dead bracken.

Dave glared at the map, then at the horizon. He did not look at me or Sophie.

We began to climb. The path soon vanished but we could see a pillar marking the summit. Dave said it must be a trig point, whatever that is, and we could see our way from there.

Without a path, it was damned hard going. The dead

bracken was often thigh-deep and soaking wet and everything below my waist squished unpleasantly. I was reminded of Bheathain's first scene in *Book One*. All that was missing was a scarf and a lost sheep. Dave set a murderous pace and Sophie scampered after him like a goat. I followed rather more cumbersomely.

At the summit we found the pillar and Dave was able to identify where we were. But he was still unhappy.

"I don't get this bit. That's where we're meant to be." He pointed into a neighbouring valley. "And we're meant to get to there." He pointed again. "But in between is this." He pointed at the map. I had no idea what the map said, and Sophie explained.

"It's all rocks," she said. "Are we supposed to climb down?"

"What with?" Dave said.

"I think if we know the way they want us to go, we'd better just follow it or we'll be sleeping here tonight," I said.

It turned out we were going to be climbing down, but Kedden and Clive were waiting for us. Or rather Sophie spotted them, and Dave deduced we were one valley too far over from where we were supposed to be.

"Simple mistake," I said encouragingly. "One hillside looks the same as another to me."

"Surprise to find you out here," I said jovially as we hove in range of Kedden.

"We've been waiting for the groups to pass through," he said.

"Are we the first?" Dave asked.

The man's too competitive for my liking.

"Third," Kedden said.

Dave shrugged. Sophie looked pleased. I didn't care.

"Are we abseiling down?" Sophie asked.

"That's the idea."

"Sailing?" I asked.

"Abseiling," Clive said. "On ropes. You walk your way down the rock face."

I had not noticed that beyond Kedden was a sheer drop.
"Oh Lord."

"Vertigo, Nevil?" Kedden asked.

"Just a little surprised. My word, it is steep."

"Safe enough once you're roped on," Clive said. "Just pay attention to your feet and you'll be fine."

All very well for him to say, but I don't generally pay much attention to my feet.

"Who wants to go first?" Kedden asked.

Sophie was the keenest, so they strapped on a helmet, roped her up, gave her instructions, and then she let herself down. I peered over the edge to see how it was done and saw her sliding down the rope and guiding herself with her feet. Another chap at the bottom unhooked her, and the safety rope was hauled back by Kedden and Clive.

"Nevil, I think you go next," Dave said. "Don't want to be last do you?"

I wouldn't mind, frankly, but I wasn't going to chicken out. Besides, Sophie had managed perfectly all right.

"Don't want any jokes about the ropes holding my weight," I said as Clive roped me up.

"Breaking strain of five thousand pounds," he said. "I think it will survive you. Remember. Take it easy. You're not as light as Sophie so no jumping off the rocks or you'll damage yourself."

"I shall be stately as a galleon," I said.

I leant back to descend, but nothing happened.

"You have to let the rope slide," Kedden said. "Stop gripping it so tight. The safety rope will hold you."

I eased my grip and felt my way down. It was awkward as I couldn't see to plant my feet, so I was either leaning too far backwards with my feet higher than my head, or else the opposite and nose to nose with the rocks. Anyway, inelegant as it was, I made it and was unhitched.

The rope whizzed upwards for Dave to descend.

In retrospect, Dave had sent Sophie and me down first,

so he had an audience as he descended, and this was his chance to show what a childhood in the Boys Adventure Corps does for one.

Clive payed out the rope and at first Dave leapt nimbly from rock to rock until about a third of the way down when there was a cry from Kedden for him to slow down. Next moment the safety rope came taut and, instead of alighting nimbly on his feet, Dave was thrown lengthways against the rock with a sort of 'ooof' noise.

For a moment he just hung there. Kedden was calling from the top and eventually Dave responded with a sort of splayed gesture and various grunting noises. It was obvious something was amiss, and he was lowered the rest of the way on the safety rope.

"Shit," was the verdict of the instructor.

Dave muttered something though a bloodied mouth.

"You went too quick," the instructor said. "Take it slow, we said."

Dave swore and said something about getting on. Quite rightly, the instructor forbade anything of the sort. Dave was a mess and when he tried to stand it was obvious his left knee wasn't working. He sat down again and groaned some more. I will admit to a degree of schadenfreude having toiled after him up hill and down for the previous three hours.

"Think you two can find the way from here?" the instructor asked Sophie and me.

"I think so. Just point us in the right direction," I said.

Fortunately, Sophie rose to the task and she and I were a much happier team now Dave was out of the way. No more charging up hills like a madman. It would have been pleasant, if not for the weather. Of course, pain aside, Dave has an even pleasanter night having been patched up in Brecon and driven back to Midsummer Hill. And I suppose I have a pleasanter night for his absence.

Getting late and no idea what tomorrow will bring. I shall try to sleep.

3am; still forest

The rain is appalling and the tent's shaking. No chance of sleep. Sounds like a storm but recall it always seems worse inside a tent than it really is. Also, something has bitten me on the crown of the head, and it throbs horribly. How in hell is this good for my health? Or anyone's health?

Bloody ridiculous idea.

GLOOM AND DESPOND

28 March; campsite, Brecon

We were woken at five-thirty for Sun Arising. Though perhaps roused from whatever pretence of sleep we had mustered is a more appropriate way to describe it.

I had thought it was absurd, given we were in a forest and so had no sight of the dawn, but having gathered us in the stygian gloom cast by the trees, Nica and Kedden led us down a path and into a field. The sky was dull as pewter and dawn looked unpromising as we gathered beneath an old oak. An owl hooted from above while Nica intoned. She had, slightly to my disappointment, found some pyjama bottoms this morning. In fact, most of us had dressed with warmth in mind, for the night in the forest. Then Nica led us onto the field where we all gambolled sedately until she and Kedden were satisfied. I had hoped that was the prelude to breakfast, but we were led down to a lake for Wild Swimming.

Ye Gods it was cold. I ventured out no further than essential—by which I mean both feet were off the bottom—and did my best, but all the pale bobbing heads in the gloom reminded me of a Hadean etching of the lost and forlorn nursing their sins for eternity.

Breakfast was prepared over the campfire and for once the morning's tea was almost pleasant, though it didn't penetrate down to my feet. Dave, Nica informed us, had a suspected broken kneecap, in addition to the obvious injuries I'd seen the day before, and would not rejoin us at

Midsummer Hill after all. A shame as I had almost become used to his dawn presence.

Now, we have just been instructed to break camp so I must leave off.

Lunchtime; Midsummer Hill, Malvern

I had intended to write more on the trip back from Brecon, but as it was the first warmth and comfort I had known in twenty-four hours, I promptly fell asleep—I was not the only one—and woke as we pulled up at Midsummer Hill. Then, as if in answer to my prayers, we were taken to the sauna.

After last night's privations this was a long overdue respite, or it would have been had it not been one of those ridiculous unisex arrangements where neither sex is comfortable owing to the presence of the other and all in the spurious name of equality. No one wanted to thrash themselves with birch twigs and instead we all lay like beached seals. My feet finally came back to life with excruciating pins and needles. Afterwards it was time for a massage which brought some relief to aching limbs.

Then matters went sharply downhill. An entire day of damp and cold and we come back to a fast day. I wasn't the only one put out and even Madeleine, who usually only picks at her food, looked unhappy. How I am to face any kind of medical exam on my final day when I am utterly exhausted, I do not know.

No idea what this afternoon will bring but I hope it is restful and quiet. Naturally, it is bound not to be.

BLIND LEADING THE BLIND

Quiet time; Midsummer Hill, Malvern

The afternoon weather turned out pleasant with bright sunshine and hardly any wind. I wouldn't call it warm, but it was springlike as we convened under the cedar tree. Perhaps the week is having a therapeutic effect after all, or I am merely becoming inured to pain. Hard to tell the difference I suppose.

What happened next was truly bizarre. Kedden went among us handing out large brown paper bags, of the sort one gets groceries in, and then led us along the verge beside the driveway. No one had explained anything, and it was all very mystifying when Kedden put an arm on a chap's shoulder—his name is Martin, and he was the one who almost passed out during the hydrotherapy—and asked him to remain where he was while the rest of us moved on. After a few more were left behind in this manner, those remaining were led down to the lakeside and then up into the woods beyond. At this point Kedden picked on me.

"This is your position," he said. "Instructions are in the bag. Open them when you hear the church strike the half hour. You are being watched."

Kedden led those remaining into the trees, and I lost sight of them. I could just about see two of our members down on the lawn, but otherwise I was alone and couldn't tell if I was really being spied on or not. I decided against sneaking a look inside the bag and waited for the clock to strike.

The wait was interminable but when it came, I lost no time opening the envelope. I quote: *shamanic walking is a spiritual practise requiring trust in one's inner senses and the goodwill of others. You will put the bag over your head and convene once more under the cedar tree. You may call to each other but must not remove the bag from your head. Your movements are being watched and your safety is guaranteed.*

Fear is the only enemy.

Fear and, of course, falling over one's feet, or walking into a tree and taking a dip in the lake. I took a good look around me and feeling utterly idiotic put the bag over my head.

"Well, this is a fine mess," I said. "Suppose I get off the hill for a start. Only way is down."

After a moment, I realised I was not wholly blind. The lip of the bag allowed a glimpse of my feet and the ground immediately under them. That was a relief as I had envisaged falling over every tree root. People were calling for each other but there were so many calling it was impossible to single one out and make for them. Even assuming they were moving towards me. I made certain I was always going downhill and worried I would walk straight into the lake, before recalling a path between the hill and the water which I surely could not miss.

Then a voice called startlingly near.

"Hello. Anyone close?"

"Madeleine? Is that you?"

"Nevil?"

"Afraid so. How the devil did you move so fast?"

"This is the jogging route. Where are you?"

"Still on the hill, I think. Can't be far though. I'll head down a bit further. Must meet the track soon enough. Ah!"

I slipped the last few yards onto the path and stopped dead. I couldn't work out why Madeleine was getting nearer to me when she was already nearer than I was to the rendezvous point.

"Wait there," she called. "I'll come to you... this is only for convenience. It's easier with two."

"Not sure I know what you mean," I said. "I certainly don't think this is anything more than practicality. Have you noticed you can see just enough not to fall over your feet?"

"Of course. How else do you think I was jogging?"

"Jogging? Gosh. I'm barely putting one foot in front of another."

"You have to trust your inner sense," she said.

I wasn't sure I had any. Never had any sense of direction, or indeed much sense of self-preservation.

"Nevil?"

"You're getting closer. But surely, you're going the wrong way. Tell you what; if I keep talking you can home in on—oh!"

"Found you."

Madeleine had unintentionally poked me in the ribs.

"Now to find the others," she said. "This way I think."

"Didn't you come that way?"

"It's quicker," she said. "We can follow the path round the lake."

"If you say so. Obviously, your inner sense is better than mine."

We started walking and then, for no reason I can think, I ducked. At the same moment, or I suppose it must have been just before, Madeleine squawked in surprise.

"Are you hurt?"

Something tapped the bag on my head, and I reached up to find a branch.

"No, just surprised. Willow tree," Madeleine said. "Overhanging the path."

"We should call out," I suggested.

"No. I'm fine really," Madeleine said.

"I mean so we can find out where the others are," I said.

"Oh. Yes of course. Hello!"

Madeleine's call was rather quiet.

"Bit louder," I suggested. "Stand back. HELLO! Anyone nearby?"

Someone replied but to be honest it seemed far away and I've no idea if they were calling in reply or calling hopefully.

"We should keep going," Madeleine said.

I agreed. At least the footpath was easy walking. No chance of tripping over anything and so long as we stuck to the gravel no chance of falling in the lake. Apart from the damn silly bags on our heads it was easy-going.

"I've forgiven you about Nica," Madeleine said after a moment. "She told me she fainted in the pool. I thought..."

"Thought what?" I asked. "You mean a romantic engagement? It's a flattering idea, but I can't see a woman like Nica interested in a chap like me."

There was a long silence and, once again, I had the nagging sense I'd said the wrong thing. Then someone called close by.

"Who's that?" I asked. "Nevil here. With Madeleine."

"Not interrupting, am I?"

"Sally? Is that you?" Madeleine asked.

"Yes. That's three of us then. They do like having a laugh with us, don't they?"

"I suppose," Madeleine said. "It's meant to be spiritual though. Inner sense."

"Nonsense. Just a case of using your ears," Sally said.

Sally was one of the frightfully active ones. I assumed she was a jogging pal of Madeleine's but there was a slight chill between them. Anyway, the three of us went hand in hand—it was the easiest way to keep contact and stop anyone lagging or tearing off in front—beside the lake and we were soon back at the cedar tree where a handful of the others had gathered. Blessed relief to take the bag off but a bit of a bore waiting for everyone else to arrive. One chap got completely lost and had to be turned back at the end of the drive.

Happy to report that was the last activity of an exceptionally tiring day and I had a shower and then dinner. Rice and roasted vegetables have never been so agreeable, but I fancy I would have eaten anything they put in front of me.

Managed an hour on MacGregor before tiredness overcame me and I decided to jot down my thoughts on the day before making for bed. It's only nine o'clock but I am utterly exhausted and it's another pre-dawn start in the morning.

29 March; Midsummer Hill, Malvern

Half an hour to grab, post-breakfast. We are to gather shortly for silent humming and immediately after we are back in the minibus for a short drive to somewhere called Holt Fleet. It's on the River Severn but that's all I know about it. Hope it's not more wild swimming as I've had my fill of that.

Cloudless sky this morning. Probably the prettiest dawn I've seen here. One does get a sense of what one is missing by not getting up before the sun. The quality of light is quite breathtaking. I doubt I shall maintain the habit though: too much of the night owl in me. Happy to say Nica was back to her usual self, bum-flashing and all, but it was subdued without Dave. We all found him a figure of amusement, but now he's gone Sun Arising had a serious side to it: as though it were a ritual rather than a bit of nonsense. Quite sure the sun will rise whether I'm out there in my pyjamas or not, but there is something of the holy, or unholy about it. Right now, it's Sacred Space and as my journal is something of a confessional I'm catching up.

Madeleine ignored me at Sun Arising. Can't understand the woman. Sometimes I wonder if she's sweet on me, then next moment I get the cold shoulder. Quite certain it's nothing I'm doing. I suppose people do have flings on weeks like this. It's such a suspension of the usual that anything might happen. But it's home tomorrow, so even if you were inclined—and you're not—it's too late.

Better get going or they shall start humming without me.

PLEASANTLY ADRIFT

Lunchtime; River Severn, near Worcester

Today is easily turning into the most enjoyable day of the whole week. True, my lunch' is nothing to write home about, but I am relaxing on the bank of the River Severn and quite alone in the world, apart from a herd of cows gently grazing behind me and the tower of Worcester Cathedral rising above the fields beyond. My only complaint is the canoe seat is hard on the buttocks, but after the last two days that seems a small thing to worry about.

The 'bus collected us from Midsummer Hill, but unlike our trip to Wales we were only half an hour on the road. Nica graced me with her company and reminded me I had still not signed her copy of *This Iron Race*. I said I'd be delighted to do it there and then if she had it with her. She hadn't but insisted I sign it tonight.

"The last day is always a bit of a rush, and you'll forget it," she said.

I said I would make a bargain with her.

"You recall certain items were removed from my room the first evening," I said.

"You were told everything would be returned and they will be, but not before tomorrow."

"I'm not asking for anything. I've decided that I will happily forego the sausage, the wine, and the beer. I have, despite appearances, discovered a few things these last few days and some sacrifices are in order. I suggest you feed the sausage to the dog. The wine is probably perfectly palatable and you're welcome to that. The beer is dreadful stuff so be warned. But I will insist on taking the cheese and tea home with me."

"You surprise me," Nica said.

"Gresham's cheddar is excellent," I said.

"Not that. I had put you down as a lost cause."

"Appearances are deceptive. Can't say I've enjoyed everything this week, but I am enjoying the effect it's had on me, and I really think I want more of life than my father had. I feel..." At this point I paused to find the right word. "Liberated, maybe, even verging on daring. I shall never be one of the Daves of this world—though it did not end at all well for him—but I do not have to go back to old Nevil either."

No idea what the new me will be like at Avebury, or whether old me will be restored. But I do feel a changed man.

Nica said she was sure 'Bonnie' would enjoy the sausage.

"You do know she's the one that snitched on you?"

"'Snitched'? No."

"Sniffer dog," she said. "Was she friendly when you arrived?"

"Now you mention it, yes. How do you feel about Italian sausage?"

"I don't eat meat."

"Ah, well. I suppose Bonnie can have her reward."

Madeleine gave me a filthy look when we reached Holt Fleet. She'd been sat in the back gossiping with Sophie. Can't imagine what they had to talk about as they are completely unalike.

At Holt we were passed into the care of an instructor who gave us lifejackets and paddles and led us to the canoes.

Initially I was apprehensive. Never done it before and the only time I've seen it done the canoes were frightfully narrow and chaps were shooting rapids in them. Can't recall where I saw that, but it was during my book-signing tour of Quebecque a week after meeting Van Zelden at the Koningin.

Anyway, these were Canadian canoes which are much broader and harder to fall out of, though I took the precaution of wrapping my journal in a plastic bag. Furthermore, the river is only a little swollen from yesterday's rain but otherwise placid. All I have to do is steer with the paddle and the current does the work. The instructor suggested we might stay together as a group, but I suspect some of us have had quite enough of each other and they paddled into the distance. I elected to travel more sedately and for a time it was bliss letting the meadows glide past while herons prowled the banks and glittering blue kingfishers flashed along just above the water.

I was not the only one dallying and shortly before the lock at Bevere I was hailed from behind. I paused and swung the canoe round to see Jackie, an older woman, with hips like a carthorse, but good natured and game for anything.

"Anything wrong?" I asked.

"No. It's bliss. Thought we might team up through the lock. Easier portage with two of us."

"Portage? What do you mean?"

"Didn't you hear the instructor? You don't want to go through the lock, not in one of these. Water is too turbulent and likely to swamp you."

"Ah. Now you mention it, I heard something like that."

I agreed with Jackie it would be a great help to have someone to help carry the canoe. Of course, she spoiled it by saying it was "all in the Midsummer Hill spirit of mutual cooperation."

"Indeed," I said, "though I don't think they can take all the credit for the principle of 'you scratch my back and I'll scratch yours.'"

Jackie looked at me as though she were weighing matters, then she said, "It's no business of mine, but if you're going to scratch anyone's back, I think it should be Madeleine's. I'm sure she'll return the favour."

What was I supposed to say? Madeleine had scarcely looked at me all morning.

The lock when Jackie and I reached it was enormous and I was jolly glad Jackie helped carry my canoe around it. I then helped her, and we got ourselves afloat without mishap.

Those cows are getting rather close, and my canoe is in their watering hole. Best close now and paddle on.

Later; Upton-on-Severn

Waiting for the 'bus to take us home. There's been a delay. No one's sure what's happened. Very unfortunate as I could do with a shower. My earlier confidence is feeling a bit soiled. Literally.

It was all going so well immediately after lunch'. Paddling through Worcester was a delight as I was in a tranquil bubble surrounded by all the bustle, though I admit the outskirts were a little drab. No sign of Jackie—I assume she was well ahead of me as I had delayed over lunch'—but when I arrived at a second lock a jolly couple with one of those canal boats gave me a hand and I was soon on my way.

Then, in a field a few miles south of the city I met my nemesis in the form of a sheep.

The dumb brute was stuck in a muddy hollow below the bank and up to its belly in water. Can't have been there long or it would surely have perished. Again, it put me in mind of Bheathain Somhairle, minus the Scottish hills and the gale, and like Bheathain I could not let matters alone—though I noted all my companions had done so or had not seen it—and I paddled towards the bank.

The sheep, alarmed, attempted to regain the field beyond but the bank was too steep, and it slumped back into the water. Its eyes rolled and it bleated pathetically.

162

I was now troubled by getting out of the canoe to help the sheep as there was only the riverbank which, close to, was above my head. Luckily, I found a shallow and managed to ground the canoe securely and clamber out. Of course, relieved of my weight, the canoe promptly refloated, and I nearly lost the blasted thing. Sensibly, the chaps at Holt had fitted it with an anchor and I threw that overboard to hold it steady and got up the bank.

It's an odd perspective being on a river in a canoe. Everything is water with the land monstrously high. It was disconcerting to now look down and see how small my canoe was. Behind me, sheep grazed completely indifferent to the fate of their fellow trapped in the river.

I walked back along the bank till I came to the hollow with the sheep. It saw me coming and immediately tried to scramble away, which took it further into the water. Any moment now its feet would come off the bottom and that would be that. Unlike Bheathain I would have failed. I hung back to let the sheep calm down, and reasoned I could get back in my canoe and use that as a ram to urge the sheep up the bank, but there was no guarantee of success, and it would only delay things. So, like Bheathain, I scouted out a safe way down and lowered myself over the bank into the same hollow as the sheep.

It did not go well. My feet slipped and I fell onto my backside and then slid down into the water, which was around six inches deep. The sheep, meanwhile, bolted up the far side having decided that I was a far greater threat than a slow death from cold or drowning. In doing so it scattered a considerable quantity of dung, much of which fell on me.

I got cautiously to my feet and as I did so a good deal of mud and filth fell from my shorts which had ridden up uncomfortably in my descent. My top half at least had stayed dry, and I remembered that among the equipment in the canoe was a towel. Presumably, the instructors anticipated some of us falling in the river and needing to dry off. I, however, could have done with a good wash before drying out, but I was not about to wade into the river. Instead, I clambered back up the bank and then to my canoe. I have apologised for the state of the towel, which might well be unsalvageable. As might be my shorts.

The last six or so miles were unhappy. Despite towelling vigorously there were parts of me that stayed damp and the all-pervading smell of mud and sheep was awful.

Ah. Here's the 'bus. Must find something I can sit on that won't spoil.

SOMETHING HAS CHANGED
Evening—last one; Midsummer Hill, Malvern

Home tomorrow. No chance to relax when I get there as I still have the talk to finish off for Sunday's reading at church. I wonder if they will notice any change in me. I believe something has changed. Can't put my finger on it.

Had a much-needed shower on my return, followed by dinner. Jackie asked me what had happened earlier, and I explained about the sheep. One or two had noticed it but decided it could get out by itself. Sophie said I was brave to go and help, but Jackie—who is one of those unbearably hearty women—pooh-poohed it saying the sheep would be more afraid of me than it would be of dying on its feet. Which was true.

A few other stories circulated at the table, including two in our group who had tied up their canoes in Worcester and enjoyed a pizza for lunch'. I admit to envying their nerve—it had never occurred to me I could cheat—but at the same time I rather disapproved. It's hardly a trial to wait one more day and then one can eat whatever one likes.

Dessert was fruit salad with strawberry sorbet. Easily the best thing I've eaten all week.

From seven o'clock onwards it was Quiet Time, but this being the last evening it was anything but. Nica took a dozen of us humming while she tinkled her bell. At first, I was frightfully self-conscious but then I slipped into it and thirty minutes flew by. Afterwards I felt quite rested. Someone mentioned we should have a swim together, but I withdrew at that point feeling peculiar. Perhaps it was only the memory of what happened last time, but I had no appetite for it. Nica didn't go either and with only a few of us left in the room it seemed a moment to ask what had really happened that evening in the pool.

"I fainted," she said. "It's happened before."

"I understand... I mean, when I asked Kedden how you were, he said you sense or hear voices. I didn't mean to pry."

"It's true," she said. "My grandmother claimed she had clearsight. I never knew if it was true. But sometimes I am aware of... I can't really explain what it's like."

"Is that why you enjoyed MacGregor's book? After all, that is what it's about."

"I suppose it is. And I must do. I brought it down with me. If you wait here."

"Of course."

Nica was only a moment.

"If you could write, *To Nica, Midsummer Hill, March*, and sign it."

I scribbled away and handed it back. She held it close to her chest.

"I was actually wondering what you meant by *I will be rewarded*. You said it just before you fainted."

"Honesty, I can't recall anything after I got into the pool. I'm sorry."

"Oh well. I had thought..."

"Go on," she encouraged, "I do sometimes have insights. Not real ones like a spaewife, but an inkling. I might remember."

"We were talking about writing and my father's poetry. I said most of my writing is in the service of others and you said I would be rewarded."

"Sorry. I must sound frightfully stupid; I really don't recall anything. But you should be rewarded, shouldn't you?"

"Well. I'm paid if that's what you mean?"

"It isn't. I mean you bring work that's almost forgotten back to an audience. You bring it to life again. And you do it selflessly. I hope you are rewarded, even if I can't recall saying it."

"Oh well. I hope so to."

"You've enjoyed your week here, haven't you?"

"It's not the exact word I would use. But I am glad to have done it. I needed a change. More than I ever knew. Perhaps things are a little clearer now. Thank you."

Nica had other people to say goodbye to and she left me alone. I sat listening to the hubbub of voices elsewhere. Someone, it was Madeleine, or Sophie, appeared in the doorway but didn't come in. It was now almost nine and having been reminded of MacGregor I thought I might get in forty minutes editing before Lights Out. It would, I decided, be good preparation for next week when I'd have to really get to grips with it and make up for lost time.

So, I returned to my room and sat down to it. Then I broke off and wrote up my journal instead.

30 March; Midsummer Hill, Malvern

Grabbing a few moments before I head down for Sun Arising. Need to write this while the memory is fresh.

Madeleine knocked at my door last night. It must have been almost ten as I was just finishing off my journal. She asked if she could come in. I said that was unwise given the lights were about to go out.

"I have a torch. From the night in the forest."

"Thought we were supposed to hand them back."

"I kept mine. Just in case."

"In case of what?"

I realised, with a jolt like icy water, that she was about to proposition me. I suppose there had been some hints. And, of course, Jackie's shove earlier that day. But even so, I hadn't expected anything to materialise. And now it had.

166

"It's awfully late, isn't it?"

"I know, sorry. I just wanted... you know..."

She let the words trail of. I felt a damned fool standing there in my pyjamas. She was still dressed in day clothes.

"You're not married?" she asked.

"Err, no. Sort of not. Divorced. Recent. Two years, actually."

"Then can I come in? I don't bite."

"Thing is. Err. No. Sorry. It's just—"

"It's me, isn't it."

"What? No, heavens no. I mean No! It's... Lord, I'm sorry; it's not the right time."

And so, she went back to her room, and I went to bed.

You bloody, bloody, arse.

HOME AGAIN
Late evening; Avebury Trusloe

Utterly exhausted and cannot write more but the reading for church tomorrow is finally finished. Must apologise to Prue as I was supposed to post it to her.

Thought I would be happy to be home but feel curiously deflated. Cats are ignoring me, and the house is too quiet. Even the hourly chime of St James sounds hollow.

Still thinking of Madeleine and what a fool I was. Good night sweet lady, wherever you are. You deserved better than to be rejected in a doorway.

AFTERTHOUGHTS
31 March; Red Lion, Avebury

Haven't written yet about the last day at Midsummer Hill. I suppose the main thing was I passed the medical and my contract will, hopefully, be renewed by Creative Havens. After all, that was the object of going.

The day started overcast with light rain. Rather a damper and Sun Arising was an anticlimax. Everyone tried hard but it was a difficult start to the day. Even Nica seemed subdued, and I scarcely saw Madeleine. Jackie tried to show some spirit, but it was a sombre group that returned for Silent Humming and then breakfast.

Breakfast was the same dreary stuff it has been all week. Had hoped after the previous evening's offerings it would be a little more relaxed and for the first time in a few days, I yearned for a proper cup of tea.

Had intended to spend Sacred Space working on this morning's talk at church but went for a wander by myself in the grounds. Despite the dampness, it was lovely and in spite of the indignities and privations inflicted on me, I knew I should miss the place. It was like one of those medieval tales where people vanish down a rabbit hole or walk into a mysterious wood, encounter strange creatures, and emerge changed. I suppose that is the point of those tales.

Speaking of changed, the first activity of the day was Sky-Dancing, which was like Sun Arising only completely naked and in daylight on the lawn. Oddly, I did not feel at all self-conscious. Dave had been naked from day one and Nica half-naked every morning, so it seemed natural to let it all hang, and flop about. Rotten luck to find myself only a few yards from Madeleine, though. Talk about having a missed opportunity thrown in your face. Suppose there's nothing at all I can do about it now. Water under the bridge, the sun set on the day, the ship has sailed, and all that.

Can't imagine what Prue, the Chadwicks, and dear Molly would have thought of me dancing naked on a lawn. I suppose one had to be there to understand. Chadwick's sermon was an utter bore this morning. Something about the Chinese. It was both too far away and too familiar at the same time. I wonder if Peter has ever done anything as daring as Sky-Dancing, or had coffee hosed up his backside. Probably not.

Then it was skinny-dipping in the pool. There was a suggestion we would use the lake but really it was too chilly and there is a rumour of eels. Eels are not well-disposed to swimmers.

With all of us in the pool there wasn't much space for reflection or indeed motion and there was as much talking as swimming. Jackie engaged me in conversation.

"You seem quiet this morning," was her opening gambit.

Talk about putting a chap on the spot. I suspect she believes something happened between myself and Madeleine and was either being kind or seeking information.

"Last day and all that," I said, feebly. "Real world is fast approaching."

"I thought you'd be only too keen to get away. Had you down as a reluctant hostage from day one. What made you come?"

"Employer asked me to. Needed to prove my fitness. My employer is the company that own this place. They also run writing retreats and I'm a tutor."

"Really? Fascinating. I dabble. I must look them up. They have a name?"

"Creative Havens," I said.

After that she droned on about horses and grandchildren and it was all a bit of a bore, as I dislike one and have none of the other. I suppose that's her real world, as this is mine.

"Do you suppose," I said to Jackie, "This could become a habit? Something one does often?"

"You're not serious?"

"I think I am. Of course, realistically I couldn't afford it. But I am tempted."

"Well, you are a surprise. I have no intention of ever darkening their door again."

It's strange, but had Nica proposed there and then that we could extend our stay another week I think I would have been in favour. Fantasy of course. The real world cannot be deferred.

After swimming we had a massage, and then it was lunch'—the first point in the day everyone got dressed— followed by another of those bizarre games of chess. We were in blindfolds for most of it, moved around on a chessboard until it's one's turn to take the blindfold off and direct a move.

I realise now it was about trust: even blindfolded, we must trust the hand guiding us because they can see the larger picture. Madeleine wasn't wearing hers at my door. I, alas, was.

Tell a lie. Sauna first after lunch', then, chess.

The rest of the day passed in a blur. Kedden did my medical assessment and passed me fit. Or at least fitter than when I arrived. He asked about the items confiscated the first night and I said it was all resolved.

"You're taking them back with you?"

"No. Only the cheddar and the tea. you can all enjoy the beer and wine. The dog is getting the salami. I don't care what happens to the biscuits."

"We will gift them to the church. For their coffee mornings," he said.

"Then I approve. I am aware I need to make sacrifices. I do wish to enjoy a long and useful life."

"I am glad to hear it. You may go."

Last item before dinner was a group assessment, which was just like at a Creative Haven where attendees assess the staff and facilities.

Sophie suggested the training for abseiling might be better, which, given she witnessed Dave's accident was reasonable. Clive scowled, but Kedden agreed with her. I suggested, to a certain amount of laughter, that the information sent to clients should make it clear that private hoards of food would be confiscated on arrival.

Nica said this would deprive the dog of its function.

"Oh, I love the dog," Sophie said. "So intelligent."

"No one is proposing we lose her," Nica said. "Are we Nevil?"

"Perish the thought," I said.

There were a few ideas about alternative diets. That our trip to Wales involved too much travelling. That the Wye was a more interesting river than the Severn to canoe down, but nothing remarkable came out until Martin, the chap who nearly passed out during hydrotherapy, suggested that for all the focus on the sacred and on meditating, there ought to be more prayer and more sense of the Divine.

"Do you mean 'God'?" Nica asked.

"By one name or another," Martin said. "But some sense that we are a part of something greater than ourselves. That there's more to life than a healthy mind and body."

Madeleine agreed vigorously. "Perhaps it should change how we feel and think about our lives as well."

"We hope it will do that, in the longer term," Kedden said.

"I mean now," Madeleine persisted. "I..." she paused a moment and, so help me, I'm certain she was thinking of last night. "I know I need to change, and I think I have changed, but not everyone has. We need to be braver. Brave enough to change."

"You're asking a lot from one week," Jackie said. "I'm only too happy to get home to my family. Not that I haven't found it interesting. But my place is at home."

"There isn't really anyone since my mum," Madeleine said.

Oh God. I swear if they had listened quietly, they would have heard my heart breaking.

Don't want to write any more. Not much left to say, and what there is can wait. Jonathan is expecting me to order lunch', but there's nothing that appeals. The thought of a mixed grill turns my stomach.

Postscriptum: weight fifteen stone, twelve, as recorded during yesterday's medical.

Later; Avebury Trusloe

Quiet afternoon getting back to *Book Two*. All feels a little alien still: as though at any moment Kedden or Nica will appear and demand something extraordinary of me. No idea where the cats are, and the house is quiet as a morgue. While making tea I put the wireless on, something I rarely do. Caught the weather forecast—continuing unsettled, what do you expect of March—and then a witless radio drama I gave up on after ten minutes. So, I put the gramophone on instead and listened to Bach, which made me maudlin, and then a Vivaldi concerto.

After tea I returned to MacGregor, but my concentration was disobliging. I may simply be too weary; yesterday was a long day. After group assessment, which, as I mentioned, left me feeling awful for poor Madeleine, we had our final dinner, or "The Last Supper," as Jackie put it. Martin said she was being sacrilegious, but no one minded.

Afterwards we all gathered in the hallway for farewells. The dog reappeared and everyone, including me, I might add, made a fuss of it. Then Nica kissed us each on the cheek and Kedden, Clive, and Maeve, along with a few others I haven't named—if I'm honest I cannot recall all their names—hugged us or shook our hands and we were off into the night.

Turns out I wasn't the only one caught smuggling. Martin received back a bottle of scotch and Sophie a bottle of sherry. I added the cheddar and tea to my bag and followed everyone to the car park. I didn't see which way Madeleine drove off. Someone said she lived near Gloucester, but I could be wrong.

Gone nine when I got home. Bone weary but managed to finish the talk for Prue. Then I slept like a baby until the alarm woke me this morning.

During the church social Prue thanked me for the talk and offered her thoughts, which were mainly critical and mainly deserved. Then Molly came up and gave me what I thought was an approving eye.

"Has your week changed you?" she asked.

"It's left me quite exhausted, if that's what you mean."

"It isn't. You look, I wouldn't say slimmer, exactly, but you stand straighter, if that makes sense."

"It was an adventure. I'm not sure I would recommend it, but it was worth doing."

"You mean you will still be employed."

"No. Not that. Though yes, I am passed fit for work. I can't deny it wasn't hard work at times and some things were just too horrid to ever talk about, but do you know, I would do it again."

"Well. I never thought I'd hear you say that. But I approve of the effect."

"I met someone," I said, the words blurting out of me. "First time really since the divorce. Lovely. I mean she was lovely. I made a hash of it."

"Oh." Molly took a step away. "Oh well. Two ships on an ocean, isn't that what they say. Passing but never meeting."

Somehow, I had hurt her feelings but couldn't say when or how. I wanted to say the two ships had got about as close as they could without colliding, but I just said she was probably right, and I should forget all about it.

I won't of course.

EVERYBODY'S HAPPY

1 April; Avebury Trusloe

Just had a telephone call from Pea. She was her usual excitable self and took a moment to get to the point.

"Anyway," she said after a preamble, "Dessie asked me to call and say he's heard from Hare & Drum about the interview." She has a strange habit of ending sentences with an upward inflection, which always leaves me wondering if she's asked a question.

"Interview?" I said, momentarily lost.

"In Oxford, Dave Carnation, was it?"

"Ah. Chase Carnadine and Dave Bratt. I had been expecting to hear something after that fiasco."

"Silly, no one's called Carnadine. Anyway, Dessie was on the 'phone for simply ages. I think he was desperate to get away."

"Oh, God. Was it that bad?"

I admit my heart had sunk. I could only suppose O'Brien or whoever had spoken to Desmond thought it as bad as I did.

"He was worried about missing his golf."

"What?"

"He's playing this afternoon. That's why I'm phoning."

"Oh, I see. My agent has interesting priorities."

"Do you like golf?"

"No. But—"

"You said it was interesting."

"I didn't mean golf is interesting. So, what did they say about the interview?"

"They loved it," Pea said. "You got so cross. It made great radio."

"Great radio? People getting cross with each other? Well, one person getting cross. Bloody Carnadine's so laid-back he's barely conscious."

"Shilling, Nevil."

"Shilling what?"

"In the swear box, next time you visit. You can take a girl out of the convent school—"

"But you can't take the convent out of the girl. We have been through this before, Pea."

"You still owe a shilling."

"What did b—" I bit my tongue this time. "What did they actually say about the interview?"

"It was just what they wanted. Loads of publicity and it was hysterical when you wet yourself."

"What! I did not piss— I mean, I did not wet myself."

"Shilling, Nevil."

"That was a verb, not an obscenity."

"But how do we know you didn't? Anyway, if you had it would be an even better story."

"No, it would not. So, my publisher is happy the world heard my humiliation and that I lost my temper on the radio."

"Yes. It was funny."

"Was it. Well, in my next interview perhaps I'll drop my trousers and offer a re-enactment."

"Would you?!"

"Absolutely not. I am glad they are happy and hope they are right about sales. Anything else?"

"No. Oh, yes. Dessie might have a commission, but I'll let him speak to you. Pub reviews. Interested?"

"Pays well?"

"Not bad."

"Then I look forward to him finishing his golf."

"I'll pass on you're interested."

Pea hung up with a girlish giggle. Two shillings is light in the circumstances. Hare & Drum are obviously using my disagreement with Van Zelden to push sales. Inevitable, I suppose, if disagreeable.

Pub reviews. Could be worse. Could be much worse. Dr Saunders won't be pleased. Nor will Nica and everyone at Midsummer Hill. The real world is encroaching.

Lunchtime; Avebury Trusloe

Coincidentally, Dr Saunders has just telephoned. It seems my trip to Swindon and the indignities of that fiendish contraption were to no avail.

"Good afternoon, Mr Warbrook. I've received the scans from Swindon GH."

"Err, have you? You might need to remind me I'm afraid. I've had an interesting week."

"The MRI scans at Swindon Hospital. Two weeks ago?"

"Oh, crikey, yes. The boom-boom machine. Not going to forget that it a hurry. Can I assume there's no bad news?"

"That's why I'm calling. Unfortunately, the results are inconclusive. You were lying perfectly still while it was operating?"

"Still as a rock," I said. "The nurse was most insistent. Frankly, I wouldn't have dared move."

"How odd. I'm afraid the images are badly ghosted and unusable. If you wish, I can book you a second appointment, but if you have had no recurrences since you last saw me, it isn't a matter of necessity."

"Well, to be honest, I would rather not. Frankly, the whole thing was rather alarming, and it took me all day before my nerves recovered. If *you* don't think it essential I certainly don't."

"Then I'll keep these scans on file for the time being. The hospital did have one question. You are quite certain you do not have clearsight and that no one in your family has it. That is correct, isn't it?"

"Absolutely. I have the psychic perception of a doornail."

"Then it must be a fault with the scanning. Nothing to worry about. Goodbye."

While I am certain there really is nothing to worry about, hearing it from another person makes me suspicious. I have no special perception, but can I really say that of everyone in my family?

But if Dr Saunders doesn't think a further test essential then I do not either.

Later; Avebury Trusloe

Afternoon on MacGregor. Think I'm getting back into the swing of things. Still have a dislike for strong food and I've not even touched the cheddar. One can take some pride in frugality, but I wouldn't mind getting my taste for pleasure back.

Maybe it's not the food. Perhaps I'm missing Malvern. And Madeleine.

2 April; Avebury Trusloe

Dr Claude Crabtree was born this day one hundred and thirty years ago. I never met him—he cut his throat, age fifty-nine, in his estranged wife's boudoir in Paris in 1948—but his literary work on MacGregor is as familiar to me as Mummy's voice. Even though we are so different—he was a communist and repressed homosexual—whenever I read *The Wizard of the North* a wave of fellow-feeling engulfs me. We are like brothers, sharing the same passion.

That doesn't mean I agree with him on MacGregor, not at all.

I did meet his widow, the actress and socialite, Liberty Pearl, but that was many years later. I was in my last year at Ripon Preparatory so it must have been only a few years before her accidental overdose of morphine. Mummy and Daddy were attending a film premier in Lunden and, though

Daddy disapproved of the kinematograph, Mummy insisted I came along. Of course, I had no idea the tiny woman meeting my parents was Crabtree's widow, but I can say I am a handshake away from the only other literary scholar to devote himself to Sir Tamburlaine.

Alas, Claude, I am presently teetotal and must toast you with tea.

And so, the day's editing begins.

Nota bene: best to add that while Professor Evelyn Bishop's work is of the highest standard, *A Writer's Life* concerns itself with MacGregor's domestic life and only references and analyses his texts in support of Professor Bishop's claims.

Bedtime; Avebury Trusloe

Still feel out of sorts but satisfied with today's work. Heavy rain and wind tonight: I can hear it in the trees. Cats refused to go out and instead slunk into the dining room and hid. They have the litter tray in the kitchen so I hope there will be no accidents.

And so, to bed. This is the only time of day I miss a drink. A nightcap rounds the day off nicely. Looking forward to the end of Lent.

3 April; Avebury Trusloe

Found another black feather in Gerald's room but suspect wind dislodged it from the chimney. It was a high old night. Branch came down in the garden and made a bit of a mess on the lawn. No damage done and I tidied it up. Cats behaved themselves last night so no unpleasantness underfoot.

Must shop today or I shall have nothing in the house. After the frugality of last week, the prospect of Budgitts' cornucopia may leave me reeling, but I shall do my best not to let old habits return.

Later; Market Street Tearooms, Devizes

Pleased to say I have resisted everything except a scone, which I am enjoying with my coffee. Market Street makes excellent coffee. I am also pleased with my resolve in Budgitts, though their selection of rice leaves something to be desired. While at Midsummer I found out that the variety they were feeding us is called Bulgur wheat, which may not be a type of rice at all but was certainly tasty. What I bought in Budgitts looks skinny by comparison.

The truth will be in the eating I suppose. How odd that a week in Malvern should have such an effect. Edith spent most of our marriage trying to get me to eat healthily.

I have decided to write to Madeleine. That absurd scene with her at my door haunts me, and, if nothing else, I want to apologise for my ineptitude: I mean cold feet, attack of nerves, call it what you will. It is two years since Edith left me and I cannot act like a fool every time a woman comes near me. God knows, it's not as if they're going to come near very often.

I shall write to her and enclose it in a second envelope addressed to Nica at Midsummer Hill asking her to forward it. They must have records of their guests.

That being said, I have no idea how I shall begin writing it: should it be a grovelling apology? Or a request that anything she left unsaid to me will now be welcomed? I was a student when I last declared my feelings for someone in writing, and I didn't have much of a knack for it then. Daddy famously won Mummy's heart with a poem: 'Lilac Rose' is still popular in modern collections of love poetry.

Even if Madeleine doesn't reply, even if Nica says it would be unprofessional of her to forward it, I may resolve my own feelings just by writing them down. I shall keep it simple. An apology. A request that contact need not end now. But no declarations of passion and no intimating that she holds anything more than platonic interest in me.

I am certain that during our ridiculous blindfold walking Madeleine went out of her way to find me, rather than making straight for the rendezvous point. Surely that means something.

Might call on Gresham's and ask if they have heard of bulgur wheat. If I can resist the cakes here, I can certainly resist the cheese and cooked meats there.

Midnight; Avebury Trusloe

"What have you done with the rest of you?" Sid asked me tonight at The Red Lion over his pint of Slaters.

"The rest of me? Oh! Yes. This is what a week of healthy living and exercise does for a chap," I said.

"I'd hate to see the effects of a month."

Sid's idea of healthy living is drinking cider instead of beer, but it is strange he should notice the weight loss when those at the after-church social on Sunday hardly mentioned it. Sid is not perceptive of life's finer points—he was once caught vigorously blowing his nose on a pair of his wife's bloomers, having mistaken them for a handkerchief—and takes no care in his own appearance, but he saw the change in me quicker than anyone else.

We proceeded to lose to The Crown at Broad Hinton. Bert Tanner mentioned that The Red Lion had won handsomely away from home the week before.

"You should be away more often, Nevil," he said cheerfully. "Not that you play badly, but we play badly when you're here."

"A jinx, you mean?" Sid suggested.

"I mean nothing of the kind," Bert said. "Only it's a fact that we win more when Nevil's not playing and it's not that he always loses his game. He won tonight!"

Indeed, I contributed half of our miserable two wins to The Crown's seven. They didn't even have the run of the dominoes, so we cannot blame ill luck.

"I suppose it must be my witty conversation that distracts you," I said.

Bert told me to go fornicate.

The evening ended most peculiarly. A couple having dinner in the dining room suddenly ran into the bar saying they had been attacked. Jonathan went to see what had happened and returned with a dead jackdaw.

"Did it get down the chimney?" Bert asked.

"No idea," Jonathan said. "They were sitting round the well when this came hurtling down and broke its neck on the tabletop."

I should add, the well is possibly the oldest part of the pub and has been converted into a dining table by the addition of a glass tabletop.

"Well, birds break their necks flying into my windows," Sid said.

"But why would it try to fly down the well?" Jonathan asked.

"To see if the grass was greener," Bert said.

"I'll have to refund them," Jonathan said, still holding the defunct bird. "Ruined their dinner and scared them out of their wits."

I said that I had mentioned the birds were getting too territorial.

"You did," Jonathan said. "I'll have a word with Abel Samwise, see if we can't teach them a lesson."

Abel manages Manor Farm and is often seen with his shotgun.

"You should get a buzzard or summat," Sid said. "That would scare them off."

A black feather dropped to the carpet. I picked it up. It was identical to the one I found in Gerald's room this morning and, of course, the same as all those in Conchita's jam jar at Crossstones. I am back at Crossstones tomorrow so must try to find out if it's stopped.

"Perhaps it saw its reflection in the glass," Jonathan suggested.

"But why would it attack itself?" Sid asked.

"It wasn't. It thought it was a rival male," Bert offered.

"You're thinking of Robins," Sid said. "Robin does that. Jackdaw is sociable. Only too happy to hang out with its own."

"Well, no more hanging for this one," Jonathan said and took it out the back for disposal.

"See," Sid said to Bert. "He is a jinx."

BLACK FEATHER

4 April; Trucker's Rest, Marlborough Road

This establishment is a comedown compared to The Ginger-bread House, but it serves a decent cup of tea and that's all I want. I don't like to drive straight home after visiting Mummy. It so often puts me in a gloomy mood, and I don't want to carry those feelings home with me. One might consider the crown I gave in payment as a votive offering and the tea a soothing balm, despite the ghastly plastic cup.

Mummy was the worst I have seen her in many months. Her eyes were dull, and she seemed sunk into herself. I remembered her distress last time and could only assume her phantom caller had not returned. For once it was I who kept up the conversation with a steady stream of chat about my week at Malvern. I even, desperate by then to make some connection with my mother, admitted I may have fallen in love with someone, but even that failed to get a response.

I couldn't leave without talking to Judith Malmsey. She was in her office and one of the carers knocked for me and showed me in.

"I only need a minute," I said. "I'm worried about my mother. The life seems to have gone out of her."

"Her condition is not stable, Mr Warbrook," Judith said.

"I understand. Even so I can't recall ever seeing her so low. Had she mentioned anything more about Mr Rookwood, or any other visitors?"

"No. She has been very quiet for three weeks now."

I decided to admit the existence of the feathers.

"A carer, I cannot give her name, removed them from my

mother's room. With the best of intentions, I am sure. But I think they should be returned if you see no harm in it."

"Do you mean Conchita?" Judith said.

"As I said, blameless. I would have done the same. But is it possible to return them?"

"Do you have them?"

"I know where they are: the broom cupboard, off the main hallway. I believe it's locked."

"We can't have our residents drinking the floor polish," Judith said. "But I see no reason they can't be returned to your mother. I have the key."

However, when the cupboard was opened the shelf was bare.

"Ah. That's torn it," I said.

"We do keep things tidy."

"Of course, of course. Is Conchita here today? She might know—"

"I'm afraid she had to return home to Malaga. Her mother is unwell. We don't know when she will be back."

"Oh dear."

"If it doesn't have to be the same black feather, I'm sure you could find one in the garden."

I began to say something, and then I remembered.

"Good heavens! I *have* a feather in my pocket. Forgotten all about it."

It was the feather I picked up at The Red Lion yesterday. Admittedly a little battered but it straightened out nicely.

"I think that is called serendipity," Judith said.

I didn't say that life has been rather full of black feathers lately, in case she thought I was as mad as Mummy. There was no point my giving the feather to Mummy as it had to appear to come from her night visitor. Fortunately, she was still in the sitting room where a few residents were watching a golf tournament on the television—I suspect all the green is soothing—so I had my chance.

Mummy's room is on the third floor, tucked under the

eaves. When she first came here, she took one look and said it was like being halfway to Heaven. The window overlooks the back garden, but it's small and though the casement opens out steel bars prevent egress. Just as well I suppose. It was odd to see mementoes of family and home—the family home—on her dressing table and bedside cabinet. A gilt framed photo of Daddy. A large photo of everyone at Daddy and Mummy's wedding at St Aldgate's in Oxford. I have a hazy memory of Mummy telling me who everyone was, but I've forgotten almost all the names now. Alongside it was a colour photo of Edith and me on our wedding day. Mummy asks after her occasionally. Beside that was a photo of Gerald in his school uniform. Like Mummy's thoughts, the gallery leapfrogged from one decade to the next.

I left the feather on her bedside table and hurried away. It's started to rain.

Later; Avebury Trusloe

Arrived home about one and after lunch' I got a decent bit of editing done. Gradually getting back into the swing of things and memory of Midsummer Hill is fading. Even starting to get an appetite back and thoroughly enjoyed cheese on toast for supper. Tempted to wander into the village for a pint of merit, but the rain is persistent.

Went to bed early and read.

GOOD NEWS

5 April; Avebury Trusloe

Postman delivered a letter from the Skye Historical Society this morning inviting me to give a talk on MacGregor's visit to Skye. It is my reward for the talk I delivered last year on MacGregor's depiction of Skye. One chap gave me a particularly hard time, arguing that MacGregor romanticised highland life. Organisers couldn't apologise enough and said the chap had a chip on his shoulder and offered to make it all up to me. This second invite must be their way of delivering.

Fee is a pittance of course, but all travel and accommodation expenses are covered, and Skye is always a joy.

Talk isn't until early September so plenty of time yet. Would be pleasant to see if I can spend a whole week on Skye and make a proper break of it. Must check how long the midge season lasts as the little blighters can ruin one's plans. Hopefully, the worst of it will be over by then.

Later; Avebury Trusloe

Just taken a telephone call from Judith Malmsey. She reports that Mummy is much more like her usual self today. Apparently, her gentleman caller dropped by last night and waltzed her round the garden. I jokingly asked if they checked the bars over the window.

"The window was wide open, but your mother prefers that. I assure you she had not escaped," Judith said. "I did wonder though. You said you had a black feather."

"Yes. From the day before. Can't recall why I kept it. Why do you ask?"

"We found six this morning. Three in your mother's room and three in the sitting room."

"Ah, you can't blame me for those," I said. "One black feather only. I left it on her bedside table."

"How strange. I'm afraid that if it happens again, we will have to investigate. It distressed some of the residents."

"Of course. Please keep me advised?"

Judith said she would, though I have no idea what I am supposed to do about Mummy's phantom visitor. Or indeed where the feathers are coming from. Though presumably the open window is to blame.

At least Mummy is happier.

AN INVITATION

6 April; Red Lion, Avebury

A pleasant day for the annual exhibition by the Avebury Society of Painters, or ASP, for short, at the manor house.

Sun is shining and the bunting strung across the High Street is fluttering brightly.

Angela Spendlove had invited me to hand out the prizes this year. Purely, I think, because she liked one or two of my Lent talks at the church and this year's exhibition is themed on Resurrection. I must admit that some of the entries were a little outré and I'm not sure mushrooms growing in an old shoe really represents the Risen Christ. Overall, though, it was all very credible and reminded me of my own brief daubings under Mr Primula at Ripon. That wasn't his real name, but he was Italian, and I never quite got the spelling of it. Tall, round chap, with a beard and a bib permanently streaked with paint. Knew his business though. Of course, Ripon was famous for its rugger and being good at art was frowned on, so my inclinations went undeveloped and unfulfilled.

I can't recall when I mentioned my early experiences in art to Angela, but she has long-determined to get me into the Avebury Society of Painters.

"I hear you've had a hard time lately," she said.

"Hard? How so?"

"This health thing you went on. Cotswolds, wasn't it?"

"Malvern," I said.

"One hill is much like another," she breezed.

"I wouldn't say it was hard; rather enjoyed much of it. Quite different from the usual run of things."

"You mean Avebury is boring you?"

"Not at all."

"Well, what do you mean?"

"I meant nothing by it. One doesn't have many adventures. Not at our age."

She looked disapproving. I have no idea how Angela spends her time, and for all I know she may be kayaking in the Himalayas next week.

"Well," she said. "If ever you feel the need for a creative adventure, ASP will welcome you. I know Edith was always saying you had talent."

I did once draw Edith. It was during our student days at Oxford. Don't suppose she's kept it. Anyway, I recalled something Madeleine said about change, and rather than forestalling Angela, as I have every other time she invited me to ASP, I relented.

"I am away next week. But perhaps—"

"Our next meeting isn't until after Easter. The twenty-sixth. A Friday."

"I can only say that I will see if I am free," I said. "But there is one slight problem. I suffer from colour-blindness. Reds and greens especially."

"Oh, I shouldn't worry about that," she said. "I swear at least two of our members are blind as a bat."

I thought that unlikely but let it pass.

"Well, if you accept I might find some things a little challenging. Do I need to bring anything with me? Only, I don't own a paintbrush smaller than two inches."

"We have some materials for people who are trying things out. All you need bring is yourself," Angela said. "I look forward to seeing you there."

So that's that then. Still, handy for The Red Lion afterwards and I'll enjoy a proper pint by then, rather than this Merit stuff. Awfully gassy and I fear the free radicals are wreaking havoc.

7 April; Avebury Trusloe

To church this morning and my penultimate Lenten talk. Drew comparisons between the long barrow at West Kennet and the tomb of Christ. Seemed to go all right, though I sense the talks are outstaying their welcome. Only one more to go and I don't think I shall be tempted to continue them next Easter. Didn't stay for tea and biscuits and headed home for cheese on toast.

Busy packing this afternoon. My second Creative Haven of the year tomorrow and, for once, they have booked me somewhere local. Uffington is a pretty village below the Berkshire Downs famous for its ancient white horse on the hillside above. At a mere twenty miles, I could easily return home each evening, but am required to be available at all hours.

My fellow tutor is Philip Strutt, acclaimed author of *The Paris Quartet*, and recent winner of the MacCarnegie Prize for something or other. There's no point attempting to compete with him; the man is a natural leader. But I am content to sit in the background next week as I am still trying to catch up on MacGregor after my week at Midsummer Hill. Happily, Uffington attracts less exotic Castaways than Glastonbury, so I should have a straightforward week.

Not surprisingly, I am apprehensive about the Inspirational Walk. We usually take the 'bus up to the Ridgeway as it offers a fine view over the Vale of the White Horse and plenty of talking points, but it is exposed up there. Better take a woolly hat so I can cover my ears. Having said that, I survived orienteering in Wales, so perhaps my worries are unnecessary.

Our reader is the delightful Tamsin Ridewell. Her *Rocky Rocket* series is immensely popular with children, but, unlike Strutt, she hasn't developed the ego that goes with success and has a pleasingly down-to-earth attitude to writing.

Must call in on Mrs Pumphrey later and remind her I am away next week.

Postscriptum: weight fifteen stone, twelve. Gratifying to see I haven't put anything back on since Malvern.

STRUTT

8 April; Woolstone Hall, Uffington

The Rover behaved itself and I arrived in good time. Strutt, as he usually does, had arrived early and I spotted him smoking in the doorway as I turned off the main road. He didn't notice my arrival, being occupied by a young woman.

Strutt was still there when I returned from the car park. His frame filled the doorway, blocking my way, with one hand holding his cigarette and the other resting on the lintel above his head. He's well over six feet and likes to emphasise his height. I didn't recognise the woman with him and assumed she was one of the Castaways. I had no choice but to approach as it was the only entrance.

"Nevil! Saw you signed up for another year in the madhouse." He turned and smirked at the woman who tittered girlishly. "And I hear congratulations are in order."

"Are they?"

I wondered if he had heard of my week at Midsummer Hill, but it turned out to be something else entirely.

"Your MacGregor thing," he said. "Admittedly, it's ventriloquism, rather than original work, but I assume it pays well."

Ventriloquism, indeed! I bit my tongue and said it paid the mortgage. The young woman clearly had no idea what Strutt was talking about, and I didn't care to enlighten her. Opportunity for that later. Strutt languidly stood aside and allowed me to pass through his cigarette smoke and inside.

My room is familiar enough, but the bed is new and rather hard. Unpacked and hung my things in the wardrobe, then arranged the en suite bathroom as I like it.

Tamsin Ridewell arrived just as I was passing through to the dining area. To my surprise she called my name as soon as she saw me and rushed across to embrace me.

"Oh, I'm so glad to see you. And you look really well, considering."

"Thank you, Tamsin. An excessive greeting, I must say. Considering what?"

"Still the same prickly old Nevil," she said and laughed. "Hope you don't mind. Deedee told me what happened at Glasto. The helicopter..."

"Ah, yes. Bit of excitement at the time. False alarm."

Tamsin had ceased embracing me and we were in the awkward, post-unexpected intimacy stage.

"You're sure?"

"Oh yes. Something to do with my ears. Sense of balance was a bit wonky. All better now."

"Good. We would miss you."

"Are you sure?"

"Of course. But you are looking well. Have you lost weight?"

"A little. Company was worried about me so packed me off to one of their health farms for a week. Only just let me out. I suffered unspeakably, but I think it did some good."

"You, a health farm?"

"I would have said the same thing, but you never know until you try things. Shall I see you at lunch? I'm just on my way there."

"Five minutes," she said.

Lunch' was pleasant enough. Tamsin quizzed me about health spas—she is rather knowledgeable having researched them for one of her murder mysteries—while I glanced over this week's Castaways. Unexceptional looking bunch, apart from a young man who appears to have some kind of skin disease and carries a shepherd's crook. Never seen anyone that shade of green before. One woman, I think her name is Deborah, got talking to me but was only interested in saying how wonderful my father was. Ghastly Midlands accent.

Must go as Strutt and I are taking this afternoon's induction session together and we ought to compare notes.

After dinner; Woolstone Hall

The afternoon was a success. Strutt was his usual loud self and spent much of the time swinging from the ceiling joists like a talkative gibbon. I do wish he'd wear something other than white tee shirts. All that armpit hair puts one off. Everything about him is testosterone to the power of ten.

189

"Writing," Strutt said in his favourite introductory speech, "demands that we wrestle with the world, subdue it, anatomise it, and only when it is at our mercy turn it into words. Any writer who attempts to describe the world without having first conquered it, will only portray their fear of reality."

It sounds impressive but I suspect it's arrant nonsense.

The Castaways were hanging on his every word, except for the green-skinned chap who scribbled in a notebook, as though oblivious to everything. Suspect he's one to watch. When Strutt finished, I quickly ran through the workshops I'd be taking for the week and then it was time for the exercise. Strutt chose the old chestnut of describing their journey to the Haven and gave them twenty minutes.

Leaving Strutt swinging from a beam I grabbed a coffee and took a moment to look at the register. Young chap with green skin is Robin Ruddy.

I was back in the room in time for Strutt to invite people to read their work. Only about half did and four of them were utterly dreary. One was an alarming-looking chap with a shock of grey hair and a liverish complexion. Piece was well-crafted but world-weary. Suspect he's a friend of the bottle. Name's Brian Glad. An exception was a young red-haired woman named Ellen who did her piece in the style of a thriller, which was interesting if not very successful.

Glad to say Robin Ruddy was one of those who read, and he gave us the only spark of originality, albeit his journey was geographically very odd.

Strutt then asked everyone to offer feedback. Brian Glad was the first to speak.

"You're trying too hard," he said to Robin. "You're over-complicating things. But I liked it."

"I didn't understand it," Ellen said. "I mean, who would read it? Who is your reader?"

"You are allowed to reply," Strutt said to Robin.

"I don't think about the reader," he said. "I write as it comes to me."

"But how would you market it?" Ellen said. "Publishers demand something they can sell."

I could sense a little animosity creeping in so stepped in.

"Not everyone has the same reason for writing," I said.

Strutt glanced my way and winked. He enjoys these little disputes. Personally, I think they can be very destructive, but happily Robin wasn't to be beaten.

"I know who I write for," he replied. "I write for the wind and the stars."

Ellen glared at him, but I admired Robin's attitude.

Only two Castaways are hopeless cases. Unfortunately, one of those was Deborah. She may approve of my father's poetry but has a tin ear when it comes to her own. Her account of arriving at the Haven was in rhyming couplets and even Strutt's relentless bonhomie struggled to say anything positive.

An hour to wait until they serve dinner. Time to drive into the village for a newspaper. Normally I'd call at the pub, but Lent is still with us.

UFFINGTON MATTERS

Later; Woolstone Hall

Bought a copy of *The Evening Chronicle* in Uffington, along with a packet of ginger snaps. Lady serving me asked if I was attending the meeting.

"Meeting?"

"Tonight. Ogmore Homes want to build four hundred houses just outside the village."

"Good Lord. There aren't four hundred houses in Uffington."

"That's why we're fighting it. You're not local, are you?"

"Avebury," I said. "Local-ish. I'm here most years."

"Then you can sign this. We're taking names objecting to the plan."

"By all means."

I signed and gave my address.

191

"Surely it will destroy the view from the White Horse," I said.

"They tell us no one has a right to a view. Not even an ancient white horse. Thank you. That's ten shillings."

Ginger snaps proved essential as dinner was dismal. Afterwards, Strutt announced he was off to the pub with several of the Castaways. Tamsin cried off, citing a headache.

"But you'll come, won't you?" Strutt said to me. "Never known you refuse a drink."

"I've refused a good many, lately. Given it up for Lent."

"You? Good Lord."

"He has something to do with it, yes. And I'm behind on work. But don't let me put you off."

"It won't. Come along, gang."

Strutt and his entourage left. Brian Glad was among them, as was Ellen and the pretty girl—Alice her name is—from the doorway earlier. Robin was not with them, which has only increased my estimation of him.

I settled in to editing and managed two hours before tiredness overcame me. It's now eleven, and I only hope Strutt, and company don't wake me up on their return.

9 April; Woolstone Hall

Woke with a sore neck. Suspect the bed is to blame. Night was disturbed by dreams, though I can't recall anything specific other than a sense I was not alone. Not that that is entirely disturbing. Breakfast passed in a bit of a blur. Tamsin was upset with Strutt as he had woken her up on returning from the pub. I confessed I had heard nothing. Alice was even more attached to Strutt's side, and I suspect neither spent the night alone.

I took the first session this morning. Theme was literary connections and how all authored books are linked to earlier books, whether deliberately or through the osmotic principle where each writer is the sum of what they have read. The literary terms are conscious and unconscious intertextuality but Creative Havens frowns on technical terms, so I use Russian matryoshka dolls as a metaphor for texts inhabiting texts. All a bit dry and arcane for the first session but I don't arrange the schedule. Most of the Castaways want to hear the Ten Rules for Popular Fiction. Not that there are ten rules. Or any rules.

Castaways are supposed to enter the first session of the week in a state of innocence, which means removing jewellery, ostentatious clothing, expensive pens, watches, and other items. Nonsense of course, but Creative Havens wants them ready to give themselves up to the creative muse.

Most had read the notes and done as requested, but Robin entered carrying his shepherd's crook.

"Excuse me, Robin, isn't it?"

"Sorry. Have I done something wrong?"

"No. Well, yes. Could you leave your crook outside, please? We're supposed to leave our usual persona at the door and begin anew for the first session. No vanities."

"It was my great-grandfather's," he said.

"Well, there aren't any sheep here. Everyone else has arrived as requested."

Robin asked if he could lean it against the door where he could see it.

"It's the only thing I've got from my family," he said. "The rest burned in a house fire. This goes everywhere with me."

What was I supposed to do? To only have one tangible link to your family must be awful. I let him hang it on the door.

Robin sat down but all through the session I noticed he had one eye towards the door.

After a half hour of lecturing, I got them writing. Theme was people in the landscape.

"And I want you to write this piece in the style of your favourite author."

Robin put up his hand.

"It's all right. We aren't formal, Robin. Please speak."

"I don't have a favourite," he said.

"Then write in the style of a writer you don't like. Can you do that?"

He nodded.

"Good. Twenty minutes."

I left them at it and raided the props cupboard. Bit of a ragbag collection, but I found a box-full of things and returned just as the twenty minutes were up.

"Everyone finished?" I asked. "Good. Who is pleased with what they've written?"

"It's derivative," Brian said.

"Of course," I replied.

"I hate it," Robin said. "It feels cheap."

"I really like mine," Ellen said. "I wrote like Dan Black."

"You admire Dan Black?" Brian asked.

"No need to be judgemental," I said. "I'm sure Dan Black has his fans."

"Millions of them," Ellen said. "Are we reading these out?"

"No," I said. "I want you to tear them up. This was an exercise in getting rid of any desire to mimic. Real writers do not copy other writers. Go on."

Brian and Robin tore up their paper with glee and sprinkled the pieces on the table.

"I chose Baudelaire," Brian said. "But I can't write like him, so why bother?"

Ellen toyed with her paper.

"Go on," I encouraged.

"But I *can* write like Dan Black," she said.

"So can anyone," Brian answered.

"That's not true," she insisted.

"Ellen. Surely one Dan Black is enough," I said. "Write the way you want to write. Dan Black didn't copy anyone."

"Wasn't he accused of plagiarism?" Brian said.

I said we shouldn't get distracted. Though he is right. Anyway, Ellen finally tore her page in two.

"Good. Now. I've got a box of oddments here and we're

going to use them to create characters. One item and one character each."

I emptied the box on the table.

"Eww," Ellen objected. "It's all old."

"Patina," Brian suggested.

"More like mouldy," Deborah said. "Is it damp?"

"Possibly," I admitted. "The hall used to be a watermill and the millstream still runs under it. But new things don't have much of a story attached to them."

"It's like product placement," Ellen said. "You can make good money from it. Dan Black does it all the time."

"No, not product placement. Take this." I held up a wooden horse with a missing head. "Who owned it? How did they play with it? How did they break it? That's for you to decide. Anyone want to try a headless horse?"

To my irritation Deborah put her hand up. I am not looking forward to her versification of poor Dobbin.

"I'm not sure what this has to do with intertextuality," Brian said.

So of course, I then had to explain what intertextuality was and how it linked to what we were doing.

"Strictly speaking, intertextuality only refers to literary works," I said. "But we are taking a holistic approach and looking at how stories connect and ways that we can create our own stories. As you found, Brian, attempting to mimic another writer's style is unsatisfactory, yes Ellen, it is, but stories are all around us. Now, after everyone has found something to inspire them you have thirty minutes to create, and then we'll break for coffee."

"But it's all old," Ellen objected. "Contemporary readers demand relevance."

"Dan Black writes about ancient history, doesn't he?" Deborah said.

"There you are," Brian added. "And some of this stuff is ancient history." Brian glanced my way and winked. Ellen did not answer back.

While they wrote, I returned the unwanted items to the box and then wandered around the tables seeing what everyone had chosen. Brian had chosen a wine bottle—empty—and Deborah had the horse, while Ellen had a pair of stiletto shoes and Robin a silk scarf.

Of course, the whole idea of creating a character from an object is hopelessly simplistic, but it is entertaining, and everyone has to start somewhere. Always curious to see who regards the item as character dressing, and who considers the character's psychology, since in the fictive world the items are their choice, not the author's. I let them scribble for another fifteen minutes and then we broke for coffee. After yesterday's dismal readings I was not looking forward to the next hour, but it proved more entertaining than I feared. Robin especially excelled, though his description left me and everyone else behind. Pirates were involved. Brian's was an all too realistic description of a drunk at the end of his wits. Deborah imagined a child grieving over his toy (thankfully, not in verse this time) and Ellen's shoe-wearer was a murdered prostitute, which was predictable, if gripping. I fear Ellen will likely achieve her modest aim of adding to the vast quantity of junk fiction.

Three others read, though their pieces were dull and unadventurous and too reliant on stereotypes. Must try to develop everyone's imaginative capabilities, though Ellen may be a lost cause.

Hopefully, today's lunch' will be better than yesterday's offering. Strutt and Tamsin are taking this afternoon's session, so my time is my own. Sorely tempted to take the manuscript to the pub and do some editing. They must serve something non-alcoholic and drinkable.

THE SOURCE
Late afternoon; Woolstone Hall

Feeling glum and out of sorts. I may have ruined my shoes and that blasted roaring in my ears is back again. Hurts if I move my head too quickly. Explain all that later.

Walk into the village was pleasant enough but I'm afraid the White Horse has gone downhill since last year. Most of the locals are retirees or commute to Lunden, and I suspect the pub is too upmarket for the few here with roots in the ancient chalk. Shame really, but everywhere seems to be losing touch with its past. At least the bartender was sympathetic to those fighting Ogmore Homes, and I told him I had already signed the petition.

With little conversation to be had, I took my glass to a comfortable sofa near the fire to mull over MacGregor's text. Fortunately, it is relatively uncorrected and legible, but it continues to surprise me. The difference between this text and that which was published is immense, and there is no doubt in my mind that, unlike with *volume one*, MacGregor wrote them completely separately. Quite how readers will react I cannot tell. I'm not even sure how Hare & Drum will react. They will both need assurances that I am following MacGregor's text and not engaging in fiction of my own.

I am also surprised, even appalled at times, at how daring MacGregor is. I never thought I would have sympathy for Sidney Beresford and John Lucas, but I must continually remind myself MacGregor was writing in the eighteen-sixties and not the twentieth century.

I had been sitting for about an hour when one of the staff wandered over.

"Is there anything else I can get you," she said busily.

"Err, no thank you. Quite fine as I am."

"Anything to eat at all?"

"I had lunch' before I came. No really. I am fine."

"Is this finished with?"

She had clasped a grim little hand on my empty glass, and with it, my justification for occupying their furniture.

"Yes, thank you. I might have another later."

I sensed a certain antipathy towards my presence. I understand the need to make money and a pint of Merit isn't going to pay the rent, but really.

Eventually, her hovering presence became too much, and I packed away my papers and began making for the hall when I remembered that one of my Israel College professors had retired to Woolstone. Old Josh would be in his nineties now, and never looked a well man, so I immediately thought of wandering down to the village church, which is a rather pretty late-Saxon survival which hasn't suffered too much messing about. It was open and proved rather pretty on the inside, albeit almost completely unadorned. Saxons, once they gave up their pagan ways, were an austere kind of Christian. Quaint looking font as well.

Outside I had a wander round the churchyard, with an eye for some of the newer graves, and sure enough, found the resting place of Old Josh. Lived to be eighty-seven which was more than I expected for him.

I could have returned to the hall at that point, but it was still only four and another two hours until dinner, so I pressed on and took a path down to a pretty lake. A large sign warned against swimming while a smaller sign said No Fishing. This, I realised, must be fed by the River Ock, which rises to the south of Woolstone below White Horse Hill. It is this river, or a side-stream, which goes under Woolstone Hall. I followed the lake upstream and soon it narrowed into little more than a brook flowing over clean gravel. Small fish lingered in the shadows under the bank or flashed in the bright sun. I had a notion that I must be in the shadow of the White Horse itself, though it was invisible in the folds of the escarpment, and I was now following the brook towards its source. Presently a footpath joined the stream, and both entered a patch of woodland.

I slung my bag across my back, and clambered over a stile, but the path immediately bore away from the stream, which occupied a narrow defile. The path climbed to higher ground and then ran parallel to the water. The sun had disappeared behind the trees, which grew close and gave a heavy shade. Insects whirred but I heard few birds. Nor did the breeze, which had been brisk a moment ago, make much among the branches. I could, though, hear the stream below, so walked easily, knowing I had only to follow it to find its source.

Then the path dropped again and bent round a small gully bearing a trickle of water. This led onto a bank of soft earth crowded with spent primroses and alder saplings. Water oozed from the mossy ground, but not in sufficient quantity to be the source of the stream, or not the ultimate source, so I stepped as nimbly as I could across the damp ground to where it rose again. This happened twice more, each time the spring gaining a little in size and the ground in dampness. Eventually, the inevitable happened and my foot sank, and my shoe filled with muddy water.

I swore, but I had become convinced the headwaters could not be much farther. I had an image in my head of the slope above and this slim patch of woodland dividing me from it. Where my determination came from, I cannot say, but I pressed on until the stream broadened into a circular pool set within a hollow, rather like a small amphitheatre. In turn the pool was fed by several small streams, none more than a foot broad and none more significant than the rest. Together, the streams did not match the outfall from the pool, and I surmised a stronger source lay within the pool itself, a fact proven when I noticed the faint rippling on its surface indicating a strong underground current.

I continued around the pool, discovering signs of ancient masonry. Here a stone wall covered in moss; there a pillar, partially broken; beyond it a fallen statue, defaced and anonymous. It was not ancient, perhaps only the last century but one, though it had through decay an ambience, a sense of being lost in time.

I was halfway round the pool when I heard an animal running. I did not see it, but it was farther into the trees, between me and where I surmised the wood ended below the green slope of the hills. By its speed, I think it must have been a deer.

Distracted by the sound, I again found myself sinking and had now got both feet wet. The air was heavy and cool. Wild garlic grew in profusion, but had not yet flowered, instead making great beds of broad, strap-like leaves. The deer, or whatever it was, had not gone and I heard it again, beyond the amphitheatre surrounding the pool. It sounded nearer, or possibly larger, than before, but again I saw nothing.

It was then I became aware of how foolish I had been. I had slung across my back my most precious possession, the only known text of MacGregor's first draft, and here I was, sliding around on wet ground and jumping streams in shoes that were completely inappropriate. I continued around the pool, reasoning I was now closer to returning to the path than if I doubled back. I crossed one more spring, finding more remains of masonry and a broken arch that had once been a bridge. Once, I supposed, this had been someone's ornamental garden, perhaps with a folly, though the house that ruled it had long gone.

I regained the beginnings of the Ock, though now on the opposite bank from the path, and headed downstream. Presently, it narrowed, and I was able to take a short run and land on the far bank with a squelch. My bag thudded into my back and knocked me to my knees. I now had muddy trousers to add to my damaged shoes, but I was on the path. It was then a simple matter to return to the stile and the open air beside the lake.

I reached the hall with barely twenty minutes to shower and change before dinner. Quite what I hoped to achieve I cannot tell. I found the source of the River Ock, or as close as one can get, but I cannot say why or what I gained by it.

Over dinner someone said that the Ock was once the village's water supply, but having seen where it rises, I would not be tempted to drink from it. Even now I can smell the dampness, though perhaps it is only my socks drying on the towel rail. I shall be sociable this evening and join everyone in the bar. Tamsin is reading later.

Tamsin informs me that we have lost a Castaway. Strutt said something unkind, though probably accurate, about Deborah's poetry and she reacted badly. Said that Creative Havens didn't know how to treat their clients and then she was off.

"You'd think he'd learn," Tamsin said sotto voce.

"It's not the first time it's happened."

"That's what I mean."

"Her poetry was pretty dismal."

"Not the point," she said. "You criticise the work, not the writer."

"And did he?"

"More or less."

"Ah. Anyone else in the group upset?"

"Yes. Don't know his name. Tall. Bloodshot eyes."

"Think that's Brian Glad. Suspect he has a drinking problem."

"He's organising a petition saying Philip was unprofessional."

"If you ask me, sleeping with the clients *is* unprofessional."

"Is he?"

"Alice. She must be half his age."

"I didn't know that."

"That, also, wouldn't be the first time," I said.

"What should we do?"

"Us? Does this petition mention me?"

"Not that I know. Why would it?"

"Well, in that case, I intend doing nothing. Wouldn't be sorry to see Strutt leave us. Not one bit."

"That sounds vindictive?"

"He's only got himself to blame."

Tamsin didn't say anything more. Strutt has a curious effect on women, and I wonder if she secretly fancies him. Only explanation I have for defending the fool. Of course,

I've sometimes had to bite my tongue in class, but you absolutely cannot upset the clients.

Only bonus is, I won't have to hear Deborah's ghastly rhymes.

Strutt then joined us, enforcing a change in subject. It was now almost eight and time for Tamsin's reading, so she left to get herself ready. The reading would be in the social room next to the bar.

"I hear we lost a Castaway," I said to Strutt as we took our seats for the reading.

"Silly cow. Couldn't take advice."

"Is that what it was? I'd heard some of her poetry. Pretty desperate stuff. But with a bit of encouragement," I said.

"Not everyone should be encouraged," Strutt said darkly.

Tamsin read well. Her work isn't to my taste—it's aimed at children, after all—but it is entertaining. Certainly, the Castaways appreciated it and there were several interesting questions.

But enough now. I am exhausted after my exploits and need to sleep. Hopefully, my shoes will be dry by morning.

4am; Woolstone Hall

Woken up in a complete funk. Horrible dream the details of which are even now escaping me. I was back at that pool in the wood, only now there was something in the water. I had this palpable sense of it rising up and me stumbling across the boggy ground, feet dragging, and then the thing broke the surface. It was brilliant white, like bone, and when it turned to me it was the grinning skull of a horse, but like no horse... no, it was exactly like The Horse—the horse on the hill.

Then I woke up.

I'm going to have to get a towel. The sweat is dripping off me and I can't sleep like this.

10 April; Woolstone Hall

Couldn't get to sleep properly after that awful dream and woke up still exhausted and with an unpleasant ringing in my ears. Complete befuddlement during breakfast and somehow contrived to drop my tray while taking it from the counter to my table. Scrambled eggs ruined. Coffee everywhere. Broken crockery. Strutt asked me if I had a hangover. Afraid I lost it and called him something rude in front of at least six of the Castaways.

"Bad night's sleep," I said. "As it happens, you slimy shit, I was not drinking last night, or the night before. Nor am I fucking any of the clients."

Can't exactly tell them I'm in a state because the effing White Horse of Uffington gave me a nightmare.

Tamsin, fortunately, was not at breakfast, so didn't hear my tantrum, but I suspect word of it will get around. Counter staff couldn't have been kinder, and I still got my breakfast, albeit a few minutes after I had expected. Worst part—apart from losing my temper with Strutt, I suppose— was listening to some poor lackey sweeping up the remains. Broken crockery makes the most awful noise.

After breakfast, I took a lesson from Midsummer Hill and popped outside to try and find my 'sacred space' before this morning's session. No cedar tree on the lawn, unfortunately, so all I managed was a brisk trot around the car park with a bit of arm waving. It's turned colder overnight and the wind's from the north, but at least the awful ringing has stopped. My best shoes are still damp, so I've not yet been able to clean and polish them. Wearing an old pair today. Bit down at the heel.

This morning's task was leading a viewpoint and narrative workshop. Thought we had lost another Castaway, but someone said Alice had a headache and would join us this afternoon. I began with classic first-person viewpoint, and all went swimmingly until we got to omniscient, when

Ellen argued that the development of individualism initiated by Freud and Jung meant the modern reader no longer accepted the 'god's eye' view of the author. I could barely follow her reasoning but, though I suspect it's hogwash, I was in no condition to debate. Fortunately, Brian Glad knows his stuff, and mentioned a string of recently published popular novels written in omniscient. After that, I couldn't wait to get the blighters writing something in a variety of viewpoints, so I could nip out for a lie down. Then we all broke for coffee and the last hour was them reading their work. Several of the Castaways are getting into the swing of it and don't hold back when it comes to critiquing. Gratifying to see them picking on Ellen, and even Robin, who is usually a sweet boy, was waspish.

Eventually I had to order restraint, saying: "We have already lost one Castaway due to unpleasantness. I'd hate to lose another."

"I'm not going anywhere," Ellen said.

"Glad to hear it," I said, as sincerely as I could.

Robin's piece was excellent and the only one written in the unusual second person. Took me some time to realise the unnamed 'you' in his piece was the White Horse and when I did realise, I found it vaguely unsettling.

Brian Glad gave us the first-person view of a drunk gazing through the bottom of an empty glass. I would say it was predictable, but it rather sums up how I'm feeling.

Then it was time to break for lunch'. Fish pie with peas and chips. Looked perfectly pleasant, but I had no appetite for fish.

Inspirational walk this afternoon. Feel like death and would excuse myself, except I'm worried word might get back to head office. Given their concern over my health, I don't want to worry them. By which, I mean I'd like to keep my job.

Before dinner; Woolstone Hall

I have not woken up in hospital so must consider this afternoon's walk a partial success, though cannot remotely consider it an enjoyable experience. The frost had gone by the time we piled into the minibus for the short ride to the top of the Downs, but it was still perishing.

I had sensibly wrapped up in jacket and coat with a long woollen scarf Edith knitted for me one Christmas. My shoes were still damp, but I had nothing else suitable for walking so wore an extra pair of socks to keep my feet warm. Strutt is impervious to the cold and had only a tight denim jacket over his T shirt, while Tamsin had several layers and a woolly hat. The Castaways had all dressed sensibly. Robin had brought his shepherd's crook, which didn't look at all out of place.

It was only a five-minute drive onto the Downs, but even so I was exceedingly warm by the time we arrived, and it was a relief to get out. Of course, without so much as a hedge to shelter us, my relief didn't last long and I was soon pulling my scarf over my ears, lest I suffer another attack like at Glastonbury. In fine weather, the view north across the Vale of the White Horse is magnificent, but today most of it was lost in a yellow haze.

A footpath of worn grass and exposed chalk took us across the slope of the Downs towards the White Horse, though from our angle it took considerable imagination to see it as anything more than lines in the chalk. Tamsin, who has a degree in archaeology, was in the lead and would be giving a talk when we got there. Strutt was alongside her and I was trailing behind, cocooned in my little world. Ellen and Robin were some distance behind me and seemed to be continuing their argument from earlier. I ought to have been the backmarker to ensure no one was left behind but was too preoccupied with staying warm. Then Alice dropped back and walked alongside me. I had noticed her glancing at me suspiciously in the minibus and wondered if word of my altercation with Strutt had reached her.

It had.

"It's not what you think," she said over the wind.

"I'm sorry. Can't hear you," I replied, freeing an ear from the scarf.

"I said it's not what you think."

"Ah. Well. I'm not sure I think a great deal," I said. "I mean, you are old enough to make your own decisions."

"But it's not like that. I'm his niece."

"His what?"

In my defence it was very windy, and I was worried about another attack of psycho-whatever it is.

"Philip is my uncle. So, I'm not... you know. We're not."

"Oh! Oh Heavens! My apologies. But I mean... well, I mean that he has, in the past."

"But he hasn't with me. It's disgusting to even think about. He's my mum's brother. I've known him since I was three. Why did you even think he and I were doing it?"

"Well. I mean. He umm. He seemed to be showing you a great deal of attention."

"Because I'm nervous as fuck about this week, and because he's my uncle. My famous writer uncle. If you thought he and me were... well, it says something about you, don't you think? Anyway, you owe him an apology."

I admitted that I owed them both an apology, and Alice rejoined the group ahead. Meanwhile Ellen and Robin seemed to have formed a truce as I couldn't hear anything more from them.

We crossed a road and climbed above the white horse. Behind, and to my left, the slope dropped steeply into a sheltered coombe, beyond which lay a small wood, and beyond that the roofs of Woolstone. The white horse, itself, still looked nothing like a horse, which was fortunate as I worried it would remind me of last night's dream. At least the wind had blown away my headache and fatigue. I can't say I was at all lively, but I no longer felt like death. Having made their truce, Ellen and Robin had begun walking faster and now stepped past me, leaving me trailing everyone. Ahead, Tamsin had gathered everyone together. I hoped she wouldn't wait for me to join them but of course she did, and I had to speed up, so they weren't all kept waiting.

"We're all here?" she asked.

There was much nodding of heads.

"Good."

She took out a piece of paper which the wind promptly ruffled. Fortunately, she was only going to crib from it, and launched into her piece.

"Folklore and myth are our earliest stories," she began, "and their themes and motives are common in literature even today." She then said when the horse was first cut and that anyone standing on the eye might make a wish.

I recalled hearing her say all this the last time we were at Woolstone, but then she caught my attention.

"Each night on the full moon, according to local legend, the horse, and its foal—you cannot see the foal—gets up and walks down to the Manger, which you see below you. There it drinks from the springs in the wood before returning to the hill at dawn."

Of course, it made ghastly sense of my dream, even though I saw the horse emerging from the pool rather than drinking from it, and I shivered horribly. I really didn't feel at all well and shifted sideways and behind Brian Glad to get out of the wind. Didn't hear the rest of Tamsin's speech, and then we were shuffling back along the path.

The walk, I remembered, took us to a burial chamber, like that at West Kennet. Tamsin led us and Strutt dropped back to walk beside me.

"Thought you might like a bit of company," he said.

"Really? Whatever gives you that idea?"

"Tamsin, actually. She said you were unwell at Glastonbury. Asked me to see you were all right."

"Ah. Thank you. I am fine. Well. Not wholly fine. Wind is bitter."

"I hadn't noticed."

"You may be immune to the cold; normal folk are not."

"I have hypermetabolism," Strutt said. "Means I run at a higher temperature than most. If I dressed like you, I'd keel over."

"I didn't know. It seems there's a lot I didn't know. I owe you and your niece an apology. I have apologised to Alice. Now I apologise to you. Put two and two together—"

"And got sixty-nine. I know. Been waiting for a moment to tell you."

"But why didn't you say so earlier?"

"Not easy when you want to be a writer and your uncle is the prize-winning *Philip Strutt*."

He didn't say it arrogantly, but with a hint of mockery, even sadness.

"She didn't want any expectations," he continued. "I thought you, of all people, would know the burden of having a famous writer in the family."

I took his point.

"Anyway," he said, "the whole group knows now."

"Sorry about that. And Alice?"

"Oh, she's fine with it. Had to come out some time. You sure you're all right? Look a bit pale."

"Bad night's sleep. Got lost in the woods down there yesterday. Rather unsettling."

"Those woods?"

I said I had been looking for the source of the River Ock.

"You found it?"

"Oh, yes. But it left me feeling a bit queer. See this dry valley, leading down to the wood. When Tamsin said the horse goes down there to drink, it gave me a turn. Reminded me of a nightmare I had. But I'll be fine in a bit."

"Well, I'll keep you company just in case."

"Thank you."

I really was rather grateful to him.

Bell's rung for dinner. Wanted to finish describing the

rest of the walk but must leave it for later. Hope it's something appetising tonight as I'm starving.

WAYLAND
Later; Woolstone Hall

Dinner was dull, but I have been tempted by an invitation to the pub this evening. That leaves only a few minutes to finish reporting on the walk to Wayland's Smithy.

Shuffling along with my head down out of the wind, I was oblivious to everything around me. Strutt had rejoined his niece and I was following at the rear. One of us should have been keeping an eye on the weather, but I think everyone was trying to stay warm. Everyone except Strutt, of course. We were now on The Ridgeway itself and I was musing that if I kept walking, I'd arrive back home, or at least in sight of it. The thought rather appealed, but of course it was twenty miles away and out of the question, even had the weather been tolerable. Still, it made walking a little easier, knowing I was nearer home with every step.

Wayland's Smithy is an ancient long-barrow, and a fine example if you like that sort of thing. It probably surpasses that at West Kennet for sheer presence and drama, but the main attraction for me was the beech trees surrounding it which brought some respite from the wind. Tamsin stood in the entrance to the stone chamber, and everyone gathered round to listen. I had heard the tale before, so only paid cursory attention to the myth of Wayland the Smith who would supposedly shoe any horse left overnight, in exchange for a shilling left beside the entrance.

Wayland, Tamsin said, was a figure from myth, distantly related to the Norse Völundr and the Germanic Wieland, also known as Alberich, but it was a mystery how he became associated with a Neolithic burial mound pre-dating the legend by three millennia.

Tamsin then told of John Gorst, a farmer, who wanted his horse shoeing, but only left a penny in exchange. He arrived the next morning to find both penny and horse missing but heard a whinnying from within the tomb. Reluctant to enter himself, he sent a commoner's lad in to fetch the horse. The boy was never seen again, except on May nights when he rides at the head of a faeric procession along the track.

Robin asked who had been buried in the mound.

"The excavators found eight skeletons in the tomb you can see, but below it was an earlier tomb with a further twelve bodies," Tamsin said. "They all dated from around 3,000 years before Christ."

There was a palpable change of mood among the Castaways, which I attributed to the number of dead and the immense age, but which may have been a harbinger of what the weather was about to do. The trees shielded us from the wind, but also from what was brewing in the skies. Suddenly, an immense thunderclap broke overhead, and the next moment an icy blast descended, and we were in a snowstorm. The snow came vertically at great speed and rebounded without laying, so we were struck from all directions. Tamsin reacted first and began ushering the Castaways inside the tomb. I was at sixes and sevens because that ghastly ringing in my ears had returned with a vengeance. Philip and Brian Glad were coercing everyone inside, while Robin Ruddy had leapt to the top of the mound and was waving his shepherd's crook at the skies. For a moment, I thought I saw someone in the trees beyond him, but Philip grabbed me by the arm and pulled me inside out of the wind.

Tamsin was calling everyone, asking for names.

"Nevil, Nevil are you there?"

"He's here," Philip replied for me. "Bit dazed I think."

"I am," I replied as loudly as I could. "Robin is outside, and one other. Did anyone see him?"

No one had, and it was quickly apparent everyone except Robin was accounted for.

"Christ," I heard someone say, and next moment Ellen was pushing past everyone. "Silly sod. I'll get him."

"He's an idiot," Brian Glad muttered. "If he gets cold, he gets cold."

"He isn't," Ellen said determinedly, and ran out into the blizzard. Philip and I glanced at each other. I think he was wondering if we should stop her, but frankly I was in no state to stop anyone. My ears hurt and my head hurt. I could only pray I wouldn't need a helicopter again, for that would surely end my career with Creative Havens immediately and permanently.

Fortunately, Ellen returned with Robin who had to be restrained as he was waving the crook over his head.

"Did you see him?" he asked urgently. "Did you see?"

"Who?" Tamsin said.

"Bonkers," Brian Glad muttered.

Robin waved the crook again, bashing it against the stone slabs overhead. Someone had a torch with them, and a shaft of light cut through the tomb, revealing his greenish face.

"Herne," he said. "In the trees. Herne. Like a stag."

I had seen someone, or something in the trees, but I did not back up Robin's story. It seemed too absurd. Fortunately, the storm quickly blew itself out, or moved on, and we emerged into fresh snowfall. Alice threw a snowball at her uncle and then others joined in, what I suppose, was an outpouring of relief.

Robin climbed to the top of the mound again and gazed intently into the trees. I looked also but saw nothing. Then I shivered and wrapped my coat about me. Philip saw I was in a bit of a state and, to my relief, ordered everyone back to the car park.

Not wanting to linger behind, I found a place in the middle of the group and kept up best I could. Presently Robin found me. Ellen was beside him and I realised they had struck up a friendship, or perhaps more. It made sense of why she had run outside to get him and been so short with Brian.

Robin was not about to introduce me to his girlfriend.

"You saw him, didn't you?"

"Saw who?" I said.

"The man watching us from the trees."

"I can't say," I said. "It was all very confusing."

• "But he was looking at you," Robin said.

"Surely not. Me? No. No I can't think that."

But I can't help feeling that I did see someone. Not a man with horns, but someone spying on us from the trees.

Best go. I am expected downstairs.

QUIET NIGHT OUT

Bedtime; Woolstone Hall

Now that I am aware Strutt is Alice's uncle I can see the familial resemblance. Apologised to both this time and explained I had been feeling rather under the weather at the time. Tamsin joined us at the White Horse, along with Brian Glad, which was a bit of a worry as he has all the signs of a serious drinker. Robin and Ellen accompanied us to the pub but soon found a table to themselves.

"The odd couple," Tamsin said.

"Those two? Yes," I agreed.

"The pair of them might knock some sense into each other," Philip said. "Too idealistic."

"Ellen is idealistic?" Alice asked.

"In her way," Philip said. "They both have only one measure for success."

"Ah, true," I said. "But you have the luxury of 'The Hammerbeam,' *and* decent sales."

"Not as decent as they were," he said. "*Paris, Trains* hasn't done as well as the others. Prizes are for the books one has written; not for what one is writing."

"But you're only forty-two!" I protested.

"Much too young to be past your best," Tamsin chipped in.

"Thank you for your confidence," he said.

"And what about you, Alice?" Tamsin asked. "What is success to you?"

Alice smiled and glanced at Philip.

"Not being compared to him."

"You'll have your own readers and fans," Philip said. "But what is it like for you, Nevil? I mean with your father?"

"I suppose difficult," I admitted. "In my youth I had hopes that the seed had dropped close to the parent, but experience soon taught me otherwise. Of course, I always envisioned my life would be around books, but not in the same way as Daddy, I mean my father."

Alice smiled. "When I was young, I couldn't say uncle or Philip. Even now I sometimes call him Nunkie Lilip."

"But not in public," Philip said.

Tamsin laughed.

Brian had been turning from one to the other of us as we spoke. His eyes were grey and glassy. He began to speak and even though he wasn't quite within our little group, we listened politely. At first, anyway, then with a sense of guilt.

"I can't claim any famous relatives. Infamous, yeah. Big family, South Lunden, that's what you get. Not what I wanted to follow, though came close once or twice. Success? Well, it's relative, innit. Pardon the pun. Scar here," he ran a thumb down his breastbone. "Open heart, last year. I'm alive. Anything else, well, it's prize enough being here."

"That sounds awful," Alice said.

"Does it? Only if you don't consider the alternatives."

"You have real talent," Strutt said quietly. "But most readers only want so much darkness."

"You're saying I should lighten up?" Glad asked.

"Light and shade," Tamsin suggested.

"What's that Italian word?" Alice asked.

"*Chiaroscuro*," Glad said. "See, I'm not thick."

"No one ever thought you were," Strutt said. "But Tamsin's right. Shadows are stronger when thrown by light."

"Maybe. Sorry. I need to go," Glad said. "Can feel the need for a pint, but it won't stop at a pint. Won't spoil your evening. I'll be in class tomorrow."

"You needn't leave," Tamsin said.

"It's all right," I said. "I think Brian knows what's best for him."

Philip agreed and Brian left us.

"A shame," Tamsin said.

"It would have been a shame had he stayed, and things got out of control," I said. "My father... well, I haven't said this often, or ever. There were times when things weren't going well. Of course, it wasn't beer with him, but brandy has the same effect."

"I didn't know that," Strutt said.

"He managed to keep it private, most of the time. Mummy, I mean my mother, saw it more than I did. I only overheard things."

"Was he violent?" Alice asked.

"Only in word. Sometimes he would disown me, saying I wasn't his son. Nonsense of course, but hurtful all the same. He would make up for it at other times. And once I had grown up, and was doing well at college, we got along swimmingly. Then he became ill."

"That's awful," Tamsin said.

"I had hoped for some encouragement for my niece," Strutt said affectionately. "Evening hasn't worked out."

"It's fine, Nunkie."

"But you have an advantage," I said to Alice. "You don't share Philip's family name, so only the critics will try to compare you. And you don't seem to be following in his footsteps. You are after a different reader to those who buy dreary literary volumes that win serious prizes. You want to be more like Tamsin."

I had glanced at Philip with a friendly wink, to show I was not to be taken seriously and he took it in good heart.

"I do want to be liked," Alice said shyly.

"I'm liked!" Philip protested in mock indignation.

"No one said you weren't," Tamsin agreed. "But writing for children is so rewarding. You'll be fine, Alice. No one will compare you."

I wasn't as confident as Tamsin. My experience of critics is they always seek a comparison, but it was best not to say so.

We left the pub shortly after closing time. The moon was up and the sky clear. We're having a late dose of winter.

"Least it's not snowing," Tamsin joked, but no one laughed.

"Did anyone see where Ellen and Robin got to?" Philip asked.

"I saw them leave earlier," Alice said.

"Sensible. They'll be snug and warm by now," I said.

"Probably in the same bed," Philip said.

"And good luck to them."

Come August when we're off to Rocamadour I shall long for a dose of this weather to escape the heat, but right now winter has overstayed. It's been a long and exhausting day. Can't imagine what came over me tonight. Never told a soul about Daddy's drinking. Don't intend to repeat it any time soon.

GOOD ENDINGS

11 April; Woolstone Hall

Brian has apologised to Philip and dropped his petition. That explains why he was friendly with him last evening. Apparently, Deborah telephoned yesterday afternoon full of regrets over storming out. What with my faux pas regarding Alice, it seems Philip has been hard-done by this week.

That came out over breakfast this morning. Yours truly is always the last one to find out these things. Alice filled me in on the details as we shared a pot of tea. It seems I am forgiven.

She had ulterior motives, though well-intentioned. I had worried her last evening and she wanted to check up on me.

"I'm really sorry to hear about your father," she said.

"Sorry?" I asked. "He has been gone an awfully long time."

"I didn't mean that. I meant what you said last night. It must have been awful for you."

"Ah. To be honest, I wish I hadn't mentioned it."

"I understand it must have been painful."

"Well, it's more that I want to protect Daddy's memory. So many people loved his poetry. They still do. I'd rather not spoil it for them."

"Wouldn't the poetry be more real if people knew? I mean everyone knows Asher Hughes was awful to his wife, but people still love his poetry."

Actually, I'm not sure anyone does love Asher Hughes' poetry, and it's not hard to believe the author of 'Crow Night' and 'Roadkill Rhymes' wasn't a pleasant chap, but that's by-the-by.

"I suppose I don't want them to know," I told Alice. "And I'd very much appreciate it if you treated what I said as private. I was rather tired last evening and said more than I intended to."

"I didn't mean to pry."

"Much of my childhood was idyllic and I prefer to remember the best bits. Besides, it's bad enough being overshadowed by my father the poet, without being overshadowed by my father the drunk poet."

"I understand. Are you teetotal because of him?"

"Tee—? Oh! No, nothing like that. Given it up for Lent."

"Oh. That might explain it."

"Explain what?"

"Why you are so cross with people."

"I am not cross with people," I protested.

Alice did not pursue the accusation. It's true I am a little shorter of temper at the moment, but I have been under strain lately. Anyway, it will be Easter soon and life can return to normal.

Now, I should get my things together. Tutorials this morning and I need to know who I'm seeing.

Afternoon; Woolstone Hall

Off to *La Traviata* in Faringdon later to mark the last evening of the Haven. Everyone will be on their way home this time tomorrow. Can't say I am looking forward to this evening. Sooner a quiet night in, but the food is presentable and Creative Havens are paying, so I cannot complain.

Impressed, and pleasantly surprised, by Ellen and Robin whose tutorials I took this morning. I do believe they may be a good influence on each other. Robin's work was as imaginative as ever but had a certain discipline that made his individual style even more striking. Ellen, meanwhile, seems to have reined in her desire for formulaic success, and produced a touching piece about her mother. After them I saw Brian Glad and, while the start of his piece was a depressing account of a man buying a bottle of gin, it then became something quite different when he climbed to the Downs and sacrificed the bottle by pouring it onto the eye of the White Horse. Not sure what the Antiquities Trust would make of it, but it was a moving account of a man almost at the end of his strength and finding hope. Relieved he kept it realist throughout and did not have the horse cantering down the hill.

Lunch' was a cold meat platter with jacket potatoes (done correctly in an oven), and afterwards I led a class discussion on the 'fictive dream' and how to maintain it. Personally, I like the author who drops the occasional aside, but Creative Havens are thoroughly modern and eschew traditional narrative in favour of 'immersive fiction' where the author never intrudes.

Brian Glad pointed out that this approach contradicts most of the great novelists of the nineteenth and early twentieth century—which it does—and then Ellen remarked that many popular novelists are equally intrusive, albeit their voice is neutral and does not register with the reader.

It all led to an interesting discussion on the nature of author and text.

Final two tutorials after that and then I had an hour free so drove in to Uffington for a copy of the *Evening Chronicle*. I was also curious to hear about the meeting with Ogmore Homes.

A young lad, probably moonlighting after school, served me, and I asked him how the meeting had gone.

"What meeting?" he asked.

"I heard the village were meeting with someone from Ogmore Homes."

"Oh, yeah."

He had taken my Crown and was now giving me change.

"Well?" I asked.

"Depends, dunnit."

"On what? I'm only asking how the meeting went. The lady I spoke to seemed very worried by it."

"Y'mean here?"

"Indeed, in this very shop."

"She's plush," he said. "Nice house and all."

"And?"

"Not everyone objects to Ogmore. Only them that have nice houses. Others think people need places to live. Local people."

"Ah. So, you would be happy to see these homes built."

"Too right."

I suppose he has a point. A view spoiled for one is a home for another. Apparently, the meeting ended fractiously and Ogmore Homes are having second thoughts. The lad was glum and said he would have to move to Swindon if the village didn't grow. I sympathised but hope Ogmore do not get their way.

After I got back, I managed an hour on MacGregor. Making fair progress and noting that Bheathain's predicament is far more clearly drawn than in the published text. In particular the depiction of Prince William's ghost is more poignant and presented in a realist manner. MacGregor intends the reader to accept his text as a depiction of reality, even when describing that outwith human perception.

Only wish I had longer to work upon it, but I wanted to write up my journal before we depart for the restaurant.

The highlight of the evening at *La Traviata* was Ellen reading a poem. Admittedly, it was hardly a cheerful offering, but that Ellen wrote a poem at all is something. I think I should be able to recall how it went.

> *Twenty-two they laid*
> *High upon the hill.*
> *Twenty-two they laid,*
> *And lie there still.*
>
> *Twenty-two they cast,*
> *The fair and the grue.*
> *Twenty-two they cast*
> *Under sod to rue.*
>
> *Twenty-two are bound*
> *Below beech and gorse.*
> *Twenty-two are bound*
> *In sight of the horse*
>
> *Twenty-two wait on*
> *Eternity's tide.*
> *Twenty-two wait on*
> *The final ride*

It's amateur stuff of course and I suspect someone helped her with the rhymes—I doubt she has ever heard of 'grue'—but simply that she wrote it from the heart rather than for a readership is enough.

The food was excellent, though I managed to get sauce all over my tie, and Philip gave us a short speech at the end. Apparently, the wine was also excellent but I, along with Brian, abstained.

Once back at Woolstone Hall we gathered in the lounge for more reading and storytelling until people began to drift off to bed, where I am now.

This time tomorrow I shall be home and most likely asleep.

A QUEER THING HAPPENED
12 April; Woolstone Hall

Weather's miserable. Torrential rain and gusting wind; looks set to last the day. Breakfasted in a peculiar mood. It's only ever in the latter days that a group seems to come together, and by then, of course, it's nearly time for everyone to go home. Not that I am averse to going home. Haven't had a decent night's sleep since my encounter with the spring. Dreamt of that horse again last night; took me up on its back and we went racing along the Ridgeway. Woke up trembling, and me legs like jelly.

Then something very queer happened during this morning's session—should add I am writing this just before lunch'—which was on setting and sense of place; or *Genius Loci*, to use the proper name.

I had done my usual talk, using examples from MacGregor—*The Barra Bride* this time—and Emile Breton's Gothic romance, *Windy Heath*, together with the French-American author Kent Duchaine who writes so well of the southern states, before setting a thirty-minute exercise to complete before the break.

I, feeling rather tired, sat back, and glanced through *Windy Heath* while the class wrote; but I was soon aware of a chill in the air, and one or two of the female Castaways noticed it too, for there was much pulling on of cardigans and the like.

I got up and walked around the room to check the windows. It was windy outside but inside the air was perfectly still, so they were not to blame. The radiator in the room was scarcely tepid, and I wondered if the boiler was on the blink. I reasoned it was best to continue and mention it to one of the staff during the break.

I sat down again, but now the chill gradually became a feeling of utter dread, close to that with which I had woken after my dream last night. This lasted five minutes before Brian Glad spoke up.

"Is anyone else writing about that tomb?"

I glanced up from *Windy Heath*. Several Castaways were looking awkwardly at each other.

"I'm turning my poem into a screenplay," Ellen said.

"Mine is a about the horned man I saw... or thought I saw," Robin said.

Brian was working on a retelling of John Gorst. Six others were also writing poems or short stories set at or near Wayland's Smithy. The other three were writing about the White Horse.

"You don't suppose..." Ellen said.

One chap quietly tore his page in half. A woman copied him then scattered the paper on the floor.

The dreadful feeling eased, and then everyone was tearing up their work, until all we had was confetti.

During the coffee break I checked the radiator, and damn near burned my hand. Then I gathered up the bits of paper and put them in the bin.

After coffee I set a twenty-minute exercise, but suggested people focus on a place they felt good about. No one objected.

"I'm afraid there won't be time for everyone, or even many of you, to read. But before you all go, I suggest leaving details that can be shared with the group so you can all stay in touch. There's also the Creative Havens forum where you can talk to other Castaways, though I suspect some of you have already made arrangements."

I am happy to say Ellen smiled.

Damned peculiar, though. Could they, by all writing about it, have brought the tomb, or the ghost of Wayland down from the hill? Perish the thought. I prefer a simpler explanation.

Rest of the morning was spent on tutorials. Everyone seems to have found it all immensely rewarding, and I must admit that several of the Castaways had impressed me, not least Ellen.

Must close as the lunch' bell has rung.

FINDING TIME

Later; Woolstone Hall

Almost ready to depart. Weather is still appalling, and it will be a miserable drive home. Had thought of popping into Swindon, as it's only a few miles out of my way. Chance to do some shopping for next week and save on a trip to Devizes; but everything will get wet through, including yours truly, so home it is.

Last tutorials were rather quiet, as they often are. With the end approaching, enthusiasm has dropped as people turn to their domestic concerns. Havens are just that, a short respite from the seas of life, and for many those seas leave little time for writing. One woman owned to me that she scarcely has a half-hour free in the day. "Before the children wake up," she said. "Even then I feel guilty; there's always something I think I should be doing."

"I don't think anyone should be guilty over a few hours each week devoted to what they love."

"But there's no reward," she said. "My husband thinks I should give it another six months and then pack it in."

"And what does he do with his free time?"

She said he had a season ticket at a football club. "But that's good because it gets him out of the house."

Other people's lives are a complete mystery to me. I tried to persuade Claudia (not her real name if my future self is reading this), that she had nothing to feel guilty about, and that she wasn't untalented and should stick with it.

"It's all right for you," she said, though not with any venom. "You went to Oxford, and your father was famous. You were born to it."

"I promise you, having a famous father doesn't make it easier."

"No? But this is expected of you, to write and stuff. I'm expected to look after kids, and maybe work down the check-outs. I had to beg my husband to let me have a week here."

It is a different world for some. Her children were at their grandma's, as her husband works shifts and can't manage them on his own. She expected tears and tantrums when she got home. She didn't say if they would be from husband or children. I said she should keep writing.

Strutt and I joined forces for the last session. The topic, oddly enough, was discipline and setting targets. I could see poor Claudia almost welling up, as Strutt described his typical 'working' day. I, in turn, downplayed my habits and mentioned that, far from living a glamorous writing life, I sat at my desk for hours on end most days. I'm not sure that helped either.

Session ended with everyone filling out the dreaded feedback forms. Strutt collected them so I've no idea what was said. If there's anything bad, I shall hear from head office soon enough. At the end Strutt sent them off to pack their things and reconvene for goodbyes in the entrance hall.

Which is where I must be heading.

Evening; Avebury Trusloe

The weather must have affected the Rover as it refused to turn over. Fortunately, Strutt, and several of the Castaways, gave me a push to get her moving and I left in a cloud of spray. Only hope I didn't inadvertently soak anyone.

Miserable drive home and I dared not stop in case it wouldn't start again. Have to hope it works tomorrow, as I can hardly call on Mr Pumphrey for a push. He must be nearly eighty. If all else fails, there's always the 'bus, I suppose.

House feels damp. Lit the fire soon as I got in, but it hasn't made much difference. Wind is from the wrong quarter, and it isn't drawing properly. Gerald's old room was especially cold. Gave me goosebumps. At least there's no sign of anything untoward while I've been away. No mysteriously open doors or jackdaw feathers.

Nothing on the gogglebox this evening, so I'm listening to Latin Jazz on the gramophone to cheer myself up. Otherwise, the house is deadly quiet. Cats are ignoring me, as usual.

Fridge is low on almost everything. Milk's sour and there's no bread. Luckily, I had a few eggs, so scrambled them for supper. Not the same without toast, but it will have to do. Go shopping tomorrow so hope the weather is decent. Wind is howling in the chimney breast, and I think most of the smoke is blowing back into the room.

Provided I don't get asphyxiated, I will try to get in a couple of hours editing before bed.

13 April; Avebury Trusloe

A bright start to the day. How often after wind and rain, the next day begins bright and clear. It is as though a great broom has swept everything clean.

Though on closer inspection it seems to have swept rather a lot into the garden and I shall go out later and tidy up. Probably have to wait until after I have been shopping. Speaking of which, I ought to make a list. Nothing more enjoyable than making a list. It feels as though one is really getting things done.

Last night was my first decent night's sleep since that business at the spring. Comfort of one's own bed, no doubt; that, and knowing I don't have to face any tutorials today. Though I shall have to get on with MacGregor, if I am not to fall disastrously behind.

Speaking of writing, I must deliver tomorrow's Lent talk to Prue. She gets quite irritable if I don't give her opportunity to correct me. Tomorrow is the last one, I'm glad to say. Better print it off while I remember. There. One click and done.

Blast. Warning light on the printer means I need more ink. At least my talk printed okay.

Meanwhile, the telephone answering machine has been chirruping. Didn't bother with it last night; it's too depressing to arrive home late to a barrage of problems and demands. Always leave it to the next day when I am fresh. I ought to see who's called before I go shopping.

But before that, I probably— ah: interrupted by the doorbell. Expect Mrs Pumphrey is eager to tell me what bad boys my cats have been.

CARP
Lunchtime; Market Street Tearooms, Devizes

Crossstones have telephoned. I called them back and was informed that Mummy has a bad cold. Judith Malmsey also said they have found more feathers in her room. I suggested they check their eaves, or get in a pest control officer, but she was not amused. Otherwise, Mummy was in good spirits. I asked after Conchita, but her mother's illness is serious, and she is unlikely to return. A shame, as I believe she knew Mummy better than anyone else at Crossstones.

The next message was from Desmond.

"Nevil, old chap. Thought Pea had told you there's a job going. Decent rates and nothing too arduous. Give me call after eleven."

I telephoned him.

"Talk of the devil," he said amiably, "almost gave up on you and passed the commission to Dommy (that's Dominic Manners, a hot new talent, according to Dessie). You're just in time."

"I was away earning money," I said. "Uffington."

"You were what?"

"Not what. Where. Writer's retreat at Uffington."

"Oh, Creative wotsit."

"That's them, anyway, this job—"

"You know they've been taken over?" he said.

I wasn't sure who he meant.

"That lot, Creative whatever. Poseidon Travel has bought them out."

"I knew it was a possibility."

"Doesn't bode well. Though you know more about all that foreboding than I do."

"The commission," I said. "The one you telephoned about."

"It's for CARP."

"Fishing?!"

"Canal and Riverside Publications," he said. "They're doing a guide to the inns of our inland waterways. When I saw it, I immediately thought of you. Know you like a tipple. Only one drawback, you have to do it on a boat."

"Do what?"

"Visit the pubs of course. CARP want a boatman's view."

"But there must be thousands of them."

"You only have to do Wiltshire. I assume there are canals in Wiltshire. Do you know how fast those boats go?"

"Not very," I said. "Look, I'm not sure I'm the right man for this. Don't know a thing about canals, and my doctor has ordered me to cut down on the booze."

"And you're not ignoring him?"

"Her, actually, and no."

"Good lord. Well, I'll see if Dommy will take it."

"Is there anything else?" I asked hopefully. "I have four weeks before the next writing retreat."

"Nothing on the books. Tell you what; I did see something I thought was you. Teaching position. Not great pay, but bed and board included. Three days a week."

"Where is it?"

"I'm just finding it. They advertised in The Gazette's Education Supplement. Here it is: Belshade College, Oxford. You were at Oxford, so you must have heard of them."

"Belshade? Yes, I've heard of them. Place for oddballs. Did you say bed *and board*?"

"That's what it says. It's in today's edition. I can post it if you want."

"No trouble. Got to go shopping so I'll get a copy. The Gazette, you say. Bit leftist for you, isn't it?"

"But has the best literary section. Use the rest of it for firelighting."

"And it's Belshade College."

"They're looking for a Master specialising in Scottish poetry of the Middle Ages."

"Good lord. Well, that is me! But it's a bit obscure."

"Is it? Not my field, old boy. But good luck. Wouldn't want you starving."

Belshade College rings a bell but for the life of me I can't recall why. Anyway, I know have the advert in front of me, beside my toasted teacake. Three days a week, bed and board. Lecturing in Scottish poetry. Other subjects to be discussed at interview. Of course, were I accepted it might queer my pitch with Creative Havens—can't be in two places at once—but three days a week term time is a lot more regular than a week here and there and Oxford is easier to get to than, say, Pembrokeshire where I'm due next.

It would also be a rare opportunity to emulate my father, though Belshade can't hold a candle to Israel College.

The only other message was from Sid Morris, reminding me there's an away match on Wednesday at the New Inn in Winterbourne. Made a note in my diary.

Remembered to call at Prue's on the way into Devizes. Said I'd been away all week, and this was the earliest I could get to her.

"Not that I think I've said anything out of line. Anyway, last one."

"Oh. I had hoped for a proper read of it," she said. "One or two of the parishioners had mentioned that some of your talks have been rather more about Avebury, and less about The Passion."

"Well, I'm sure next year they will be happy to step forward with their ideas," I said. "Even Jesus couldn't please everyone."

"That's in very poor taste, Nevil."

"I just wish those who complain most would do more. It's only too easy to carp."

227

Mentioning carp reminds me of Dessie's canal pub gig.

Can't imagine there's too much involved in driving one of those things. See enough idiots doing it. And there are worse ways to spend a day. Job at Belshade, assuming I get it, won't start until the autumn term and that's four months away. Have a think on it.

Now, the serious business of finishing my pot of tea and teacake before I plough my way through the rest of the Literary Supplement.

Postscriptum: weight, fifteen stone, ten. Seems the stresses of Woolstone have taken another two pounds off me.

Later; Avebury Trusloe

Some people are never satisfied. Prue has telephoned insisting I change part of tomorrow's talk. Claims I have lapsed into idolatry, or worse. Utter nonsense, of course, but I will have to do as I'm told or never hear the end of it.

Had hoped for a few hours on MacGregor but will have to postpone that till later. Thing is, with the Parochial Committee poised between those who value St James for its antiquity, and those who would be happier praising the Lord in a shed, I can't afford to be too unpopular, or I'll be ousted at the next elections. That would allow Peter to put another of his apparatchiks into office and then all hell will break loose.

I have, though, found time to refresh my knowledge of Belshade College. Oliver Bearskin's *Guide to Collegiate Oxford* has much to say about it and, while it's not as disreputable as I thought, its origins are deeply peculiar. Will gather my thoughts on the prospect of employment later, though I must remember to update my CV. Can always turn Belshade down if the job doesn't appeal. Now, need to appease Prue before I do anything else.

On second thoughts, time for a cup of tea.

Bedtime; Avebury Trusloe

Windy again. Didn't get around to tidying the garden, but no matter as the weather is only going to untidy it some more. Wind is rattling the windows and the fire is sulking again. I'm sitting here with a blanket over my knees as I write. The cats were skulking by the back door earlier so at least I didn't have to round them up before sending them out. They were only too willing to be off. Complete mystery where they go to at night.

Reasonably happy with the changes I made to tomorrow's talk so Prue should be mollified.

Four more days of Lent and I can enjoy a proper pint again. Nights like this I really miss a snifter before bedtime.

What on earth made me go teetotal?

Going local

Palm Sunday, 14 April; Red Lion, Avebury

Thank God that's over with. Prue made a beeline for me during the church social. Said I had ignored her objections and brought idolatrous paganism into the church, and on Palm Sunday, to boot. Peter Chadwick overheard her and came to my defence, which made me feel even worse. To have Prue disagree with me is one thing, but to find common cause with our head druid is quite another.

Molly was visiting her mother in Swindon so she wasn't there to defend me, and I couldn't wait to get away. At least I shan't be asked to do anything like this next year and, considering the amount of time it's taken, they should consider themselves fortunate for what they got. Dessie would be most unhappy to learn I was giving away copywriting for free!

Emerged from St James's into a typical April shower. Didn't fancy a wet walk home, so turned for the pub. On passing the Henge Shop, I spotted one of the Tree sisters inside, but no customers, as far as I could tell. That reminds me: must ask Prue at the next PCC meeting if she's contacted the New Barn School. It wouldn't surprise me if she let it slip her mind. In fact, I'll remind her next time our paths cross.

Called in at the village store for a copy of the Sunday Mercury. Had already thought that if I was going to the pub I might as well enjoy lunch' there, rather than going hungry for an hour or two before I get home. Angela Spendlove, one of the volunteers, was behind the counter. She beamed as I entered.

"Just The Mercury," I said, having taken the paper from the stand.

"Are you quite sure?" she asked. "You have lost a bit of weight and I'm not the only one who's noticed. We had a delivery of flapjacks in, and I know you like them."

The shop's flapjacks are, it must be said, a favourite of mine, though my thoughts were divided while I wondered who else had noticed my recent weight loss.

"Have you?" I replied. "Oh, that is awfully tempting. But no. It is still Lent after all."

Lent was a feeble excuse, but I refuse to admit that I am watching my diet. That's the sort of thing silly young women and tedious sports people do.

"Only until Thursday, Nevil. Are you still coming a week on Friday?"

"Coming to what? I don't recall."

"ASP, Nevil. You promised you would join us."

"Ah, yes. I did. Week on Friday. Provided nothing comes up, I shall be there."

"Excellent. But are you certain I can't tempt you with flapjacks? The shop doesn't make a great deal selling newspapers."

Social obligations are one of the problems with living in a small village. Not only does everyone know you, along with most of your business, but it requires a commitment to localism that the average town-dweller cannot imagine. One ends up buying things from the shop which one doesn't need, or want, just to ensure the shop's survival and continuing ability to sell you things you don't need or want but buy out of some collective desire to see the village do well. Or perhaps one just buys them out of guilt. I imagine they keep a list of customers who have failed to give sufficient support to the volunteer-run shop, and I do not wish to be on it.

I am certain the flapjacks will immediately result in the re-addition of several pounds I have quietly lost.

Ah. My lunch' is arriving. Glass of house red is called for, but, alas, The Red Lion does not offer alcohol free wine... what am I saying? At any other time, I would mock the very idea of alcohol-free wine. It's as much a parody as the seedless grape. I shall enjoy a pint of alcohol-free Merit. As Angela said, Lent is almost run.

Later; Avebury Trusloe

Got home about half two. No rain, but a blustery wind blew away any warmth I had gathered at the pub. Someone had left a horse in the meadow beside the river. Beast trotted after me and I had to shoo it away before it got too close. Out again later: Procession from Windmill Hill this evening, followed by readings at St James's to mark Christ's entry into Jerusalem. Might drive into the village, though it always feels a bit feeble as it's only a mile or so. See what the weather's doing. Managed two hours on MacGregor. Am about halfway through the revisions, which still leaves me a week or two behind what I had hoped. Life keeps getting in the way of work.

At least I seem to have stopped thinking of Madeleine. *Tempus fugit, fluit aqua*, and all that.

Bedtime; Avebury Trusloe

Surprisingly joyous and moving evening. We convened just before seven on Windmill Hill, a mile to the north of the village. Once it had a small stone circle, but no trace remains. Nor is there anything left of the windmill, but it does give an excellent view over the valley and Avebury.

231

I was a little late, though there were one or two stragglers behind me on the track to the summit. Once arrived Molly gave me a cardboard palm leaf. The members of the PCC were all present, and about thirty others, including most of the Tree family. Only Elder, the youngest daughter, was missing. I glanced westward where the sun was still an hour from setting, and then eastwards to the Downs. It was all very lovely while we waited for the last few people to arrive, though I was glad to have dressed for warmth as the wind was brisk.

Peter Chadwick was waiting to welcome us at St James', so Pauline Lamb had charge and read from Matthew 21.

"And when they came near Jerusalem, unto Bethphage, by the Mount of Olives, Jesus called two disciples, saying unto them, go into this village and find ye an ass and bring the beast to me."

At *Jerusalem*, Pauline had waved towards St James', and at *Bethphage* her arm had swept around to mean the hill where we stood. I had glanced behind me at that point and, as I expected, approaching from the west was a young man leading a donkey, with Elder Tree riding.

Pauline continued.

"The disciples did as Jesus commanded and brought the ass and set Him thereon.

And the multitude spread their garments beneath the ass's feet and others cut branches from the trees and strewed them in the way."

There was much waving of cardboard leaves, but no strewing them just yet.

Our Jesus was already on her ass, so we only had to wait for her to arrive. The young chap with her is, I think, her boyfriend, though I can't recall his name. The ass was a donkey from the sanctuary at Cherhill but seemed plucky enough.

"And the multitudes that went before, and that which followed, cried out Hosanna to the son of David: Blessed is he that cometh in the name of the Lord; Hosanna in the highest."

We all joined in with the salutation, as donkey and rider joined us. Redwood Tree, the pater of the genus, looked insufferably proud, and I suppose Elder is the prettiest Jesus there ever was, even with the wind blowing her hair across her face. But it was all charming as we walked off the hill and towards Avebury. Even the donkey behaved itself, though a few of us were worried about the weather. which was increasingly blustery and the sky cloudy.

The last few yards of the procession took us up the High Street where our crowd of thirty-strong was swelled by those who hadn't the energy, or willpower, to get to Windmill Hill, and now the palm leaves were well and truly strewn and the donkey walked, unfalteringly, on a sea of cardboard fronds, up the road, through the lych gate, and into the churchyard.

Here Elder dismounted, and as her boyfriend led the animal aside and towards a horsebox parked outside The Red Lion, we entered Jerusalem, via the porch of St James'.

Sometimes the church is a rock, but tonight it seemed more like a ship, serene upon a troubled sea, and in the quiet interludes between word and prayer the wind swirled noisily around the tower and linden trees.

Molly had done an outstanding job with the flower arrangements and Peter singled her out for thanks. I've no idea where she could have found actual palm leaves.

It was ten when we left, with the moon shining half-full and high in the south. I was jolly glad to have taken the motor-car as it was no night to be walking. Boris and Tusker shot through the front door even as I entered. Made the best of the rest of the evening and settled down with a pot of tea and a flapjack to watch an old Frederick Banistaire and Margarethe von Brunnen musical. 'Gentleman Thieves' is a few decades older than I am, but delightful nonsense. Afterwards, I wrote up my journal and presently I shall head for bed. House is chilly this evening. Hope we're not in for a late frost.

15 April; Avebury Trusloe

The day began with breakfast and just as I had set myself up for a morning's activity, the postman came with doom and gloom in the form of a bank statement. It was not pleasant reading and payment for the Uffington Haven cannot come soon enough. I was considering telephoning Desmond and finding out when the next payment from Hare & Drum was due when the telephone interrupted me. To my surprise, it was Pea, and she was whispering.

"Nevil?"

"Yes."

"Can you talk?"

"Err, Pea. Is anything wrong?"

"No, no. I mean yes. A bit. Dommy's ill."

"Gosh. Is it serious?"

"No! Not for him anyway. Od'd on chill pills. Gone into hospital but he'll be fine. It's Dessie. Dommy was down to do that pub article. The one with the boat. Dessie's frantic. I suggested you might step in, but he said you turned it down. You didn't, did you?"

"Actually, I did. Don't know a thing about boats and my doctor would not approve of a pub crawl, however slowly I crawl."

"You're not going sober, are you?"

"Not forever, no. But it seemed wise—"

"Oh, that's awful." Pea sounded almost in tears. "I was sure you'd do it."

"Can't he turn them down? I mean CARP are doing the whole country. They must be dealing with loads of agents."

"That's just it, Dessie has signed the contract."

Pea paused a moment, then said.

"And it's a really good contract. They know how to pay."

My eye flirted with the bank statement on the breakfast table.

"How generous is this contract?"

234

"You mean you'll do it?"

"I'm only asking what the fee is."

"Twelve hundred plus expenses."

"Crowns? And what's Dessie taking?"

"Yes, Crowns. Gross is fifteen hundred. Dessie's taking twenty percent. I tell him he should take more."

"More? So, I, not that I am making any promises, would get twelve hundred."

"Twelve."

"And when do they need this by?"

"You'll do it?"

Pea's powers of recovery had kicked in. She sounded almost buoyant.

"I asked when they need it. I do have other commitments."

"Thing is," Pea prevaricated. "Dessie's already booked the boat-thingy."

"Narrow boat, I believe they are called."

"That's it. Waterfowl Cruisers in Bath. You need to be free from May twenty-seventh to first June. Can you? Pretty please. Love you forever, mwah, mwah."

"But that's six weeks away! How long is Dommy going to be ill?"

"It's not that simple. Dessie had to let him go."

"Ah. I thought Dommy was the new wonderchild."

"It's complicated. You know Cecily, Dessie's youngest daughter?"

"Slightly. Why?"

"She and Dommy were... you know. It all came out when he was rushed to hospital."

"I see. And Dessie doesn't approve."

"Can you blame him?"

"From what I've heard of Dommy, probably not. This canal gig, how long is it?"

"Only a week."

"I mean how many miles?"

"Oh. No idea. But you need to get to Reading."

"Bath to Reading. Tell Desmond I'm thinking about it. Meanwhile send me everything you have from CARP and the boat people."

"Thank you!" Pea trilled. "Oh, I knew you'd do it."

"I have <u>not</u> said I will do it. I'm only saying I will think about doing it."

"But you will do it for me? Only Dessie said he might have to let me go if things don't pick up."

"You? It would fall apart without you."

"That's sweet of you to say."

"I assure you, Pea, I'm not being sweet. The thought of Dessie trying to run the agency by himself is terrifying. Might as well say goodbye to any work from him. No, Pea, he will not let you go. Now, send me everything and I promise I *will* think about it. Can't be too hard driving one of those things."

"Oh, Nevil. I do love you. One more thing, are you free on Saturday lunchtime?"

"Probably. It is Easter so rather busy at church, but lunchtime shouldn't be a problem. Why?"

"Hare & Drum want a catch-up."

"What do they need to know?"

"They didn't say. Just that they'd like to meet you, same place as last time. I assumed you'd remember?"

"Of course, I do. Though I don't know what I can tell them."

"Good, I'll say you can do it. Got to go. Dessie's coming back."

"Back?"

"Shhh. Bye."

So, there we are. I have checked my diary and am free that week in May. I have also got the road atlas from the Rover and found what looks like a canal between Bath and Reading. Hardly any distance on the map, and I have a week to do it. Probably get a decent bit of editing done in the evenings. Only so much pubbing a chap can take and there's sod all else to do on a canal.

And I still have six weeks to wriggle out of it, if it's not to my liking, and meanwhile Pea is in my debt.

Plus, the twelve hundred will come in very handy.

Meanwhile, I need to think of something to tell Hare & Drum. Assume it will be the same man of mystery as last time.

Later; Avebury Trusloe

Telephoned Belshade College after lunch' and spoke to the secretary, a Mrs Purge. She didn't recognise the Warbrook name, so I casually mentioned that my father had been a don at Israel College. That did the trick and suddenly she couldn't do enough for me. Accommodation is an attic room, but it's spacious and all mod-cons. Three days a week, full board. Initially lecturing on Scottish medieval literature, but they have hopes of extending the curriculum. Of course, I must satisfy the college of my credentials, to whit there is an application form and interview to be considered. No doubt, I shall find something ghastly in the paperwork, but I can't think there are many more knowledgeable on Scottish medieval literature. Mrs Purge promised to put the details in the evening post, so I should have it tomorrow.

Afternoon spent editing. Decided against asking Dessie when the next payment from Hare & Drum is due. If I'm seeing them on Saturday, I can always raise it then, or perhaps better not to mention it at all, as I still have some catching up to do. Plus, I don't want to betray Pea, as her call earlier was surely made without Dessie's knowledge.

BELSHADE

16 April; Avebury Trusloe

Began the day by recalling everything I knew, or could immediately discover, about Belshade College. In part this is preparation for my application, but it may also serve as a warning. The postman interrupted my deliberations with delivery of the college prospectus and the form for my application, with a note from Mrs Purge thanking me for my interest.

Belshade is one of Oxford's less established colleges, dating only to the 1850s when it was founded by the Glass manufacturer Epsilon Belshade and his brother-in-law Lodovico Settembrini, a one-time prelate in the Roman Catholic Church who rose to become Prefect of the Vatican Apostolic Library before a spectacular fall from grace involving the copying of condemned texts and allegations of sexual vices. Neither of these appear to have concerned Epsilon Belshade, who appointed Settembrini as Belshade's first Principal. Epsilon, or rather his manufactory, is, of course, famous for the development of spectral glass through which one can observe the behaviour of magnetic and other energy fields, including the human aura.

The prospectus is unusual; though, given my speciality in medieval Scottish literature, I am in no position to object! If accepted, I shall be dividing my time between the Faculty of Language and Histrionics and the Faculty of Irrational Inquiry, with a title of Magister non-Tenure. I approve that they have retained the proper Latin. Courses are, provisionally, Rough Magic: Scottish poetry of the Middle Ages—Oh Heaven! —and The Golden Bough: The Wildwood in Jungian psychology— Oh Hell! Other courses, the prospectus informed, were in development. Just as well, as I would struggle to sustain an academic year on woods and poetry alone.

The one sour note is that, unlike every other Oxford College, Belshade does not permit alcohol on the premises. Ah well. Dr Saunders will approve.

Of course, should I get the position, it will present a problem with the cats. Not sure I can rely on Mrs Pumphrey every week, and I doubt Belshade will be amenable to cats. Cross that bridge when I come to it.

I'm also puzzled by recollection of an association between Belshade and Sir Tamburlaine. Can't think what it could be, or where I might have read it. Must look it up.

Nothing in the post regarding the canal gig. Probably Pea forgot to post it. If it's not here tomorrow, I'll telephone her.

Spent the rest of the morning editing, then walked into the village for milk, bread, and today's *Marlborough Times*. Pleasant weather. Mild and with only a trace of spring dampness. I was in good humour, until a ghastly shock outside the Henge Shop.

The Henge Shop sells nothing needful for the Avebury locals, if one discounts rock crystals, ley line finders, facsimiles of ancient books of magick, and candy rock with the name of Avebury down its centre, as needful things. But we all must make a living, and I cannot complain too much, as I am certain many readers of *This Iron Race* are exactly those who would find such things essential!

Nevertheless, I was taken aback by the effigy painted on the side of a delivery van parked outside. No doubt many of Heart of Albion's books are 'terrifyingly good' but the ghastly image was unsettling in the extreme.

It was, I suppose, a type of faun, but shaggy-haired, or prickled like a hedgehog, and antlered. The eyes were bright red and the rest entirely black and white.

Whatever it was, was not the classic image of the Devil Himself, for He, it is well known, has cloven hooves and this creature had toes. Perhaps it has no clear identity and is only the work of the artist's imagination: indeed, MacGregor writes that the uncanny never appears as it truly is, but manifests as what we suppose it to be. I only hope if it ever shows itself to me, it will take on a more pleasant form.

Along with milk, and bread, and the *Times*, I got a ham and cheese pie, a tin of peas, and treated myself to another four of their Wiltshire-made flapjacks. The pie and tinned peas will provide my lunch' and means I don't have to cook later. Church this evening.

Only hope that blasted van has moved on by then. Not the sort of thing one wants to see in the dark.

I dropped into the pub to see if Sid or Bert were about. Dominoes at The Winterbourne in Winterbourne Bassett tomorrow evening, and one or other of them will want a lift. No sign of them so left a note at the bar. They can always telephone if they are desperate.

Ought to get home as I'm helping Fred Thirsk and Terry Woodson up at West Kennett long barrow with the bonfire for Dawn Service on Easter Day. Then it's straight Evening Prayer after that. Can say goodbye to getting any work done today.

Bedtime; Avebury Trusloe

Dreadful night. Heavy rain and wind. Hopefully, we did a decent job making the bonfire, and we won't wake to find it blown all over the Downs. Terry had borrowed a trailer and we drove up the track to the barrow with the firewood and straw bales. Terry mentioned the weather was forecast to be bad, so we stowed most of it in the entrance to the tomb. After we finished, there was just time to get home for a wash and brush up and bite to eat before it was out to Evening Prayer.

Afterwards, I escorted Molly from the church to her door. Poor thing has come down with 'flu and I said she should have stayed home all wrapped up.

"But it's Easter," she said. "It's once a year. And if He can suffer then so can I."

"Noble, very noble," I said. "But you might have half the village down with the ague."

"Will you come in, just for tea?"

"Sorry, I must be getting home. And I don't think the weather is going to improve. If anything, it might get worse."

Our exchange took place in the Linden Tree's porch, and though the roof kept the rain off, it was scarcely sheltered. Molly opened the front door, and I had a sense of warmth and comfort within and even the lingering scent of muffins. Domesticity tugged at my senses, but the reality was I could hardly spend the night there, so must, at some point, face the weather. It was better to do so now, before I caved.

"Another time is surely more suited to us both," I said. "Goodnight, and sweet dreams."

"Nevil, you are such a goose at times. But you are a gentleman."

"One tries to keep up standards," I said. "Cocoa and bed for you. Take heed. Now, I must make for my own door."

"Take care, dear."

I don't think Molly has ever called me 'dear.' I wonder if the influenza was affecting her. The wind was certainly enough to make one light-headed. Utterly chilled when I got back to the motor car, and I sat a few minutes with the engine running and the heater on full, just to warm up. Then drove home cautiously, watching for fallen branches. It was well after nine when I arrived home and the cats were waiting for me at the door. They shot into the night leaving me to get myself a pot of tea. Decided to light the fire, though the wind is playing hell with it. Air in the sitting room is getting rather smoky.

Must have a chat with Peter Chadwick some time. Recalled this evening that he and his good wife have holidayed on the canals. Can't imagine there's anything too taxing about steering a narrow boat, but it wouldn't hurt to ask.

BOATS
17 April; Avebury Trusloe

Details of the canal job arrived in the post with a brochure from Waterfowl Cruisers. Who knew canal boats were so well appointed? There I was, expecting a hammock and a paraffin stove, and instead there's a bedroom fit for a sheikh and a galley better equipped than my kitchen.

Of course, one will have to get used to a certain restriction, owing to the narrowness, but that isn't a hardship. Almost telephoned Pea straight away to accept but best to have a chat with Peter Chadwick just in case there's anything to worry about. No church this evening, so I might call on them at lunchtime. I suspect Pea, and of course Dessie, want confirmation sooner rather than later, so mustn't delay.

The envelope from Pea also included a copy of CARP magazine, presumably so I can familiarise myself with their readership and house style. Given the number of advertisements for boat fittings, wood-burning stoves, varnishes, and boat paint they have an odd sort of readership. More interested in maintenance than the alleged pleasures of actually going anywhere. Still, I think I can see the kind of reader they appeal to. These are people who wear woollen jumpers in the evening and amuse themselves by painting floral designs on buckets. The men all have beards and smoke pipes, and the women are all fat and jolly. No point writing of the baroque pleasures of The Gingerbread House or devilled kidneys with bitter chocolate mousse and tempura seaweed—not that The Gingerbread House is anywhere near the canal, thank heavens—for these are people who prefer the plain and simple life.

Well, I rather approve of that.

Now, put this aside and get on with editing. Halfway through *Book Two,* and almost back on schedule.

Later; Red Lion, Avebury

Short of predicting my death by drowning, Peter Chadwick could not have been less encouraging. He claims that attempting the canal alone is utter folly as one man cannot hope to both man the boat and work the locks at the same time. I admit he may have a point, and I must investigate further. As for his prediction that I would give up within two days, and be lucky not to fall in, I can only say it stiffened my resolve. If I took the week at Malvern in my stride, then I can jolly well cope with a week on the canals.

Having prophesied my failure, he did have one useful suggestion. Apparently, the biggest challenge on the canal is a flight of locks just outside Devizes and warned that if sight of it didn't put me off, then more fool me.

I'm shopping in Devizes tomorrow, so I may jolly well do as he suggests. I can call at the library as well and see if they have anything on boating. Best to know what I'm letting myself in for.

It would be so much easier to do with a partner, or a shipmate. Even if they are only there to hold the steering thingy when one needs the lavatory or wants a cup of tea. Alas, no one springs to mind. No, that is not entirely true: none suitable, who would be willing, is a more honest view. I do miss the camaraderie of Malvern. It seemed anything was surmountable, no matter what the elements, or Kedden, or Clive, or whoever, threw at us, we, together, would overcome it.

Blast. Now I'm thinking of Madeleine again. I rather hoped I was over her. She would be ideal company on this voyage. Except, now I recall, for her fear of water. What was it? Yes, her baby brother drowned in a pond. Canals wouldn't be her thing at all.

But twelve hundred Crowns. Think of that and be brave.

In other news, Sid Morris left a message at the bar requesting a lift to Winterbourne this evening. I am to collect him from Beckhampton. Bert may well be with him. If I leave for home now, I'll fit in two hours of work before teatime. Drink up.

A QUEER NIGHT
Bedtime; Avebury Trusloe

Extraordinary end to the day. I'm sitting up in bed, feet frozen, hands shaking and mind leaping like a damselfly from one thought to the next. Heaven knows what state poor Sid and Bert are in. Neither are at an age when running around comes easily, and Bert, especially, seemed spooked by the whole thing.

We had been soundly thrashed by the Winterbourne team and, after nursing our wounded pride over several pints of Slaters, Baxter's Ale, and, for me, two pints of Merit, we departed via the gents which was out the back in a corrugated tin shed. It was raining.

"What a bloody night," Bert shouted over the noise on the tin roof.

"We did not do ourselves proud," I replied.

"Sod the dominoes. I mean listen to it," Bert said.

The rain drummed and the wind swirled through the

243

entrance and around our ankles. What had been a decent enough day, weather-wise, had turned ugly soon after sunset.

"That wind is cold on my arse," Sid said. "But it's an ill wind blows no one some good and there'll be a few callers tomorrow wanting roof repairs and such. There's always money in misery."

"A cheerful soul," I said.

"A realist," said Sid.

"Buggeration," said Bert as the light failed, plunging us into darkness.

"Reckon I'm nearest," Sid said.

"Nearest to what?" I asked.

"Light switch. Here it is. Ah. Fused maybe. Hang on. Pub's dark an' all."

"Line must be down," I said. "Let's hope it's just here, and not back home. Hang on. I have a torch. There."

"Watch where you're pointing that thing," Bert objected.

"Sorry, didn't realise you hadn't finished."

"At my age the bladder is not to be hurried."

Ablutions completed; we stepped out into the rain. It was quieter away from the tin roof, but the wind took one's breath away and made communication difficult.

"You wait here, and I'll bring the motorcar round," I said.

"'Ere why don't Bert and I wait here while you fetch the car?" Sid said.

"That's what I... never mind."

I stumbled around in the car park for a few moments, finding at least one puddle, until the Rover materialised out of the gloom, and I got the door open. The ignition groaned and, at the second attempt, the engine fired into life. I put the cabin light on for Sid and Bert's benefit and met them as close to the gents as I could. They dashed in, Sid in the front with me and Bert in the back.

"Good of you to drive us tonight, but I think soonest over soonest best," Bert said.

"Couldn't agree more," Sid said.

"All in?"

"Drive on, I reckon," Sid said.

The motorcar lurched over the potholed car park behind the pub, until we joined the lane through Winterbourne Bassett. The wipers could barely cope, and the windows had misted up as soon as we got in. I turned left for the main road and after what I thought was an appropriate distance turned right onto what I thought was the Avebury road.

"'Ere that 'ent right," Sid said moments later when the road bore further right.

"It's a bit narrow," Bert said. "Is that the church?"

The headlights had caught a large stone building. I couldn't tell if it was the church, but certainly it should not have been there.

"I know what I've done. Haven't been here for a while and lost my bearings."

"You drove here not three hours ago," Sid said.

"That's as may be. Once we're on the main road we'll be fine. Just need to retrace our steps. Bert, don't suppose you can see out the back? Need to turn round."

Bert could not and, after a bit of toing and froing, Sid lost patience and stepped outside to guide me backwards until I had the motorcar turned round. He got back in, considerably wetter, and we set off again. This time, I made no mistake and got us to the junction with the main road and turned south. There was not a house light or streetlight to be seen and the headlights reflected off the wet road in a dazzling glare.

"I'll have to slow down," I said. "I can't see a thing. Sid, can you watch the verge and let me know if I'm wandering across the road."

"Doing fine," he answered. "Haven't seen a night like this in a while."

"What was that?" Bert said.

"Where?" I asked.

"Summat white, by look of it. Caught a glimpse out the side window. Gone now."

"Watch the turn," Sid warned.

"Must be nearly in Berwick Bassett," I said.

"You wouldn't know it," Sid said.

"Rotten luck this power cut. Yes, there we are, that's the turn for the village."

"Black as the devil's coal cellar," Sid muttered.

The road turned again for the south. The wind howling across the Downs pushed against the motorcar, trying to force us into the verge. It even penetrated around the edge of the window and chilled my ear.

"There it is again," Bert said. "Look out!"

"Bloody hell, what's that!" Sid shouted.

I braked, putting the motorcar into a slide, as something large and dazzling in the headlights ran across the road.

"Cow," Sid said. "Must have escaped."

"Too big for a cow," Bert said. "And the way it moved. Reckon it's a horse."

"Where'd it go?" I asked.

"Up the road," Bert said.

"Bloody hell," Sid said.

"I'll take it slowly." I drove on at fifteen, or so, and presently something large and white glimmered in the night. As Bert said, it was a horse, and it was in the middle of the road.

"That'll be the death of someone," Bert said.

"What we supposed to do?" Sid asked.

"Catch bugger and get it in field," Bert answered.

"Easier said than done, even in broad daylight," I said.

"Well get nearer to it, but slow."

I drove on, no more than five miles an hour. The horse shifted on a dozen yards at a time, but we were slowly getting closer.

"It's a big bugger," Sid said.

"That Glendale has stables round here," Bert said. "Looks like the sort of beast he'd have."

"*Rupert* Glendale, you mean," I said.

"Now, now. Not the horse's fault that bugger ran off with your missus," Sid said.

"Even so," I muttered darkly.

"One of us should get out," Bert said.

"I don't think it should be me," I argued. "I have to drive."

"Wait by then."

Bert got out and tramped into the night, his coat catching in the headlights.

"Daft bugger. Better give him a hand," Sid said. "If it bolts, drive up behind, but for fuck's sake don't run us over."

Sid followed Bert. The horse moved away down the road. I drove on, trying to keep Sid in my headlights, and trusting Bert was ahead of him. It was a devil seeing anything and I couldn't hear over the engine noise. Then, the horse turned and came towards us at speed. It was dazzlingly bright, Bert jumped aside as it passed him, and then Sid too. I swung the Rover across the road, hoping to head the creature off, but I was already thinking something was wrong. The horse was too bright. Nothing should seem that bright, just by reflection alone. Too late I put the Rover in reverse, and tried to back away, but the creature was upon me, and I had the strange sight of it leaping overhead. I glanced in the mirror, and it was as dazzling behind as it was in the headlights, even though the Rover's taillights are red and little better than candles.

My hands were shaking. Tales of the ghost coach at The Red Lion suddenly seemed less than fanciful. I got the Rover straight again, then picked up Sid and Bert. Both were shaken.

"Queerest damn thing," Sid said.

"Get us home, Nevil," Bert replied.

I drove on as fast as I dared.

"It leapt clear over me," I said.

"We saw. That weren't no ordinary horse."

"The ghost of a horse, mebbe," Sid said.

"'Ere is that a light?"

It was. Someone, somewhere, had thrown a switch or rerouted the power, and the village of Winterbourne Monckton had lit up like a cluster of stars at the roadside.

Ten minutes later I had dropped Bert by The Red Lion

and then put Sid outside his door in Beckhampton.

"Queer night all round," he said. "G'night."

Bright Thursday; Avebury Trusloe

Woken with a fearsome headache, as though someone were drumming on my skull. Only hope I have not come down with a chill after last night's misadventures. Ought to find out how Sid and Bert are. I could telephone them, but they might think I am worrying unnecessarily. I expect to see them both at the vigil tonight, so can ask then.

Over breakfast—two pots of tea and an extra slice of toast with jam—I reread my journal entry from last night. Cannot believe I wrote so much, as I was exhausted, and my nerves shredded. It is all true, or as well as I can remember, but can't help thinking I would have been better off with a cup of cocoa and making immediately for bed. Must have wanted to get it down while the memory was fresh, but haste doesn't militate in favour of my recollection being true. Sid and Bert should be able to confirm.

One snippet that must have slipped my mind while writing last night is that Bert Tanner had an uncle who was a bargee. Of course, that was in the days when the canals still had industrial purpose, but Bert did say that his uncle was plagued by rheumatism in old age on account of the canal damp. Hardly suppose I am at risk from only a week aboard. He did mention the camaraderie among boating folk and said I shouldn't be put off by Chadwick's dire warnings, as one could usually find someone to lend a hand.

In any event, I must let Dessie and Pea know, one way or another, by this evening. That gives me a chance to look at the locks at Devizes. Funnily enough, Bert said something about them as well; he claimed they were a wonder of the waterways and took half a day to navigate from top to bottom. I cannot believe that.

But first I must make a shopping list. Saturday marks the end of Lent so I can indulge a little.

Later; Market Street Tearooms, Devizes

Something has trampled through my front garden. I did not notice it from the window earlier, but when I stepped outside, the vandalism was obvious. Hard to say what has done the damage, as I could not make out any footprints. Deer are the most likely culprits, though their hooves are narrow and tend to make an obvious impression. These were larger, but the outline was unclear. Several bedding plants are very sorry-looking, and the lawn is badly dented. Hard to say what else is damaged, as I am not a gardener. Nothing I can do about it for the next few days, as the ground is sodden after last night's rain.

It put me in a bad mood for my drive to Devizes, so it wasn't the best day to get my first proper sight of the canal.

It seemed best to look at the locks first, as I knew I wanted to lunch' at Market Street after shopping. Shopping first, then driving out to Caen Hill, and back here for lunch', would mean parking twice, requiring either two parking tickets, or a stroke of luck finding a space on the streets.

I left the Rover in the car park at the Black Horse pub— they weren't open at that hour, so I doubted they'd complain—and crossed the road. The road soon took me over the canal, and from the bridge I could look down the length of it. At first sight, it seemed unimpressive, but following Chadwick's advice I took a footpath down to the towpath. This led past one set of lock gates, and then another, each separated by a larger basin where boats might pass.

The third basin was occupied by a boat which had tied up, and across the canal was a small café reached by a foot-bridge. I was considering whether to make a change from my usual appointment at the Market Street Tearooms, when my eye returned to the canal and, having now reached the brow of the hill, I saw why Peter had wanted me to come here.

I do not know how many locks there are in total, but I could see at least a dozen, one after the other. Halfway up a boat was leaving a lock and it looked tiny amidst so much water. This, it was clear, would be a challenge. I glanced back at the moored boat, hoping for a friendly face and advice, but it was deserted, so I decided to enquire at the café.

No one was on the wooden patio, but inside there was a family of four around a table, an elderly couple with a pot of tea, and one man with a dog near the door. I decided against interrupting anyone eating and approached the chap at the counter.

"Excuse me."

"Morning. What can I get you?"

"I'd like to know more about the locks."

"Such as?"

"Well. Are there any attendants? Canal workers who can help?"

"With a boat you mean?"

"I shall be travelling this way in month's time. Commissioned to write a piece for Canal and Riverside Publications. Heard of it?"

The chap indicated a rack of newspapers and magazines. CARP was on display.

"Excellent. Only I'll be navigating on my own, so naturally I'm keen on all the advice I can get."

"No attendants here. Get them on the Thames, but not here. Excuse me, sir. Customers must take priority."

Two young men in cyclists clothing had come in. Both were whippet thin and wearing skintight squeaky clothing.

"Of course. Understand." It was annoying but as I was not ordering I could hardly argue. I turned to leave.

"Excuse me," said the wife of the family foursome. "I overheard. The easiest thing is to wait for another boat and go up together. The locks are wide enough, and it saves a lot of work."

"Especially if you're boating alone," her husband said. "We've come from Banbury, on the Oxford Canal. We'll be tackling the locks here this afternoon."

"Ah, so you don't yet know how long it takes to get to the bottom?" I said. "Or from bottom to top."

"It's around five hours, four if you're lucky," he said. "We're boating all the time. This is our third time on the K and A."

I deduced this was the boaters' shorthand for Kennet and Avon. Clearly, they were both mad, but I kept my thoughts to myself. Annoyingly, it had confirmed what Chadwick had said: five hours to cover barely a mile seemed a Herculean labour.

"But find someone going the same way, and it's much easier," the wife said. "And fun too."

I took 'fun' advisedly.

"I'm completely new to all this," I said. "I'm a writer. Commissioned to do a piece for a magazine on canalside pubs. Want me to do it by boat."

"You'll get paid to go boating?" the woman said.

"That's the idea," I confirmed. "It's for Canal and Riverside Publications."

"My sister's a travel writer," she said. "For Passepartout, the travel company?"

I had heard of them.

"She's in the Seychelles reviewing luxury hotels and beach resorts. Three passports in five years. She keeps filling them up with visas."

I wasn't entirely certain where the Seychelles were, but luxury beach resorts sounded more fun than canals. Meanwhile, neither child had said anything. They were about the same age, both boys, and might even be twins. One was engrossed in an electronic toy and ignoring everyone. The other stared over a slice of uneaten toast at the debris of breakfast plates. His eyes were balled nearly as tightly as his fists.

"We're going soon," the mother said quietly to the unhappy child.

"Do we have to?" said the other.

There was an unspoken antipathy between the children whose nature, being a single child, I could only guess at.

"We do," the father said.

I had, meanwhile, asked how well their boat was appointed, and, between reprimands to the children, learned it was just like home, except for the lavatory, which was chemical, rather than a water closet.

"It stinks," interjected the happy child.

"You get a different view each morning," the mother added.

"It's the same view," the sullen child said. "It's always boring. Boring!"

"Sorry," the mother said. "Someone dropped their Game-Pod in the canal this morning."

This is what the happy child was playing with, and I understood the source of antipathy.

"You could share," father said to the cheerful child.

"Shan't."

"It's boring!" the other child exploded. "I want to go home!"

Before either parent could move, the boy slipped from the chair, and ran out the open door. The mother chased after him.

"Mind the water, Litton! Don't go near the water!"

I rather thought going near the water was unavoidable in a canal holiday.

"Sorry. Better go." The husband stood up. It was the end of the conversation.

"Thank you for your time. I am much informed," I said.

The cyclists had settled at a table in a chorus of fidgety squeaking from the skintight clothing. I followed the husband out. Mother was standing beside the unhappy child, who was lying in a puddle and thrashing his arms and legs.

"I suppose the boats do have showers," I said to her husband's back.

He turned and said they did.

"That's fortunate."

Five hours to travel one mile beggars belief. But if that is the worst the canal has to throw at me, then the rest cannot be so bad. I also have a handful of books from the library, one of which has maps conveniently marking all the pubs, so I can brush up later. For the moment I am content to sit here with my tea and bacon sandwich, having decided that I will telephone Dessie as soon as I am home and accept the commission.

Whatever the perils of Caen Hill, twelve hundred crowns cannot be ignored, but I shall have to have a word with Dessie. Why am I not reviewing beach resorts in the Seychelles?

CONTRADICTIONS

1.30am; Avebury Trusloe

Not long been home. Completely exhausted but need to write this down before bed. Sid and Bert utterly contradict my recollection of Wednesday night. There was no horse. Instead, they say I simply fell asleep at the wheel and was nearly the death of them. Luckily, the Rover only mounted the verge, and they were able to wrest the wheel off me and bring us to a halt.

"We were a bit worried when you got us lost, even before we'd left Winterbourne," Bert said.

"Must've been some kind of brainstorm," Sid said. "You imagined this horse, I reckon."

There were around fifteen of us keeping the Midnight Watch at St James and we were taking it in turns to kneel and pray at the altar. Most of us were elderly and age takes its toll on the knees. It was after nine and Sid, Bert, and I were taking tea in the vestry. My remark on Wednesday evening's events had turned into an awkward conversation.

"We didn't know what to say," Bert said. "I mean, you could lose your license for something like that."

"It's never happened before," I said. "And I can't even say for sure it happened then. My memory of events is quite different."

"It's a worry, see," Sid said. "I mean, you could have swerved across the road and hit something."

"What we'd like," Bert nodded at Sid for confirmation,

"is for you to get yourself checked out. We know you had that funny turn down in Somerset."

"It was not a 'funny turn'," I protested. "I was in hospital for a few hours, that's all."

"Even so, Bert and I are happy to keep this between us, but we think you ought to get yourself checked out."

Bloody infuriating. I am quite certain I saw a horse. My journal entry for Wednesday night is clear and cogent. I can only assume Sid and Bert were so disturbed by the event they have invented this false account.

It all put me in a bad mood for the rest of the watch, which is a shame as I usually enjoy the peacefulness of the church at that hour.

Earlier, it had all been quite jolly. Holy Communion was at seven-thirty and Lucy Chadwick presented everyone with a raffle ticket at the door. Molly was tweaking her flower displays, and trestle tables had been set up in the north aisle for supper. There were about fifty of us when I arrived, and at least a dozen entered after me.

We began with Peter reading from Corinthians. "For I received from the Lord that which I deliver unto you; that the Lord Jesus on the night of his betrayal broke bread, saying, Take, eat: this is my body, which I break for you: do this always in remembrance of me." Then Fred Thirsk read from John 13. This was followed by Apple and May Tree singing Psalm 116, which they did beautifully and with only the slightest of hesitation.

I took out my raffle ticket, more as part of a collective ritual than in expectation or hope. I didn't especially want my feet washing, but I rather enjoy seeing the parishioners put the clergy in their place. Prudence read the numbers, and fortunately mine was not called. We sat as Peter washed the feet of a dozen parishioners, while Prudence read from John 13.

After the ritual, the tureen was brought from the kitchen, and we sat for supper. It was only leek and potato soup, but the simplicity made it even more pleasurable. Elder Tree, our Jesus from last Sunday, read Grace.

Most of us then departed home, while the core of dedicated watchmen, and watchwomen, settled in for the long evening.

Oh dear. I don't think I can finish this. I am yawning my head off. Must go to sleep.

Long Friday; Avebury Trusloe

Overslept badly and missed Matins. Pounding headache again. Have not drunk a drop for over a month yet have all the symptoms of a hangover. Scrambled eggs and bacon have put a little life in me, but I am out of sorts.

One thing I am clear on: I cannot possibly go to Dr Saunders and say that some friends are convinced I fell asleep at the wheel. The possible repercussions are too grave. I must find my own remedy, assuming that Sid and Bert are correct, and my own memory of Wednesday evening is lax.

I'm tempted to telephone Sister Ethelnyd, she being the highest authority I know on such things, but will see out Easter first. Doesn't feel right to consult a soothsayer during Holy Week.

That reminds me to telephone Dessie again. Only got through to an answering machine yesterday afternoon, and I never know if the blasted things have worked. Meanwhile, a second pot of tea will go some way to making me feel human. Then I ought to sit down and work, as I have fallen behind again these last few days. Out again later for Evening Service and won't be home before nine. Simply must get to bed early tonight. Tomorrow is the all-night vigil, followed by breakfast *al fresco* at dawn, and it will demand all my powers of endurance.

At least tomorrow is the last day of Lent.

Later; Avebury Trusloe

Managed a couple of hours editing before the headache defeated me and I retired to the sofa for an hour. It was then time for lunch', but I telephoned Dessie first, with what I hoped was good news. He was out.

"But I can give him a message, if it's a nice one," Pea said.

"I have reconsidered that commission you mentioned. CARP."

"What?"

"CARP! The canal pub people. You were desperate for me to take it."

"You will! Oh, I'd almost given up for thinking you wouldn't."

"I thought it was life or death that I did."

I was a little aggrieved that Pea seemed to have forgotten quite how desperate she was that I took the commission.

"Anyway," I continued. "I think I can cope with the worst the canal can throw at me."

"Oh, thank you. I'll pass it on to Dessie."

"And where is my agent?"

"In hospital."

"What?"

"He's visiting Dommy. I think they may be making up."

"Oh dear. I mean, oh good."

"Cecily has been distraught ever since. She swears she can reform Dommy."

"Hope over experience. And Dessie's going along with it?"

"Well. Dommy is a brilliant writer."

I must admit he has a certain flair, but typical of Dessie to have one eye on business. Even if, according to Pea's dire prognosis, all is not well.

"Tell Dessie to pass on anything I need to know, such as where I might find the boat. And no surprises."

"I'll tell him. Thank you. Mwah!"

I assume her last remark was a kiss. Now, something to eat.

Late afternoon; Avebury Trusloe

After lunch', I decided a bit of fresh air might shake off my headache and recalled the garden was still a mess. Surprised Mrs Pumphrey hasn't drawn it to my attention, as her houseproud tendencies often stray across our borders.

Wrapped up warm against the wind and set to with rake and trimmers. The bedding plants have survived better than I feared, and most are bouncing back already, but at least one shrub was severely damaged. Had to cut back all the broken stems, which was a pity as the buds were showing. No idea what it is but has pretty yellow flowers at the end of summer. Not much I can do about the lawn. The Englishman's affection for his personal green sward is a complete mystery to me. I'll have a word with Sid and see if he might have an hour or two free. He might even have the remedy in his shed of mysteries in the churchyard. Certainly, has the grass there under control.

I was bent over the shrub when Bill Pumphrey interrupted me.

"Spot of bother, I see," he said.

He had a bowl of bread crusts which he was scattering across his lawn.

"Something has been through here and left a mess," I said. "Suspect it was deer, though I haven't seen any hoof prints."

"It was the faeries," he said. "Don't see 'em so much nowadays, but that was them all right."

I began to laugh, believing he was humouring me, but his face was earnest.

"It's the old stone avenue," he said. "Reckon it passes under your house, and that's where they ride."

"Ha, ha. Yes. Very good. But I would have thought the wee folk would be kinder to the flora, wouldn't you? They've made a mess of this shrub."

"That's St John's Wort, that is. Faerie folk don't like it. Whoever planted that there must have wanted to stop the faeries riding."

"Then it didn't work."

"They've ridden here for years, and they won't be stopped."

"Bill, is that you?" Mrs Pumphrey called from their house.

"Coming dear. Just talking to Nevil. Reckon faeries have been riding."

"You let that poor man be. These potatoes want seeing to."

"Duty calls," Bill said. "If I were you, I'd dig that out and be done with it. Faeries don't take kindly to big folk getting in their way."

Bill went inside to peel Mrs Pumphrey's potatoes. I finished tidying up the St John's Wort but decided to leave it standing. Anything with a good Christian name is a friend of mine.

The telephone rang just as I got in from the garden. It was Pea again.

"Sorry, Nevvie, just had a call from Hare & Drum. They've cancelled tomorrow's meeting. Hope it's not too late to change your plans."

"I had no plans," I said. "Did they say why?"

"Something about trouble on the roads. They hope to reschedule."

"Never mind. It's not like I had much to say to them. Any news from Desmond?"

"Dommy's been discharged, but the police are sniffing around, so who knows?"

"To be expected, I suppose. Thank you, Pea. And please would you not call me Nevvie, I know you think it's endearing, but it isn't."

She giggled and hung up.

Must get something for tea, and then it's church at seven for Evening Service.

Bedtime; Avebury Trusloe

Suitably mournful service this evening. Someone, probably Terry Woodson or Sid, had dressed the altar with candles and set them in the wall niches. With the overhead lights off, the church had the feel of an old oil painting, and the heating was turned down to the minimum. I didn't take off my coat the whole time.

Afraid I let the side down and dozed off during Peter's reading, which, I think, was from Isaiah. Fortunately, Bert noticed and gave me a nudge just as everyone stood to sing Psalm 31. "Lord be my rock of safety," was especially appropriate, as lately I have felt all at sea.

Still, I suppose a rock isn't altogether welcome for those at sea.

Molly accompanied us on the piano. Glad to hear she's feeling a bit better. Apparently, the survey team who cancelled their booking after the snow have booked themselves into the Linden Tree for the week. Can't imagine there's anything left to discover after so much digging.

Naturally, after what Sid and Bert had said the previous evening, I was a little concerned about driving home in the dark, so I put the radio on. Something soothing by one of the French romantic composers wafted from the speaker, but I knew it had no chance of keeping me alert, so I changed channel and found the National Programme, hoping it might have the news or current affairs. To my surprise a familiar voice boomed out, but it took me a few moments to recognise Philip Strutt reading from his latest cure for insomnia, *Paris, Trains.*

Of course, it was utter tedium, but I turned the sound up and drove home accompanied by his mellifluous baritone.

Bed soon, as tomorrow will be a long day.

BEER!

Holy Saturday; Red Lion, Avebury

I am enjoying my first proper pint in six weeks and have steak and kidney pie and chips on order. God may be absent from the world this day, but I am less inclined to dwell on spiritual despair, when there's Cropwell's Bitter and puff pastry to enjoy.

I woke early this morning, but rather than allow me to

roll over and go back to sleep, the chattering birds, including what sounded like a battalion of jackdaws, drove me into the bathroom and then to the kitchen. Glad to say the faeries left my garden alone last night, though there was a dead mouse on the lawn. The cats were sound asleep on the sofa, conscience free and indifferent to suffering, but I let them be and made a pot of tea and scrambled eggs on toast.

The weather this morning was indifferent, but I am more interested in what it will be doing at dawn tomorrow when I breakfast with bonfire bacon beside the long barrow at West Kennet.

Admittedly the tomb at West Kennet is some three thousand years older than that occupied by Jesus, but it has been village custom for longer than anyone can remember to witness dawn on Holy Sunday beside its ancient stones. Tonight, however, is the Reverend Peter Chadwick's idea. Can't help thinking an all-night vigil is optimistic given the average age of the congregation.

Rowan Tree approaches with my lunch'.

"GOD IS DEAD"

Later; Avebury Trusloe

Rereading my last entry, I began wondering when I first learned that God was dead over the Easter weekend. It must have been one Long Friday or Holy Saturday, aged twelve or thirteen, when Daddy found me praying at the foot of my bed. I can't remember what I was praying for; it might have been for Edwin, my imaginary friend who I'd recently lost, or for a poorly auntie, but I remember praying fervently.

"Nevil," Daddy said from my bedroom doorway. "You do know God is dead."

"He's dead!" I said, awestruck. And I mean in the old sense of awe.

"Yesterday He died on the Cross and now he lies in the tomb," Daddy said. "Today we are alone as we are never alone. You must pray He is reborn. He depends on you."

My father left. I got up from my knees and fell on my bed crying.

God is dead. On this one day of the year, from sunset on Long Friday until dawn tomorrow, God is out of this world.

I shouldn't have spent so long in The Red Lion at lunchtime. One pint turned to four, and I'm at sixes and sevens making sandwiches for this evening. If I wasn't on the PCC I might take the night off, but we must make a good impression. Due at St James's at eight for the Lighting of the Fire.

I'll take my journal with me as, Lord knows, the hours will drag.

Postscriptum: four pints Cropwell's Bitter.

11pm; kitchen, St James's, Avebury

I have been delegated to make tea, which gives me a few minutes to compose my thoughts while the kettle boils.

As intended, I arrived early at St James. Sid Morris was busy gathering logs for the Paschal Fire, and I gave him a hand for a few minutes.

"Not too many," Sid said. "It'll be a long night. Didn't see you park."

"I walked down," I said.

"Sensible of you, what with the other night. You should get yourself checked out."

"Damned impertinence," I said. "Anyway, there's no point driving to church as we'll be at the barrow tomorrow morning."

Sid did not reply. so left I him to his logs and went into church. Molly was there but she couldn't stay for the vigil as her guests would want their breakfasts in the morning.

I was determined to see the night through.

"Is that wise?" she asked.

"Why ever not?"

"There was your accident at Glastonbury," she said. "And you do look tired. Your father died far too young."

"If I appear tired, it may be that I am tired of people

asking about my health. Yes, I was poorly at Glastonbury, but I passed my week in Malvern with flying colours."

"I only meant you should take care of yourself. There's no need to get upset with me."

Of course, I felt awful after that. Molly means well, as does Sid, in his way, but all this concern for my health is tiresome.

The church is freezing tonight. Pauline Lamb suggested we turn the heating up, but Peter Chadwick said something about no comfort for Jesus in the tomb, so I presume we must make the best of it.

Kettle's boiled.

3am; St James's, Avebury

Redwood Tree and his daughters Apple and May gave us a delightful performance of Moses crossing the Red Sea. Redwood played the Pharaoh—it was taken from *The Dramatised Old Testament* by Falkirk and Watson—while Apple and May played Moses and the fleeing Israelites. It ended with Apple and May tipping a bucket of water on their father's head, with great delight. Exodus 14 is always part of the Easter Vigil, and it was nice to see something novel done with it, though I don't think Peter Chadwick was happy with the impromptu flooding.

Their performance perked me up no end, as by then I was feeling rather fragile. Only to be expected at this godforsaken hour, and while Prudence is mopping up the nave, I've popped into the kitchen for a cup of coffee. This is morning, after all.

Something odd happened earlier. Fred Thirsk was minding the fire in the churchyard, and I joined him to warm up a bit. Fred assured me there was enough firewood to last till dawn, and then, for some reason, wouldn't stop talking about rabbits. Eventually, bored by rabbits, I wandered up the High Street to stretch my legs. I had passed the pub and must have been somewhere in the middle of the stones, when I heard a low rumble, like timpani, or the bass note on a piano. Then, up from the great ditch beyond the stones, galloped a magnificent white horse. It shone in the starlight—the moon had set by then—and as soon as I saw it, the noise redoubled. It was the same creature I saw on Wednesday night, the same that Bert and Sid denied. Well, here it was, large as life, but oddly, I wasn't at all frightened.

Next thing I knew, Fred was shaking me awake, claiming my snores were disturbing people. I was back in the church and the drumming sound was Sid on the piano, accompanying Paul Durdle reading from Genesis chapter 1.

I'm not the only one who's frayed around the edges. No, that's not what I mean. People become more themselves when they are weary: less guarded. Lucy Chadwick surprised me earlier. I was sitting behind her during Peter's reading from Genesis 22—Abraham sacrificing Isaac—when I noticed tears streaming down her face. I went to pass her a handkerchief, but she waved it away.

"Think of Jesus," she said, "all alone in the darkness."

I didn't know what to say, except to apologise. But later, just before Redwood's performance as Pharaoh, she collared me in the kitchen.

"I'm really sorry," she said.

"Whatever for?"

"I wasn't honest," she said. "One should be honest, shouldn't one?"

"A white lie never does any harm," I said.

She smiled.

"I wasn't crying for Jesus. Peter and I, we had a son. He died before entering the world. I could hear Peter remembering that as he read."

"Gosh. How awful for you," I said.

Words are so ineffectual at times.

ARISE!

Easter Day; Avebury Trusloe

I am glad to be home. Have made myself a pot of tea but can't decide whether to continue with the rest of the day as

263

normal, or crawl into bed for a few hours. Seems wrong to go to bed in broad daylight—it is now eight—but I'll feel wretched the whole day if I don't.

We emerged from St James's at five o'clock this morning, with the eastern sky paling to grey. Exhaustion had forced a kind of solemnity on everyone. Sid dislodged an ember from the fire and dropped it into the thurible, ready for Paul to carry to West Kennet. Pauline Lamb took a stick from the fire to light the Paschal Candle.

Peter Chadwick asked us to pray over the candle.

"Sanctify this new flame and grant that our minds made pure we may be inflamed with heavenly desires as we welcome You, Our Lord, again into our lives so we may attain festivities of unending splendour. Through Christ our Lord, amen."

"Amen."

Peter would carry the cross at the head of the procession. Pauline would follow with the candle. Then Paul with the thurible. Fred handed out tarred staves to a dozen of us, including me, and we thrust them into the fire to get them going. Most of the rest had battery torches which took away some of the atmosphere and ceremony. Then we set off for West Kennet in near silence, with Paul swinging the thurible like a pendulum, releasing clouds of incense and the ember glowing in the darkness.

A flaming torch is something of a hindrance in a crowd. Lowering it, so one can see one's feet, risks scorching the backside of whoever's in front. Fortunately, there were enough torches that I could see well enough on the narrow path behind the cricket ground, and once across the Devizes Road, it was a simple matter to follow the path besides the River Kennet. Dawn was approaching, but night lingered under the hedges and the river only revealed itself through gentle mutterings. Birds, newly woken, whistled and chirruped in the willows and alders above our heads.

It was a beautiful if chilly dawn. The eastern sky had

silvered and the darkness of Silbury Hill rose from its marsh. A few yeas ago we would stop to light a fire on its summit, but the Antiquities Trust forbade the practice. I'm not sorry, as the climb is a beast with weary limbs.

"Would you Adam and Eve it," Sid muttered.

"I beg your pardon," I said.

"Them. Devizes Road."

I had been aware of a distant noise, but now saw a cluster of lights travelling at speed.

"Motorcycles?" I asked.

"Ravens, by sound of 'em. And on Holy Day."

I was vaguely aware that Raven is a marque of motorcycle, but apart from the headlights I couldn't make out anything. The noise was intrusive.

"Hell's Angels," Fred Thirsk muttered behind me. "Well named. Hell rides while God sleeps."

"But soon to wake again," Sid said and grabbing hold of my torch, thrust it in the air where it collided with a willow branch. Flaming debris descended on Fred who urgently brushed it off hair and clothing. The motorcycles continued north, and the sound faded. Silbury Hill grew larger before we skirted its flank and crossed the Marlborough Road.

Now we had only a steady climb to the long barrow. The eastern sky now had a golden hue and only the brightest stars remained. Behind me a trumpet sounded, bright and clear and banishing. I couldn't see who played it. Then Peter at the head of the procession began reciting.

"This is the night, when once You led our forebears from slavery in Egypt, dry-shod through the Red Sea.

"This is the night when a pillar of fire banished the darkness of sin.

"This is the night, that sets aside our worldly vices and the gloom of sin, and leads us to grace, for by Your death is Adam's sin redeemed!"

We had arrived outside the tomb. The ancient sarsen stones flickered with the light of our torches.

"O truly blessed night, at this time and hour when Christ rose from death."

Peter touched the cross on the wicker gate covering the entrance. The gate fell aside, and Elder Tree, her white gown shimmering, stepped from the darkness of the tomb and spread her arms.

"Praise the Lord!"

"Praise the Lord!"

"Halleluiah the king is returned."

Paul opened the thurible and spilled the ember onto the Celebration Fire. Those of us with torches assisted, and soon it was burning.

Some had brought chairs up yesterday, and now sat to await dawn. Elder Tree, as our risen Jesus, went among us and gave blessings, which may not be entirely orthodox, and possibly blasphemous, but no one objected. Others, of a more practical disposition, prepared bacon, and bread for toasting.

Then the sun rose on Easter Day.

9pm; Red Lion, Avebury

Holy Communion was at 11.30; later than usual on account of the all-night vigil. I'd managed two hours sleep and was feeling rather wretched. Couldn't face walking to church, so drove and left the motorcar at the pub before walking down to St. James's.

The Paschal fire was still smouldering. Decent pile of logs left over. I asked after them, but they've already been promised to Molly. No sign of Lucy Chadwick at the service.

It all seemed a bit of an anticlimax after our dawn procession, and I was glad to get out and call in here. Pub isn't too busy for a Sunday, and I've had a chance to speak to Jonathan. Those bikers I saw this morning were playing on my mind.

"Ravens?" he said.

"That's what Sid Morris called them."

"I suppose he should know," Jonathan said. "Our usual crowd ride Berliners."

"You haven't seen them?"

"This was at five this morning, was it?"

"About then. Just before dawn."

"Bit early for the pub, Nevil. They'll have long gone. Not seen a chapter riding Ravens since, ooh, must be two months ago."

"You mean Hells' Angels?"

"That's them. February it was. Nasty looking bunch. If it was the same bunch, I'm glad they kept going."

It was February when I saw O'Brien. And I was supposed to be meeting him this weekend. Curious coincidence. Can't see him being a motorcycle enthusiast.

Now. As I am driving I ought only to have no more than two pints, but the saving on beer allows something decent for lunch'. Can't face cooking later, so what shall it be? Christ is risen and original sin is no more. I think gammon with all the trimmings. How long ago Malvern seems.

Postscriptum: two pints of Bishops Snout. Managed a few hours editing this afternoon but am now going to bed. Expect to sleep like a stone.

CAT TROUBLES

Easter Monday; Avebury Trusloe

I woke later than usual, despite my early night, but was feeling considerably refreshed, right up until I opened the front door to let the cats in. Boris shot past me into the living room, but Tusker entered slowly, and then brushed up against my leg in something almost like affection.

Of course, I was immediately suspicious, and it was soon apparent that Tusker was reduced to three legs, with one back paw scarcely touching the ground.

I knelt and tried to lift the offending leg. Tusker growled and firmly pulled the leg away. I said something fatuous about allowing the doctor to treat the patient. Tusker glared at me. I tried again and with one hand firmly behind his neck managed to lift the paw long enough to see the basal end of a thorn sticking out of the pad. Tusker's growl rose just slowly enough for me to get both hands clear in time.

"You're really not the ideal patient," I said, and went to get the first aid box from the cupboard under the sink. Edith was always particularly good at stocking up on things for doomsday scenarios, so I knew there would be something useful in the box, and, once I had managed to deal with its childproof lock—how is one supposed to cope when suffering from an injury? —I found a pair of tweezers.

Tusker was still in the hallway, backside on the doormat and one back leg cocked in the air. His intensive licking of the offending paw paused just long enough to give me a cold stare.

Neither of my cats take kindly to humans, unless they are bearing food, so this promised to be a difficult encounter. I would need one hand for the paw, and one for the tweezers, but that left me dangerously exposed to the malevolence of an aggrieved cat. I recalled once seeing a vet stuff a cat into a gumboot to castrate it without being torn to pieces in the process. Alas, while I have a pair of gumboots, Tusker is much too large to fit. But the principle sounded good, so I retrieved my leather overnight bag from the hall cupboard. It has been a stalwart of many a Creative Haven, but this was the first time I had packed a cat. It seemed wise to wear gloves.

The valise opened as wide as its old leather would allow, I coaxed Tusker to stand up and then, without thinking too much of the consequences, put my hand and arm firmly underneath him and lifted. The general grumbling became a howl of rage. I gripped his chest as best I could, but my leather gloves proved slippery. Teeth penetrated my gloved typing finger and all four legs shot out and grappled with the jaws of the valise. I attempted to lower away, pushing the valise wider open and thrusting each paw down in turn until I had Tusker's head inside. Perhaps the relative darkness was comforting, because something of the struggle dissipated at that point, and I managed to close the valise in such a way that only his tail, and paw requiring attention, protruded. I secured the valise and checked my finger. There were several pinpricks of blood. Sensing my distraction, Tusker attempted an escape, and the valise began to hop slowly down the hallway. I retrieved it and grasped the extended leg, knowing that if it disappeared inside the valise, I would have no chance of retrieving it without injury. The growling became a howl and the tail thrashed like a snake.

I knelt with my knees either side of the valise, adjusted my reading glasses, and grasped the paw in one hand and tried to clasp the end of the thorn in the tweezers with the other. Tusker was having none of it and at each attempt jerked the paw away. Eventually I had the valise on its side, which allowed me to see both thorn and tweezers at the same time and managed to grip the blasted thing long enough to pull it out.

The valise howled and then coughed, as though suffering an asthma attack. I released the paw, and it vanished inside. The thorn was tiny.

I was now feeling rather proud of myself. I had averted major disaster, wearing only my pyjamas and dressing gown, and before even a single cup of tea. Anything else the day might throw at me would pale into insignificance. All that remained was to stand well back and release the clasp on the valise.

The chink of daylight was all the encouragement Tusker needed, and a mass of fur and indignation streaked into living room, leaving behind a disgusting smell.

I peered into the valise, discovering a slimy headless ball of fur, surrounded by yellow mucus. I couldn't face that, not before breakfast, so opened the front door and flung it onto the lawn to deal with later, before grappling with the childproof cap of the antiseptic bottle.

What with it being a public holiday, and no telephone calls, I had intended an industrious day's editing, but I have been an hour at breakfast and still not moved. My finger throbs horribly and may be beyond use for some time.

6pm; Avebury Trusloe

After lunch' I managed two pages of typing, before I admitted defeat. Apart from the discomfort, attempting to touch type with my ring finger left the page littered with mistakes. I read instead, comparing the text of MacGregor's first draft with the published edition. I should do that more often, as it allows a degree of oversight. Gillanders Neave, Lord MacDonald's dutiful manservant, may be the most sympathetic character in the entire work. Or at least, what I have read of the first draft so far.

Breaking off now to make tea, though anticipate that also will be difficult. Only hope I can drive, as I am calling on Mummy tomorrow afternoon. The wretched cat has spent all day curled up on the sofa and will no doubt accept a bowl of Kitty Nibbles without shred of apology or concern.

Postscriptum: apologies for the handwriting. I'm forced to use my left hand. Weight this morning, fifteen stone, eight.

1am; Avebury Trusloe

Just been woken up by some insufferable lout riding a motorcycle up and down the lane. It's not just the noise, which is appalling, but one always worries about the cats. Usually, the road is peaceful between the evening commute home, and the dawn chorus.

Sounds like a large motorcycle too. One of those Ravens.

23 April; Gingerbread House, Manningford Bohune

Managed the drive to Amesbury with only a tolerable degree of pain. My finger has swollen, and I could only just get my driving glove on. It's also red and hot, except for the tip which is pearl-white and numb.

Still attempting to write left-handed, so if you're reading this at some later date, apologies. I am doing the best I can.

Lunch' is on its way, and, in an esprit d'aventure, I have ordered langoustine poached with Normandy pears and a side salad of quail eggs, sautéed cavolo nero, and toasted almonds.

I was tempted by the canard au chocolat, but that might be a bit rich for lunch'. A pint of Hainaut Grand Cru will pass the time while the chef performs his magic. What the French know about cooking, the Belgians know about beer.

Mummy was in good spirits today. That pretty Spanish girl was still on leave, so no update on the black feather situation. Hopefully, the ghost of Mr Rookwood is leaving well alone. All in all, the usual pitfalls of visiting Mummy failed to materialise; it was the unexpected that did the damage.

I had just settled in the Day Room with Mummy. The sun was streaming through the French windows and, for once, the entire room seemed bright and gay. Of course, it didn't do to dwell on the faces of the residents, but there were enough visitors to give a semblance of compos mentis to the assembly and I was anticipating a calm half hour of dutiful affection.

It all went rather wrong. Mrs—I assume she was once married, though I've never looked to see if she has a wedding ring—one doesn't past a certain age—so I have no idea one way or the other—Bean dropped her teacup over the side of her armchair. Her visitor, I think a daughter, was herself in a wheelchair, so could not reach down and I obliged by leaning over. The cup had shattered on the chair leg, and I managed to lance the end of my already damaged index finger on a shard of porcelain.

As I mentioned, the tip of that finger was completely numb, so it was a moment before I registered the blood. This created a scene, and I was suddenly the centre of attention for about three carers of various languages, who then passed me to a fourth who, thankfully, was as English as Norwich mustard.

"Dreadfully sorry," I said once in a side room being patched up. "My finger is having an unfortunate few days."

"It is very swollen, Mr Warbrook. Can you feel this?"

Mrs Mustard tapped the end of my finger.

"Completely numb I'm afraid. Has been since yesterday evening. Bitten by one of my cats."

"A cat?" Mrs Mustard said, with the keenness of a lawyer seizing on a vital slip of the tongue.

"Persian, name of Tusker. I was removing a thorn from a paw. Bit of a misunderstanding."

"They are disgusting creatures, Mr Warbrook. I would not have one in my house. They carry disease. The numbness is a sign of infection. Any pain in the wrist?"

Now she mentioned it, I had noticed a slight stiffness while I was driving. This was also confirmation Tusker had left more than bite marks. I suppose, vomiting half a mouse immediately after biting me does indicate a lack of feline hygiene.

"I cannot urge you strongly enough to see your doctor. The wound is infected. If the infection spreads, it might result in amputation."

"Of the finger?"

"As far as necessary, Mr Warbrook. It appears already to have affected the entire hand."

I confess, I flinched. I am not terribly brave. Then I remembered I intended shopping in Devizes tomorrow.

"Would it wait until tomorrow?" I asked. "Only it is three o'clock and I have still to drive home."

"It is your limb, Mr Warbrook. But tomorrow at the latest."

My finger bandaged, I returned to the Day Room, but I admit my mind was feverish, and whatever nonsense Mummy said passed me by. Frankly, I was only too happy to make my goodbyes and get out of there.

Ah, this looks like my lunch'.

7pm; Avebury Trusloe

The langoustines were not shelled. Keen not to get seafood and *jus de poire Normandie* on my newly-bandaged finger, I eventually accepted defeat and asked a waiter to de-shell the creatures for me. Waiting like an imbecile, while the chap patiently prepared my food, took some of the pleasure out of eating, though it was tasty enough.

Afterwards, worried I would arrive home after the Devizes

surgery had closed; I used the telephone at the front desk in The Gingerbread House to make an appointment for tomorrow. Dr Saunders: ten-fifteen sharp. I shall take my notebook with me just in case she wishes to see my account. Speaking of which…

Postscriptum: one pint Hainaut Grand Cru.

Had hoped to get some editing done this evening, but it's impossible to concentrate.

TROUBLE IN BORNEO

24 April; Avebury Trusloe

Up early this morning. Finger was painful last night, and I slept fretfully. Put the wireless on during my scrambled eggs on toast and heard report of a coup in Borneo. Unfortunately, I didn't get all the details and can only hope Gerald is unaffected. No doubt I shall soon hear if he is not.

Due at the doctors later but had hoped to get a couple of hours work in, such as I can while impaired, but a telephone call interrupted events. It was Mrs Purge of Belshade College. I am invited to interview at one o'clock next Thursday. Of course, I accepted, and asked Mrs Purge how many had applied for the position, but she gave nothing away. Between now and then, I must brush up my knowledge of Belshade and re-read the prospectus.

Lunchtime; White Bear, Devizes

Dr Saunders is a cat lover and assured me Mrs Mustard was overstating the case against them.

"I don't think we'll have to amputate," she said lightly. "Nor are you going to die of plague."

"Plague?"

"Bubonic. Cats are carriers for the plague, but not, happily, here."

"So, I have nothing to worry about. False alarm."

"I didn't say that. It is infected, but nothing antibiotics won't clear up. I'll write a prescription and you can collect it at Dollywhites on the High Street."

She handed me a slip of paper.

"How long before I can use my finger again?"

"It rather depends on what you want to use it for."

"Typing is the most pressing. And writing. It's inconvenient for eating as well. And ablutions, though I won't go into that."

"The swelling should go down within a week. If it doesn't, see me again. The course of antibiotics is twenty days. I'm afraid, it's no alcohol."

"A blow," I said. "I abstained for Lent; rather looking forward to a modest tipple now and then."

Inside, I was seething at the cruelty. Lent had barely been over a few days, and now this.

"How has your weight been?" she asked. "As you're here, I thought we might catch up on progress."

Rather than present her with my entire journal, I had written out the relevant information for just this moment. Dr Saunders studied the page intently.

"Noticeably weight loss at the end of March," she said.

"I was at the health spa in Malvern," I said.

"It was obviously good for you."

"It may surprise you, but I am tempted to do it again one day. It was a liberating experience."

"You do surprise me. But you stopped recording your drinking."

I explained about Lent.

"It ended only a few days ago, so you understand that having to forego on account of the antibiotics is something of a blow."

"I can only advise you, Mr Warbrook."

"I understand, but is it really so essential?"

I disliked the wheedling sound in my voice, but having kept rigidly to my Lenten promise it seems extremely unfair to prolong my abstinence on account of a sore finger.

Dr Saunders glanced at me through her black-rimmed glasses.

274

"Unfortunately, alcohol impedes the effectiveness of the antibiotics. You don't want the infection to spread, do you?"

Having been defeated yesterday by oversized prawns, I accepted, with reluctance, the soonest mended the better. More pressingly, until I can type properly, editing will be painfully slow, so I really cannot afford not to help Mother Nature on her way.

Dr Saunders seemed happy with my progress, weight-wise, and, I suppose, I am too, having shed over a stone since February. As yet, I have not needed to re-equip my wardrobe, but have taken my trouser belt in a notch and found that some of the older trousers and shirts at the back of my wardrobe now fit rather well.

Called in at Dollywhites to pick up the prescription. Young lady at the counter repeated Dr Saunders' warning re alcohol. Tablets to be taken twice daily on an empty stomach. Oh, joy.

Dragged myself around Budgitts. I had never considered before how much food is packaged in such a way that only the fully-dextrous stand a chance of opening it. Utterly depressing. Even a tin opener is presently beyond me. The time was then eleven thirty and I decided on lunch' at the White Bear, and a valedictory pint before my three-week enforced sobriety begins.

Even more depressingly, I am travelling to Edenborough in a fortnight and must forego the excellent selection of whiskies at the Stuffed Cock.

I hope Tusker is feeling suitably apologetic.

FOG

Bedtime; Avebury Trusloe

Not been home long following dominoes at the Waggon and Horses in Beckhampton. Took my first capsule of Phloxy-mycin just before six, so my three weeks of enforced sobriety had begun when I collected Bert outside The Red Lion.

"Reckoned it was a risk, but didn't fancy the walk," he said.

"Risk?"

"Of you nodding off."

He slammed the door with what I thought was unnecessary force.

"I think that unlikely," I said. "Not that I am admitting my guilt for last time. My memory differs from yours. As it happens, I am in some pain" —I waggled my sore digit— "so sleep under any circumstances is difficult."

"Put it where you're not supposed to?" he asked with a queasy grin.

"Bitten by a cat."

"Unforgiving creature, cats," he said gnomically.

"Onwards? Or is it not too late for you to call a taxi?"

"I'll take my chances," he said. "Mind, reckon fog later."

I said that even I would be hard-pressed to lose my way between Beckhampton and Avebury. Though I suppose I might have said that about Winterbourne Bassett.

The tables were laid out ready in the backroom of the Waggon and Horses when we arrived. Sid, living practically next door to the pub, was already ensconced by the fire.

"Made it safely, then?" he asked as we sat down.

"Thank you, we have," I said stiffly.

"Supposed to get foggy tonight," he said. "Who knows what might appear in the fog."

"I hope your own journey was satisfactory," I said.

"Very," he replied.

The Beckhampton team turned up, en masse, some ten minutes later, and after the usual friendly banter, we set to. Bert was matched with Doris Knightly while Sid played her husband, Tom William, or 'Twice' as he is usually known. I had Lancelot Trail, a biochemist, and the best player in the Beckhampton team. I didn't fancy my chances and they quickly turned worse when I found that I could barely pick up the damned tiles on account of my finger. Had to play left-handed, which interfered with my concentration. Low point was when I tried to pick up the double-blank and managed to flick it into the middle of Bert and Doris's game. I lost badly. Then lost to Twice.

"Off night?" Doris asked as we settled down for what would be my third game.

"Not been sleeping too well," I said. "Bitten by my cat."

"Oh dear. Whatever did you do?"

"Pulled a thorn from its paw. You'd have expected a bit of gratitude. Instead, I'm on antibiotics and off the booze for three weeks."

I led with the double five, scoring two. Doris, po-faced like the expert player she is, could only lay a five-three, scoring zero. I followed with a three-two scoring four. That was my last spell of decent scoring and Doris gradually overhauled me and drew ahead. I rallied and it was close at the end, but I lost by eight points.

"Sorry chaps," I said to Sid and Bert. "Not been my night."

"Just as well it's been ours," Bert said.

Bert had won all three of his games, and Sid had won two. Between us, or rather, between them, we were five-four victors on the night.

Bert got himself another pint and Sid was nursing his glass of porter. I joined them with a bitter lemon.

"Looks wrong, a bloke drinking something like that," Sid said truculently.

"I didn't fancy Merit," I said. "Had quite enough of that during Lent. Sorry I let the side down this evening."

"Team needs a minimum of three," Bert said. "They also serve, who only lose their games."

"A bit harsh," I said. "I don't always lose. But I wouldn't mind stepping down if you find someone willing. I admit I'm not in your league."

"You're safe for this season," Bert said. "Can't put another player on the team sheet till September. Kennet Valley League rules: all players on a team must be registered at the start of the season. Substitutes only allowed in cases of death or infirmity. I assume you've nothing planned?"

"Actually, now you mention it, I might have something planned and, if it happens, I'll have to step down come September. Interview for a position at Oxford. Comes with accommodation, so I'll be staying up there half the week."

"Nice work for those that get it," Sid said. "'Ere, what about the church committee?"

"Cross that bridge when I get to it. Very much hope I can continue."

"Reckon a few of us hope so too."

"It's three days a week, Tuesday till Thursday. Depending on how quickly I can get away, I should still be able to make Thursday evenings for the council meetings."

"Suppose you can't get back here for Wednesdays?"

"Have to be an exceptional reason," I said. "Peter trying to relocate the tower or install wind chimes instead of bells. I might be able to negotiate with the college, but don't want to say anything at interview in case it queers my chances."

"So, it's not certain you'll get it?"

"By no means, though I think it's likely. Interview's next week, so I'll know soon enough."

Bert and I left soon after: stepping out from the snug bar into a damp and chilly night. The prospect of driving a few miles home was quite bad enough. Oxford to Avebury, and back on such a night would be unthinkable. I had not expected Sid to be quite so concerned at the prospect of my missing council meetings. It is only once a month and if the meeting is on a Thursday, I can't see any problem. That said, the modernisers would be only too happy to see me step down, so that's one reason not to.

"It has got foggy," Bert said. "Hope you can remember where you parked."

I had my torch out, but it only changed things from deep brown to yellowish-grey.

"Should be along here," I said. "Look out for potholes."

Fortunately, the Waggon and Horses had been quiet, and I had parked near the entrance. The Rover was tucked in behind a large black workman's van, which was parked closer than it need be, and I had to sidle down between the two vehicles to unlock my door. Bert was on the far side.

"Strewth almighty," he said.

"What is it?"

"See this beggar?"

I shone my torch across and saw a small white van.

"Ah. Albion Books. Saw that outside the Henge Shop the other day. It is a bit startling."

The hideous, red-eyed creature looked even worse on a foggy night.

"Give a chap bad dreams, that will. Come on Nevil, get us home."

I got in and leant across to open the door for Bert.

"They could have left us a bit more room. Hardly a lack of space in the car park," I complained. "Now, home."

The headlights showed only a pale wall of fog and the top of the stone wall bordering the main road. I tried them on dip, but it didn't improve the view.

"Remind me why we do this," I said.

"For the pride of *The Red Lion*," Bert said. "Generations have stepped forth to defend its honour. But I take your point."

The engine turned over and faltered.

"Doesn't like the damp," I said, and tried again.

This time it churned asthmatically, the lights dimming as the starter motor whirred.

"Come on old thing."

I tried again, and this time the engine caught and spluttered to life. I revved and dropped the clutch. The car rocked backwards, and the engine died.

"I suppose if it comes to it Sid could put us up for the night," Bert said lugubriously.

"Perish the thought. Try again."

This time, the engine caught, and I was gentler with the clutch and reversed out smoothly.

"You started those antibios, then?"

"This afternoon. Yes."

"Do they say if you're safe to drive with them?"

"Very funny. Might be worthwhile sitting here for a minute, let the engine warm through. Then, when we get to the roundabout it would be useful if you kept an eye on the exits. Easy to miss our turn."

"I thought you reckoned you couldn't get lost from here."

"That was before I knew I'd be doing it blind. Right, I think that's warm enough."

The engine had lost its rasp and was ticking smoothly. Entering the main road took blind faith, and hope no one was driving at speed on such a night, but we were heading for home. At the roundabout, I slowed down to a crawl and Bert wound down his window and picked out the road signs with my torch. It would be easy to end up on the Cherhill Road, or even travelling back the way we had come, but we did not. Bert wound up his window, but it stuck an inch from the top.

"Never mind," I said. "Fix it in the morning."

"It's not your bloomin' ear it's freezing. 'Ere, you hear that?"

I couldn't hear a thing, but next moment a dazzling white light appeared behind us, hesitated a moment, then overtook at speed. A single red light vanished into the dark.

"Ruddy lunatic. Motorcycling on a night like this."

"Perhaps, like us he has no choice," I said. "But I'll take it steady, just in case we find his mangled corpse in the road."

"Big bike an' all," Bert said. "Horton, or a Raven. Hard to tell."

There was no other traffic and presently I dropped Bert outside The Red Lion, then swung round and headed home. An owl hooted as I got out the car, but I suspect he had no hunting tonight. Should have worn something a bit warmer this evening, as I was shivering when I opened the door. The cats greeted me by streaking out into the darkness, and I wagged a finger after them warning against thorns.

Warmed myself up with a cup of tea and put on the

news. Wasn't paying close attention, but Borneo was mentioned and there was film of tanks rolling down a street. I've no idea if Gerald is still there. Either way, there's nothing I can do tonight.

And so, to bed.

25 April; Avebury Trusloe

Up early again. Remembered my tablet and waited a good twenty minutes before making a pot of tea. Am sitting with my second cuppa of the morning at my writing desk and flexing my wounded finger. I doubt the antibiotics have kicked in, just yet, but it is less painful, and I will risk typing later. Do not want to fall further behind.

Last night's fog is lingering. Due at the village hall this evening, so I hope it clears before dusk. House is cold this morning.

Enough blathering: to work!

THE BELLS

Late evening; Avebury Trusloe

Things began promisingly at the village hall tonight. Prudence Turnstone, reporting for the Spiritual Outreach Committee, said they had received over fifteen letters congratulating everyone on the success of the Easter celebrations. Dawn at West Kennet had been especially popular, and it was hoped we could do it again next year.

"We'll need a new Jesus," said Sid.

"I thought Elder did very well," Pauline replied.

"Y'didn't see her boyfriend then?"

"What of him?"

"She won't be a virgin twelvemonths time, will she?"

"I can't see that's relevant," Paul said. "Jesus was hardly a sixteen-year-old girl, so if we're going for authenticity—"

"I say it sits wrong with me. Whoever plays Him should be above reproach."

"Honestly, I don't think the world cares," Lucy said.

"But Jesus was not of the world," Sid said.

"Surely we can leave this discussion until the new year," I said. "Perhaps she'll be only too happy for someone else to have a turn."

"I agree with Nevil," Fred said.

Fred had been unusually quiet up till then. We found out why later.

"Any news on the crèche at the New Barn School?" Molly asked.

Prudence said she had written and was awaiting reply.

"Written?" I said. "Surely, you only need to call in and ask."

"Best to go through proper channels," Paul said.

I glanced at Molly. This sounded like delaying tactics.

"I could speak to Jenny Atkins," Molly said. "She volunteers there. I know her through the Egg Collective."

That's the village's community of chicken keepers.

"Sounds good to me," Sid said. "Motion moved. We're a small place and most of us are friendly."

"I second Molly to approach Jenny Atkins," I said.

There was a show of hands. Prudence voted against and Paul abstained, but it was carried.

"I'll report back at the next meeting," Molly said.

Terry Woodson was our chair for the evening. He, like Fred, had been quieter than normal. He asked Prue if she had anything else to report, but all she had was the takings and expenditure for catering. We had made a modest profit.

Molly reported on the flowers in the church. One of her volunteers was retiring and we agreed to offer a small gift in thanks. Budget of ten crowns. Then it was Fred's report on bell-ringing matters, but he declined to speak, saying Terry Woodson would present a joint report later. This raised a few eyebrows.

Paul then passed on Peter Chadwick's thanks to me for writing the Lenten talks. Prue gave me a steely look, but Paul was effusive, and I almost felt it had been worthwhile. Sid said that some of my talks had been too little on Jesus and too much on "wicket folk."

"They too are seekers of truth," Prudence said, and though I winced, I was happy to see Sid back down.

Then it was Terry's turn to report on Fabric and Works. Normally this is the dullest part of the evening, as it's difficult to enthuse about guttering and drainage and electrical repairs. It's also something we usually agree on, as it's commonsense to keep the place in good order. Tonight would be different.

"This is speaking for Fabric and Works and for the bell-ringers," Terry said, with a nod to Fred. "You will recall that in January Peal Services inspected the bells and associated machinery. It's once every five years, so I think only two or three of you will recall that the last report highlighted problems with the bell frame. There were recommendations attached, but nothing's been done about it in the interim."

Fred glanced at each of us in turn. I admit to taking the church bells for granted. They sound in the same way that birds sing.

"January's inspection indicates that damage to the main bell frame, which is oak and two centuries old, requires urgent repair owing to dry rot where it sets into the walls of the tower. The inspector is of a view that it can be done in situ, without dropping the bells, but it can no longer be ignored."

"Gosh," I said. "Can they still be rung?"

I was beginning to understand Fred's gloominess. Running the tower is his main hobby.

"For the time being, yes; however," Fred continued, "our insurance is up for renewal in September and the inspector cannot recommend coverage for bell-ringing until repairs are complete. That means, if nothing is done, the bells will fall silent."

"Had we acted five years ago, we wouldn't be in this position," Fred added.

Paul coughed. "The obvious question is, what will it cost to repair the, err, bell frame?"

"We'll have to get estimates," Terry said, "but the work

is similar to what they had done ten years ago at All Saints, and that came to 60,000 crowns."

Prudence pursed her lips.

"The bells are part of the village," Sid said. "They are the voice of the church."

"There is nothing in the Bible to say bells are an essential part of worship," Paul said. "Many modern churches have dispensed with them."

"St James is hardly a modern church," I said.

"We are aware of your affection for its history," Paul said. "There are other ways of summoning the faithful. Bells can be recorded, for example."

Fred looked ill.

"It's hardly the same," I said.

"I only observe that 60,000 crowns would go far in the community," Paul said.

"It would fund the Outreach budget for ten years," Prue said.

"There are grants for bell-work available through the diocese," Fred said. "They paid for part of the work at All Saints."

"'Ere," Sid began. "If Fred's against recordings of bells, and I don't blame him, why not send Peter up the tower with a megaphone and he can summon us like them Mohammedans do."

"That is in poor taste," Prue said.

"You'd have a job getting him up there," Lucy said. "He has vertigo."

"Ha! Y'mean our vicar's afraid of ascending?" Sid said.

"You're being cruel," Paul said.

"Well, it's bitter news, is all," Sid said. "I've heard them bells, baby, boy, and man. When I got back from the army, the bells told me I was home, and when I got married, they tolled for me again."

"If Sid speaks for the village as a whole, we might look at setting up a fund," Terry said.

"I think it would be popular," Paul said. "But what do you propose we do next?"

"We know what needs doing, so we should start inviting tenders," Terry said. "Can someone motion that we begin that process? And might I suggest, Fred, that it not come from you?"

"I'm only too happy to put my hand up," I said.

"Someone to second the motion?" asked Terry.

"I will," said Paul. "As you say, we must have estimates before considering what to do next."

"Motion passed."

"And there's nothing in the inspector's report saying we cannot continue to ring the bells, pending repair or the renewal of insurance," Paul asked.

"He recommends we stop using the twenty-eight-inch bell," Fred said. "It cramps our style, but we can still ring."

The meeting ended soon after and we departed into the night. Eleven o'clock is now approaching and I'm waiting for the church clock to sound the hour. On any other night I would barely notice the peal, but tonight I am listening.

I shall put this down and pray.

26 April; Avebury Trusloe

I woke in a bad mood. Of course, as I lay in bed mulling things over, the church bells chimed the quarter hour, which only made things worse. Thus far, the old-hands have managed to thwart the modernising tendency at St James and kept things as they were. But this will be a bigger challenge, because keeping things as they are will be expensive.

Toast and marmalade for breakfast. Need to get eggs and milk at the village shop. Off to Lunden tomorrow, so won't manage to do a proper shop until Monday.

During my second pot of tea, the postman delivered the contract for the canal gig. Everything looks in order. Pea kindly included a brochure from Waterfowl Cruisers. My boat is a forty-foot-long 'Wader Class' called Snipe. Company provides tuition for the first few miles or so, which, happily, includes the first lock.

Less happily, it transpires that CARP accepts advertising from many of the establishments I will be visiting *en passage,* and my reviews must be encouraging and positive, while being always truthful, rather than filled with the kind of withering put-downs delivered by Eglantine Pierpont, restaurant reviewer for the Sunday News. A shame, as I think I would be rather good at scathing witticism. I suppose, I can always reserve my true opinion for the pages of this journal.

I signed the agreement slip included and put it in an envelope. I'm due at the New Barn School this evening for my first session with the Avebury Society of Painters, so can post it then.

Finger is notably less painful this morning. Either time or the antibiotics are working. Managing a fair job of writing with the proper hand this morning. It promises well for a productive day's editing.

THE JOY OF PAINT
Evening; Red Lion, Avebury

I can't imagine why I never joined ASP before. Well, perhaps I can. Edith was always so busy at her various social events; committees for the eradication of scrofula; the embroidery network; and riding lessons; that I valued those evenings she was at home. Of course, she was always encouraging me to get out of the house, saying it was unhealthy to spend so much time sitting at a desk—she was quite right on that account—but if one is married, oughtn't spouses spend some time together?

In retrospect, one suspects she had a different perspective on events.

But I am now a gay divorcee, and as the cats have no need of my company, what is to keep me at home in the evening? The company at ASP is certainly more enjoyable than Sid and Bert, and so far, my colour blindness is not causing difficulty. I may even be a more promising artist than I am a dominoes player.

I suppose that should be less of a surprise than it was. I dabbled in the fine arts while at college, even joined an art club during Freshers' Week, though I didn't attend many sessions. Perhaps I should have taken art more seriously, rather than trying to write poetry. I would have felt less worthless if I weren't competing with my father.

Anyway, forty years on, I am putting things right, and I was pleased with my efforts, even though I failed to persuade a single member to join me afterwards in the pub.

As one might expect, they were mostly women of a certain age—my age—and several were familiar faces, even if I had a job remembering everyone's name. There was also a younger woman, thirty-something, who was very proficient with pen and ink. The youngest female was Apple Tree. Of the three chaps, beside myself, one had come down from Broad Hinton, one I learned nothing about, and the other was a young chap who I vaguely recognised. Said his name was Wilf, or something like that, and was exuberant with the paint. His canvas looked nothing like the objects laid out for us to depict, but it was enthusiastic; though I don't think I could live with it.

Fortunately, there was none of that dreadful earnestness one so often encounters in such company, and the evening got off to a jolly start when Angela handed out smocks and artist's hats.

"To get us in the mood," she said, looking rather fetching in a straw boater and gingham artisan's outfit. "To be a true artist, one must break free of convention."

That's the kind of freedom I yearn for but find terrifying in the flesh. Fortunately, I know from my week at Malvern that initial apprehension fades, and I fully anticipate enjoying it when it happens. If, for the time being, I am stuck trying to create 'likenesses,' as Angela disparagingly calls them, instead of liberating colour and tone and creating an original work rather than one that imitates reality (I'm paraphrasing Angela), then so be it: it will pass.

Somehow, I have a splodge of green paint on my shoe. Evidently, the smock does not protect everything.

The evening also gave me my first ever look inside the New Barn School. It's rather cheerful, much nicer than any school I remember, though I can see why Prudence turns her nose up at it. There's a distinctly 'new-age' tone to some of the inspiring quotes and artworks decorating the place. One wall was entirely covered in unicorns, and there was a portly Buddha in the corner of the room.

The session ended with Angela saying that I should keep a sketchbook and use it to develop ideas. Ideally, it should be small enough to travel everywhere with me, but large enough that my hand is never cramped. I should also invest in a set of artist's pencils.

"These," she said, "will allow you to develop shade, and with shade we create form."

"Light and shade," I said. "Chiaroscuro: the Italians have a word for it."

"They will be especially useful for next week," she said. "We have a life model."

"Oh, really. Gosh. Haven't done anything like that since college. Male or female?"

"Does it make a difference?"

"Of course not. I didn't mean anything by it. We are drawing, not admiring."

Not one of my better moments and Angela gave me such an odd look. Only hope it's no one I know, as it will be awkward looking them in the eye next time we meet.

Ten o'clock, already. Just heard the bells. Funny how I've been hearing them all day. Barely notice them usually.

27 April; Avebury Trusloe

I removed the bandage with trepidation during morning ablutions. My finger is much recovered and has gone from a

288

sullen red to milk-pale. Tusker's lacerations are almost healed and, apart from stiffness in the knuckle, it is back to its usual self.

Half a mind to stop taking the tablets, so I can enjoy the theatre interval in Lunden tonight. Though enjoy isn't quite the right word, as I may need a stiff drink after an evening of Van Zelden.

But Dr Saunders' warning is still ringing in my ear and, even if the finger looks better, that doesn't mean the infection is out of my system. So, it was a dose of Phloxymycin and then a twenty-minute wait before bacon and eggs.

The theatre program mentions that Van Zelden likes to surprise the audience by appearing in the foyer during the interval. Leaving aside that it can hardly now be a surprise, I suppose he does it for the attention. Any sane performer would be only too happy to escape to the green room for a bit of respite. I shall have to keep my wits about me, as I do not want to be recognised. Tonight is very much a reconnaissance of the enemy's position, so I must stay undercover.

Catching the four-thirty from Swindon. Arrives Lunden shortly before six and the evening performance begins at seven. That leaves plenty of time to get a tram from Hyde Station to the Hyperion Theatre and visit the gents before curtain-up. I shall want something substantial for lunch', as there's no time for an evening meal, but that still leaves the morning for work.

Nota bene: might want to wear old shoes for art class. Green paint is surprisingly difficult to remove.

Afternoon; Lunden Train

The parking fees at Swindon Station are extortionate—almost as much as a taxi home—but I cannot rely on a taxi late on a Saturday evening. The train is at least clean, and reasonably quiet, though that might change at Reading. I've often found that people are noticeably coarser the nearer one is to Lunden.

Decent morning on *This Iron Race*. It is curious that the whole enterprise, along with a substantial part of my earnings the last nine months, is due entirely to Van Zelden and his ridiculous allegations about MacGregor. One might almost consider it ironic, in the same way that German National Socialism inadvertently advanced scientific discovery and technology by several decades, in only a few short years of destruction and murder.

A crass analogy, but I cannot help being apprehensive about the evening. Van Zelden is meddling in forces he does not understand and cannot hope to control. Beneath that veneer of entertainment, there is something very dark.

Train announcer advises the buffet will be closing in twenty minutes due to staff shortage. How can there be a staff shortage, unless whoever is currently working the buffet is jumping off the train?

I shall go in search of a cup of tea.

IN THE SPOTLIGHT

Late evening; Swindon train

My hopes of passing incognito were dashed in spectacular fashion only twenty minutes into the performance. It's not enough that the audience see Van Zelden as the enormous success he has become, but they must also learn of his humble roots in Old Amsterdam, and upbringing by devout Catholic parents, and the horrible beatings he suffered when his abilities first manifested, and then his running away to Heidelberg. These he delivers as asides and mock-confessions, between, and during, his elaborate, and admittedly clever, artifices.

He also thanks those who abused him, including his father, from whom he is estranged, because in punishing him, so he claims, they were compelling him to further his talent.

It was during an account of his expulsion from Heidelberg that he mentioned reading MacGregor's *Willoughby Chaste,* and how this almost forgotten novel (his words) had shown him that he was not the first to have known magick and been despised for it. And then, as though waking from a familiar performance, his address to the audience changed and he looked up and, I swear, spoke directly to me.

"I don't often say this," he began, "and I don't know if he will welcome me saying it—"

My blood ran cold. How could he possibly know I was there? Could he sense my presence?

"—But when it came to understanding what MacGregor was; as a poet and author, and as a loving husband and father; one man showed me the way. Ladies and gentlemen, he is in the audience tonight. Without Nevil Warbrook I would not have begun to understand MacGregor and, if I had not understood him, I would not be here tonight. Please, Nevil Warbrook, stand so I can applaud you."

A spotlight swung across the audience like a beam of destruction and settled on me. Those sitting nearby, knowing it could not be meant for them, turned to me.

I opened my mouth and closed it. It was like the very worst moment at Malvern, only magnified. I could not remain seated—it would only make me stand out even more if I seemed churlish—so I stood, and bowed awkwardly left and right. Van Zelden applauded. Then everyone applauded. More people applauded me than I think have ever applauded me in my life. It was deeply uncomfortable, and then exhilarating. Extraordinarily so.

Van Zelden brought the applause to an end and indicated me to sit. The spotlight turned back to the stage, and the moment was over.

I could not imagine why he had done it. Even allowing his story is true, and I have no reason to suppose it isn't, it was such an extraordinary shift from his treatment of me at the Koningin in New Amsterdam and his criticism of *Book One*. What was it? Something about not sending a blind man to count the stars. If he intended this as a peace offering, it was like being beaten over the head with an olive branch.

Answers, at least in part, came during the interval. As we exited the auditorium, other audience members asked my connection to MacGregor. One asked if I knew of my influence on Van Zelden. Had I met Van Zelden?

"It must be so great knowing you influenced him. Oh, he's so wonderful."

"Say, were you a mentor to him?"

"Didn't I read somewhere you and he don't see eye-to-eye?"

I gave noncommittal answers. What could I say? I could hardly admit that at our last meeting he had nearly caused me to wet myself, or that I suspected he had left his sanity in the Reserved Manuscript Depository at King James University. I even, feebly, said that any scholarly work I had contributed on MacGregor was itself in the shadow of Professor Evelyn Bishop and Dr Crabtree.

Worse, it was one of those rare occasions people queue up to buy me a drink, and I had to refuse because of the blasted tablets.

"Do you suppose he'll appear among us?" a woman said, obviously eager for him to do so. I wanted to mutter he was hardly Jesus.

Then, just as I had accepted a young chap's offer of a soda and lime, an usher appeared and asked if I was Nevil Warbrook.

"Seat number 211?"

"I believe so. Would you like to see it?"

"This is the guy you want," the chap with my soda and lime said helpfully.

"Mr Warbrook, would you come this way."

"Of course. May I take this?"

"I'm afraid no drink allowed backstage, sir."

"Alas."

I handed back the soda and lime with an apologetic shrug. I was being summoned.

The attendant led me into the auditorium and then to a side door. At once the plush furnishings were replaced with a workaday corridor. I had, by now, realised my booking had revealed my presence. Seat number 211 in the name of Nevil Warbrook must have been a giveaway. I wonder at how many shows he had looked for my name and found it absent? One almost feels sorry for him.

The corridor became more glamorous, and I realised we were passing dressing rooms. For this show, only one counted. It was ajar and voices came from within. The attendant knocked and the door opened fully.

"Mr Van Zelden, sir. I have Mr Warbrook for you."

"Great. Send him in. Excuse, Danny."

That was Danny Rich, his agent. The room was brightly lit with a mirror taking up all of one wall. In addition to his agent, a young woman was attending Van Zelden's makeup.

"Nevil, hope you enjoyed the attention."

Danny Rich looked at me with boredom.

"Thank you, Hendryk. It's surprising how many people wanted to buy me a drink simply because we are acquainted."

"Don't be so stuffy. What I said was true."

"Then it is equally true that I would not be here, and *This Iron Race* would only be available in a butchered text had it not been for you and your silly claims about Mac-Gregor. I suppose Mr Rich also owes me some thanks, since if you wouldn't be here then he wouldn't be your agent."

"I have many clients, Mr Warbrook," Rich said.

Van Zelden ignored him.

"What did you think of the show? Meet your expectations?"

"It was... not what I feared," I said.

"Never believe a man's publicity," Van Zelden said.

"I still think you are dabbling in things you don't under-stand—that is no slur on you; no man *can* understand them—but you're not as reckless as I feared."

"I'll take that as a cautious *yes* if that's okay. You're wondering why the peace offering."

"I admit, I am curious."

"I admire what you're doing with the book."

"But what about *blind men and stars*?"

"They quoted me out of context. But I will say there's material in those books which anyone not attuned to magick will not get."

"I see. And you would *get it*, assuming it's there."

"I'd have a better chance. I mean, I think I would."

"Then it's unfortunate, for you, I mean; that I am the chosen editor."

An attendant put her head around the door.

"Five minutes Mr Van Zelden."

Van Zelden acknowledged her, then sat still for the makeup girl to finish him.

Danny Rich spoke.

"My client wishes you to know he has been contacted by your publisher. They are enquiring whether he would be willing to collaborate."

"Collaborate? They asked him if...? Good Lord."

"They haven't spoken to you?"

"No. And I mean they really ought to have done."

"My client was concerned they had not done so. He was also concerned to gauge your reaction."

"Well, I think you can *gauge* it here and now. I am contracted to edit and restore the first three books of *This Iron Race*. If that goes well, I anticipate a contract to do the rest."

The attendant returned.

"Three minutes until curtain."

"You'd better take your seat for the second act," Van Zelden said. "You do know the book would sell better with my name on it. My name *and* your name."

"I would object," I said.

"It's the publisher's decision."

"Two minutes until curtain."

Van Zelden stood. "You'd better get back, Nevil: wouldn't want you to miss the start."

Must leave off there. Train attendant has announced the buffet car is closing in ten minutes and I'm parched.

EMISSARY

28 April; Avebury Trusloe

Arrived at Swindon Railway Station last night to find the premises deserted, and the lavatories locked. Frustratingly, I had avoided the squalid facilities on the train, so my situation was now urgent. Fortunately, I hung on until I'd reached the outskirts of town and stopped by a convenient hedge.

Inevitably, while I was indisposed, at least three motor-cars and one motorcycle passed and illuminated me in their headlights.

It was long after midnight when I got home. The cats were waiting on the doormat and disappeared into the night without a hint of greeting, and it was odd after the crowd at the theatre and the distractions of the journey to settle back into an empty house. One notices every creak.

Normally I would have relaxed into the armchair with a glass of whisky, but it hardly felt worth it when the only thing to drink is bitter lemon, so I went to bed and read until drowsiness overcame me.

Dreamt that I was desperately searching for somewhere to urinate and eventually found a large potted geranium. I had just relaxed, when an audience applauded me and the geranium disappeared. One of Van Zelden's acts involved a geranium, but the meaning of the rest escapes me.

Holy Communion this morning. You would have thought Peter might have focused on the plight of our bells, but instead we had a homily on the simplicity of faith among the Coptic Christians and how their faith relies solely on the Word of God. I can see what he's doing: why worry about bells when you have the Bible? Bah, humbug, I say. Bells are as traditional a part of our worship as, I'm sure, camels are to Coptic Christians. But I confess, I was not paying close attention.

Matters improved during the social afterwards, where it

was clear news of our bells had got around. There were lots of bright, and occasionally eccentric, ideas for funding the repairs, which at least showed parishioners' concerns. I doubt Peter will get away with ignoring all of them.

I was on the point of leaving when the devil himself, which is to say the Reverend Peter Chadwick, along with Pauline Lamb, collared me by the cake stand.

"Just the chap I wanted to speak to," he said.

"About the bells?" I asked.

"No, no. But I understand the matter is in hand. I wondered if you knew what Tuesday marks."

"Tuesday?"

I couldn't think of anything further to say.

"April thirtieth," Pauline said unhelpfully.

"Well, yes. I knew it was the end of the month," I said, still none the wiser.

"I understand the date might not hold much significance in the Christian calendar," Peter said. "Nevertheless, for other faiths, or rather one faith in particular..."

I had, by now, realised where this was going. April thirtieth marks, for some, the end of winter and May first the beginning of spring.

"Beltane's Eve," Pauline said.

"A prelude to the Midsummer celebrations," Peter echoed. "After your talks on The Passion, and its associations with Avebury, we thought you might like to work with the Spiritual Outreach Committee. Join with the celebrants on Tuesday evening and write something for the parish magazine. You know how fuddy-duddy some of the parishioners are about the faith-free."

"I think they prefer to be called wiccans," I said demurely.

"Wiccans are one sect among many," Peter said. "The faith-free are a broad church, like our own."

"Would you?" Pauline said. "We really are hoping you will. There's so much misunderstanding. And it would raise money for the bell fund."

296

"Would it? How?"

"Fred is organising a ringathon for Tuesday night," Pauline said. "Two teams of ringers working in shifts from sundown to sunrise. Paul and I will ask for donations towards the bell fund. But really, we'd like you there because we know you'd do such a good job describing the evening."

"And where is the head of our Spiritual Outreach Committee in all this?" I asked.

"Prue doesn't feel able to commit," Pauline said.

"Ah. Spiritual Outreach only reaches so far," I said.

If I was being asked to do something so ridiculous, I might as well get a few barbs in.

"Sid offered, but we thought he might be too aggressive," Peter said. "Fred is busy with the bells and Terry said he needs to be on watch in case a night of ringing proves too much for the bell frame."

"Well, the last two have noble excuses," I said. "Fortunately, I am free that evening."

"Oh, thank you. We knew you wouldn't let us down," Pauline said.

"I don't suppose you know the weather forecast for Tuesday?" I asked.

"I don't recall any hurricane warnings," Peter said.

So, there we have it. I am a reporter for the evening. Let's see. 'Beltane marks the beginning of summer when the cattle were driven out into pasture. Although originally local to Eirish and Scots Gaelic culture, it is now celebrated among new-age communities worldwide. On the evening before Beltane a great fire marks the end of winter, with sacrifices of bread and beer, and at dawn embers are sent into the community to light the next season's fires.'

Says nothing about bells.

Evening; Avebury Trusloe

I was anxious to get some work done this afternoon, so did not lunch' at The Red Lion and instead called at the village shop. They can be a bit hit and miss with their suppliers, but I now have six Manor Farm lamb and rosemary sausages, a dozen eggs, and a bag of barn-grown mushrooms.

Something very satisfying about a proper fry-up. Keeps one going for the rest of the day.

Editing continues well-enough, but the significant differences between the new edition and the published text are worrying. The magick is so much more pronounced that in a recent scene they are almost two separate texts. Given I wish to disassociate MacGregor from Van Zelden's accusation, I wish he were more helpful. But professionally, and morally, I must produce a text as close to his intentions as I can determine. Even if it results in a work with which I am not altogether comfortable.

In Edenborough next week and have telephoned King James University Library to reserve several boxes of the Mac-Gregor archive. No hope of locating the fair copies for books two and three, but I hope to find a clue to their fate in Lady Helena's correspondence following MacGregor's death. I also have one or two questions relating to Booth Scryers and if I cannot find what I want in the library, I may have to seek advice from a practitioner. Assuming I can find one who isn't a complete charlatan.

Also intending to call at Arbinger Abbey. The MacGregor Society have helped fund a small museum dedicated to him, including a few rooms restored as they were in MacGregor's time. As society secretary, I am hoping for a guided tour of the whole property, but given it is still in use as a retirement home I may be unlucky.

Anyway, best not get ahead of myself. Interview at Belshade on Thursday, and it's a busy week elsewhere too.

29 *April; Avebury Trusloe*
Planning a staying-in-and-working kind of day and putting my misgivings behind me. I am contracted to restore three books and cannot afford to renege. If I then decide not to

continue with the rest, I am sure Hare & Drum will make other arrangements.

Stopped for lunch' of cheese on toast and listened to the radio. The coup in Borneo continues, with reports of clashes between factions in the army. I have heard nothing from Gerald, or from Edith on Gerald's behalf, so assume he is unaffected. No idea what I shall write about Beltane, but the weather report for tomorrow evening is dire.

BELSHADE CONNECTIONS
Evening; Avebury Trusloe

Pending my interview at Belshade, I have read up on the college's history. I knew there was a connection between MacGregor and Belshade, but until this evening the details had eluded me. I have now found it in Dr Crabtree's *The Wizard of the North* and thought I would describe it here as an aide memoire.

The association did not occur until after MacGregor's death, which is probably why I could not recall it immediately, and concerns his first-born son, Lorcan.

Once widowed, Lady MacGregor divided her time between Arbinger and an apartment in Lunden's Bayswater district, where she became the friend of Mrs Delta Harnoncourt. Mrs Harnoncourt, née Belshade, was the elder sister of Epsilon Belshade (naturally, this eccentric family included an Alpha, Beta and Gamma) and prior to her marriage was a noted society beauty, and the mistress of James, Prince of Wales (son of King Charles VII and later King James IX of Scotland and III of England): a liaison which, allegedly, continued after her marriage to George Harnoncourt, and his to Princess May of Saxony.

It was this friendship that led to Lorcan's enrolment at Belshade, but quite what persuaded Lady Helena that Lorcan was suited to Belshade's eccentric curriculum, I do not know. The college has received a great deal of green ink in its one-hundred-and-fifty-year existence, but it was not then, and is not now, a school for witchcraft and magick. Albeit its interest in the Old Craft was well known, and, perhaps, why so few of its alumni achieved high office in church or politics, or other station in public life. However, to its great and lasting credit, it has always been an establishment open to all levels of society. A seat of learning where even the son of a labourer might make the best of his abilities, by talent alone. This point may be pertinent to young Lorcan's acceptance at Belshade, for, in the decade after MacGregor's death, Lady MacGregor's finances were not secure—Arbinger was ever a money pit—and perhaps her friendship with Delta Harnoncourt secured reduced fees.

In any event, regardless of inducements, and whatever talent young Lorcan might have possessed, the effect was not long-lasting and within three years he had left, if not in disgrace, then with insufficient achievement to satisfy Lady MacGregor, who promptly enrolled him at King James University, Edenborough, whose fees were paid through an endowment from the Edenborough Merchant Adventurers.

I do not know the circumstances that led to young Lorcan's removal from Belshade College, but it brought on a cooling of relations between Lady MacGregor and Mrs Harnoncourt, to the point where neither woman spoke to the other for some twenty years, until the funeral of Mrs Harnoncourt's husband, who had died in a macabre mountaineering accident in the Swiss Alps.

It is a curious coincidence that I, some one hundred and fifty years later, am to be a tutor at the college once attended by MacGregor's eldest son, and, as a researcher and chronicler of MacGregor's life and works, I cannot but hope that surviving report of young Lorcan's schooling remains in the college archives. Not least an explanation for why Belshade was thought appropriate for his talents, and why he was so abruptly removed from its influence.

REVELS

30 April; Avebury Trusloe

Glanced out of my bedroom window first thing to see five revellers dancing around the Longstones. They are exceedingly early, as I believe the festivities will not begin until dusk. I certainly do not intend heading out until seven, at the earliest. Clear blue sky, but it's not forecast to last beyond lunchtime.

My garden is still bedraggled. I suppose I'm stuck with it looking seedy until everything gets properly growing, and then I shall have to protect the shoots from the local deer population.

Just gone upstairs to check, and the revellers have departed. Presumably, they are now camped in the main circle. Not looking forward to this evening, but I shall take my Instamax camera, and do my best to capture the depravities. Still, at least I'm not ringing bells all night.

Have taken my tablet of Phloxymycin and am waiting twenty minutes before I make breakfast. Promised myself a decent day's work between now and lunchtime.

Postscriptum: weight this morning fifteen stone, seven. I am slowly wasting away.

Late evening; Red Lion, Avebury

Only called at the pub to dry off before driving home. Utterly miserable evening. Wish I hadn't bothered, as the front room is full of revellers, and I'm stuck in the back with a few locals. When Jonathan offered a pint of Beltane Mead, I nearly said something rude. Nursing a pint of Merit, but not enjoying it. If ever there was a time for a brandy, this is it.

Place is swathed in greenery with sprigs of may blossom and sprays of gillyflowers. Half the women in the front room have garlands in their hair, and the men are all green-faced like elves. I glanced into the restaurant, and the well is practically festooned with vines. It's like an invasion.

I'll write it up properly tomorrow, so this is really first impressions and strictly off the cuff.

The rain didn't help, and mounting the May Pole on the back of a truck (the Antiquities Trust forbid digging holes within the circle) was a sorry spectacle, and if another idiot shouts 'Happy Beltane' at me, I shall swear.

Happily, I bumped into Pauline gamely gathering donations for the bells—which rang the whole time I was there—and learned she had received a measly fifteen crowns, ten.

"Is Paul doing any better?" I asked.

"I haven't seen him," she said.

"Must be around somewhere," I replied.

"I hope so. This isn't going to pay for tea and sandwiches for the bell-ringers."

"Peter will tell us it's the thought that counts."

"Doesn't it?" she asked.

"Dry rot is immune to prayer," I said, more acidly than I intended.

"Everyone is having a good time, though," she said.

I begged to differ and, leaving Pauline, I homed in on the impressive Beltane fire. There was an enormous guy dressed as Jack Winter, with a white beard and red hat, and people were toasting marshmallows and baking potatoes in the hot ash. I managed a few photographs, but no idea how they will turn out. Then I watched a pair of jugglers tossing flaming torches between them, followed by a bevy of women gyrating, with rather too much innuendo, on their broomsticks.

I couldn't help feeling out of place. I was dressed all wrong, by which I mean sensibly, like Pauline. Everyone else was garlanded with spring foliage, beshawled, bejewelled, be-wigged, and leather-tasselled, and at least one chap had a fine spread of antlers. Just as at Malvern, I was torn between disapproval, and aching to join in.

It didn't take me long to see everything, so I made for the pub. I suppose none of it is any odder than a teenage girl pretending to be Jesus, but it has no substance; there's no theology, no tradition of belief. However sincere those women are, they're not the sort of witches that worried King

James. I doubt any of them has cast an actual charm, raised the tiniest demon, or divined anything that I couldn't judge simply by glancing out of a window. They are, for want of a better phrase, making it up as they go along.

Mustn't be cynical or I'll get an attack of the glums. Peter and Pauline want something upbeat and inclusive. You can manage that, can't you?

Postscriptum: down to the last few pages in my journal. Must call at W B Jones tomorrow for a replacement.

1 May; Caen Hill Café

There were a dozen revellers at the Longstones this morning. They had draped something over the stones, and were prancing around it with drums, before, with a great hurrah, they threw whatever it was aside and embraced the stones. Utter madness.

Had considered popping back into the village to see the jollities continue, but I had a busy day ahead with shopping and a hair cut in Devizes, so thought better of it. This afternoon I'll finish brushing up on Belshade for the interview, and then dominoes at The Red Lion this evening.

Eustace of Scrub-Up & Co. has done a decent job of making me look presentable—he trimmed my ear whiskers at no extra charge—but I have no idea what passes for professorial at Belshade. It might be that ragged denim and hair down to one's backside is perfectly acceptable. But I know my own standards and shall feel easier at interview having made the effort, even if it goes unappreciated.

As Scrub-Up is at the west end of town I continued west, rather than to my usual haunts on Market Street, and returned to the café at Caen Locks. Hard to believe, from the picturesque scene below me, that this is the pinnacle of canal boating, but I shall discover the truth soon enough. I also have a convenient view of the nearest lock and hope to watch someone take their boat through it. I may even take notes. Speaking of which, my new journal, not yet started, has a faux-leather cover in a pleasing shade of lilac.

Peter Chadwick telephoned just before I left for Devizes. He asked how I got on last evening.

"The weather put a damper on it," I said. "Only hope Pauline and I don't catch a chill. How much did Pauline raise in the end? And was Paul actually there?"

"Pauline raised nineteen crowns, three shillings. I'm afraid Paul got involved in an argument and ended up with blood all over his face."

"What happened?"

"A reveller took exception to the bells. Said we were trying to take over their night. Paul ended up in the mud."

"Ah. Wonder if Paul said anything untoward. He can be a bit keen."

Keen to proselytise, I meant. It pays to know when to advance the cause and when, for self-preservation, to stay quiet.

"He hasn't said. But I would applaud him for spreading the Good Word."

"Really? I thought last night was about building bridges."

"One-way bridges, Nevil."

"Ah. Anyway, I'll have something for the magazine in a day or two."

One-way traffic, eh? It seems a bit shameless. Yes, there is no tradition to what I saw last evening, but it seems harsh to dismiss it. Of course, Peter would quote John 14:6 at me, but I've never gone along with a rigid interpretation. Jesus spoke to those about him at a certain place and time. I'm not sure he spoke to all men for all time.

Who are we to judge?

Anyway, I shall endeavour to be sympathetic in my piece for the magazine. And I must admit after a few hours even I was getting fed up with the ring-a-thon.

No sign of a boat coming and it's clouding over. Don't want to get rained on before I've shopped at Budgitts.

Postscriptum: Narrow 5-4 victory over The Bell tonight. I was on fine form, winning two matches and narrowly losing the third. Now for bed, as I have a long day tomorrow.

2 May; Eagle and Child, Oxford

The interview went very well. Not only am I the only candidate for the position, but the work promises to be tolerable, accommodation is fair, and the pay reasonable. A regular income will be welcome.

To begin at the beginning—though as my father once wrote: *All beginnings are known by their end and the end is known by the beginning*—the drive was agreeable, though the Oxford traffic was especially bad, but I confess as I left St Giles behind and drove north through the suburbs and into open country, my heart sank a little. Belshade's claim to be an *Oxford* College was shrinking by the second, but I suppose the nature of its curriculum demands a degree of isolation from the city, and the nights will be peaceful.

In fact, Belshade Hall is only three miles north of Oxford and overlooks the wetlands of Ot Moor, being quite exposed to the north and east. The landscape reminded me of the Cambridgeshire Fens, though on a smaller scale. The original building is impressive, if austere, but was significantly, and unsympathetically, extended post-war and again some twenty years ago. The halls of residence are on-site (so many colleges today house the students in dormitories in the cheap districts of town) and accommodate around three hundred students. A modest number, as colleges go, but quite a lot so far from the city, and especially so when it maintains its founder's hostility to alcohol in all forms. Even the windfall apples in the orchard are not allowed to ferment.

This titbit was passed on by the threadbare usher, name of Digby, who escorted me to the principal's office. I like to befriend the menial staff, as they are the ones you can rely on in a pickle.

The principal's office was small and made smaller by bookcases on two of the three walls. The plan was that of an equilateral triangle and one's eyes were continually getting trapped in the corners. The third wall had a window, half covered by a black shade; an old-fashioned copper radiator; a large pot plant; and a tall birdcage. At least, I assume it was a birdcage as it was covered with a purple cloth. In front of the window was a desk and from behind it rose Audley Stonebreaker.

"Mr Warbrook, I presume."

"I have the pleasure to be such," I said.

"Please. Take a seat. I assure you this is a formality. There are no other applicants, and your knowledge of the curriculum subject is exemplary. Think of this as familiarisation: you with Belshade, and us with you."

I sat, as did Stonebreaker. This was better news than I thought possible, though there was something odd about his words. One shouldn't be too familiar with one's superiors. It can leave them with the idea they are free to take liberties that only friends can take with friends.

Stonebreaker took my application from his desk and appeared to read it, though I suspect this was mere theatrics. I could not see his face, other than in silhouette against the window light, but he is a large, well-built man, and his features, what I could see of them, heavy-set. I couldn't help thinking that Dr Saunders would have him on a diet.

"Very satisfactory," he said. "Tell me of your involvement with the church. St James's, isn't it?"

As he put my application down, his hand caught in the window light. The fingers were unusually long and feminine. The question had thrown me a little.

"I am secretary on the Parochial Church Council," I said. "Note taking at meetings, that sort of thing."

"Belshade also has secretaries," he said. "I meant at a personal level."

"I worship regularly and enjoy the tradition. I wouldn't call St James 'High Church,' but we like to keep the old ways."

"There are older ways than those of the church," he said with a glance at the bookcases.

The penny dropped.

"Of course," I said. "I am a Christian, but not the kind who objects to other faiths, or wishes to challenge them. Much of the church's dealings with magick has been deplorable."

"I am glad to hear it," Stonebreaker said. "Belshade is an inclusive college, and all beliefs are welcome. We believe there is only one answer to life's mysteries, but many questions and many quests."

That was his only concern, such as it was, with my application. We spoke, thereafter, about my ambitions as a poet and writer. I touched on my father's legacy, and on MacGregor. I decided against mentioning Lorcan's schooling at Belshade—there will be time to follow that up during autumn term. Then I spoke of my tuition methods at Creative Havens, and Stonebreaker said the college holidays would allow me to maintain my work with them, indicating a welcome tolerance for extra-curricular activity.

Then he summoned Digby and instructed him to show me the accommodation.

"I trust you are satisfied with us," Stonebreaker said. "We are a friendly college. Considering the powers we work with, it is unwise to bring hostility into the lecture room."

I didn't have time to dwell on the remark before he rose and embraced me warmly. I attempted to do the same, but found his girth greater than I had supposed, and my hands ended up on his hips.

"I must confirm the matter with the heads of faculty," he said. "But that is a formality. Welcome to Belshade College."

"Thank you," I said. "I confess, I am surprised, and delighted to be here."

That was not entirely true, as I still have doubts about my exact role, but gift horses and all that.

Digby led me slowly up a flight of stairs. Then up a second flight, narrower than the first.

"Staff accommodation... is in what used... to be the attic, sir," he wheezed.

"This keeps one fit," I said.

Perhaps that was a little unthinking, as Digby was far

from fit and had to catch his breath once we reached the landing. This led to a windowless corridor, lit only by a skylight. Doors led off either side, and I assumed this was in a flat-roofed section between two pitched roofs.

"This will be yours, sir," Digby said, and produced a large bronze key. I realised all the metal fixtures and fittings must be non-ferrous.

"Iron," I said. "No iron in the college."

"None, sir."

"What about motorcars?"

"Staff parking is beyond the orchard, where the East Drive meets the road. The apple trees absorb, so they say, the harmful effects of iron and protect the college."

He winked in an easy-going manner I didn't approve of. I suspect Digby is not wholeheartedly behind Belshade's pedagogic philosophy. That makes two of us.

"The rooms are furnished, but if you would prefer to have your own things brought up, we can find storage for what you do not require."

The room had everything I would need to survive for three days of the week. The view was northward, across the moor to distant hills, but at least it admitted plenty of light. There was a desk, large enough to write at; a dressing table; somewhere to hang a few clothes; a mirror, somewhat tarnished; a comfortable chair; and an old-fashioned bed with copper and bronze filigree. A second door led off the room.

I tested the mattress but thought it impolite to check for any staining. If needs be, I can replace it, but no sense being awkward at this stage.

"And bathroom through here?" I asked of the second door.

"Indeed."

Everything was functional and clean, though the window had no blind.

"Is there anything else, sir?"

"No. This is very satisfactory. A home from home," I said.

Austere though, now I think of it. I shall want a few

creature comforts with me, and a bookcase wouldn't go amiss.

Digby showed me back to the entrance hall.

"Give my regards to Principal Stonebreaker and say everything is very satisfactory." I said. "Actually, there is something you might help me with. I'm heading back to Oxford to the Eagle and Child. It was a favourite haunt of my father when he was at Oxford. He was a don at Israel College. But I was wondering if there is a hostelry nearer at hand."

"An Israel Man, sir. As were you, no doubt, for father is followed by son. I can speak for the Abandoned Arm. Very homely. Not like the city pubs."

"Sorry, I didn't catch the name."

"Abandoned Arm, sir. In the village of Beckley."

Digby pointed toward the hills behind the college. I made a mental note. At least he is a drinking man, even if Stonebreaker isn't.

This brings me to the snug at the Eagle and Child, and a satisfactory outcome to a very satisfactory day. It could only be improved by a pint of proper ale.

Evening; Avebury Trusloe

Been home some two hours. Time enough to make my tea and settle down for the night, as the strain of travelling has caught up with me, even if my mood continues jolly. Naturally, the cats suspect something is amiss, and are ignoring me steadfastly. Mrs Pumphrey, my neighbour, will care for them the three days of the week I am away. She has done so before on occasion, and both she, and the cats, seem quite happy with the arrangement. Mr Pumphrey will be less pleased. I only wish Mrs Pumphrey would not refer to Boris and Tusker as 'my boys,' when it is I who pay their vet's bills.

The post was waiting for me on the doormat when I got home. I have my ticket from Great Northern Railway for Monday and return on Friday. As requested, they included a receipt, which will be handy for claiming expenses, as the exercise is largely for the benefit of Hare & Drum.

Nota bene: find time tomorrow to ensure I have everything I need for next week laid out ready to pack.

Returning to today's concern. Having now seen the college, and knowing the position is all but mine, I have been reading up on the local history. Ot Moor is the site of the Battle of Otta's Mere when, in 1076, Baldwin, the local Saxon lord, led an uprising against Danish Rule. He briefly besieged the town of Oxenaforde, long a well-defended frontier town between the Saxon earldoms of Mercia to the north and Wessex to the south, and put much of it to flame, before a force of Danes from Banbury routed Baldwin's men and he fled to Otta's Mere, where, perhaps, he intended to hold out, much as Hereward had done at Ely in 1074. However, Otta's Mere was far smaller than Hereward's Eel Island, and Baldwin was soon defeated and forced to swear loyalty to the Danelaw. At that point, Baldwin disappears from history, but there are tales from the villages of Beckley and Charlton-on-Ot Moor, that he will ride again when England is in peril, and there were reports in the years before the Great War of his war party flying above the marshes.

Ignis fatuus, along with inebriation, has much to answer for when it comes to folktales.

I think that's enough history. An early night is called for.

3 May; Avebury Trusloe

Spent part of the morning preparing for next week. Edenborough can be bitterly cold, even in late spring, so, although if it is a little shabby, my coat is essential. I shall not want for proper food next week so no need to worry on that score; books, however, are essential, and I'm taking Crabtree's *Wizard of the North* and Bishop's *A Writer's Life*, along with a street map of the city. Still toying with Louis S Robertson's, *A Literary History of Alba vol. viii.* It has some interesting remarks on MacGregor's legacy, and on Lady Helena's life after his death, but it is too general to be of much use in my search. It is also by far the heaviest of the three books. If I need to consult it, King James's University Library will have a copy.

I need my camera, though I will have to buy a roll of film in Edenborough, as I exhausted the last roll during Beltane Eve. A portable radio as well, as my hotel room is bound to only have a television. And my slippers for evenings when I am not tempted onto the Royal Mile. It is astonishing how easy it is to forget one's slippers. Evenings are not the same without them.

I'm taking recent correspondence for the MacGregor Society. Diane Dickinson of Dorothy Parkin Homes is extraordinarily supportive, and the society may have secured a grant from the Alban Literary Foundation, which will allow us to expand our ambitions. I'm also hoping to climb the Madeleine Shrine. It has recently been restored by the Trustees of the MacGregor Estate, and this will be my first opportunity to get a look at their work.

I have all the essentials for next week. Anything else I think of I can add tomorrow. Lunchtime now and then back to the editing.

IN THE PINK

Evening; Avebury Trusloe

I have now seen more of Mrs Pumphrey than I ever anticipated. I appreciate that the contours of the larger lady are more challenging than those of a slimmer, and younger woman, but aesthetically—and I have the weight of art history on my side—few can have attempted to capture quite so much flesh on a single canvas at any one time.

Of course, I was as unexpected to her, as she was to me, but she carried off the change in our relationship with insouciant ease. I, on the other hand, gawped like a fish, as she disrobed and sat for us.

"Focus on the line," Angela said. "Line and tone."

Tone was not a word I associated with Mrs Pumphrey's

311

rolls of flesh, but, curiously, I suddenly lost any desire to capture a likeness, and instead attacked the canvas with great smears and daubs of colour. The artist's smock took its fair share of splatter, and I had taken the precaution of wearing my gardening shoes, so splashes on them are not a problem. I did get a smear of pink on my spectacles, but that cleaned off once it was dry.

At the interval, when we broke for tea and biscuits, Mrs Pumphrey slipped on a dressing gown and inspected our work. It was clear she had done this many times before, and most of the students were well acquainted with her geographies. When she came to me, she leant across my shoulder to examine the canvas and I averted my gaze as her dressing gown gaped, revealing a cavernous cleavage.

"It's very... violent," she said.

"Violent?" I said. "I had hoped for something impressionistic. Even exuberant."

"But you're stabbing the canvas with the brush," she said.

Angela must have overheard us, because she stepped in with an apparent dislike of the model taking over the tutoring. Though, were Angela to take over the modelling I should have no complaints.

"You're breaking free of representing reality," she said. "An excellent improvement."

I felt a glow of satisfaction. Praise is all too rare, in my experience, and praise from a woman even rarer.

"But focus on brush control," Angela said. "Every stroke must be deliberate, even if the effect is spontaneous."

Deliberately spontaneous, or spontaneously deliberate, I thought. Now there was a puzzle. I can achieve the effect in literature well-enough, but what appears to be spontaneous in a text is carefully wrought through editing and honing. I have yet to effectively edit paint. I must ask about technique at the next meeting.

Good lord. Am I really taking this seriously? I think I must be.

4 May; Avebury Trusloe

Early start to the day, as I must be at the village hall for the flower show. Put the radio on to catch the news. Situation in Borneo is still volatile. Not heard from Gerald. Mind you, I wouldn't expect him to think of reassuring his parents of his wellbeing.

The flower show has been on my calendar for months. Can't say I have much interest in flowers, but it falls to me to write the report for the parish magazine. The cake stall and selection of preserves, however, is another matter; there are some excellent bakers and jam makers in the village.

Nothing in the post from Belshade. Early, I know, but if I don't receive anything by first post on Monday, I won't know until I'm back from Edenborough. Of course, Audley's reassurance should be enough that the position is mine, but a contract would be welcome.

Better get my skates on and finish breakfast.

CAKES AND ALCOHOL-FREE ALE
Afternoon; Red Lion, Avebury

The only advantage to the prohibition on alcohol is driving to the pub and back on a clear conscience. I drove, rather than walked, because there are only so many cakes and jam jars one can carry any distance. I have a walnut and ginger cake from Mrs Westmacott, one of Mrs Hartmann's Schwarzwald plum brandy cakes, and a chocolate and nutmeg roulade from Angela Spendlove. The roulade won't keep beyond the end of the week, so will have to go in the freezer, but the plum brandy cake is practically pickled and will last a month. I have also jars of quince jelly, gooseberry, rhubarb, passion fruit, and figgy jam, and three jars of honey from the hives at the manor gardens.

Molly won best in show for an ikebana arrangement of dead hawthorn, flowering gorse, and miniature sarsen stone; which the judges said captured the spirit of the Downs, even if I thought it a bit austere and prickly. Prudence Turnstone

313

came second with her interpretation of the Passiontide in Flowers. May and Elder Tree combined to win 'most promising newcomer' with an intricate arrangement of grape vine and razor wire they called 'blood and hope,' while Apple Tree earned a runner's-up prize with an apfelstrudel cake.

I congratulated Molly after the prize-giving.

"Thank you, Nevil. And how did you get on?"

"I haven't an entry," I said.

"At your job interview. It was this week, wasn't it?"

"Oh yes. It went very well. I have all but been promised the position."

"So, you'll be leaving us?"

She looked downcast, which didn't sit well with the small plastic and brass cup she was carrying.

"Wherever did you get that idea from?"

"I assumed as the job is in Oxford."

"Oh, no, no, no. I shall room at college three days a week, but I won't be leaving Avebury."

She brightened at the news.

"Only we can't stand to lose any more people from the council," she said. "You've heard about Fred."

"No. Not a thing. What's happened?"

"He was taken poorly during the ring-a-thon. They think it was a stroke."

"Good Lord. He's not...?

"Thankfully, no. But he's very shaken up. He's standing down with immediate effect, both as Captain of the Tower and council member."

"I suppose as the bells are in such a parlous state—"

"We can't think negatively. Not now," Molly said. "The ringers are appointing a new Captain next month."

"Do we know who they will choose?"

"Not yet. But you see what I mean about you not leaving."

"Oh, quite. Just as well I have no intention. Though it slightly depends on the college letting me go early on Thursday afternoons, so I can get back in time."

"And Wednesdays? What about Wednesday meetings?"

"Won't be able to make them, I'm afraid. But plenty of time. Term doesn't start until end of September."

"It's not very reassuring."

"Best I can do. Can't afford to ignore this opportunity. It will be my first regular income in years. And I'll be following in my father's footsteps: Oxford don and all that."

"Of course, you must go for it. Is it nice?"

"Nice?"

"Where you'll live."

"Tolerable. Not like home of course, but I shall manage."

"Good. I do worry about you sometimes. On your own I mean."

"I get by perfectly well. Look" —I showed her the cakes and jam I had bought— "I am fed for a month. What else shall a man want, but cakes and jam," I paraphrased the playwright.

"You are losing weight," she said discouragingly.

"At my doctor's request," I said. "And I feel better for it. You are forbidden to worry about me, dear Molly. I am perfectly well. Now, enjoy your prize."

If Fred Thirsk has stood down, it leaves the traditionalists on the council exposed. Only takes one batty bell-ringer with modernist tendencies, and St James's could be in dire peril. Question is, what on earth to do about it?

UNCERTAINTY

Later; Avebury Trusloe

Managed to settle down this afternoon and edited for three hours. Still uncertain whether I wish to continue beyond my contract for three books. Wonder if H&D will entertain a meeting next week while I'm in Edenborough. Worth a telephone call to Desmond, I think.

Putting off calling on Mrs Pumphrey. I need to remind her I am away next week so she can look after the cats, but after Friday's revelation I am uncertain of our new relationship. Perhaps I shall be all right if I look her determinedly in the eye.

Disappointingly, Paul Durdle seems not to have a mark on him. That, or he heals exceptionally quickly. He claims to have raised eighteen crowns and five shillings, prior to the attack on Beltane Eve, but that this disappeared in the melee. He did not get a good look at his attacker.

I suppose it is entirely plausible. Too aggressive in his proselytising among an unsympathetic crowd: the collection bowl jingling a little too loudly.

"Nor everyone I spoke to was happy about the bells," Pauline admitted. "One said we were scaring away the spirit of summer."

"Wicket folk. What d'ye expect," Sid muttered.

Pauline, Paul, Sid, and I had made an informal PCC gathering in the corner of the social room after Holy Communion to discuss Fred's retirement, but until we had a new Captain of the Tower there wasn't much to say. Everyone agreed he had seemed in excellent health. Molly was busy serving tea and coffee, but I could see her keeping an eye on us.

"Eighteen Crowns wasn't going to make much of a dent on the repair bill," I said.

"That isn't the point," Pauline said. "Prudence has taken it rather badly."

"How so?" I asked.

"What happened to me, of course," Paul said. "So much for spiritual outreach."

"He outreached you," I said.

"Very droll. I can't see you taking a thump for Jesus."

"Hardly what we were called to do," I said. "I witnessed, and the parish magazine will have something on the Beltane celebrations. That was my part in events."

"Soon, I hope," Pauline said. "Going to print on Friday."

"Really? Ah. Thought I had a bit more time. I'm off to Edenborough tomorrow so it will keep me occupied on the train journey."

"You'll post it in good time?"

"Of course. If I can, I'll send it by electronic mail."

"What are you doing in Edenborough?" Paul asked.

"Research. This book I'm editing. Restoring the text, actually. I'll be working at King James University."

"MacGregor's *This Iron Race*," Molly said, having now joined us.

Paul's eyes narrowed.

"It's not a Christian book, is it," he said.

"I'm an editor," I protested. "Not all books are *expressly* Christian."

"But the rumours about him. Don't they worry you?"

"Indeed, they do! That is why I am refuting them by restoring his text," I said, showing more intention than I truly fear is the case. They are not in any shape or form books a Christian can wholly admire, but I could not admit it in company. Heaven knows what Paul would say if he knew I was shortly to be employed at Belshade College. But of course, he will know soon enough.

Nota bene: there is a small risk that employment at Belshade might threaten my position on the PCC in more ways than scheduling clashes. I shall have to tread carefully and emphasise that I am teaching Scottish poetry. The less said of the other material on the curriculum, the better.

"More cake, Nevil?" Molly asked.

"Is that Mrs Hartmann's date and whisky cake?" I asked.

"Fresh from the show."

"Ah. No. Better not. Having lunch' at the pub in a bit. Then I must pack for tomorrow. Don't want to bother cooking anything this evening."

"I shouldn't have too many at the pub," Paul said. "Don't want you forgetting your toothbrush."

"Fat chance of that. Antibiotics following a mishap with one of my cats. Haven't touched a drop all week."

"You don't seem wounded," he said.

"The bite marks have healed." I held up my finger for

examination. "I was thinking the same of you. Peter said you had blood all over your face."

Paul did not answer.

Postscriptum: left the pub in a bit of a hurry. Crowd of bikers arrived and made the place less than salubrious. I went home and packed for tomorrow. Nuisance having to get the piece done for the parish magazine so soon. I had hoped for a pleasant snooze on the journey up. Instead, I must revisit Tuesday night.

Should have given Paul a piece of my mind earlier. How dare he cast aspersions on my faith? Just because I don't pretend to be holier than thou all the time, does not make me any less a believer.

THE TOLLING OF THE BELLS
Evening; Avebury Trusloe

My bags are packed and sitting in the hall, and I'm having an early night as I will be up with the sparrows. Not that that guarantees a decent night's sleep. Changes to routine always make me restless. Can't even enjoy a proper nightcap. Like a child, I am reduced to a glass of milk at bedtime.

Been an unsettling day, what with worrying Molly like that, and Paul Durdle coming over all sanctimonious. Then those motorcyclists ruined what had been a pleasant lunch'. It all feels as though I am leaving for Scotland on a sour note.

If I am honest with myself, I would sooner not be at Belshade three days in the week. But the income is regular, and I can't rely on Creative Havens any more, not with this takeover business. God knows poetry doesn't pay, and employment with Hare & Drum is hardly secure. If that means fewer evenings at the PCC, then sobeit. I can't see any of the others foregoing fifteen thousand a year to sit in the village hall once a month.

Ah, there they are. The bells are ringing eleven. Third night I've found myself listening to the bells at this hour. I suppose one only pays attention to familiar things when one fears losing them. But, as I reach the last page of my journal, I'm reminded that if Dr Saunders is to be believed, I too might fall silent earlier than expected.

What a glum thought to end the day. I shall close this and put my pen down before things get any worse.

Printed in Great Britain
by Amazon